PAMELA
HART

A Letter from Italy

piatkus

PIATKUS

First published in Australia and New Zealand in 2017 by Hachette Australia
An imprint of Hachette Australia Pty Limited
First published in Great Britain in 2017 by Piatkus
This paperback edition published in 2017 by Piatkus

1 3 5 7 9 10 8 6 4 2

A CIP catalogue record for this book
is available from the British Library.

ISBN 978-0-349-41712-7

Text design by Bookhouse, Sydney
Typeset by Bookhouse
Printed and bound in Great Britain by
Clays Ltd, St Ives plc

Papers used by Piatkus are from well-managed forests
and other responsible sources.

MIX
Paper from
responsible sources
FSC
www.fsc.org
FSC® C104740

Piatkus
An imprint of
Little, Brown Book Group
Carmelite House
50 Victoria Embankment
London EC4Y 0DZ

An Hachette UK Company
www.hachette.co.uk

www.littlebrown.co.uk

*For my Aunty Pauline, who showed us all
what an independent woman could do.
She is greatly missed.*

'Albanian smugglers?' Rebecca couldn't believe she'd heard right.

'Mostly Albanian. A few Bulgarians as well. They're part of the resistance movement against the Austrians.' Jack grinned at her as though that were the best news in the world, and continued to fossick through their steamer trunk, removing clothes and stuffing them into his duffel bag. Rebecca sat on their bed and resisted the impulse to help him. There was a small flutter of panic underneath her heart. This was happening too fast.

'How did you find them?'

'Nonna Rosa put me in touch,' he said.

Nonna Rosa owned the trattoria where they ate dinner most nights. It didn't surprise Rebecca that she was associated with smugglers; the food in the restaurant was suspiciously good given wartime restrictions.

'Do I have any clean socks?'

Wordlessly, she went to the chest of drawers and found him two pairs. He stowed them away, and rolled up his macintosh to go on top. His shirt was pulling out of his trousers, as it always did, and his hair was ruffled. He never could be bothered to use pomade to smooth it down. There was always something more interesting to do. Like this: heading off with Albanian smugglers, for God's sake!

'But you don't speak Albanian.' She tried to sound reasonable, like a professional partner, not a wife being abandoned.

'The captain speaks a bit of English. He wants the Albanian side of the story told.' He stood up and looked around, searching for anything else he might need. 'It's a great story. But I have to go now. They're sailing with the tide.'

He grabbed his shaving gear from the wash stand and stashed it in the top of the bag, then pulled the drawstring tight and slung the bag over his shoulder. His eyes were alight with excitement; he almost vibrated with it. The excitement of a journalist on the track of a great story. She could feel the pull of it herself; but they'd never let a woman go along.

She wanted to throw herself at him and beg him not to abandon her in this foreign town, not to risk his life. But she couldn't. They were reporters, and this was a story. Excitement rose in her too. Of course he had to follow it. And of course she would be all right alone. They had been in Italy for six weeks, in Brindisi for a month now. She had a place to stay, and she had her work to continue. No room for panic or dependency; she was a New Woman and she could take care of herself, surely.

'How long will you be away?'

He grinned at her again, clearly relieved that she wasn't objecting. He was like a schoolboy let off a scolding, but that vulnerability was endearing. 'You're the best wife any man could have! I don't know. They come back every week or so. I expect I'll be back soon enough, and if not I'll send you a message.'

He pulled on a sailor's knitted cap. It covered his blond hair – suddenly he could have been from anywhere, from Slovakia or Albania or Bulgaria. What if something happened to him out there? What if this was the last time she ever saw him? She tried to memorise him, to pull every detail of his appearance into her mind and hold it. The blue eyes, the straight pale hair, the high cheekbones, the long rangy body almost too bony. None of that captured his charm, though, or his energy, or the way he made a room come alive when he entered it. She reached up to touch his cheek, tears pricking her eyes.

The duffel bag dropped to the floor with a clunk, and he pulled her into his arms. For just a moment, she felt safe and warm and comforted. He kissed her, and she clung to him. The kiss was passionate but brief, and then he set her back on her feet as though he had just given her a sop to her emotions.

'If you wanted to risk your life,' she said, a little annoyed, 'you could just have joined the Army.'

'Can you imagine me stuck in a fox hole, taking orders from some idiot officer?' he said breezily, picking up the duffel again. 'No fear! I like to pick my own risks.'

'Be careful.' She could hear a hint of tears in her voice. 'Smugglers—'

'Oh, I'll be fine!' He hugged her once and was out the door. 'Don't worry!' came drifting back up the stairs.

What a stupid thing to say. As if she could help worrying. Albanian smugglers. Resistance movement against the Austrians. The old Austro–Hungarian Empire was breaking up from within, the subject states – Albania, Bulgaria, Hungary, Slovakia – all mounting resistance movements, working with the Allied countries against Austria and Germany. They were, by all accounts, ruthless and single-minded in their work, and were involved in all kinds of bombings and killings.

And Jack was going to write a news story about how Albanian smugglers were part of the war effort.

God help him.

Her hands were suddenly cold; she rubbed them together and closed the door against the draught. Then, automatically, she began picking up the clothes he had strewn around the room. As she put his good shoes away in the steamer trunk, she realised that the small shoe-polish box was gone, and remembered that clunk as the duffel had fallen to the floor. He had taken their store of gold sovereigns with him. No doubt he thought gold was likely to loosen more tongues than Italian lire.

He should have left her a few, just in case.

Rebecca went to the window and looked out onto the blustery grey sky. Below her, the houses of Brindisi huddled under the autumn wind. Beyond them, the harbour, and the ships that had brought her and Jack all the way from Australia: the naval flotillas of Britain, France, Italy and Australia, here to stop Austrian submarines passing from the Adriatic Sea out into the Mediterranean. The Otranto Barrage, it was called.

It had been her ticket off the Women's Pages of *The Sydney Morning Herald* and into reporting real news. When Jack had been offered the assignment, he had made her part of it, part of a team reporting naval news. A great boost to her career, being a war reporter, since there were so few journalists accredited by the War Office.

She could still do that, no matter how lonely she would be without him. She *would* do that. She had been a journalist before she was a wife, after all.

She saw Jack come out into a small piazza further down the hill, heading quickly for the harbour. Gripping the window ledge, she watched him as far as she could, until he vanished into a narrow alleyway between two buildings.

Outside, a newspaper boy shouted headlines: *Germania avanza!* Germany advances. Half a continent away, the Brindisans could read about those battles in safety, and understand what was happening in the world. And just like the Italian journalists who had written those stories for their fellow countrymen, it was her job to bring the news of the war back to the readers of Australia and England. She could do that with or without Jack.

Of course she could.

Under her gloved palm, the altar rail was smooth, polished by generations of hands.

Rebecca stood uncertainly. Jack had been gone for a week, without a word ... a prayer or two was surely in order? She had no way of knowing whether he was dead or injured or perfectly all right: no messages came from behind the Austrian lines in Albania.

She was like millions of other women in this war, who had to wait and pray for the safety of their men. The beautiful stone statue of the Virgin regarded her with compassionate, knowing eyes.

How old this church was. It awed her, the casual age of Italy, where a house might be held up by part of a Roman wall, or a fountain crowned with a Renaissance statue. Coming from Australia, where a very old house was one that had been standing a mere hundred years, for Rebecca the centuries under her feet were like a raft, buoying her up, giving her hope.

The church was small, whitewashed, dazzling with sunshine so that the dust motes glowed golden in the air like small blessings. She genuflected, head bowed to the tabernacle and its red lamp; the swish of her skirts sent a susurration around the high ceiling, as though the rafters were whispering back to her, bringing her into a partnership with the walls, the ceiling, the golden dust. Into a kind of peace, where she could leave worry behind for just a moment.

She turned her face up to the Cross above the tabernacle and prayed for Jack's safety; but the act of praying for him brought all the worry back. For a moment she felt so alone, so abandoned, that tears fell onto her cheeks and trailed down.

'Our Father, who art in Heaven . . .'

•

Sandro turned from inspecting the memorial plaque on the wall when he heard the faint whisper of skirts, his fingers still touching the words, *Alessandro Panucci Requiesat in Pace*.

A woman, praying before the altar, standing straight and tall. Sunlight from a rose window above the tabernacle caught her face, so that she was standing in a nimbus of light, her profile pure and clear. She looked like an angel, but angels didn't cry, and the shaft of light caught the tears on her cheek. Sandro was struck by that curling in his gut that happened whenever he was presented with real beauty – not of the woman, but of the whole scene. Some perfect balance of elements that called out to him like the note from a bugle, which grabbed him by the throat and demanded to be immortalised.

What a shot. Could he catch it? He only had the little pocket camera, and it wasn't good in low light, but maybe . . . If he asked her first, the moment would be gone. Ruined. He would have to shoot first, and ask later.

He leaned against the pillar to steady himself and set the frame with infinite care. The click of the shutter was loud and sharp, echoing off the rafters.

She started, turned and saw him.

For a moment, confusion covered her face. A beautiful face, soft and lovely. Then she caught sight of the camera he was sliding into his pocket, and she transformed.

'How *dare* you?' she said in English, right out loud, clearly not caring this was a church.

She strode over to him and put her hand out.

'Give me that film,' she demanded in Italian.

He was a little surprised that she knew about film; most people didn't. He didn't really blame her for being angry, but he wasn't going to give up what might be the best shot he had ever taken.

'Now, miss,' he replied in English, soothingly. 'I'm sorry—'

'You *should* be sorry! Do you make a habit of taking pictures of women without their consent?'

She was blazingly angry, and the set of her mouth (*madonna mia*, what a mouth!) was disgusted.

'I suppose you take them home to, to – *gloat* over them!' The implication was clear – he was a pervert, making his own pornography. That got him angry.

'Miss, if you think men *gloat* over a picture of a woman crying in a church, you don't know much about men!' Maybe it wasn't the most sensible thing to say, but geez, he was a professional.

'I know enough,' she said, her tone damning. 'And it's *Mrs*, not *Miss*. Give me the film.'

'Or what?' he asked. 'It's a public place. You've got no rights here, *signora.*'

Her face crumpled a little, as though she were holding back tears. It made him feel guilty – but, hand over his film? Not a chance. Apart from anything else, he had some good shots on there of the Australian flotilla coming into Brindisi harbour.

'A church is a place of prayer,' she said, rallying. 'I think one has an expectation of privacy here.'

She had a point. Sure. He hadn't intended to take any shots when he'd come here. He'd just wanted to see the memorial plaque for his grandfather and great-grandparents.

'Ma'am,' he said, trying to be nice, trying to pull this conversation back to normality. 'I'm a photographer, not some . . . crazy guy. Here's my card.'

She took it automatically, and read it. 'Al Baker from New York?' Her shoulders relaxed a little, and then tensed again. 'You intend to *sell* that shot?'

'No, no!' Maybe? If he had another exhibition, he would put it in, and perhaps someone would buy it. Which wouldn't be fair to her. It would be a low thing to do. 'No,' he said. 'I promise I won't sell it. It was just – such a good shot, I couldn't resist it.'

She took a deep breath, and let it out again; he tried not to look at her chest. 'I would recommend that you not bring your camera to church, Mr Baker, if your resistance to temptation is so low. It's very unprofessional. Disgustingly so. And if I find *any* evidence that you are attempting to sell that image, I *will* sue you. If you've run to Italy to avoid the draft, you're clearly a coward, so I'll hope you'll run from a lawsuit too.'

Then she dropped his card on the floor and walked off.

What a – he didn't know any word that fitted her particular combination of upper-class authority and vitriol. He fell back on Shakespeare. What a *shrew*.

A coward. Everyone thought he was a coward because he wasn't in uniform. It ate away at him. As if he hadn't *tried* to get into the Army. *Two* armies. She'd hit him where it hurt, all right.

And now, if the shot turned out as good as he hoped, all he'd be able to do with it was – gloat over it in private.

Goddammit.

2

When is a journalist not a journalist? When she's part of a journalistic duo, and one half is missing.

```
JACK QUINN IN ALBANIA FOLLOWING STORY STOP HAS
BEEN AWAY TEN DAYS DONT KNOW WHEN HE WILL RETURN
STOP WILL CONTINUE TO FILE STORIES FROM HERE STOP
REBECCA QUINN
```

Rebecca wrote out the telegram to their editor in London, William Evans, head of the *Evening News*. Although they also wrote for *The Sydney Morning Herald*, their stories were sent via London – and moreover Evans was the one who paid them on the *Herald*'s behalf, so he was the one who mattered.

She handed it over the counter at the Brindisi post office.

'*Si, signora*,' the clerk said.

'*Grazie*,' she replied.

Jack had been gone from Brindisi for ten days, and there was still no news of him. Every day, Rebecca had done her rounds:

reading the local and English newspapers, checking in with her local contacts, writing brief updates on naval positions and submarine sightings. She sent them off by telegram to the *Evening News* in London and *The Sydney Morning Herald*, sorry that they would never make the front page. There was so much other war news, in this last part of 1917: the battle of Passchendaele, the Italian front line on the Isonzo River and the Austrian push there, the trial of Mata Hari for espionage ... The Otranto blockade of the Adriatic Sea wasn't exciting enough to make a headline, no matter how important it was to the Allies' ability to send shipping through the Mediterranean.

She couldn't continue to collect second-hand information any longer, hoping that Jack would return tomorrow and resume his role as their main contact with the navies. He had been the naval correspondent for the *Herald* for six years – he liaised with the Australian naval flotilla and had every contact they needed to get the stories. But they had come to Italy to cover these stories together, and her accreditation was as good as his, even if her contacts weren't. If he wasn't here, she would simply have to do it herself. But Evans, of course, had had to be told.

No more waiting. She put on her hat and gloves and a jacket against the sharp November wind. It was time to talk to Commander Warren.

The Royal Australian Navy flotilla was working out of the 'British base', alongside those of the Italians and the French, and she knew just where she needed to go. She made her way carefully down the steep street to the harbour, her breath misting in the cold air. Men watched her go by, she knew, but she kept her eyes firmly on the ground, fists clenched, ignoring the whispers and the '*Bianca bella!*' from every second man she passed.

Jack loved her thick blonde hair, but right now she wished she was solidly brunette, and preferably with a smaller bosom.

Of course, men had shouted at her on the street before. Even in Australia it happened, particularly if she passed building sites in the city — but not with the constant, ever-present enthusiasm the Italian men gave to it. And now, she was alone. No one to turn to, no one to protect her if push came to shove. Walking through the streets was like running the gauntlet.

She came out into the piazza before the British base with relief but with an increase in nerves. The base was in the same precinct as one of Brindisi's huge old forts, which squatted, solid and forbidding, behind a low stone wall topped with iron railings, spikes and barbed wire.

Other buildings surrounded it; some quite large and impressive, if one took the trouble to look at them. It was hard to do so, though, because the fort drew the eye, speaking of ancient times when marauding ships had sailed down this very harbour in search of plunder and glory. It made her mouth go dry.

It was the first time she had come here. Jack had always done the liaison with their naval contacts, but now she had to hope they would be equally prepared to talk to her.

There were guards on duty at the gate, inspecting a mule-drawn cart that seemed to contain straw. The wind made her pull her coat around her more securely, and brought a scent of animal and salt, which seemed to contain some essence of Italy.

The guards were Italian, so naturally they gave Rebecca the up-and-down look without which no man in Italy (and, to be fair, quite a few in Australia) could speak to a woman. They sported moustaches, of course. Every Italian man had a moustache. One of these, on the younger of the two, was a bare wisp, but the other was luxuriant and shiny, as though it had a life of its own.

'*Signora?*' that one asked politely.

She handed over her card.

'Mrs Quinn, to see Commander Warren. *Appuntamento.*' She had looked up the word for appointment last night. Her Italian had been getting quite good, but since Jack left she had found herself reaching for words she'd known perfectly before, as though her mind had gone on strike to leave space for her heart.

It had taken her days to secure a firm time to see Commander William Warren, the head of the Australian flotilla. He had been out on patrol until yesterday.

The two guards muttered to each other quickly. She was developing her ear for Italian, so much harder than speaking it, but this was beyond her. Then the older one shrugged, gave her card to the younger, and indicated that she should follow him.

It was something of a relief to see a squad of Australian sailors, with their distinctive white caps, manhandling some supplies from a cart into a low, blocky building. They were laughing and joking as they worked. A couple of them had blond hair, like Jack; silly that she should suddenly feel a sharp pain under her breast. In Sydney, she had known so many women whose husbands were away at the war; they seemed to be able to put on a good front. So could she.

The young guard didn't lead her to the fort, but to a relatively modern building, no more than fifty years old, with arched Romanesque windows.

It was cool inside, with high ceilings, and the walls were, surprisingly, painted a rich pink. She couldn't imagine an Australian naval station being painted pink, not even this dark fuchsia.

She was led to a part-open door and waved inside, as the guard announced, '*La signora Quinn*,' with a dazzling smile.

'*Grazie*,' Rebecca said.

She took in the room quickly. An antechamber with a small desk, a sailor sitting behind it, a solid dark-haired man – boy, really – with a cupid's bow mouth that made him look even younger. He had a plain anchor on his epaulettes; a leading seaman. She sent a small thank-you to Jack, who had explained all the ranks to her – at length – the summer they'd met. She'd even found it interesting, because he did.

The leading seaman stood to greet her, looking curious but not surprised.

'Commander Warren will be right with you, ma'am,' he said. He looked around as though to find her a seat, but the office was filled with wooden boxes and a couple of tea chests. A filing cabinet stood against one wall, its top drawer open, and a box below it was half full of papers. She had interrupted his filing, but he didn't seem to mind. The Australians had only been in Italy for three weeks, and had spent most of that out on patrol. Not much time for filing.

'Thank you,' Rebecca said. 'I'm sorry for interrupting you.'

'Oh, don't worry about that!' he said. 'Gosh, it's good to see someone from home.'

The simple enthusiasm was reassuring.

'I know what you mean. It's rather nice to hear an Aussie accent.'

The door behind the desk opened and cut them short. 'Mrs Quinn?'

Commander Warren smiled at her and ushered her into his office.

She had met him once before, three years ago, just after war had been declared. A well set-up man, handsome even, with a strong straight nose and a mouth that gave nothing away. He looked tired, and more than three years older.

'Commander Warren. Thank you for seeing me.'

This office was also clearly in the process of being unpacked, but here there was a plain wooden chair, which he held for her as she sat, then went around to his own – not much better.

'Mrs Quinn, what can I do for you?' He had a pleasant Scottish accent, modified by years in Australia, but still there, burring his consonants.

She took out her notebook and pencil. 'I intend to continue with my husband's work while he's away, and I'm hoping you will keep me informed, as you kept him.'

Surprise flickered over his face.

'You've seen my credentials,' she pressed.

'Credentials?' He looked confused. But Jack had submitted both his and Rebecca's foreign-correspondent credentials when they first arrived in Brindisi – first to the British, the French and the Italians, and then to Warren when the Australians had arrived. At least, she had assumed Jack had submitted hers along with his.

'My husband didn't tell you that I'm an accredited journalist? With *The Sydney Morning Herald* and the *Evening News*? And *Le Monde*, for that matter!'

Warren now looked embarrassed, as a man might who had walked in on an argument between husband and wife. How could Jack have forgotten to show her credentials? A cold lump formed in her stomach. The simple answer was that he wouldn't have. Couldn't have. It had been deliberate. But she couldn't think about that now.

'You're not a war correspondent,' Warren said definitely. Well, of course not. There were very few accredited war correspondents. For most of the war, there had only been one Australian accredited – Charles Bean – and he had won his accreditation in a lottery run by the Australian Journalists' Association. The various defence departments liked to keep a strong hold on what was reported and by whom. But they couldn't stop journalists from just turning up and writing stories, and they had learned to work with them, mostly.

She was a journalist, not just a journalist's wife. She'd come to Italy to get away from the deadly routine of the Women's Pages, and by God she was going to do it. Although Jack's absence made difficulties for her, it also opened up opportunities to establish herself as an independent journalist, quite capable of working alone in foreign climes.

Her papers went everywhere with her, for safety. It was the work of seconds to take them out and hand them to Warren, who looked them over quickly before handing them back to her.

Neither of them said anything, but Warren nodded to her. She took a deep breath, damping down the nerves that had erupted so fiercely.

'So, I'm hoping, firstly, to interview you about the situation here in Brindisi – in the Adriatic generally – and then to get press access for any future press conferences or announcements.'

A frown went across his face, and he sat back.

'The interview . . . well, I can give you a few words, I daresay. But press access – no, I'm sorry, Mrs Quinn, that won't be possible.'

Her heart pounded. Any setback, no matter how small, seemed to overset her these days. She had thought of herself as independent, but with Jack gone, everything seemed too hard.

Oh, she hated feeling like this! So weak. So *incompetent*. Anger helped. She drew on it for strength, moistening her lips and swallowing against a dry throat.

'My credentials—'

'Fine, perfectly fine. But both the British and the Italians have a strict rule: no women allowed in the press corps. Technically, you're not even supposed to be on base. I made an exception because you'd come so far – and because you're Jack Quinn's wife.'

Jack was somewhere between an accredited war correspondent and an ordinary journalist like herself. He didn't have *formal* accreditation. He didn't need it.

Every officer in the Royal Australian Navy knew Jack, since 1911 when the RAN was formed. Jack had been the specialist journalist, the one who always reported on the Navy with respect and admiration. Obsession, even. He had travelled on an RAN ship to New Guinea at the beginning of the war, setting up in Rabaul after it had surrendered. He and Rebecca had been separated for six months. That ship had been the *Parramatta*, Warren's ship, and he and Warren had been friends ever since.

She knew she had skated into war reporting on Jack's coat tails. Women were expected to write about 'the women's side of the war' – the effect on children, on the home front, on women 'forced' to work in munitions factories and on the railways – but Jack had offered her the opportunity to do so much more when he'd suggested she come with him to Italy.

'I appreciate you making an exception,' she said to Warren.

Warren relaxed a little. Perhaps he'd feared womanly tears, reproaches. But she would show him that she was a professional.

'Do you know where he is, ma'am?'

'Somewhere in Albania,' she said. 'He went off with some smugglers; I think he was trying to contact the Serbian nationalists.'

'They're causing the Austrians quite a lot of strife.'

'Yes,' she said. 'I'm trying to carry on while he's gone.'

He blinked. Stared for a moment. She held her breath, hoping for a change of heart. But he pushed back from the desk.

'O'Neill!' he called. The leading seaman popped his head around the door.

'Sir?'

'Tea.'

'Aye aye.'

She shouldn't have expected anything else. This man was a strategist, after all, or he wouldn't hold his position.

She sat quietly and waited for the tea. Commander Warren read over a paper on his desk, frowning, but not as though he were ignoring her; rather, as though he were checking something that might be relevant to her situation.

As O'Neill came in and served the tea, in thick white mugs, the commander shook his head, and laid the papers down on the desk.

'I'm sorry, Mrs Quinn. There's no room for interpretation. Women are forbidden in the press conferences here.'

She swallowed her disappointment. This would make her work ten times more difficult. Why hadn't Jack ever mentioned it to her? Perhaps he hadn't known – or perhaps he had, which was why he'd never bothered to submit her papers. Something eased inside her heart at that simple explanation. After all, he had done the direct work with the Navy, while she had used her growing Italian to pore over the local newspapers and talk to the contacts she had started to cultivate in her first few days in the town: the Harbour Master's clerk, the Postmaster and the porter at the train station who sighed over her blue eyes, a *carabiniere* at the police station – the people who knew the local news first. And, of course, the local errand boys, who went everywhere and saw everything. She had several of them on her payroll. They made a good team, she and Jack.

But being barred from the press conferences . . . She wouldn't be able to get the sort of stories that Evans at the *Evening News* would expect. But she mustn't cry. She would never have any respect from anyone again if she cried.

The tea was good, hot and sweet. The best she'd had since coming to Italy.

'There is one favour I'd like to ask . . .' She tried not to look like she was charming him. Business-like, that was the thing.

'Yes?' He gave nothing away. A little tense, worried about having to say no to her.

'Getting my letters back to England and Australia . . .'

Commander Warren allowed Jack to use the naval mail system, which got their post back to England in a week or so; a back-up to the unreliable Italian telegraph service.

He relaxed. 'No problem there. Hand them in at the gate and they'll be put in the post bag. We *want* stories to get back about what we're doing here.'

'You're proud of the work you're doing?'

'Of course,' he said. 'It's vital to the war effort.' He paused. 'I can't give you access here, on base. But at Nonna Rosa's . . .'

He looked at her meaningfully. She smiled. Not on base. But off base? Nonna Rosa's was the trattoria where the officers ate when off duty. So did the journalists, of course.

'Thank you. No doubt I'll see you there.' She tapped her pencil on the paper. 'Now, I just have a few questions . . .'

Rebecca stood outside the gates, where a long stone wall gave a section of quiet from the harbour. She was torn between satisfaction at how the interview had gone and annoyance at being shut out of the press conferences.

No use standing around here in the cold, freezing her fingers off; she should get home and write up the interview. It felt good to get back into harness – maybe she should have done it earlier.

The hills and stairs of Brindisi reminded her of Sydney's foreshore, near her father's warehouse at The Rocks. She wished, as she began the steep ascent, past a travelling knife-sharpener and a shoe-shine lad who couldn't be more than ten, that she was climbing to his office, to sit down and have a cup of tea and laugh about her brother Linus's latest adventure.

She had gone only a little way up the hill when she saw Mr Baker, the American man from the church, coming down towards the gates. In the church he had moved with circumspection, but now he walked with a controlled, athletic grace.

He stopped when he saw her and raised his hat. In the sunlight, she could see him properly for the first time. Around thirty, well dressed in a tan suit and brown gloves. Tall and elegant and good looking, with dark hair and eyes. Clean-shaven, unlike all the Italian men with their moustaches.

'Mr Baker.' It was barely an acknowledgement.

'Visiting your husband?' he asked. He was trying to be polite, clearly, and just as clearly he couldn't think of any other reason a woman might be near the naval base. She should end this conversation – but it was a relief to speak in English and be understood.

'No. Conducting an interview with the Australian commander.'

He raised an eyebrow.

'You're a journalist?' The astonishment in his voice just made it worse. 'I didn't know women could be – what, a foreign correspondent?'

'And the Italians don't think we should be! Women apparently aren't allowed in the official press conferences.' She knew her tone was bitter, but why shouldn't it be? 'I'm reporting on the Otranto Barrage for the *Evening News* and *The Sydney Morning Herald*, but they won't let me in the press conferences even though I have proper press accreditations.'

His look sharpened. Surprised, yes, but there was something else, some alertness, in his gaze. But he shrugged, complete with spread hands.

'Well, it's natural. War's not something you want women involved in.'

Rage surged up and out her throat.

'My husband is away behind enemy lines because of this war, Mr Baker. And I'm not supposed to be *involved* in it?' Her hand swept up and across the hill reaching up from the harbour, full of houses and shops and restaurants. 'Go up there. Go find the mothers praying for their sons at the front. And the girls who are afraid they'll never see their sweethearts again. Go find the widows, and the orphans who know their father will never come home again. And tell *them* they're not involved!'

She almost spat the words; she couldn't remember when she had last been so angry. Even angrier than she had been in the church. Turning on her heel, she walked away, up the hill. Towards the widows and orphans.

Waiting on the corner for a donkey wagon filled with casks to go by, she cast a quick glance back to him. He was standing with his hat in his hands, staring after her as though she had shocked him.

Good.

Now she would go home and write her story and send it off.

But as she climbed the steep stairs that led to the next level, the piazza, she stopped on the middle stair. Perhaps she hadn't been fair to Mr Baker. Her emotions had been so up and down since Jack had left, and her confidence had been shaken by Commander Warren's revelation that her papers hadn't been presented. Sometimes she felt like hitting Jack for going on that fishing boat, for sailing off into the darkness on a dangerous mission. But really, she just wanted to lean into his shoulder, and feel his warm arms around her.

Gosh, how she missed him.

A Letter from Italy

Australia joins the Adriatic fight!

A Royal Australian Navy flotilla of four ships has joined British, French and Italian flotillas in Brindisi to take part in the Otranto Barrage. The Barrage is a collection of naval drifters (boats resembling fishing boats, each armed with a 6-pound guns and depth charges). Together, the drifters deploy steel nets that entangle any submarine attempts to move from the Adriatic bases of the Austro–Hungarian Empire into the traffic-rich Mediterranean.

Commander William Warren, of the Australian flotilla, told our correspondent: 'Our job is to keep the Austrian U-boats from making it out of the Adriatic into the Mediterranean, where they target convoys.'

When asked how the arrival of the Australian flotilla would change operations, Commander Warren said: 'We're used to long patrols and being at sea for days on end. In the past, patrol ships have put into harbour during the night hours. But our allies have agreed to four-day patrols, and I'm confident that we will be able to significantly improve the results of the Barrage.'

Early differences in approach between the Italian and British navies appear to have been resolved by the Australian contingent.

3

Sandro stood and watched her walk away. Well, he'd tried to be polite, and look what it had got him. Another tirade. She just didn't like men, that one.

She was going with her head high and her back straight. *Madonna mia*, she had a good figure. She sure had It. But she was hard, not a shred of warmth. Had to be like that, he supposed, if she was really a reporter.

A woman reporter. He couldn't help but wonder at that. And he couldn't get a single newspaper interested in his photographs!

He turned up the hill, heading for the market square, to collect the day's meagre shopping for Nonna Rosa. Shopping. This wasn't the life he'd expected when he came to Italy. He had thought he'd be fighting, had been sure the Italian military system wouldn't reject him as the American one had. He was fit, he was strong, he was determined. He'd even been a champion boxer in high school. Army regulations – and Army doctors – were ridiculous.

He was tempted to simply take his cameras and go to the front anyway. For a moment, he imagined it. The terrible, stark beauty of No-Man's Land. The camaraderie of the trenches. And, yes, the fear and the ever-present danger. But a shared danger, and a shared purpose. Maybe he'd stick with an American battalion. There were days he'd have killed to hear a US accent.

The market square was sparsely populated – Wednesday was the proper market day, but there were a few daily stalls. There wasn't much on offer. Most of the produce around here was bought by the navies; the townspeople had to make do with the leftovers.

Eggs, greens, autumn fruits – apples and pears – onions, leeks, garlic, chillies . . . it reminded him of home, of going to the greengrocer with his mom when he was little, clinging to her hand in case he got lost in the big city. Brindisi was so *small*. There wasn't a building of more than three storeys. Even in Little Italy, where he grew up, there were four- and five-storey houses, and close on the horizon there had always been the skyscrapers of central Manhattan. New York was a hell of a home town – there wasn't anywhere that could stand up to it.

The light was different here, too. Harder; it gave everything a sharper edge. It made focusing easier, but any blurring was more obvious. The depth of field was completely different.

Some things were the same as Little Italy: the washing strung between houses in the back streets. The aroma of red gravy, always simmering in the background. The voices, bickering or gossiping or fighting in Italian. But no cars, no steam from the subways, no buses or trolley cars. It was too quiet. He'd considered doing a series of photographs of the town. Call them something like 'The Real Italy', get up an exhibition when he went home, build on the success he'd had in that group show last year.

That exhibition had made him think that he might really be able to make a living as something other than a studio photographer. He didn't know how to describe what he did. 'Art' photography usually involved semi-naked girls. But what he wanted to do was make art with the camera. To show the world what he saw; its beauty *and* its ugliness. The critics at the group exhibition had seemed to think he could do it. The critics *and* the buyers. He'd not only sold everything in it, some of those prints were still selling off the walls of Lorenzo's pizza house.

Thinking of Lorenzo's made him homesick – and hungry. He could just tuck into a pizza Neapolitana right now. Instead, he bought an arancini from a stall near the steps and ate with satisfaction.

At least the stall holders had got used to him over the past couple of weeks. No more questions about who he was, where he was from, why he wasn't in the Army.

It still felt odd to be called Alessandro Panucci, though. He'd been simple Al Baker all the way through school, and hadn't that made things easier! His English was accentless, and half of his schoolmates hadn't even known he was Italian. No one shouted 'Itie!' at him as he walked home from school. No one on the other team yelled 'Dago!' when he went out to box for the school, as they had to Guillarmo Bartolacci.

Alessandro Panucci. Al Baker. He'd never been able to make up his mind which he preferred; which he really was.

'What's Rosa cooking tonight?' the wizened old man on the tobacco stall asked him. Dario was a regular at Nonna Rosa's, a widower who'd never learned to cook.

'*Arrabbiata*,' Sandro said. 'And *scaloppine con funghi*.' Darn, he'd forgotten the mushrooms. He turned back and bought them: porcini, portobello, champignon. At least there were plenty. Perhaps she'd do *funghi trifolati* instead of *arrabbiata* for the pasta course, and *scaloppine limone* for the *primi*. They had a lemon tree in the backyard and this far south Nonna got lemons all year round.

'*Bene*,' Dario said, smacking his lips. '*Delizioso!*' He grinned at the woman on the next stall, a widow of about thirty. 'So, Serafina, you'd better snap this one up before one of the young ones gets him. He's a good catch!'

Serafina eyed Sandro up and down with relish. He was taller than most Italian men – most of the first-generation Italian–American children were taller than their parents – but something about the way Serafina assessed him made him wish he had a squint and a limp.

'Well, he knows where to find me,' she said, with a wink and swish of her skirts. She was joking, but there was a real invitation beneath the joke. She was pretty enough, but not overly bright.

'*Domani*,' he said. 'I'll see you tomorrow.'

'I'll be here!'

Dario laughed and laughed.

Sandro took the vegetables back to the trattoria, thanking God that the mild autumn sun was shining. It brought out the cream and gold of the plastered houses, the burnt orange of the terracotta roofs, lit up the little grottoes to the Virgin Mary which nestled in nooks and crannies throughout the town. The blue of the Virgin's robe was the same blue as the sky.

He was the only young man not in uniform in the streets. Sailors everywhere. He knew that the news of his unfitness for service had gone the rounds, but that just made it worse. *Not a real man*, that's what they all thought. He could tell by the way they looked; the small half-smile of pity lurking under those Italian moustaches.

He refused to grow one. Most of the Italian men in New York had moustaches too, but he didn't care. His bare upper lip was a declaration of nationality. He might look Italian, he might speak Italian, but he was an American, and proud of it.

'*Ciao, Nonna!*' he called as he went through the front door.

His grandmother came out of the office. If he was taller than most Italian men, then so would she have been in her youth – even at seventy she could almost look him in the eye. He wondered if his grandfather had cared; her husband, his father's father, had been shorter by far, according to the photographs.

'So, what did you get?' Her Italian was different to the normal Salentino he'd heard in the market. A little more refined, less guttural. But her critical assessment of food was the same as every other Italian *nonna*.

He unpacked his canvas bag onto the kitchen bench, Nonna Rosa watching as he placed each item carefully on the bench. Finally, she sniffed. The onions were small, he knew, and the apples had spots.

'*Spazzatura*,' she said. Garbage. He could feel himself tense, but he knew she wasn't blaming him. Just the war. Nonna Rosa was a tough old bird, but she didn't take things personally.

She sighed and began to put the food away. He was used to the routine of the place now, so he took off his jacket and hat and began to set the tables for the night's meal.

'You know La signora Quinn?' he said.

'Yes.'

'She's a reporter. A journalist.'

'She herself, not her husband?'

'That's what she said.'

'Hhha,' she said. It was more an expulsion of air than a word; a noise that meant she was thinking and he should not talk to her.

Not for the first time, he thought of his father's description of her, his mother, given as a kind of warning before he left for Italy. *Your grandmother, she's a good woman. But she's not an easy woman to live with.*

His mother had smiled and patted his arm. 'I'm sure he'll be fine with her. What woman wouldn't love a grandson like Sandro?' she said softly, in that gentle tone she always used with her children. Even when they were naughty, she chided them gently. He and his brothers would have done anything for her, anything to bring that lovely smile to her face. They perfectly understood why their father doted on her – she was everything a wife and mother should be.

His brothers were older. Giovanni was in the Army, based in France, and Marco worked as a translator at the Defense Department. Marco had been able to stay in the States, which was a comfort to their parents. Their mother hadn't liked it when Sandro had decided to go to Italy. His sisters were still in the old neighbourhood, though, with their families.

He set out the forks and spoons for the pasta course, noting the contrast they made with the dark wood. A gleam of light on the blade of the knife. Hard to catch that in an image, and he didn't have time to try. At least he wasn't only helping his grandmother anymore, now that he was working with Marcio Fabrini.

And at least he was near the sea. Growing up on Manhattan meant that the sea was always there, the backgound noise to everything, the salt smell even overtaking the garlic of Little Italy and the five-spice of Chinatown.

'Fill up the carafe, *nipote*,' his nonna said. *Nipote*. Grandson. He was the only one here – would it kill her to use his name?

'Sure, Nonna.'

She had a barrel of cheap Castel del Monte red in the back and some bottles of good Brindisi Rosso – a local wine that packed quite a punch.

He filled the carafes with the Castel del Monte and placed them ready in the office. Nonna was unusually quiet. She was up to something, maybe. She often reminded him of his brother Marco – the same trick of staring silently at him, the same lack of patience for stupidity. When Marco was quiet like this, something was brewing.

No doubt he'd find out in her own good time.

4

Nonna Rosa's was three blocks back from the harbour, in one of the old stone buildings so common in Brindisi. It had one large arched window, but no sign, except a small blackboard on the wall near the door that said simply: *Trattoria Famiglia*.

Rebecca hadn't been there since Jack had gone to Albania; more than two weeks. She wasn't quite sure why not. Something to do with being the only woman at the table. When her husband had been there it had been unremarkable. Alone, though . . .

Of course, she had worked with men before. At *The Sydney Morning Herald* she had been one of only two female journalists – the other was Louise Mack, her boss, the editor of the Women's Page. Louise was a genuine celebrity, having written a book about her experiences as a war correspondent, going behind enemy lines to report on the German invasion of Belgium in 1914. As a consequence, the editors and male reporters accorded her a guarded respect. You only had to read her book, *A Woman's Experiences in the Great War*, to see that she was utterly fearless.

As Louise's protegée, Rebecca had been treated with a wary courtesy, which had grown into respect after they realised that, although she was the daughter of a red-ragger feminist mother, she wasn't going to harangue them about politics, nor did she think she knew everything there was to know about journalism.

Her marriage to Jack, who was already working at the *Herald*, had helped. As a single woman, there had been too many equivocal situations; as a married woman she was safer to work around.

Wearing any old thing to dinner had been fine when Jack was with her. Alone, she armoured herself with a good dark-green woollen suit and a white silk blouse, under her winter coat. A nice felt hat, a pair of green leather gloves she'd splurged on in Rome, and she was ready for anything.

Outside Nonna Rosa's was a long bench table filled with men in overcoats and hats, all smoking cigarillos. They ignored her, until she passed them by to go through the arched doorway. Then one said, '*Bianca bella!*' in a tone of astonished gratification, and they all turned to look.

She walked past with her nose in the air, cheeks faintly warm. It was worse, somehow, than merely passing them on the street.

One step through the doorway and the smell of good food hit her. She was accustomed to garlic by now; was beginning to enjoy it. She could smell it: garlic and tomato and beef, fresh bread and vinegar. The wood-and-stone room was redolent with it, as though the aroma had soaked into the walls, along with the tobacco smoke from the hand-rolled cigarettes every Italian man seemed to smoke after dinner.

The smell took her back to her first dinner here with Jack; his eyes bright across the table as he told some story. Her stomach clenched and she was momentarily angry with him for not being there. Perhaps it would be easier to go home. But she was conscious that her suit was loose on her; she couldn't remember when she had last eaten a full meal. She'd been buying rolls and soft fruit and eating them in their room at the pensione. She just hadn't wanted to front up alone, to navigate the intricate waters of a woman trying to eat in a respectable restaurant without a man.

She should eat. More, she should take her place in the world. Damn Jack, encouraging her to come to Italy and then rabbiting away to Albania.

Inside, it was crowded. Three long tables and two smaller ones. The tables were full of sailors – officers, mostly. French near the door, Italians in the middle and, yes, the Australians and British on the far side. Conversations in a number of languages rose around her, Babel-like.

Overhead, strings of salami and Parma hams hung from the beams, and carafes of wine were lined up ready on the back counter.

And there was Nonna Rosa, coming out from behind the counter to greet her. A woman almost as tall as Rebecca, and still striking; iron-grey hair, snapping brown eyes . . . not the motherly, comforting figure she had expected when she first read the sign.

Rebecca tensed. In most places, a woman alone would be shown the door, assumed to be a prostitute. At least, at Nonna Rosa's, they knew her.

Nonna Rosa nodded. '*Signora Quinn, buonasera.*'

'*Buonasera, Nonna Rosa.*' It had taken her a week or so to get used to calling a stranger 'Grandmother Rosa'. But everyone who came here did the same.

'*Vieni.*'

29

Rebecca followed her to the table at the back where the journalists sat. Where she had sat with Jack and the others, laughing and talking and happy.

This time, she was conscious of every male eye in the place on her. Commander Warren was there, at the front near the window. He nodded to her, a smile at the corner of his mouth. She hoped that was a good sign.

'*Bene*,' Nonna Rosa said. The three other journalists in town were there, as they usually were at this time of day. She looked at them with new eyes; not as Jack's friends, but as potential rivals, now she was working on her own.

Ambroise Lemaitre, from *Le Figaro*, a dark-haired man who, somehow, didn't look French. Perhaps it was his glass eye, which gave him an air of absent-minded distraction. Mark Coates, also brown-haired, with clothes that were definitely English, from the *Daily Herald*. And Christy Nolan, a redhead-turning-grey who looked up with twinkling blue eyes – Irish eyes – and said with a pronounced brogue, 'Begorrah, Mrs Quinn, it's good to see you!'

'Hello, Christy,' she said, sitting down next to him, but with a sudden qualm. Was it right for her to call him by his first name, without Jack being here, especially since he was so much older than she – old enough to be her father, in fact? She had no guide to etiquette for a working woman who was married but without her husband – a situation, she reflected, that thousands of women must be finding themselves in.

'M'sieur,' she said, nodding. 'Mr Coates.'

'*Bonsoir, madame*,' Lemaitre said automatically, but his good eye was alive with curiosity, looking her over with no trace of male appreciation or sympathy. All business.

'A farewell dinner, Mrs Quinn?' Coates said. 'I suppose you'll be going back to the Women's Pages now your husband has gone off.'

Water off a duck's back. She'd had that dismissive reaction from so many people, men *and* women, that she barely registered it anymore, except for the flicker of the anger she had poured out on Mr Baker. She was faintly ashamed of how she'd berated him.

'No,' she said. 'I'm staying.'

At that they all stilled, looking her over in an entirely new way. As competition. It was very satisfying.

From behind her, Nonna Rosa demanded, 'Spaghetti or penne?'

'Penne,' she said quickly, not wanting to struggle with the long strands of spaghetti in front of these critical eyes. She'd got used to the way trattorias worked: no menu, just one pasta for *primi*, the first course, and sometimes two choices for *secondi*, the main course. If you wanted choice, you cooked at home. Although Italians normally ate a big lunch and a small supper, Nonna Rosa's had adjusted to the routine of the foreign navies, where the officers, while in port, worked mostly during the day and came out to eat at night.

The big evening meal meant that Rebecca rarely ate breakfast; a soft roll and a cafe latte mid-morning, while she read the local papers, was all she needed. It helped with the finances, which were doable, but tight.

'Good choice, lass,' Christy Nolan said. It was easy to think of him as Christy, just as it was impossible to think of Coates as Mark. Lemaitre was harder to read.

Christy poured her a glass of wine and she took a sip to gain some breathing space. As she set the glass back on the table she noticed an Italian officer coming from the back, where the men

31

went to relieve themselves – she, of course, had to wait until she returned to the pensione; she was careful to drink very little at meals. She recognised Tenente Somma, a man with whom Jack had been quite friendly. She nodded to him and smiled. He stiffened in outrage, and spoke in Italian.

'Signora, what are you doing here?'

'Having dinner,' she said quietly.

His face softened and he tried to speak in English. 'Ah, signora, you not know, *si*? Only the . . . the, the *puttana*, the bad women, they eat in *pubblico* with men.'

Another moment, another choice: to stay, or to be a good girl and go home.

'There is no food at my pensione, Tenente,' she said simply. 'I must eat.'

'*Si, si,* but . . .' He cast a look of loathing at the men. 'Not like *this*.'

'This is the journalists' table. I am a journalist.' Italians put a gender on their nouns. Journalist, oddly, was feminine. '*Sono un giornalista,*' she said.

His mouth worked; for a moment she thought he was going to spit at her.

'*Puttana,*' he hissed. '*Si vergogna tuo marito.*' *Whore. You shame your husband.* A flush swept over her; she could feel it move up her chest and face. He took it for shame, and satisfaction sparked in his eyes.

She stood up, her chair scraping in a sudden silence. Every eye was on her.

'I'm a journalist, sir,' she said loudly. 'And my husband is proud of my work.'

Tenente Somma sneered at her. 'Excuses for behaving like a strumpet!' He turned his back on her and walked away.

The officers all stared at her, Italian and French and British and Australian.

'*Signori*,' she said, nodding to them all. 'When men leave for the war, women must do their jobs, or you will have no homes to go back to when it is all over.'

Whispers, as those who could speak English translated for those who could not. Somma turned to stare at her with a kind of hatred in his eyes, but most of the others relaxed, or shrugged agreement, or simply sat with bland, blank faces. A couple of British ensigns, in a corner, sniggered and ogled her, but she stared them down, as she'd seen her mother stare down hecklers at suffragist meetings.

When they were quiet, she sat again.

Coates was watching her with much the same expression as Tenente Somma. Lemaitre was unreadable, his dark gaze merely thoughtful. But Christy patted her hand like an uncle and said, 'Have a drink, *acushla*.'

For once, she drank thirstily, shaking a little. She'd met with male hatred of a working woman before, but that had been in Australia, where she had the fortress of her own home and her friends and family to retire to. And Jack, who had laughed away anything dark, who had urged her to get her correspondent's credentials. Yes, she should remember that, that it had been his idea for her to become a journalist in the first place. He *would* be proud of her being here.

Someone coughed softly to get her attention. She sat back to let the waiter put her plate down, glancing up over her shoulder.

'Mr Baker!' His unexpected presence rattled her. What on earth was an American photographer doing serving tables in an Italian trattoria? He had taken off his suit jacket and was working in waistcoat and shirt sleeves.

He nodded to her, a waiter's nod, with no warmth behind it, as he placed her pasta on the table.

'It's Alessandro Panucci here, ma'am.'

'Nonna Rosa's grandson, *non*?' Lemaitre said.

Nonna Rosa's *grandson*? Pretending to be an American? No, he came from New York. He *was* an American. Italian–American. But why call himself Baker? Fraudulent, she thought.

'That's right,' he said. 'I'm just helping out because Nonna's regular waiter has been called up.' Mr Baker – she *couldn't* think of him as Il Signor Panucci – tried to keep an expressionless face, as a good waiter should, but failed to hide his lack of servitude. Too much *presence* for a waiter, who should be unobtrusive. You couldn't ignore Mr Baker.

She realised that the three men had relaxed, even Christy Nolan, as though having someone of the 'lower orders' in the conversation made them stronger. It was the reaction of a class-based society, and she hated it.

But that didn't mean she had to like *him*.

She nodded coolly to thank him for the pasta, and he withdrew, face set. So, he had come running to his grandmother to avoid the American draft? As an American citizen, the Italian government couldn't conscript him. She'd been right to call him a coward.

A flicker of unease reminded her that Jack had also not joined the Army, or the Navy. In Australia, there was no draft to avoid; all the ANZACs were volunteers. Journalists served in their own way; Jack had nothing to be ashamed of. But when she considered it, she realised that all three of the men with her had other reasons for not fighting. Lemaitre had that glass eye – he would have been rejected for military service. Coates was a conscientious objector, a pacifist. And Christy – well, Ireland

34

was only in the war because it was notionally part of Britain. It hadn't decided to join in, as Australia had, but had had the war forced upon it. There was no conscription there, either.

The penne was delicious, and so was the pan-fried veal that followed it. The fight with Somma, the astonishment over Mr Baker, had given her an appetite, the first time she had felt hungry for days. She had been eaten up with worry about Jack, which was only natural, but she knew she couldn't keep up that level of anxiety. She needed to adapt.

Small servings, just enough to fill her up. Every time Mr Baker's tanned hand came past her to the table, she tensed, but he continued to serve with noncommittal efficiency. After the meal itself, some dried apple and cheese, the discussion switched to business: the war, the Navy's work in blockading the Adriatic, the Australian arrival. It was restful, although the men sounded her out, tested her – which revealed to her how little they had spoken to her when she'd been there with Jack – trying to find out if she had access to Jack's special sources of information, and how much she knew about politics, ships, personnel. She held her own, thanking Jack silently more than once for all those late-night discussions about the RAN. The men hadn't spoken like this to Jack; they had accepted him automatically as one of their own – and accepted her simply as his wife.

Of course, none of them expected her to get her hands dirty.

'I'm thinking of going up to the front,' Coates said. 'That's where the real stories are.'

'Surely, lad, go and get yourself killed by a stray bullet for King and Country when you don't even believe the war should be happening,' Christy said.

'The war is a conspiracy of capitalist warmongers,' countered Coates.

'I'm not saying you're wrong,' Christy replied, a glint in his eye. 'So, why report on it at all?'

And they were off on that familiar debate. Christy delighted in baiting Coates, who was torn between his patriotism and his socialism. Lemaitre smiled at her and toasted her silently with his wine glass, a gesture that seemed to be a simple compliment on how she had handled herself so far. She nodded in return, but she didn't raise her glass.

Nonna Rosa arrived at the table with small cups of dark coffee.

'*Grazie, no, Nonna Rosa,*' Rebecca said. If she had that coffee she'd be awake half the night. Not to mention needing to use the necessary here, and there was no WC for women. The men – the Navy men – had been going past them to the back door all night. No doubt Nonna Rosa kept a barrel for their convenience in the alley behind.

At the thought, Commander Warren walked behind them towards the alley, and paused, as if seeing her for the first time.

'Mrs Quinn,' he said. 'Nice to see you.'

'Commander Warren,' she said, shifting her chair so she could look at him more easily. He nodded to the men.

'We're off in the morning on patrol, so we might have something for you all in a few days,' he added, including her impartially, and she felt a rush of gratitude. It would have been so easy for him to ignore her and speak only to the men.

'How about an interview, Commander?' Coates said.

'One a week is my limit,' Warren answered, moving towards the back door.

The men looked at each other, and then turned to her in astonishment.

'You got an *interview* with Warren?'

'I think he thought I was going to ask about getting back to Britain. I – er – surprised him.'

'Typical!' Coates snarled. 'Womanly wiles!'

'But yes,' Lemaitre said. 'Of course she used her wiles. Would we not do so, too? And what doors would be closed to her beauty?'

Christy gave her a long, considering look.

'We all write for different rags,' he said. 'We help each other out. Sure, get the scoop, but don't leave the rest of us out in the cold.'

She understood that. It was the way Jack had worked with them, although he had kept back more than he had shared.

'No worries,' she said, deliberately using the phrase Jack would have used. 'There wasn't much.' She gave them the information she'd already sent off and they all took notes. 'But that door's closed,' she added. 'Women aren't allowed in press conferences.'

The three men relaxed immediately, and she felt rather proud that they considered her so much a rival, but she also worried. If press conferences were so important, how was she to do her job? Jack had better come back with a smasher of a story, or she would know the reason why.

Mr Baker removed the last of their plates and presented the bill silently to each of the men in turn.

It was only ten o'clock, but the Italian government had mandated that all restaurants close by ten-thirty. Rebecca watched the journalists merely sign across their bill. Of course. Jack had kept an account here, too. Mr Baker, standing behind, formed a stark contrast to Mark Coates: Coates a little stout and florid, Mr Baker lean and dark; Coates full of self-satisfaction, Mr Baker . . . well, he clearly wasn't used to being a waiter.

'We add an account for you too, eh, Signora Quinn?' Nonna Rosa said as she approached the table.

'Thank you,' she said. She signed the bill, and something in her settled. If she had been asked in Sydney, she would have said that she disliked routine, but here, alone, where so much was strange, the idea of routinely eating at the same place, somewhere she was known, held a good deal of comfort.

As they rose to leave, Nonna Rosa detained her. Assuming it was something to do with settling up whatever Jack had owed, Rebecca nodded goodnight to the others and followed the signora to the back room – a small office-cum-storage room, where bags of rice and flour lined the walls.

There was a desk, with nothing on it except a spike on which papers had been impaled, and a big blotter and inkwell. Nonna Rosa moved around it and waved Rebecca to the small visitor's chair, but she didn't sit down herself. She stood, tall and suddenly imposing, dropping her smiling Italian-*nonna* persona.

Mr Baker followed them, out of sheer curiosity it seemed, and leaned against the door jamb, crossing his arms. Behind them, the noise of the departing diners faded. The air smelled of garlic and dust.

'You need my grandson,' Nonna Rosa said.

Rebecca blinked. What could the woman mean? Using him as a translator? A local guide?

'Nonna!' Mr Baker protested.

'I heard,' she continued. 'No press conferences for women. *Sì?*'

'Yes,' Rebecca said, and Nonna Rosa nodded, as if vindicated.

'Alessandro, he is *fotografo*. How to say . . . photographer. Not *giornalista*. You are a *giornalista*, but no press conferences. *Presto!*' She threw up her hands, as if pulling off a magic trick.

Rebecca looked quickly at Mr Baker. A *press* photographer? His card hadn't said that. It had just said *Al Baker, Photographer* and an address in New York.

He shrugged, his expressive face showing a great deal of reserve. She knew he didn't approve of her, not from the moment they met, and now she had the impression that her public facing down of her detractors had put her beyond the pale with him. Annoyance grew in her; but she might need him.

'So, you think Mr Ba— *Signor Panucci* can go to the press conferences on my behalf?'

'For you, *si*. And you—' Nonna Rosa stabbed a finger at her, 'you get him the . . .' She appealed to Mr Baker. 'How you say it?'

'The press credentials.' He hesitated, and flicked a glance at her. 'Could you do that?'

'Get you a press pass?' She considered. 'Yes, probably. The *Evening News* would likely do it.'

They looked at each other, assessing the potential for partnership.

Despite her dislike for him, she couldn't quell the spiral of excitement that climbed inside her abdomen. Perhaps this was the solution, a way around all the barriers, until Jack came back. The fact that Mr Baker disliked her – well, she had worked before with men who disapproved of female journalists, and no doubt she would again.

If only she knew how long Jack would be away! Or if he was likely to go off again, following the exciting stories. If she teamed up with Mr Baker and Jack came back next week,

39

what then? A small, cold voice deep in her mind asked, *And if I don't team up with him and Jack never comes back, what then?* Journalists had been killed more times than she could count in this war. She pressed her hands together in her lap to stop them shaking, and focused on reason, on practicality. A photographer's work would be helpful to Jack as well as to her. There was no drawback to getting Mr Baker credentials.

'I can go to the Italian press conferences, and translate afterwards,' he assured her. His tone was odd; as though he were determined not to be too enthusiastic. Not to plead.

'Why don't you have credentials?' she asked, trying not to get swept up in the possibilities. Was he even a photographer?

He pulled a stool over and sat on it, shrugging.

'In New York, I was a studio photographer. I sold a couple of photographs to the news agencies, but I wasn't a press photographer. Since I can't fight, I thought – war photography. I've got the equipment. I can do the job. But getting access, and selling what I shoot . . . that's a different ball of wax.'

She'd never heard that expression before, but it was clear enough. And reasonable. He'd said, *can't fight*. Perhaps he wasn't medically fit? There were illnesses that didn't show, she knew, like heart murmurs. But he did look very strong; and he moved quickly and surely, like a man in good health. Well, it was none of her affair. If Mr Baker – Signor Panucci; Rebecca really didn't know what to call him, even in her thoughts – wanted to pretend he couldn't fight, that was his business.

Nonna Rosa said something rapidly in Italian, and handed a manila folder to Mr Baker. He spread the contents across the desk. Photographs. A few studio portraits of young men in uniform, an older couple on their wedding day. Standard.

Not very inspiring. And then . . . a series of ships coming into Brindisi harbour, flags flying.

'The Australian flotilla coming into port,' she said.

'Yeah. And here . . .' He uncovered another, of men, sailors, loading boxes of ammunition onto a ship.

They were good. Sharp, clear, well composed. As good as any she'd seen in *The Sydney Morning Herald*. Underneath them, something else entirely . . . she pulled out an astonishing image of a park (could it be Central Park?) in winter, icicles hanging from tree branches, an unbroken sweep of snow echoing the curve of a pond, the whole thing a composition of light and shape. Art, not mere photography. She opened her mouth to say something – she didn't know what – but Mr Baker quickly slid that one beneath the portraits, and put the flotilla shot firmly on top.

'Well?' he said.

Rebecca held out her hand. 'It's a deal, Mr Baker.'

Nonna Rosa sniffed loudly. 'Alessandro,' she said.

Rebecca nodded, but really, she barely knew him. She couldn't possibly call him by his first name.

'We can send these two to the *Evening News*, and I'll request credentials for you. I'll write an update to go with them. Might as well start with a sale. They pay through bank drafts.'

He opened his mouth, clearly to ask a question.

'I'm sorry,' she forestalled him. 'I don't know what they pay for photographs.'

He shrugged again, that high-shouldered Italian shrug that seemed so foreign to her. 'Well, more than I'm getting now, eh, Nonna?'

The older woman watched them with deep satisfaction on her face. '*Si. Bene*. And I teach *you* Italian. Salentino.'

Salentino was the local dialect of Italian. Rebecca blinked.
'I—'

'I heard, you have been asking for a teacher. I teach. You come, help me in kitchen one hour every day, I teach. Not peasant Italian. My father was an *avvocato*.'

A lawyer for a father. Perhaps that explained the hauteur; Nonna Rosa had come down in the world – and was determined her grandson would make his way back up. Fair enough.

'*Grazie, signora*.'

Nonna Rosa sat down behind her desk and placed her two hands flat on it.

'Out now.'

'Yes, Nonna Rosa.'

Rebecca smiled on her way out; there was an odd kind of comfort in being told what to do by a grandmother.

•

Mr Baker walked her back to her pensione, past the rectangles of light cast by emptying trattoria doorways, into the dark streets beyond. The men who were still clustered around the cafes and trattorias in the piazzas kept their distance. Of course. She was with a man now. Relief warred with annoyance, and annoyance helped her to be businesslike and crisp.

'I'll have these images posted to the *Evening News* tomorrow.'

'Use the post here and it'll be a year before they get there.'

'Commander Warren has said I can use the naval postal service.'

He whistled in astonishment. 'Well, you certainly went over big with him.' There was – not quite disapproval, but a kind of restraint in his voice.

'Nonsense.' She hesitated; but if they were going to be partners in this enterprise, he should know. 'My husband is a friend of his.'

'Ah ha. Nothing like a bit of personal pull.'

He was right, of course, but did he have to say it so baldly? Americans! So brash.

The Damonicas' house was down a small street, and off a tiny square. Before the war, it had housed mostly travelling salesmen. Now, Rebecca was often the only guest, and those who did stay there were superannuated *nonnos* who had been called back as salesmen by their old employers; men who toddled through occasionally and went off again. The only other woman she saw there was Angela, the owner's daughter.

'This is my pensione,' she said, and offered her hand. They shook hands and Mr Baker tipped his hat. She couldn't see his face underneath it, despite the small lamp burning next to the gate.

'Goodnight, Mrs Quinn,' he said, his voice alive in the darkness. 'I'll call on you in the morning and we can discuss our next move. *Buona notte.*'

His Italian accent perfect, the lilt in his voice clear, Mr Baker suddenly seemed more Italian than American. A dago, Jack would have called him. It unsettled her.

'I'm looking forward to working with you,' he added.

She reached up to turn down the lamp – part of her agreement with Signor Damonica – and went through the gate, holding it open just a moment to say, 'Goodnight, Mr Baker,' conscious that she was repressing her own emotions in response to his enthusiasm. That British reaction to emotion she'd been brought up with. *Foreigners* were emotional. If you were part of the British Empire you controlled yourself. It was something to hold on to in this foreign place.

He waited until she had closed the gate and then she heard his footsteps move away. She stood still until they had faded into the distance, wanting a few minutes to herself, to let the day and its ups and downs settle in her mind.

Tomorrow he would come and they would plan a story. His pictures, her words. No. Her words, his pictures. An image rose in her mind of a wonderful partnership; of the two of them producing magnificent journalism, so that Jack, when he came back, was astonished by how well she had done. Mr Baker certainly had the talent, even if she didn't like him very much. She mocked herself, imagining glory like a child. She would have to be careful not to rely on him too much, just because Jack was away. And he was, after all, a foreigner.

5

'Alessandro! Come here!'

'In a minute! I'm in the middle of developing!'

He'd learned the Italian for that in the first week he was here. Nonna insisted that he always speak to her in Italian, even though she often despaired of his accent. Sandro slid the developed film through a bowl of clean water to wash off the stop bath and pegged it up on a line to dry, then set the door of the little room open so the fumes could dissipate.

He could do only the most basic of photographic tasks here, developing and contact printing, but it was better than nothing. He went down the stairs, whistling. Even just developing a film was a pleasure.

Nonna Rosa was waiting for him by the kitchen counter.

'Here,' she said, sketching a quick map of the harbour on the back of an old envelope. 'See? Next to the *droghiere*.' He must have looked puzzled, because she paused, searching her memory for the English word. 'Chandler's. The ship chandler.

Ropes and lanterns and . . .' She waved her hands. 'The things boats use.'

Sandro smiled to himself. It wasn't often his nonna was at a loss for words, even English ones. She thrust the map into his hands and led him out to the back courtyard, to the shed next to the lemon tree at the very end of the property, which backed onto a tiny lane. Sandro had to help her drag the shed door open across the stone paving; the wood had swelled with the constant rain.

Nonna muttered a word he was surprised she knew. Like all Italian–American boys, he had been most interested in Italian when he was learning swear words. That one he hadn't even heard until he was in high school.

He was overcome with affection for her, and it surprised him. She certainly didn't invite it. But in the late light the wrinkles on her face stood out more clearly. He had never known anyone quite so alone, and it roused all his protective instincts. Not that she would thank him for that. She wasn't the grandmother he had imagined having as a boy – but she was far more entertaining as an adult. He wondered sometimes how she had given birth to his conservative, sentimental father.

At the back of the tidy shed was a handcart. He could barely see it in the gloom; the sun had just set, but the clouds were thick and it was almost as dark as night in the shed.

'There,' Nonna Rosa said. He grabbed the handcart – like a wheelbarrow, but with a wheel on either side at the front, making it more stable, but harder to steer. He stood in the yard with it, feeling faintly ridiculous, reduced to being a little boy playing with toys. He would have loved this handcart as a kid, its solid wooden sides and bright blue paint.

'As soon as it's dark, go to the place, and pick up what Giaccomo gives you. Cover it over with this.' She handed him a blanket. 'Don't let anyone see what you have.'

'No,' he said.

She blinked and actually pulled back in astonishment.

'I'm not going anywhere until you tell me what this is about.'

Her mouth narrowed. 'It's not illegal.'

'I'm not traipsing around town like an errand boy. What's going on?' He spoke in English, mainly because he couldn't remember the Italian for 'errand boy', but it seemed to convince her that he was serious.

She shrugged and replied in Italian. 'Supplies.'

'What kind of supplies?'

'Food.'

'Oh, for God's sake, Nonna, I'm going to find out as soon as I pick it up. What kind of food?'

'Flour,' she muttered. 'Strong flour.'

Jesus, Mary and Joseph. Flour was – rationed wasn't exactly the right word, because it wasn't that organised, but it was in very short supply. It was why Nonna had been making ravioli instead of fettucine or tagliatelle – ravioli required less pasta, less flour. Most ordinary people had been reduced to eating black bread instead of white, made with ground almonds and chickpeas and anything else that could make a paste.

Flour was like gold.

'Where are you getting it?'

'It's not illegal.' Her mouth was stubborn.

'Then why do I have to go after dark?'

'It's . . . an arrangement.'

He stood still, unmoved, and she sighed. The light was leaving; she had become more a silhouette than a person. He wished he could see her eyes.

'There are some Albanian farmers who have flour,' she said.

The Otranto Barrage patrol area included a section of the Albanian coast. God above, did his nonna know *everyone*?

'How are you getting it?'

'One of the Italian captains likes his pasta, but the cooks at the mess don't have time to make it properly. When they are on patrol, near Vlore, a boat comes out to the ship . . .'

'So, you get the flour . . .'

'Most of it goes to the Italian ships' cooks. But some comes here. I make the pasta for the Italian captain's cook, and I get paid in flour. *Legittimo del tutto!*'

'So, why am I hiding it and picking it up in the dark?'

'Because there were food riots in Milan only a few months ago. You think you'd get back here safely if people knew what you had?'

Food riots. *Madonna mia.* He was overtaken by compassion for this, his ancestral country. Always poor, always in strife. The peasants, always hungry. War just made it worse. Across the nation, the wives and widows of soldiers struggled to bring in the harvest. They were planting less because they could not do all the work themselves, which meant they harvested less . . . and flour became a commodity people would commit a crime for.

It was full dark, and Nonna Rosa wrapped her arms around herself, shivering.

'Okay,' he said. 'I'll go. But when I get back we're going through the inventory and you're going to tell me where you're getting everything. All your suppliers, including the black- and grey-market ones.'

He could tell that she was smiling from her tone of voice. 'Oh, *si, Don* Alessandro.'

Don meant 'Lord'. It was a gentle mockery. But he'd be damned if he'd let her ride roughshod over him, even if she was his nonna.

'*Ciao, Donna* Rosa.'

'Why are you saying *ciao* like a Venetian? Respect your heritage!'

She had to have the last word. He hadn't even known 'ciao' *was* Venetian. But then, as she constantly reminded him, American Italian really wasn't the same as Italian Italian.

He trundled the handcart out of the gate, the old blanket thrown in its well.

The trattoria would open soon; he would have to hurry, or his nonna would have to do the service herself. But as he turned the corner, he saw the Kythera kid from next door hurry out the front. Only fourteen, but useful. Sandro had started work at that age himself, at the meatworks, along with his father and older brother. The smell came back to him with the memory; not bad in winter, that sharp iron tang of blood, and the yeasty smell of cow guts. But in summer . . . they managed to keep most of the flies out, but the smell . . .

The memory of sudden pain made him shake his head and draw a deep breath of clean, cold sea air through his nose. He flexed his hand. Forget it. Over and done with. Think of the good times.

He had always been fascinated by photography, by the idea of catching and holding a moment before it slipped away. He had saved up the twenty per cent of his wage packet left after paying his parents board, and bought himself a box brownie and three rolls of film. The camera itself wasn't expensive, but getting the film developed and printed was. That was why he'd started doing extra work on Saturday afternoons for Signor Restelli, the photographer who had a studio two blocks from his parents' apartment and who was the only developer nearby.

The day Signor Restelli offered him a job was the happiest moment of his life. To get out of the meatworks! To get away from that back-breaking manual labour and the stink of rotting flesh, from the sharp blades and the constant sound of steel on bone. And more, to do what he loved, what he was beginning to believe was his passion.

He'd been seventeen. Ten years ago. When Signor Restelli had died four years ago, it was no surprise to anyone that he left Sandro the business. The studio and flat were rented, so it wasn't as much as people thought, but it was a good livelihood, and got even better once the war started and everyone wanted pictures of their sons and husbands and sweethearts before they went away, and the men wanted pictures of their families to take with them. And because most of his work was on Saturdays and after hours, once people had finished work, he had time for his real work. He didn't like to call it 'art'. He didn't think he was good enough to call himself an artist. Besides, could photographs *be* art?

But photography *could* pay. He had made money – enough for him to come here, to take a risk. He'd taken his assistant, Carlo, into partnership with him, and Carlo was running the studio until he came back. If he came back.

The handcart wheels rumbled over the road. No other wheeled traffic out, not tonight, at the dark of the moon. The blackout wasn't complete, here in Brindisi – too far from the front for the German airplanes to reach, and so heavily defended by sea – but supplies were short, so no one wasted kerosene on

50

lighting the street. The Brindisi council had announced that they would only light every third streetlamp, and even those would be turned down low.

The map had been clear enough, and he knew Brindisi well by now, but the place seemed so different in the darkness. As he got closer to the harbour, the weight of the handcart pulling at his shoulders, he could hear the music and laughter coming up from the brothels near the base, and from the big cafe, Leon's, down on the waterfront. The houses down here were a mixture of very old – older than America! – and hastily erected wooden shacks, flung up in any spare space to take advantage of the new business war had brought. Most of the brothels offered food as well as their other wares. Like Nonna Rosa's, that part of their business would have to close at ten-thirty – but that just meant they would take their celebrations inside.

The ground levelled out and he had to pull back on the handcart to slow it down, lest he be dragged off the shore and into the harbour's dark, greasy water.

The smell here was salt and oil, old fish and, oddly enough, shoe leather.

Under a lone street lamp, he studied the map. The chandler's should be three doors down from here, but he couldn't see a light. A narrow alley went beside the shop to the harbour, so he trundled the handcart down it and knocked on a side door only a few steps from a sharp drop-off. Close by, waves slapped against wood – a pier at the back door, maybe? That would make sense. And then, there was the distinctive clink of stays against a wooden mast. He knew now where he was; this was where the fishing boats moored, their red sails tightly furled.

A faint line of light around the door became clearer. When it opened Sandro was almost disappointed that it didn't creak.

An old man stood in the doorway, with bushy eyebrows and a long white beard that caught the light like spiderwebs caught dew. Sandro itched to photograph him; he looked a lot like Leonardo da Vinci's self-portrait.

'*Signore?*' he said. '*Sono Alessandro Panucci.*' Tonight he was definitely a Panucci. Al Baker wouldn't creep through the streets with a handcart to collect flour of questionable provenance.

'*Si, si.* About time.' The door shut in his face. A moment later it opened again, and the man stood there with a flatbed trolley stacked with sacks of flour.

A lot of them.

The old man seemed to find the look on Sandro's face funny. It was. He acknowledged the man's amusement with a wry smile of his own.

Sandro stacked the flour into the handcart carefully. The flour bags were each about the size of a pillow, and the first few didn't feel heavy at all. About ten pounds.

By the tenth, he was aware not only of his shoulders burning, but of the very high hill he would have to push this stuff up.

Fifteen. Twenty.

That was it. He covered the sacks with the old blanket and looked at his cargo dubiously. How much of a disguise was a single blanket?

The old man said, '*Salve,*' and closed the door, leaving Sandro in the dark with the equivalent of a grown man's weight to push up to the trattoria.

He was used to being on his feet all day, in the studio, but that was on a wooden floor, not cobblestones. He had to get fitter. Like most New Yorkers, he had walked everywhere, and on weekend afternoons he and his brothers and their friends had taken the subway up to Central Park to play football – American football, because almost no one in America played soccer. And if you kicked a round ball around Central Park, someone was sure to pick a fight with you. He'd been in his fair share of those – that's what had got him interested in boxing in the first place, when he was in parochial school.

More walking, that's what he needed, he decided as he finally arrived at his destination. He would find a bit of rope somewhere, and begin skipping, walking, shadow boxing. He let the handcart rest next to the back door of the trattoria and straightened, stretching his hands. His left hand was aching from the difficult grip on the handcart handles, and he rubbed at the base of his thumb. Yes. Skipping and shadow boxing would do all of him some good.

As he opened the door, Nonna came over and cast a quick glance at his face.

'All right?'

'*Sì*,' he said. 'It's a long hill.'

She smiled her dour smile, the ordinary one, and nodded. 'That's why I sent you.'

Other people had protective grandmothers. His was as protective as a bayonet to the buttocks.

6

Every morning, the journalists gathered at Nonna Rosa's to have coffee and a roll and to read the newspapers. It was easier to read them there, on the long benches near the window, than in their respective pensiones. Rebecca hadn't gone since Jack left, but today was the day.

Her body ached for a comforting embrace, for the sense that she wasn't totally alone. It was mortifying to realise how much she had relied on his lovemaking; without it, it was hard to sleep and she awoke still tired. Jack was a passionate man. Sometimes she thought that lovemaking was the best thing about being married, but of course there was more. Without Jack in bed beside her, though, it was hard to remember what that was.

She picked up her newspapers from the railway station, where they arrived from Bari. She checked in with Niccolo, the boy who ran errands for the Station Master, but he had no news for her today. She tipped him anyway; one day, it would pay off.

Making her way down to the trattoria was challenging. The cobblestones underfoot were always slippery – the small heels on her winter boots tended to skid off them – but today was especially bad because they were still slicked with rain that had fallen before dawn and turned icy. She held onto the wall for balance as she went. She probably looked drunk.

From corners and through piazzas as she passed she caught glimpses of the sea. Brindisi was a town built around hills and water – like Sydney. But Sydney had never been so cold. She had woken that morning with a tear turned to ice on her cheek. A good thing she couldn't remember the dream that had evoked it.

To save stumbling around to the front door on the cobbles, she came in through the back courtyard, where in some long-off summer days they would sit in the open air to eat. Mr Baker was there. He seemed to be fighting the biggest branch of the lemon tree, hitting at it with short sharp jabs, shifting from one foot to another, backwards and forwards, side to side.

He wore a white undershirt and something that looked a lot like a pair of black tights under cream shorts. Black socks, thin flexible leather shoes. Of course! That was what boxers wore to practice. He was *boxing*. She might have known he would do something so nasty. Learning to defend oneself was one thing, but the attack he was making on his imaginary opponent would cause serious damage in reality, and he was clearly enjoying it. Wasn't there enough violence in the world without creating more for *fun*?

Curiosity appeased, she couldn't help but feel a little heat rise to her cheeks at the way the undershirt and tights clung to his body. Even a married woman might blush at those shoulders and thighs. She'd never seen better, even on the lifesavers on Bondi Beach. She turned aside to go around the long way, but he saw her and stopped, panting. He grabbed a small towel hanging from a branch and mopped his face with it.

'Sorry, didn't see you,' he said, evidently unembarrassed by his odd, revealing, outfit.

And she, what was she doing, ogling a man's body? Shame!

'I'm just . . .' she said, indicating the trattoria.

'Sure. Morning coffee.'

She went in quickly, acutely aware of the scrape of his shoes against the stone flags of the courtyard.

Christy and Mark Coates were at the long table when she arrived, coffee and a large plate of rolls already on the table. In the mornings, they served themselves from coffee and rolls placed in the centre of the table, so she didn't have to worry about Mr Baker coming back in.

Lemaitre came in as she was sitting down and pouring her first cup.

This was a quiet, businesslike part of the day. They didn't all take the same papers, so occasionally one of them would ask, 'Does anyone have more about Mata Hari?', who was a Dutch dancer arrested by the French for espionage, a double agent reporting to Germany. A female spy! The papers were full of her. Or they asked for more about the Somme, or about New Guinea. Or, of course, the Isonzo line, the Italian front line that stretched across the top of Italy's 'boot'.

Local stories came from the Bari paper. She had noticed before that, while Coates and Lemaitre were avid for news about their homelands, Christy was more interested in local news. Of course, with Ireland not being a main player in the war, or a target for German bombs, it was rarely mentioned. Eighteen months ago, during the Easter Rising of 1916, Germany had tried to help the Irish people rebel against the British.

Unsuccessfully, as it turned out. But Germany was unlikely to reverse any public sympathy it held in Ireland by sending zeppelins to bomb there.

Her own interests were wide, and she couldn't help but look at the fashion pages as well as the war news, which predictably elicited a jeer from Coates. But the most important part of the day was reading the casualty lists in the British papers, when they came. Today, *The Times* had arrived from Rome, and she pored over the lists for her brothers' names. Not there. Not today. She thanked God every time, acutely aware that the news was old – by the time the lists got to Britain, then to the papers, and then the papers were shipped to Rome, weeks had elapsed since the reported battle. Her brothers might both be dead, and she not know.

Her brothers, tall and blond and athletic. Will, the solicitor – the reason she had met Jack, because Will had clerked for Jack's father Valentine in the university vacations. Will was working in Army logistics in Sydney. At least *he* was safe. Earnest, that was Will. Responsible, especially now that he was a father. But the younger two, Charles and Linus . . . Charles was on the Somme, Linus in Egypt.

She had to believe they were alive until she heard otherwise. As she put the casualty lists down, she realised that she had placed Jack into the same part of her mind that Charles and Linus occupied. A place of intense fear and potential grief, but not a place that she could live in from day to day. That was the way to madness.

'More coffee, *madame*?' Lemaitre asked.

'No, thank you,' she said, recalled to business.

The four of them made notes of local issues to follow up on, of local incidents, such as the sighting of an Austrian submarine just off Posticeddu, the next big town north of Brindisi. Not much today – sometimes they had good stories come out of the local papers. The nationals – well, their newspapers already had correspondents in Rome who would handle those.

The noon Angelus bell rang, picked up by church after church until the whole town was vibrating. She, Christy and Lemaitre crossed themselves automatically, and Rebecca said the words of the prayer under her breath; Coates sneered at them, but said nothing. As a socialist, he was also a proclaimed atheist – but he knew better than to air those opinions too loudly in Italy.

As the men left, Rebecca dawdled over the fashion pages of a Milanese newspaper. Really, those sketches of a new dropped-waist style were very good. She would have to get some made like that when she got to Britain after the war. She had a happy moment of imagining herself working in London at the *Evening News*, decked out in the latest style, the first woman general news reporter. It could happen. She would *make* it happen.

After they had all gone, and Mr Baker had cleared their plates and cups away, Rebecca presented herself, rather nervously, to Nonna Rosa. Mr Baker left, to go to a job he had at the Brindisi photographer's; she wasn't sure if she were glad of that or not.

Nonna Rosa looked Rebecca's black dress up and down and sniffed, then took a big white apron from a hook on the wall and handed it to her. Rebecca felt the sniff was a bit unfair. Admittedly, her dress wasn't in the latest fashion – but she had been advised by the attaché in the Australian embassy, when they had come through Rome on their way to Brindisi, that the modern skirt length of mid-calf would cause riots in a small Italian town.

Her dress was modest and smart – and if it was a bit too smart for Nonna Rosa, well, too bad!

She took off her gloves and hat, wrapped the apron around herself and washed her hands in a bowl set for the purpose. The water was pumped into the sink, and Nonna Rosa set her to washing vegetables. Carrots, spinach, other greens she didn't know the name of. Nonna Rosa chopped onions and asked her questions in Italian, then corrected her when she replied in the same language. That was the lesson.

'*La tua famiglia? Tuo padre? Vivo?*'

Her family? Was her father alive? She could speak French, thanks to a French nanny, so translating was often a matter of working out the Latin roots or the similar French word and then turning that into English, then finding the right Italian words to reply. She was slower than she would have liked, but Nonna Rosa gave her time.

'*Si. Mio padre e mia madre sono vivi.*'

'*Sono* entrambi *vivi,*' Rosa corrected. 'Both alive. Again.'

'*Mio padre e mia madre sono entrambi vivi.*'

'*Bene. Hai fratelli?*'

Fratelli? Like fraternity? Something to do with brothers?

'*Si. Tre fratelli.*'

'*Cattolica?*' Was she Catholic? An important question in Italy.

'*Si.*'

Rosa grunted and scraped the chopped onions into a big pot.

Rebecca had expected something more formal, but as the hour wore on and she was moved from sink to bench, to knead dough, she relaxed and began to enjoy it. She liked to cook, and making bread always brought comfort. The Italian flour was stronger than the Australian, and formed a smooth, glossy dough, springy and dense. The rich yeasty smell surrounded her with an illusory sense of home.

'*Hai sorelle?*'

'*Sorelle?*' She should know that word. It was on the tip of her tongue.

'*Si. Fratelli,* brothers, *sorelle,* sisters.'

Sisters. Of course. Like sorority. '*No. Nessuna sorella.*'

By the time her hour was up, she realised, Nonna Rosa knew a good deal about her.

'*Tuo marito? Dov'è?*'

Where was her husband? The question had been posed in the same polite tone, but Nonna Rosa was looking at her with more interest.

'God alone knows,' she said in English, picking up the dough and slamming it back onto the bench.

Nonna Rosa made a half-laugh sound in her throat and said, 'Enough for today,' also in English.

Mr Baker came through the back door with his camera and haversack, looking competent and workmanlike. Today, he had swapped his suit for thick fawn corduroy trousers and a brown wool jacket with plenty of pockets, the kind of jacket photographers always seemed to wear. A bright yellow scarf dangled around his neck.

'I'm going to take some wide shots of the harbour,' he said. 'Want to come?'

'Good idea.' She washed her hands and hung the apron back on its hook.

Rosa's shrewd, cool eyes assessed her. '*Si,*' she said, the barest hint of a smile at one corner of her mouth. '*Ci vediamo a cena,*' she suggested. 'I'll see you at dinner.'

'*Ci vediamo a cena,*' Rebecca repeated obediently, pulling on her gloves and making sure her hat was secure.

Nonna Rosa nodded and turned her back to stir the huge pot of soup. Bacon and barley; an autumn soup.

The air outside was cold and somehow empty after the richness of the kitchen aromas. She would need a warm coat tonight. They walked, side by side, up the winding streets, past the church where they had met, past two old ladies sitting in the weak sun crocheting, past the school where children's voices counted: *uno, due, tre . . .*

Nonna Rosa's questions had stirred up so many memories. Rebecca's mother, repeatedly encouraging her to take the leap and become a war correspondent, 'For the good of women everywhere, Rebecca!' Her father, proud and worried, but staunchly supportive, waving goodbye at the dock as her ship pulled away.

She might never see them again, or her brothers. Who knew if they would survive? Tears pricked her eyes and she wiped them away with a gloved finger, and told herself not to borrow trouble. She was conscious of Mr Baker, striding confidently beside her, and wondered if he missed his parents.

Her family had had an odd home, compared to others, but she missed it. Her mother, so involved during their childhood with the suffrage campaign, had been more mentor than homemaker. Her father, an importer/exporter, used his contacts to bring in the latest magazines, books, journals. And the meetings! Soirées – salons, her mother had called them – but really, their home had been a meeting place for all those with advanced ideas. Fabian socialists, suffragists, Free Thinkers.

There had never been any question but that Rebecca would attend university. She studied History and Classics, against her mother's wish for her to be a doctor. Or a lawyer. Or anything that would push the boundaries of women's rights.

Jack had been in the year ahead, and the only male student who hadn't tried to patronise her. On the contrary, he was enthusiastic about the women's movement. He didn't have much respect for tradition. He was studying law, like his father, and managing somehow to combine that with a cadetship in journalism. Their courtship had been a series of brief meetings, a few words, a pressed hand, and then he was off again, juggling his two worlds with consummate skill. His father hadn't even known about the cadetship until Jack had graduated and announced that he already had a job with the *Herald*, a job that took him all over Australia and the Pacific. Perhaps she shouldn't have expected him to hold still in one place for very long. She had learned shorthand in the first place because it guaranteed her two hours a week when they could be in the same place at the same time.

And then after she had finished university it had seemed so natural, with his encouragement and her mother's delight, to apply for the position on the Women's Pages at the *Herald*. She had done it for 'the experience', but she had quickly discovered a real love for the job. The journalist's curiosity and burning desire for the story seemed to come naturally; sometimes, she thought, more naturally to her than to Jack, who was in it mostly, she suspected, for the excitement. No doubt Albania was quite exciting.

Best not to think about Jack now, or she would get either teary or annoyed. She rushed into speech.

'Why do you call yourself Al Baker?'

Mr Baker looked sideways at her. 'It's my name.'

'But—'

He waved his free hand in a kind of apology, and paused, turning to her. She stopped to listen.

'When my father arrived on Ellis Island, they thought Panucci meant "baker", so they changed it.'

'Just like that?'

He shrugged. 'It's not such a bad idea, having a name everyone can say.' He grinned, and she was abruptly aware that he was a very good-looking man, with white teeth and a confident glint in his brown eyes. 'So, I'm Al Baker at home and Alessandro Panucci here. It's taking some getting used to, I can tell you.'

He was not much taller than she was. Six foot, perhaps, to her five seven. Five eight in her boots. Unlike Jack, and all the men in her family, who towered over her. She was accustomed to tilting her head right back to look into a man's face. It felt strangely intimate to be closer.

'I imagine it is,' she said, starting to walk again. So, he hadn't lied to her. Wasn't pretending to be someone he wasn't. That, at least, was reassuring. 'It took me weeks to get used to be called Mrs Quinn.'

He nodded with understanding.

'What part of England do you come from?' he asked.

She looked at him in surprise. 'I'm Australian!'

'But you sound—'

'Australia's part of the British Empire, but I can assure you, I'm not English.'

She smiled to herself. So, she had thought him American, he had thought her English. Both wrong, but both also right. She was Australian, but she had been raised to think of England as home, as no doubt he had been raised to think of Italy.

From the top of the main hill of Brindisi, near the Cathedral, there was a panoramic view of Brindisi harbour. It was an odd shape – a long main passage that split into two arms, rather like the antlers of a stag.

They looked down over the white-plastered houses, which shone in surprisingly brilliant sunshine, to a deep blue sea ruffled by the autumn wind. Rebecca had seen it so many times now, but she was still thrilled to be there. This was the *Adriatic*! In *Twelfth Night*, this was the sea on which Shakespeare shipwrecked Olivia and Sebastian. The *Mare Superum* of the Romans.

'Good light,' Mr Baker said beside her. He had set up his tripod and camera at the highest point they could find, and now was peering through the viewfinder with the focusing cloth over his head.

She had seen staff photographers work at big events for the *Herald*, and she watched him out of the corner of her eye. He knew what he was doing, that was clear. She relaxed a little, and pulled out her notebook. From here she could see all the ships in port.

The Australians were gone, as Commander Warren had said they would be. But there were a number of Italian ships: a couple of frigates, and two of the new MAS boats – so small she could barely tell them from fishing boats, but equipped, she knew, with two torpedos each. She used Jack's binoculars (so big she could barely hold them steady) and took notes.

The French contingent was smaller, moored in the left arm of the harbour. And the British seemed to be moored opposite them.

The flotillas were taking turns. Commander Warren had mentioned a four-day roster.

'Okay,' Mr Baker said. 'I've got a couple of exposures. What else do we need?'

Two French destroyers were leaving port, making way rather faster than usual inside the harbour.

'Something's happened,' she said, pointing at them.

They exchanged glances, the excitement of a new story in their eyes. Hurriedly, Mr Baker set up again and took an exposure.

Even walking as fast as they could, by the time they reached the French moorings the two destroyers were out of sight. There were guards on the gate, of course.

'*Bonjour, messieurs*,' she said. She showed her press credentials, thanking her stars that she had decided to get a press pass from *Le Monde* as well as the *Evening News*. She didn't mention it usually because she'd never actually submitted a story there – it was so much more work to write it in French that usually she wouldn't bother – but she kept the card in her purse, and she showed it to the guards.

'I'd like to see the commander, if you please,' she said in French. 'I write for *Le Monde*.'

They looked at each other for guidance and then informed her they must ask a higher authority. The younger of the guards went off at a run, and Mr Baker set up the camera while they waited. A few minutes later the guard arrived flanking a lieutenant, a beautifully turned out older man with a pencil moustache.

'Madame, I am so sorry, but the commander is unavailable. There will be a press conference soon. Tomorrow, perhaps.'

'Then a few words from you, *monsieur*? What's happened? Two of your destroyers have just left port in a hurry. It's not your turn to patrol . . .' That was a guess, but it was a good guess.

'Lieutenant,' Mr Baker called confidently, and ducked underneath the focusing cloth. The man looked up, startled, and realised what was happening. Instinctively, he straightened and sucked in his small pot belly.

'And your name, Lieutenant?' Rebecca asked in French, notebook ready.

'Morelon. Raoul Morelon.'

'Come, monsieur, tell us what's happened.'

He sighed, but spoke, as though the camera had made it an official interview. She gritted her teeth at the insult. A woman reporter he could ignore, but not a man with a camera.

'A distress call from an Italian ship. That's all I can tell you.'

'From where?'

'Near Otranto. The Australians are on the scene, our ships are joining them. That's all.'

He began to turn away.

'Was it torpedoed?'

'That's classified,' he said sternly. 'Good day, madame.'

The guards moved across the gate and presented their arms.

'Let's go,' Rebecca said. 'The post office, quick smart, before any of the others get this. I'll tell you what he said on the way. It's a scoop!'

Summary

The Australian and French flotillas in Brindisi are racing to the aid of a distressed Italian vessel in the Adriatic Sea. More to follow.

After a moment's thought, she sent the same story to *Le Monde*, in French. Why not?

Going back to her small room wouldn't get any stories written, so Rebecca set off to see her contact at the docks while Mr Baker went to develop his plates.

Sydney was a harbour city, and she was used to the mixture of races and types found near the docks – but Brindisi! So close to Africa and the Levant, it had taken over much of Venice's port traffic as travel up the Adriatic had been made dangerous by Austrian submarines. Men of every colour and size and dress thronged the streets near the public docks. Ignoring the jeers and the invitations in half-a-dozen languages, she made her way to the Harbour Master's office.

The office was always busy – an old stone building, plastered with cream stucco, it held a chill no summer could dispel, but the office was warm enough, heated by the cram of people. Men. Rather rough men, captains and first mates of ships in port, of ships leaving port, of fishing boats looking for better moorings, of tramp steamers complaining about the lack of wharf space now that so much of the docks area was taken by the various navies.

She had established, in her first few days there, that although the Harbour Master himself did not speak English, his clerk spoke quite good French and rather liked speaking to a young lady in that language.

'What's the news?' she asked him.

'Not much,' he said. He was a married man, she knew – she did like this Italian custom of the man wearing a wedding ring – it made things so much easier. But he was a flirt, and he smiled confidingly at her.

'It's the *Orione*,' he said. 'A distress call.' He spread his hands. 'That's all I know, I'm sorry.'

She slid a folded note across to him and he took it, disguising the motion by patting her hand just a little too enthusiastically.

Back to the pensione, dissatisfied and chafing. To know there was a story out there and not be able to get it!

Angela, Signor Damonica's daughter, met her at the front door. Angela was a few years older than Rebecca, a plain-faced plump woman with a discontented air that occasionally broke into a lovely smile.

'*Signora Quinn! Telegrafo!*' she called, waving a telegram flimsy at Rebecca.

It was from Walter Evans, the editor of the *Evening News*. Rebecca's stomach cramped with tension. She had no idea how he would have reacted to the news that she would be filing stories solo. Although technically she was there as a correspondent, it had been clear that Evans had seen her as an addendum to Jack.

WILL GIVE YOU SIX WEEKS TO PROVE YOURSELF STOP GET ME A SCOOP STOP EVANS

Six weeks.

Her stomach relaxed, and then tightened again. A scoop. Six weeks to get something that would impress Evans enough that he would consider her Jack's equal – and continue to pay her. Without that stipend, she couldn't afford to stay in Italy. Couldn't afford to wait for Jack. Their money was all in Jack's name, of course, and although he'd left her with enough to go on with, if he stayed away too long she would need the money Evans wired through to her and Jack each month.

So, she would do what she had come here for – she would get out of the Women's Pages once and for all. No woman journalist had achieved it yet, but she was determined to be the first to be allowed to report general news. She needed a scoop.

Was it wicked to hope that the Austrians would attack? That German troops would suddenly target the Adriatic? Yes, it probably was wicked. Then she would just wish – pray – that she was *there* when something happened.

She couldn't face Nonna Rosa's that night, curling up in bed instead with a cup of tea and some shortbread, along with her Italian grammar and phrase book. If she was going to do this job, her Italian had to be better than it was, and an hour with Nonna Rosa every day wasn't enough.

She slept little that night. A gale had been brewing and reached its peak around midnight, the wind and sleet battering at the shutters. She hoped whatever disaster had called those ships out of port was over by now, that the crews were all safe and sound.

•

Rebecca was woken, early, by a pounding on the front door.

'*Signora! Signora!*' Half awake, her first thought was for Jack, that he was in trouble or had sent for her. She leaped out of bed, struggled into her dressing gown and raced down the stairs, her hair lying in a long rope over her shoulder. Angela was already opening the door.

Outside, Niccolo the errand boy jumped from foot to foot in excitement, ignoring the rain and the fact that he was totally drenched. As the door opened, he peered past Angela.

'*Signora! Venga! Venga! Presto!*' He launched into a torrent of Italian, of which all she grasped was 'station' and 'soon'.

'*Lentamente,*' she pleaded. 'Slow down.'

'*La nave!*' he almost shouted.

The ship. Not a message about Jack. She felt tension flow out of her in a wave of mixed relief and disappointment. Surely she should have had news of him by now? Surely he could have written?

'The ship that was in—' Oh, what was the word for 'distress'? She settled for 'trouble'. 'The ship that was in trouble?'

'*Si, si, signora. Loro stanno arrivando! Alla stazione dei treni!*'

At the railway station. A scoop. This could certainly be a scoop. She marshalled her Italian.

'Go tell Signor Panucci!' she ordered the boy. He hesitated. 'I'll pay you later. Go!'

He ran.

'Angela, can you help me with my buttons?'

Angela, taking on the role of lady's maid with enthusiasm, stuffed Rebecca into her clothes in quick time, slammed her hat on her head and ushered her out the door complete with gloves, purse, jacket and an umbrella against the driving rain.

It was fifteen minutes' walk to the railway station, up and down hills, fighting the wind the whole way. By the time she arrived, all but her shoulders and bust was wet through.

The station, normally quiet, was alive with excitement, with the Station Master and several guards waiting for the train from Bari to pull in. But, she was pleased to see, there were no other reporters. Mr Baker arrived a few moments later, running with his camera clutched under a macintosh. His tie was still undone, and he'd abandoned his stylish beaver for a cap with a cape at the back, such as butchers used when carrying meat. It had kept his hair dry, at least. He shucked the macintosh and cap onto a bench and began to set up his camera, nodding to her as he did so. She nodded back.

Please God she would be able to speak enough Italian to get the story. Her notebook was at the ready.

When the train pulled in, to much clapping and cheering from the station staff, she was delighted to see that the four crew members piling out, looking half-drunk with fatigue, were Australian.

They were happy to tell their story to a fellow countrywoman.

It was an extraordinary story, full of danger and resolution and courage and sheer doggedness. After a battle with a submarine that had taken out the *Orione*'s stern, they had gone onto the ship to help salvage it.

The *Orione*'s passengers had been taken off to the waiting Australian ships, and then . . .

They had saved, the four of them, along with a handful of the original crew, an entire ship it usually took a full complement to operate, and they had done it in the worst possible weather, under impossible conditions, in a mine field.

'You're heroes!' she said. 'Let's have a photograph of you all.'

They lined up, smiling, leaning against each other, ignoring rank and protocol; just four men who had been through too much together to remember who was in charge.

Mr Baker joked with them, his long experience in taking portraits showing in his authority here and the way he allowed them to relax and be natural. When the shutter finally clicked, she knew the result would be perfect. He steadied the camera with his left hand, and with a shock she saw that his left thumb had been amputated just below the knuckle, leaving behind a stub. How had she never noticed that before? Thinking back, she realised that he usually kept that hand half curled, the thumb hidden behind his fingers. A habitual camouflage.

She felt as though she'd been kicked in the solar plexus. He was so – so *beautiful* that this disfigurement seemed wrong. Worse on him than it might be on someone else; which was ridiculous.

Was that enough to keep a man out of the Army? It would explain a great deal if it were. How awful that she had thought him a coward. And said so! Her angry words to him in the church must have hurt him so. What could he have thought of her? She wondered what accident had taken that thumb off, what terrible moment of pain and horror. She shuddered.

He turned to say something to her; saw her shudder, and followed her glance to his hand. His expression closed down and he moved away. Her face burned with embarrassment, but what could she say? *I wasn't revolted by your disfigurement.* No. Best to ignore it. After all, it wouldn't affect their working relationship if he thought she was a shallow woman who put too much stock in appearances. Would it?

She thanked the sailors and off they went to report to Commander Warren, sure of their welcome and ebullient just from being alive. Unfortunately, they weren't sure where the passengers from the *Orione* would be taken.

Trying to be helpful, to make up for her insensitivity, she held the focusing curtain as Mr Baker packed the camera into his bag. He took it from her and folded it precisely, silently.

'How soon can you get that printed?' she asked. He didn't look at her, but he answered.

'An hour, maybe two. Depends if Fabrini is using the darkroom.' He put his macintosh on and slung the tripod over his shoulder.

They began to walk back, through the rain, both of them under her umbrella. Mr Baker, she noticed, was more concerned about keeping his tripod dry than himself. It brought him close to her; she stumbled on an uneven bit of road and clutched him to save herself, his arm strong under her hand, his other hand coming around to steady her.

Unsettled, she spoke quickly, at random.

'I wish we had a photo of Commander Warren, to add to the report. It would be good to get a proper portrait of the commanders, all four of them, and have them ready for when a story breaks.'

Was it her imagination that his breathing had quickened? Of course it was. He let her go as soon as she regained her balance. She touched his hand – his left hand – in wordless thanks, and something in him relaxed.

'They all come into the trattoria sooner or later – I could set up some studio lights in Nonna's office. Back to studio photography.' He sounded rueful.

'In a good cause. Newspapers like pictures of heroes.'

'Are *they* heroes?' he asked, putting his cap back on, an edge to his voice. 'Just doing their jobs, aren't they?'

'Easy for us to say. How would you like to face down Austrian submarines every day? That *U-14* commander has already sunk eight ships this year!'

'The Austrians probably treat that captain as a hero,' he said bitterly.

'I suppose, from their point of view, he is. Facing our battleships every day.'

'Maybe you're right. But that makes every man on every ship on both sides a hero.'

Rebecca smiled at him. 'Aren't they? To their families? To everyone they protect?'

Mr Baker lifted his camera bag and hoisted the strap over his shoulder, and smiled at her. He seemed to have forgiven her *faux pas*. 'Oh, you women are too soft,' he said.

'Not me!' she said. 'But the men . . . I respect the men. And the nurses, and the ambulance drivers and all the rest.'

He looked at her with a strange smile, and she remembered his injured hand – the hand that, perhaps, had kept him out of that heroic company. A pang of sympathy went through her.

'We do a job too,' she said. 'Imagine how much more worried the people at home would be without the news.'

'Let's hope we have some good news to bring them soon.'

'Amen.' As one, they made the sign of the cross, and then laughed at themselves.

The first time she had laughed alone with a man other than Jack since their marriage. She felt guilty, even knowing that was ridiculous.

Or was it? He was handsome for a foreigner. Dark eyes filled with concern, laughter lines at their corners, dark lashes, a strong jaw. Beautiful skin, like honey. It did feel wrong to stand this close to a man who wasn't Jack. As if she were being unfaithful.

Which was absurd, of course.

•

Mr Baker spread the photographs out over the long table, and Rebecca examined them.

'This one,' she said, pointing to the image in which the young men were smiling, laughing, in high spirits.

'This is better,' Mr Baker said definitely, pointing to a more sombre version.

'Too serious. This is a better one for the story.'

'It's out of focus.'

'What?' She looked more closely at the two pictures. Yes, she could see that the laughing one was very slightly fuzzy; but the overall effect was much better. 'Once it's been published on newsprint, you won't even see that.'

'I have my reputation to consider,' he said stiffly. 'This is my first real chance to impress Evans. I don't want him to think I'm sloppy.'

'The story is more important,' she said without thinking. That was the world of journalism she'd been trained in. All egos – even the editor's – were subservient to the story.

'This is my career we're talking about, sister.' His tone was snarky. *Sister* certainly wasn't a pleasant term of address in a New York accent.

'Fine!' she snapped. 'We'll send both of them, with a note saying I made you put the laughing one in. All right?'

He nodded, his face shuttered. Very well, she thought. If he didn't want to learn from her experience, then let him learn from his own. Evans would pick that laughing one, she was certain. And then he'd see. This wasn't about the perfect image – it was about getting an image that would print well and bolster the story. He'd learn.

A Letter from Italy

Daring rescue by Australian mariners

HUNDREDS OF LIVES SAVED!

The Italian transport *Orione* was torpedoed by an Austrian submarine in the Adriatic Sea off Otranto on 16 November.

HMASs *Warrego* and *Huon* responded to the distress call and, with the *Parramatta*, began a rescue mission with Lt Mortimer from *Warrego* in charge.

In high seas and frigid conditions, the Australians managed to transfer all 400 of the passengers and crew of the *Orione*, including 140 wounded with their nurses, to safety. Rescuing those already in the water required both daring and perseverance, as the extreme cold meant that they could not assist their rescuers.

Unwilling to abandon *Orione*, which he believed could still be salvaged, Cdr William Warren of the *Parramatta* took the stricken vessel in tow, under torpedo attack from the U-boat, and with the support of the *Yarra*, which received some damage from collision with the unsteerable transport. *Warrego* and *Huon* engaged the submarine, which broke off its attack.

When an Italian tug finally took over, Warren assigned Lt Hill, Eng Lt Clarence Bridge and Signalman John Varcoe to join Mortimer and 14 of the Italian ship's crew. Bravely daring extreme bad weather and heavy seas, these men kept the ship afloat through the night, although their tug became detached and they were uncertain of their position.

Lt Hill was in command throughout. Signalman Varcoe described him to our correspondent as: 'an excellent seaman and cool'.

The 400 *Orione* passengers will be returned to Italy to await a new ship.

7

That afternoon there was a break in the clouds, so Rebecca went out to take the air, heading for the dock as if by instinct, just in case there was any news. She could see the harbour from the piazza halfway down; an Australian destroyer was almost in port, with people crowding her decks. Number 70 on her hull – the *Warrego*. The patrols had been four days each so far – the *Warrego* wasn't due back for three days yet.

A crowd was gathering, peering through the iron fence to try to see the ship come in to dock.

She hurried, but of course when she reached the gates of the British base, the guards wouldn't let her in.

'More than my hide is worth,' the corporal told her kindly, in a Cockney accent.

The crowd was too thick for her to see anything through the fence. Looking around, she found one of her most reliable allies, Niccolo.

'*Ragazzo!*' she said. '*Andare a prendere Signor Panucci, a Nonna Rosa's.*' She held out a lire note temptingly, but held it back so it was clear that it would be payment after the errand was done. '*Correre veloce!*'

'*Si, signora!*'

He took off, two of his friends at his heels.

The wind was picking up, sharp and worrying. If a ship were in distress, they wouldn't welcome bad weather.

The *Warrego* sounded her horn; not the forlorn prolonged fog horn, but a short, efficient blast. Coming around to starboard, then, which meant she would be docking, rather than tying up to the long trot line that ran across the harbour and to which the Australian ships were normally moored. Coming in to dock meant loading or unloading – what? Those people she had glimpsed on deck? Or, more sombrely, bodies?

A great bustle was happening inside the base; she edged in until she could see a sliver through the fence: men running to the dock, trundling handcarts, trolleys, all kinds of apparatus for transferring either people or goods.

The crowd was pushing her around. She lost her place, but the kindly corporal said, 'Here, ma'am,' and slid her in behind him. Probably against the rules, but she was so grateful.

'Thank you, corporal,' she said breathlessly.

The *Warrego* came in to the dock and tied up smoothly, while men were shouting to each other from deck to wharf. A gangplank came rattling down, and then a procession of wounded men, bandaged, each supported by a sailor. Oh, why wasn't Mr Baker here to catch this on film!

The walking wounded were followed by stretcher bearers, carefully negotiating the steep descent. And nurses. What nationality? She realised, with a laugh, that all the wounded men were dark haired and had moustaches. Italian, then.

They were being taken to the Italian hospital, up the harbour from the British base where they had been brought ashore.

Behind her she heard a disturbance in the crowd, and then Mr Baker appeared to her right, his camera cradled carefully to avoid damaging it in the crush.

'Can you get a shot of them?' she asked and he jumped in surprise, then peered behind the corporal to find her. She chuckled at the look on his face.

'Mrs Quinn!'

'Can you get a shot?'

'Yes. Hold on a minute.' He balanced the heavy camera against one of the stone posts, and shot through the railings.

'See that nurse coming down with the bandaged man?'

'Got it,' he said, concentrating. He took the shot and then fished his small camera out of a pocket. 'Can you hold this?'

She wriggled sideways, conscious of the press of people behind them, craning to see, and managed to get both hands out to take the large camera, carefully. She hunched over it, protecting it with her body, and he nodded approvingly before snapping several quick shots of the passengers, some wounded and some bewildered, some shaking with cold, some kissing the ground as they reached it in an ecstasy of gratitude, holding their hands up to God in thanks.

'There,' Mr Baker said in satisfaction. 'That's a good one.'

Together they peeled out of the crowd, Rebecca tossing a quick, 'Thank you!' back to the corporal.

On the other side of the press of people, the square was almost deserted. They took a breath and looked at each other. She was conscious that her hair was mussed and her dress dirty in places from the stone wall and rusty bollards, but they couldn't simply go home to tidy up.

'We need more information,' she said. 'The crew's story was good, but we need the passengers' side of things.'

'They won't let us in.' She watched as the gates opened and an ambulance drove through, heading for the Italian hospital. The rest of the passengers were walking up through the British area to a gate that led through to the Italian base and its hospital.

Several men with bandaged heads or shoulders were being supported by nurses dressed in long blue dresses with big white aprons. Some had lost their distinctive winged caps, but they all had a Red Cross armband on their right upper arm; and not all of them were dark-haired. Some northern Italians were blondes and redheads, she knew.

'I have an idea,' she said.

•

'You can't just fake your way in!' Sandro said in exasperation.

'*Our* way in.'

Mrs Quinn stood there with long strips of fabric in her hand. Bandages. Behind her, Nonna Rosa was leaning on the kitchen counter, laughing.

'I am *not* pretending to be a wounded sailor.'

'But it's the perfect disguise!'

She was consumed by the desire to get the story. He'd seen it in the other journalists, and he recognised it now. Just as obsessed. Just as determined. He couldn't help a flicker of admiration amid his annoyance, and a desire to look professional in her eyes.

'No bandages,' he said firmly. 'I'll wear a sling. I can put the small camera in that.'

'Now you're talking!' She took the widest of the fabric strips and made a sling for his left arm. She was in a blue dress, and she had borrowed one of Nonna's big aprons. She had a Red Cross armband on her right arm.

'Where did you get that?' he asked.

'I volunteered for the Red Cross in Sydney,' she said absently, going on tiptoe to tie the sling behind his neck. She smelled of elderflowers and woman. He cleared his throat and stared over her shoulder, out the window where the sky was temporarily blue, with scudding clouds promising more rain later.

'There,' she said, and stood back. 'Let's go.'

He rolled his eyes at her but he went. The need to get the story burned in him too.

•

They came to the Italian hospital from the opposite direction. The procession of wounded was tapering off, but a few were still shambling along, complete with their nurses. The women looked tired; they must have done multiple trips to ensure every man was taken care of.

Mrs Quinn brought him straight to the front door. He hung his head and tried to look sick; he *felt* sick about pretending to be someone who had genuinely been wounded in war. It wasn't right. He had to stop letting her talk him into things.

The guards at the door looked at them curiously, and one said, 'Why aren't you coming in with the rest of them?'

'We got lost,' she said. To his astonishment, she spoke with a strong Roman accent. Of course, she would have stopped in Rome before coming to Brindisi – all foreign journalists did, to get travel passes through their embassy. But he hadn't realised she'd worked out the difference between the Roman accent and the Salentino.

It was unreasonable of him to be annoyed about that, as though she had been deceiving him, but he was, just a little.

The guard waved them through.

Inside, predictably, it was chaos. Wounded men in beds, in chairs, leaning against the walls. The light was bad in the corridor; no use to try for a shot. Mrs Quinn looked at him, and he shook his head. He took off the sling. In the face of the real agony of these wounded soldiers, he couldn't continue with it.

'Sister!' a woman's voice called in Italian. He nudged Rebecca, and she turned to face the nurse coming out of a room to their right. 'Sister, bed three needs a bedpan immediately.'

Mrs Quinn froze. He tried not to laugh; some poor bastard was busting his guts in there. But the idea of Mrs Quinn doing bedpan duties was so funny. He coughed a laugh, and she glared at him.

'I'm not supposed to leave this one alone,' she said with authority, gesturing towards Sandro. 'Shell shock, and he could go crazy any minute. I'm the only one who can calm him down. Last time he almost killed two doctors.'

Goddarned woman. He tried to look shell shocked, but since he'd never met anyone like that, he wasn't sure he knew how.

'Well, you can take him the pan in, at least, can't you? I've got a septic wound in bed eleven. The pans are in the scullery over there.'

'All right,' she said. To Sandro, *sotto voce*, she added, 'We can get a first-hand account from him.' They went to the scullery, where a large bin held only a few white enamel bedpans.

Bed three was one of six in the ward. The other beds were full of men with dark hair and pale faces, and others sitting on chairs, heads hanging. The one in bed three was older than he'd expected, about fifty, with grey hair and grey streaks in his moustache. He grabbed the bedpan with both hands and thrust it underneath himself with urgency, and then relaxed as the smell began to permeate the room.

'Can't you bloody make it to the toilet?' one of the others shouted, and the man replied, 'On what?' and it was only then that Sandro registered that both his legs stopped halfway down the bed. A double amputee.

Shaken by compassion and a kind of dreadful understanding, Sandro looked in the little cupboard next to the bed. Sure enough, there was toilet paper. He handed it to the man, who took it gratefully, and used it. Mrs Quinn was standing there like a statue, looking at the man's legs.

'I'll take it,' Sandro said to the man. 'She's got some questions for you all.'

He took the bedpan to the toilet off the scullery, tipped the contents in and flushed, then left the pan in the sink and washed his hands. He needed that moment of privacy.

A war photographer. That was what he had wanted to be, purely because it would get him to the front. It wasn't that he had forgotten how devastating war could be on the fragile bodies of soldiers. No. But this was the first time he had come face to face with the consequences of war, and he had to admit to himself that he was shaken.

He expected to come back to find Mrs Quinn interviewing them all, one by one or in a group. Instead, she was giving water to a man slumped in a chair, and then went on to do the same for a couple leaning against the wall. She helped one of those slide down until he was sitting on the floor. Her hands were soft, and her face concerned. It triggered a fillip of annoyance in him; why couldn't she stay haughty and distant? It would confuse things if she became likeable.

He joined her in holding cups for men to drink from, in supporting men to the toilet, in bringing bottles to piss in for those who couldn't make it. When a trolley with drinks and food came around, he helped her to distribute them and give aid to those who couldn't feed themselves.

And he became aware, gradually, that she *was* interviewing them all. Bit by bit. Question by question, slipped in as she helped each individual man.

'So, the stern was ripped right off?'

'They couldn't steer?'

'The Australians helped?'

'Did you see the submarine?'

Tiny, unobtrusive questions. Calm, gentle questions. But questions, nonetheless.

The afternoon light had moved around and the ward was bright with it. He knew he should take a picture or two, but he couldn't bring himself to photograph these men – these brave men – through subterfuge.

'We're journalists,' he announced. 'Can I take your pictures?' He showed them his camera. Some were too far gone to care, but others nodded. Except for one man, who glared at Mrs Quinn and shook his head.

'*Basta!*' he said. That's enough. Sandro agreed with him. He took several shots of those who were willing, while Mrs Quinn glared daggers at him. Once he had finished, he went to her.

'*Basta*,' he said. 'They're fed and watered, and you have your story. Let's go.'

Her mouth was tight with anger, but she pulled off her Red Cross armband and followed him out into the loud corridor, where the sound of grown men crying with pain set his teeth on edge and made him angry with the world.

They moved quickly out the door, past the surprised guard, then up the hill to the Damonicas' house, where she would no doubt write the story she had conned those poor bastards into giving her.

At least he had been honest with them, he told himself. But the moment of self-congratulation soured. He'd stood by and let her pretend to them. Let her deceive them.

'That's no way to get a story!' It burst out of him.

'What are you talking about?'

'Lying to those men, deceiving them into thinking you were a nurse!'

'Nonsense.'

He stopped and grabbed her by the arm, forcing her to face him.

'Are you telling me that there's nothing wrong with lying and cheating to get a story?'

She glared at him, just as angry as he was.

'I'm telling you I told them all who I was while you were off with the bedpan!'

He was a fool. He stood, stock still, and didn't know what to say. She wrenched her arm out of his hold, and put her head up.

'I don't know why you want to think the worst of me, Mr Baker, but if we're going to work together, you'll have to learn to trust me.'

She walked off.

'I'm sorry,' he called weakly after her. She heard him; her shoulders moved and settled as she shrugged off his words.

Goddammit.

8

The next morning, as Rebecca arrived with her newspapers, the other three journalists surveyed her sourly, and she couldn't help but grin. They'd clearly heard of her exploit on the grapevine, and they weren't happy she'd managed to get a story off last night via telegraph. She hadn't been foolish enough to send it through Warren – he would have censored it back to nothing. Mr Baker's photos they would send today, through Warren, and another set by the regular Italian post, just in case.

Mr Baker brought the coffee and rolls to the table. He nodded at her; slightly embarrassed, as he should be. How he could have thought she would abandon every journalistic ethic in pursuit of a story! The nerve of him. But the images had turned out well.

None of the others had been let into the Italian hospital. The Italian commander had hand-picked an Italian journalist from Rome, and given him an exclusive. 'Wanted to make himself look good to the top brass,' Coates said.

So, she had the only interviews with the survivors. She tried not to be smug about it, but it wasn't easy.

'They're getting tougher with the press,' Christy said. 'Look at Venice – *everything* that's printed has to go through Admiral Thaon di Revel.'

The Bari paper covered the unloading of the rescued passengers, but in general terms. They were waiting, it said, for the shipping company to find another ship for them, and it could be some time before another convoy set out.

She felt happier today – a good day's work done yesterday, a start on establishing herself as an independent journalist, without Jack. As always when she thought of him, many times a day, a spear of fear and worry went through her from head to toe. But she couldn't let it take her over.

Christy finished with the British edition of *The Times* – ten days old, now – and handed it to her as she filled her coffee cup. She yawned as she took it; although she had slept better the night before than she had been, it still seemed as though she had a good deal of napping to catch up on.

As always, she turned to the casualty lists first, her heart tight in her chest. Most of the time she could pretend she wasn't afraid for her brothers, but every morning, there it was, the terrible possibility. It was one of the reasons she had wanted to come back to these morning sessions at Nonna Rosa's. Looking at the papers all by herself every morning had just been too hard.

So many names. The battles in France and Belgium just went on and on and on. Passchendaele, for example, and Ypres. How many times had they fought over that town? Her brother Charles was stationed near there; when she saw all the names on the casualty lists from France, it seemed like a special intercession that his name hadn't come up.

The lists were organised in descending order of horror: a summary at the top of how many killed or wounded, and then the lists: Killed; Wounded; Missing. A few months ago the War Office had stopped supplying lists of the wounded, but a few still crept through, from journalists on the scene, she suspected.

Neither of her brothers in Killed, neither in Wounded. Her heart lightened, she glanced at the Missing section. Linus Yates. Lieutenant Linus Yates. Missing, believed wounded.

Her breath seemed to have caught somewhere under her breastbone.

The Battle of Beersheba, it said. She'd never heard of Beersheba, except in the Bible. She looked again at the casualty lists. Yes, there they were, from Linus's battalion. At least he wasn't dead. At least he wasn't *known* to be wounded.

It felt as though her face had frozen. She couldn't move, could do nothing but blink at the words. Missing, believed wounded, 31 October. All Souls' Eve. She felt a sob climbing in her throat, and choked it down by taking a long breath.

She couldn't cry here. Jack should be here, to take her out of this place where people were staring at her. She could be angry with Jack, and then she wouldn't cry in front of these strangers. These strange men.

Her hand was clenched on the table in a fist. She made herself open it, gently, and smooth out the paper she had grasped.

Linus wasn't dead, that was the main thing. But it had been more than two weeks since the battle. He *could* be dead, easily, by now. The image of her parents receiving this news swept over her, and she came to her feet. She had to get out of here. Now.

'I'll see you in due course, gentlemen,' she said, and got herself out the door without falling over or screaming, which she had to count as a victory. Victory. They were calling the Battle of Beersheba a victory, too.

•

'What's got into her?' Coates asked as Rebecca left. Sandro didn't like his tone. Coates had a thing about Mrs Quinn, he suspected; his eyes had a nasty glint when he looked at her – but only when she wasn't turned in his direction. You had to watch the ones like that.

But Mrs Quinn had left in an odd way, with her head held high and her hands clenched tightly on her purse. Offended, almost. As though someone had let off a bad smell or told a blue joke.

Christy Nolan shrugged and pulled over the copy of *The Times* she had been reading.

'Women have calls of nature, too, you know,' he said.

Coates laughed nastily, and Lemaitre stared at him as if he were in a freak show.

'Oh, dear Mother of God,' Christy said. 'Her brother's name is Linus, isn't it?'

'Is it?' Sandro said, coming forward. He threw a napkin on the counter and bent over the paper, looking over Christy's shoulder to where his forefinger was planted in the middle of the casualty lists.

'Linus Yates,' he said. 'Was she a Yates before her marriage?'

'I don't know,' Sandro said. He read. 'Missing, believed wounded. That's bad.'

'*Mais oui,*' Lemaitre said. 'Worse, in some ways, than knowing the worst.'

He sounded as if he had personal experience.

'A brother,' Coates said. He sounded regretful, as if he would have preferred her to be mourning a lover, or maybe a husband. He made Sandro's stomach turn.

But her – typical of those British types. She'd just sat there for a moment, expressionless. Not a tear, not a sigh, not even *telling* them. Just out of here, and head high at that. They weren't good enough to share her feelings with. Not even important enough to be told the news.

Any Italian woman would have wailed and cried and shared her sorrow. Hell, most American women would have too.

He felt his compassion for her as a personal affront. He didn't want to be sorry for her.

'Ah well,' Christy said, sitting back and putting jam on a soft roll. 'She's a proud woman and likely didn't want sympathy.'

Or else she didn't know how to ask for it. Sandro felt another pang of compassion, but what could he do? It wasn't as though she were family.

•

In her room, she sat at the rickety rattan table by the window where she wrote her stories, her hands clenched in her lap, rocking backwards and forwards, just a little, staring at the whitewashed walls and the picture of the Madonna and Child that hung dead centre on the opposite wall.

Missing. Believed wounded.

The brazen desert sky seemed to spread above her, and vultures circled high overhead. To be wounded in such desolation; to be alone, and afraid, in the silence after the battle, when the world was full of the moans of the dying and the harsh cawing of gluttonous crows. And Linus, her little brother, smiling, lighthearted Linus, who went through life as if it were a drawing-room comedy, as if life were a delight. Linus, lying bleeding, hurt, thirsty and in pain, somewhere beyond hope.

A sob wrenched through her, tearing at her lungs, her sternum, her throat. She had to do something. Anything. Write to her parents. They would have had a telegram at least a week ago. She could send them one, find out if they had any other news.

But she knew, immediately, that they had not. They would have let her know if her brother had died. Or if he'd been found and taken to hospital; knowing, as they did, how she pored over the casualty lists.

The one great communal occupation of the war: people who had never opened a broadsheet newspaper in their lives bought *The Times* each week to check the lists.

Her thoughts were wandering. If her parents hadn't contacted her, it was because they were still caught in the torment of suspension. Not knowing was better than knowing, wasn't it, if he were dead?

She rested her forehead on her clenched hands on the table and prayed, while tears fell from her cheeks and slid through the rattan crevices to the floor.

•

A knock on the door roused her from a light doze.

'*Signora!* A gentleman to see you,' Angela called through the door. She sounded delighted, as though a gentleman calling on Rebecca were just as much fun for her.

'*Grazie*,' she called back, her voice hoarse. She should get up and go down to the parlour, but she felt a terrible lassitude.

The door opened and Christy came in, hat in hand. She sat up and drew in a breath, cleared her throat.

'Well now,' he said comfortably. 'I just thought I'd pop in and see how you were travelling.'

'Thank you,' she said. It felt more than odd, to have a man other than Jack in her bedroom, even though Christy might be old enough to be her father. It forced her to her feet. She picked up her jacket and hat and purse and indicated the door.

'Let's walk a little.'

He ushered her out and closed the door behind him quietly, and took her elbow as they went down the stairs, as if he wasn't sure she would manage it alone.

She fixed her hat on with a hatpin without looking in the mirror. The last thing she cared about today was how she looked.

As they went out into the courtyard Christy settled his own hat on his head and remarked, 'A bit of a shock, like?'

'Yes,' she said. 'My—'

'Your brother, aye, I saw. Linus is an unusual name.'

A tremor went through her at *Linus*.

'Yes.' It was as though she couldn't say anything but 'yes'. She tried again. 'He's the youngest. Light Horse. Sometimes, after the battle, if a horse has – has fallen on the rider, they can't see him . . .'

'Don't upset yourself,' he said gently. 'It might be another thing entirely. He might have got bushwhacked in the desert somewhere, or his horse went lame and he wouldn't leave it.'

Her heart lifted at that simple explanation. The problem was, there was no way to know which explanation was more likely. But she had to keep a stiff upper lip, and pretend to be brave.

'Oh, that would be Linus! He was mad for horses his whole life.'

'There you are, then.' Outside the courtyard, the full force of the wind hit them.

'Ah, it's fierce weather we're having, isn't it?' Christy said. 'I feel sorry for the men out on the Barrage.'

'Poor devils,' he agreed. They walked on for a little while, heading down and to the left, towards the inner harbour. 'Now,' Christy said finally, 'I've been wanting to say, if you don't want to work with young Panucci, I'd be happy to give you the news from the press conferences. Sure, you should have asked me before you talked to him.'

'How kind of you! But I didn't talk to him – at least, it was Nonna Rosa's idea. And, frankly,' she said, looking up at him with a sceptical glance, 'I didn't think you'd be too happy to pass information on to a rival reporter.'

He barked a laugh. 'Aye, well, if it was your young Jack-feller-me-lad I might not have been so willing, I'll grant you. But he can look after himself.'

'And I can't?' She felt the familiar irritation arise, and was sorry for it; Christy's impulse in coming to see her had been sheer kindness, after all.

'Oh, lass, you can look after yourself to here and Sunday, but things aren't set up for women in this trade, are they? I'm an Irishman, and we don't like seeing the weak put down.'

She stayed silent. What could she say? *The weak* indeed! On the other hand, he was perfectly correct – things *weren't* set up for women in this trade of hers.

'Now I've put my foot in it,' Christy said ruefully. 'I didn't mean *you* were weak.'

'No,' she said. The short exchange had cleared her thoughts, and her mind was her own again; Linus's fate was put in the special grotto of prayers and hopes she didn't show to the world. 'I'm just a three-legged dog you're helping over a stile, aren't I?'

He chuckled honestly at that. 'I wouldn't dare agree. But the stile's a high one, and the best of us can use some help over it.'

'Thank you, Christy,' she said. 'I appreciate it. But this arrangement with Mr Baker is working out well so far.'

'Fair enough. If you need my boost over the stile, though . . .'

'Yes,' she said, and smiled up at him as at a favourite uncle. 'I'll ask for it.'

They walked for a while, through the thin warmth of early afternoon, which brought striped cats out to lie along the tops of walls in the sunlight, and caused the sharp scent of the harbour to intensify. They paused at a small open space that overlooked where the fishing boats were moored, red sails furled. Their nets had been spread in the time-honoured manner to dry, and she wondered how long fishermen had been casting nets in this sea. Back well beyond antiquity, to the edges of humanity itself. That was a comforting thought; this coast had seen war after war, each as devastating to the people involved as this one was, and yet the nets were cast and brought in, century after century. Endurance, tradition, survival. After the war, they would still cast those nets, and bring them back to be dried.

After the war.

The wind rose, cold, and they turned back without speaking. Christy delivered her to her door and said goodbye, smiling.

'Remember,' he said. 'If that stile's too high . . .'

She went inside feeling comforted, and less alone.

9

His first press conference. Finally.

Sandro held his credentials – a telegram from Evans, but still good enough – and a small notebook and pencil. That was what reporters used, right? He'd seen Christy Nolan and the others going over their notes in the trattoria. And he wasn't going to hand his head to that woman for washing as he had yesterday. His mouth tightened at the memory. She had a nerve, telling him which picture was better!

All press conferences were held in the Italian base, the old fort that loomed over the harbour. The small cluster of reporters – eight of them, including a few of the local Bari reporters who had come down on the train for the day. Their reports would be syndicated all over Italy. And his – theirs – might end up all over the world. An edge of excitement went up his spine. He was glad he was taller than the Italians. The British and French reporters were half a head taller, so they literally as well as figuratively looked down on the Italians, but they couldn't look down on him. That Quinn woman would probably be surprised that he even knew the word *figuratively*. She hadn't realised that he came from the city with the greatest public library system in the world. And he'd used it.

The gates opened promptly at nine-thirty, and they went in. Sandro followed the others, his palms sweating.

Piece of cake, he told himself.

They were shown into an office at the front of the building, a section that had been built up against the solid stone of the tower. There were no chairs – just an open floor, and at one end stood the four flags: Italian, British, French and Australian. After a moment, a door at that end of the room opened and the commanders walked through. Not all of them – the French were out on patrol. Mrs Quinn had a young lad who watched every morning and reported who left the harbour and who came back.

Italy: Rear Admiral Alfredo Acton. Britain: Commodore William Kelly. Australia: Commander William Warren. Sometimes Sandro thought every second Brit was called William.

Behind them, a line of suitably serious young men, all Australian, none over thirty. Three were in officer's uniform. He recognised most of their faces from the train station.

It was Acton, the Italian commander, who spoke first, and here Sandro and the Italian reporters had the advantage. He made a brief speech about the thanks owed to the men of the Australian flotilla for their assistance during the *Orione* emergency.

Commander Warren also lauded the men's work. 'They worked like Trojans,' he said. 'In the most difficult of conditions. We are very proud of them.'

The British Commodore, Kelly, announced the thanks of the Admiralty: to Warren, and to Lieutenants Mortimer, Bridge and Hill for their rescue of the damaged ship. The young men in officer's uniform stepped forward and shook his hand as if they were in the presence of the King himself. Sandro whipped out his pocket camera and took shots – the light wasn't great but he might be able to get something if he pushed the developing. Then he realised he was supposed to be taking notes, and grabbed his pencil and book. He had to get the names right. That was a reporter's first duty, Mrs Quinn had said.

The two other ranks of men stepped forward to accept their nomination for medals. The light was too poor now to take any shots – a cloud was passing over the sun. He concentrated on writing all the details down and wished he could do shorthand like the other reporters, whose pencils sped over their pages.

The commanders didn't wait for questions, but left straightaway.

'Can we get a group shot, boys?' Sandro forced himself to ask. He wished now that he'd brought the big camera, but he hadn't wanted to stand out on his first day. He remembered Christy saying once, 'A reporter's gotta be pushy, lad,' and he could see now that it was true. 'Maybe outside, where the light is better?'

Every single one of his photographs would be in perfect focus this time.

'Sure!' one of the ordinary seamen said. They all trooped outside. The officers, giving the men their limelight, stood behind, smiling. It was a good shot – they were buoyed up by the acknowledgement of their superiors, and it showed.

'Can we get a copy of that, mate?' the signalman asked. 'Forgot to ask you the other day.'

'Sure, sure. Come up to Nonna Rosa's in a couple of days and I'll have one for you.'

'What about us?' Christy asked. 'Can we get copies?'

Sandro grinned and waved his telegram at them. 'Sorry, gents. Exclusive to the *Evening News* and *The Sydney Morning Herald*.'

'You're working with the Quinn woman?' Coates asked.

Sandro didn't like his tone. 'What of it?' he demanded.

'Better you than me, that's all I'll say. And she'll dump you like a bad smell when her husband gets back.'

Not man enough to stand up to her, that was Coates's problem. Sandro quelled a momentary doubt about what would happen when Jack Quinn returned, and winked at them, then realised a moment later that they might take that the wrong way.

'She's a very nice woman,' he said. 'My nonna thinks so, and you know, Nonna Rosa always knows best!'

They laughed at that but one of the Italian reporters cornered him as they went through the gates. 'You can sell it to me, though, eh? Don't have an Italian paper yet?'

'Would your editor be interested in a story too?'

'*Compagno, I'll* do the story.'

Sandro put aside a vision of sending his parents a proper Italian newspaper with his photographs in it. He'd made a deal, and he wouldn't renege.

'Signora Quinn does the writing, I take the photos,' he said. 'Both, or neither.'

'A *woman*?' The reporter laughed until the edges of his moustache quivered wildly, and the other Italians laughed along with him. 'Now I've heard everything!'

He walked away from the laughter with his head high. Those *bastardi* would kill to get their stories in an English paper. He was okay with the current deal. And besides, Mrs Quinn was twice the reporter those guys were. Catch them dressing up and handing out bedpans for a story! He felt the stirring of partisanship.

Mrs Quinn was waiting outside.

She had dressed in dark green today – how many outfits did she own, anyway? His sisters thought they were doing well with one to wear, one to wash and one for Sunday best, but he'd seen her in at least four different skirts and blouses. Rich parents, he reckoned. You could tell by the way she spoke, all crisp and British.

'How did it go?' she asked, but not as though she doubted him.

'It went fine. I took notes. And I got some shots.'

They went to the big cafe not far from the base and sat at a table inside, away from the wind. She looked pale, as though she hadn't had much sleep lately. Should he ask about her brother? If she'd wanted him to know, she would have told him. Better let sleeping dogs lie.

Leon, the cafe owner, came over to take their order; coffee for him and tea for her.

'A letter for your grandmother came in. Save me a trip up to the trattoria.' Leon passed a stained envelope across to him. It was stiff with dried salt, as though it had been dropped in the sea.

He had ceased to be surprised at Nonna's odd way of receiving correspondence. He was liable to be stopped anywhere – by someone he knew or by a stranger – and be handed a note or letter or small parcel for her. He had his suspicions about what it all meant, but he kept them to himself.

A big, shambling, friendly man, Leon would have stayed and chatted, but luckily another customer came in.

'Friend of your nonna's?' Rebecca cocked an eyebrow at Sandro, looking, for the moment, like a mischievous angel.

'Friend of everybody's,' he said. He filled her in on the press conference and she looked over his notes, and started drafting up the story then and there. He watched with admiration. Words had never been his forté. Art and sport, that was his school career. Math wasn't too bad, either. You needed that to run your own business. But English composition? He'd been lucky to get a C minus.

The understanding that he was dealing with a professional writer sank into his bones. He relaxed. He could safely leave this stuff to her, and stick to what he did best: listen, and shoot pictures.

'I'll go and write up a clean copy at the pensione,' she said as she finished her tea. Maybe he should follow her example: tea was more easily come by than coffee, and the swill Leon was putting up wasn't worth drinking.

'I'll make some prints,' he said. 'I'll be at Fabrini's if you need me.'

She smiled at him and let him pay, which was nice of her, because he really hadn't known how to stop her paying for herself, as she usually did at Nonna Rosa's.

He could make contact prints in his little darkroom at Nonna Rosa's, but for the kind of prints the sailors would want to send home, for the kind of prints a newspaper wanted, he needed an enlarger.

During his first week in Brindisi, he'd gone into the only photographer's in town and enquired about work, prompted partly by a desire to have access to a proper darkroom, and partly because he just flat out hated being a waiter.

Fabrini's, it had said over the door. A bell had tinkled as he opened it, and a young woman came out to stand at a wooden counter that stood in front of a dark red curtain. Sandro immediately knew that the studio space must be behind it, because the shop itself was small – just big enough for the counter, a visitor's chair, and some elaborately framed photographs on display: the typical wedding, baptism and first-communion photos on one wall, and on the other, more simply framed prints of sailors and a few soldiers, stiffly smiling. Sandro admired the way the photographer had got the light to shine so that their moustaches gleamed.

'*Buongiorno. Posso aiutarti?*' the woman asked. A girl, really, maybe eighteen or nineteen (although he found it hard to guess the age of Italian women – they seemed to mature earlier and get older faster than American women).

He switched on the Italian part of his brain and smiled at her as he took off his hat. She was pretty, with quick warm eyes and a sweet smile.

'*Buongiorno.*' He placed his portfolio on the counter – a gift from his parents when he left, it was a nice leather case with handles, big enough to hold a dozen 8-inch by 12-inch prints with room to spare. 'I'm a photographer, Alessandro Panucci.'

'From New York!' she said brightly. In Italian, 'New York' was '*La Nuova York*', and it was odd to hear his home town sound foreign.

He laughed. 'Everybody knows everyone's business here, eh?'

'Everyone knows Nonna Rosa,' she said, with a hint of reserve in her tone. He'd heard that before. Not everyone, it seemed, liked his nonna. He didn't blame them. She was a tough old bird.

'I was wondering if you needed any help here?'

She laughed, covering her mouth with her hand in a way that reminded him of his sisters. 'Oh, don't ask me! Papa is the one you have to talk to.' Then a quick, assessing look at him; at his good wool suit and nice hat. 'But it would be good – when the ships are in, Papa has to work very hard.'

From behind the curtain, Sandro could hear men talking, and a deep voice said, '*Stai fermo!*' Stay still, stay still, the photographer's eternal entreaty. A single muscle twitch could ruin a portrait.

'I'll wait for him, then,' Sandro said. He smiled at her again and leaned on the counter, not averse to a chat with a pretty girl. 'May I know who I'm speaking to?'

'Oh, I'm Natalia Fabrini. I'm the youngest. Angela and Maria are married already, and live in Bari. I'm the only one left at home, so I have to help in the shop.' She was as natural and unselfconscious as a child, and he felt a little ashamed that he noticed the swell of her breasts and the curve of her hips in her dark dress.

The curtain was pulled back and three men came out: two French sailors, complete with caps, and a man in a black suit: Fabrini, no doubt. Short, wiry, electric in movement, he ushered the men out with broken French.

'*Demaan, demaan,*' he said, nodding and smiling. 'Ready tomorrow.' As the men went out the door, he turned, the smile wiping off his face, and switched to Italian. '*Bastardi francesi,*' he said. 'Couldn't hold still. I wasted three plates.' His eyebrow went up as he looked Sandro over.

'Signor Fabrini—' Sandro began, but Natalia cut him off.

'This is Rosa Panucci's grandson, Papa. Alessandro. From *New York.*' As though he were from Mars. Or maybe Heaven.

'*Buongiorno, buongiorno,*' Fabrini said, smiling again.

Sandro went through his spiel once more, this time bringing out the photographs in his portfolio. They were all good. He'd brought some of his best portrait shots, including a couple of big groups. And a few he'd taken of Brindisi itself: the Roman columns, the steps, the harbour.

Fabrini nodded. 'Good, good. Yes. Come and see.' He led the way behind the curtain. It was the studio space, the same as you'd find in any photographer's, with props along one wall, and a camera, a Rietzschel, on a tripod. Not bad equipment, but nothing outstanding. At least he was using dry plates and not wet.

Behind the studio space was a door that led to the darkroom. Again, Sandro was reminded of his own studio in New York. He spared a thought for Carlo, his partner. Carlo wasn't a letter writer – Sandro didn't expect to hear any news from him unless things went bad.

The darkroom was about nine foot square. It held the trays, the sink, the shelves for storage, the contact printer – and an enlarger.

'*Ottimo*,' he said politely.

'*Si, si. Solo il meglio.*' Only the best? Well, Sandro thought, maybe this is the best Italy can offer. It was a depressing thought.

The girl was crowded in behind him. He felt her arm brush innocently across his back, and prayed that her father wouldn't notice the effect it had on him.

'So,' Signor Fabrini said. 'When the ships come in and the sailors come, I'll send word to you. One of us in the darkroom, one of us in the studio, *va bene?*'

'*Tutto bene*,' Sandro said. They went out to the front of the shop and discussed money. It was more than Nonna Rosa was paying him to wait tables, but he suspected that it was on the low side. No matter. He'd bring up an increase in pay after Fabrini was sure of his worth.

'Wonderful!' Natalia said. 'I hate helping in the darkroom. It makes me breathe funny.'

She put her hand on her chest in emphasis, and Sandro really wished she hadn't. It made it hard to concentrate on what her father was saying. Fabrini glanced from one to the other, but he said nothing.

'I'd better go,' Sandro said. 'My nonna will be wanting me to set up for the evening trade. I'm helping her out for a while.'

'A good grandson,' Fabrini said, not approvingly but thoughtfully. '*Bene.*'

•

Had that only been three weeks ago? After a quick visit to Fabrini's workroom, Sandro turned that over in his mind as he climbed the hill to Nonna Rosa's, his newly printed photographs of the heroic crewmen in hand. A good grandson. Was he? Since that first meeting with Fabrini he had gradually withdrawn from waiting on tables, although he was still needed occasionally. The Kythera boy, Georgiou, was helping out now. Sandro still did a lot of the prep work, and the clean-up after. Better a dish hand than a waiter. He didn't like the way the officers and journalists looked down their noses at him. Half the time he wanted to . . . well, once a boxer, always a boxer.

Was he using Nonna Rosa as she was using him? She was the least dependent woman he'd ever met – except, perhaps, Signora Quinn, who had something of the same self-control and strength. He wondered what her husband was like.

He'd waited on him only once, the first night he'd come to Brindisi, but then Jack Quinn had just been one of a group of laughing, drinking men. A man like any of the others.

He hadn't had the impression of a man strong enough to match Signora Quinn . . . but maybe she'd been hardened by having to fend for herself now he was gone. It was often so, he'd noticed. Widows became more competent, stronger, than they had been as wives.

Or weaker, he thought, remembering his own mother's mother, who had moved in with them after his grandfather's death, unable to cope.

No generalisations. He grinned. It was human nature to try to find patterns, but there weren't any real patterns to people. They were too complex, too ornery to be put into neat little boxes.

He wondered, with a sudden chill, which box Signora Quinn had assigned him to.

10

In the middle of the night, Rebecca came awake slowly, conscious of something badly wrong. Noises. Long, shrieking whistles and thuds, coming from some distance. The sound sent her to the window and out onto the balcony into the cold air. To the north, on the far horizon, flashes of light came irregularly, followed some time later by an attenuated shriek and bang.

She'd heard that sound before, when she'd done a story on the Liverpool Barracks, a nice *look how well your sons and brothers are doing* story. They'd used live ammunition on the range that day. The sound of shells whistling to their target and exploding was unforgettable. Now, it ran along her nerves like nails on a blackboard. Some warship was shelling a coastal town.

The Austrians were becoming bolder, coming further south. Shivers ran through her, not all from the cold. Was Brindisi safe? She'd never considered that this might turn into a target city – surely they wouldn't dare take on the combined Allied fleet!

Another flash. What town could it be? Surely not Posticeddu. That was too close for comfort.

From the harbour, the sound of a ship's horn sent another shiver through her. No doubt the Italian fleet was heading out to engage the Austrians. She sent a prayer after them, hoping that no mother or wife would receive bad news tomorrow.

What was *happening*? Not knowing was horrible. Nerve-racking. She was sick of waiting around for people to tell her things, of being dependent on others for scraps of information.

She was a journalist, and tomorrow she would investigate. Find out where, and how much damage. Real war reporting. Tonight, there was no way to get where she needed to. The livery stable was closed, and she had no horse or vehicle of her own, not even a bicycle. She wished she had one of the motorcycles the Italian Army couriers rode – although her skirts would be a distinct safety hazard.

But tomorrow, she would get a horse and go to find out for herself what these terrible noises meant. She would be like Louise Mack, the very first woman war reporter, who had encouraged her so strongly to take the step into war correspondence. 'Don't let them stop you,' had been Louise's advice. 'If it's safe for a man, it's safe for us. And sometimes, it's safer for us than for a man.'

Rebecca would ride up the coast tomorrow and find out the truth of tonight's attack. And Mr Baker could take pictures.

•

It was clear that Mr Baker wasn't going to stop cradling his camera in order to drive, so Rebecca took the reins of the donkey cart from the livery stable owner.

'*Grazie*,' she said, ignoring his grin at the sight of the woman doing the man's work. She clicked her tongue and flicked the reins, and the donkey, thank God, walked on. She settled the skirt of her brown dress around her. Brown, in honour of Linus. Not black, though, because, with God's grace, he wasn't dead.

It took them almost an hour to get out into the real countryside.

She was still possessed of the impatience that had taken hold of her the night before, the desire to find out for herself what had happened, which town had been shelled, who had been hurt. But this donkey wasn't going any faster than a walk, and his white whiskers and muzzle showed that he had age as an excuse. The Italian Army had commandeered all the good mules and donkeys as well as all the horses.

At least it was a nice day, so far as a November day in the northern hemisphere could be considered nice. A brisk breeze blew high fluffy clouds around, and the leaves of the olive trees rippled under it, sending waves of silver and sage across the fields to the right of them, all the way down to the beach and the white-capped sea. To the left, stubble in the field waited for the winter snow, and birds picked over the sparse grain the gleaners had missed. There were women in a far field, pruning vines. It could have been any day in the long history of Italy.

In Australia, where fields and agriculture were so new, where towns sprang up overnight to feed the growing population, it was easy to believe that women's rights were central to the advance of civilisation. Here, though . . . here women went about their accustomed duties, bowing to both church and husband, as they had done for millennia. It all seemed so *permanent*, and it shook her. Were her ideas, her mother's ideas, only good for a portion of humankind? Did they have the right to expect women here to speak up, to agitate, to join the cause when they were part of a civilisation which had stayed unchanged for so long, and endured so successfully?

From far up, along the ridge, she caught a glimpse of smoke being shredded on the wind. A steam train; the sight comforted her. Italy *was* changing, come what may, and war would speed that change. Women's rights had to be part of the change, or none of this fighting was worth anything.

She hadn't said a word since they had left the outskirts of town. But she was stuck for a topic of conversation, especially since – apart from writing the last story about the medals – all she had thought about for days was Linus. No, she couldn't talk about her brother. The very thought made her choke up, and she had to keep her wits about her today.

What else could she say? She didn't really know Mr Baker. Not as a person. He was handsome, smart, quick and competent at everything he did; he was a good grandson to Nonna Rosa; he was ambitious. That was it. Where did she go from there? She was conscious that he was looking at her.

Although she tried to control it, there were times when the journalist's itch to *know* took over her mouth and spoke of its own accord, no matter how embarrassing it proved.

'Do you mind my asking, Mr Baker – you said you "can't fight"?'

He looked at her with a half-smile that had no animosity behind it, and stretched out his left hand, showing the thumb. Its abrupt end disconcerted her, as though her eyes kept expecting it to be whole; as though it was a joke, a *blague* as her nanny used to say.

'But—' she said.

'Doesn't look much, does it? But to get into the Army, you have to be able to pick a pin up from the floor with either hand. And I can do a lot with this thing . . .' He waggled the stump of his thumb. 'But I can't do that.'

'Surely they could find another role for you? My brother works in logistics in England.'

'Each and every Army recruit has to be physically able to fight. Those are the rules.'

His voice was bitter, despite a superficially matter-of-fact air. She could see the discontent, the frustration, in his face, and it made her heart clench with sympathy. To have imagined yourself whole, and normal, and to be told that you were ... defective. What a blow to his pride.

'Is that why you came to Italy?'

He shrugged. 'I thought the Italian doctors might be less picky. They weren't.'

They fell silent. There wasn't anything she could say that would help. Despite herself, she wondered how he had sustained the injury. She couldn't ask. Could she? She took another quick glance at it, and he caught her at it.

'I was working in a meat-packing factory. My second week on the job, one of the other workers got too enthusiastic. Happens often enough. There are butchers all over the world missing the top of their thumb or finger.'

She shuddered, and he laughed, with real amusement. 'It hurt like heck, I can tell you that! But once it was over, I was fine ...' He trailed off. She finished the sentence silently for him ... he was fine until he'd tried to enlist.

She had to change the subject.

'I've always wanted to go to New York,' she said brightly. 'What was it like, growing up there?'

Strangely, Mr Baker hesitated. 'I guess,' he said slowly, 'it was a bit like growing up in a miniature world. Every nationality on earth, just a walk away.'

As they ambled along, he talked about Little Italy being next door to Chinatown and Little Germany, about his father and brothers working in the meat-packing district, about his discovery of the New York Public Library and the Metropolitan Museum of Art.

He gave the impression of a close family, a good upbringing, but there was something held back, something not said. But clearly, he had educated himself, and that ambition to improve himself was the best thing she had learned about him, apart from the clarity of his images.

'What about Sydney?' he asked eventually.

She laughed. How to describe her family? 'You've heard of Emmeline Pankhurst?' she asked.

'Sure.' He nodded. The whole English-speaking world had heard of Emmeline Pankhurst, suffragette and activist.

'Imagine having her as a mother.'

His face was comical in its dismay. 'Well, now, that explains a lot.'

'You mean, what I'm doing here? My husband was posted here, and I took the opportunity to come with him,' she said. 'If I had to write another article about fashions or hairstyles! With the war going on, and they still expected us to care more about hemline length!'

'So, here you are,' he said.

'Yes. And from here, I'm going into general news, or feature-article writing. No more Women's Pages for me!'

He nodded, and looked at her as if seeing a new side of her; it wasn't exactly unpleasant, but it did make her wonder what those dark, compelling eyes had seen.

Not long after, they passed through Posticeddu, where the road came right down to the sea to go through the little fishing village. They had set out very early but the boats were in, the nets spread to dry, the sharp smell of seaweed clear on the breeze.

A few moments, with the women of the town coming to their doorways to stare at the strangers going through, and then they were out the other side, along the sea road. To their right, now, were marshes and sea grass, and a long beach stretching out to an out-thrust spit of land. As they came closer, she could see that it was a stone fort. Old, but then everything looked old here.

Then again the sea road, but now they weren't alone on it. Traffic was coming from the other direction. People on foot, a couple of wagons piled high with household goods. A jolt through her stomach made her realise they were refugees, ousted from their homes by the shelling she'd seen the night before.

The wagons and handcarts were full, too full to take passengers, apart from one old *nonna* who perched on what was undoubtedly her favourite chair, lashed onto a mountain of chests and blankets that smelled of ash and wet wool. Children, old people, pregnant women – they all walked. There were almost no men, except *nonnos* hobbling on canes and boys too young to shave. The population of a country at war.

She had faced the journalist's dilemma before, when she had reported on a big fire that had ripped through an area of slum dwellings – set, they had said, by the landlord, who wanted to sell. A journalist wasn't there to help – or, not to offer the immediate kind of aid anyone would give from simple humanity. The journalist's help was broader, more abstract. The buttressing of civilisation through the free exchange of information.

She believed in that passionately, but it had been hard that night to leave the women and children huddling in their meagre coats in order to go back to the warm newsroom. She had called her mother from the newsroom and set in motion the charitable women of Sydney; those left homeless were helped. But still, she had turned her back on people in trouble in order to do her job.

Now, again, she was faced with the desire to help. To turn the cart around, pick up the smallest children and bring them back to Brindisi. To feed them and warm them and do whatever she could. But what she had to do was get the story.

'I wish we could help them,' she said.

Mr Baker nodded. 'Not much we can do on our own,' he said. 'And they'll have family in the area, all of them.'

She hadn't thought of that. That was the other side to a traditional, apparently stagnant way of life: the supportive networks that were the lifeblood of the culture. She was momentarily ashamed of her assumption these people would be asking for handouts.

Before they reached the refugees, she pulled the cart to the side of the road and wound the reins around the brake lever. The donkey immediately started to graze on the scant grass of the verge, and Mr Baker was setting up the tripod before the donkey had swallowed its first mouthful.

Rebecca jumped down from the wagon and approached the first family party, a group of five: husband, wife, and three children ranging from about ten to around six.

'*Buongiorno*,' she said, and introduced herself, notebook out. '*Cosa è successo ieri sera?*'

A chorus of voices answered her. It defeated her Italian at first – the accent was much thicker than in Brindisi – but gradually she sorted it out, took it down: the first shell hitting the church, the highest building in the town, and then death raining down. Frantic running, the children scattering everywhere, the hiding in the dark in the scrub around the village until the shelling stopped.

A vivid picture emerged of a community terrified, destroyed, clinging to each other in the darkness as their homes were pounded into pieces, each blow lit by the fires that sprang up.

'The smell of burning,' the wife said, 'I am a weaver, and the smell of burning wool . . .' She turned aside, hands to her mouth, and her husband curved his arms around her and held her, his cheek against her shoulder.

Others crowded around, and gave details. The time of the first shell: 11.40 pm. The number of shells: 'Forty-one. I counted them,' said an old grandpa. The attackers: 'An Austrian destroyer,' said the wife, in control of herself once again. 'As we ran down the hill I saw it.' The destruction: 'All gone, all,' a young girl cried. 'What will become of us?'

They turned their shoulders to her as they comforted each other. She waited, her heart hurting to see them in such straits. She felt so helpless. She didn't even have a home in which to offer them shelter. But she had to get their names, if she was going to quote them.

'Thank you,' she said. 'I hope you'll be able to go back soon.'

'Never!' one woman said, a broad-faced woman with a strong jaw. 'I'm not taking our girls back there!'

Rebecca nodded her understanding and walked back to the wagon.

Mr Baker waited until she was out of shot, and the people had begun to move again, before he focused.

He took two exposures, to the astonishment of those photographed, and they went on, the long flat road behind them filling up with more as the day went on.

Why hadn't they met anyone earlier on their way? She looked behind. The stream of people was turning off the main road, going inland, not far behind them.

'Where are they going?' she asked Mr Baker.

He seemed to consult a map in his mind. 'Serranova, maybe,' he said. 'It has an old fort. Maybe they think they'll be safer there. Or else the lord has told them he will feed them.'

'The lord?'

'The count. Conte Dentice di Frasso.'

The sense of living in a culture older than she had imagined rose up in her again, making her feel like a mayfly, transitory and unimportant.

'Let's go,' she said, setting the donkey in motion. It grabbed one last mouthful of grass before it deigned to walk on.

It made her uncomfortable to have the people on the road shift aside for them, but she kept the donkey moving slowly, thanking them and occasionally stopping to ask a question, but the answers were all the same. Shock, fear, anger, loss. A terrible litany. After half an hour, they began to smell something other than salt on the wind. A stale remnant of cordite, like the morning after Cracker Night.

Above the plain, the shapes of houses began to appear. There was no one left on the road but them; all the townspeople were gone, it seemed.

Rebecca let the reins drop and the donkey stood still, so that the only sounds were the waves on the beach and the mewing of the gulls. She felt a great reluctance to go further, and at the same time a devouring curiosity. This was her first real experience of war; the trip from Australia had been full of convoys and submarine scares, but no shot had been fired.

Interviewing the crew who had saved the *Orione* had been the closest she had come to action. Time to change that.

She urged the donkey on and it flicked its ear at her as though scolding her for not knowing her own mind, and walked on. It was good of Mr Baker not to comment on her pause.

At first, the damage didn't look too bad. The houses on this side of town were mostly intact. Then they came closer, and saw that the other side had been shelled; the walls to the south were only remnants of the buildings.

It wasn't a large town – not like Brindisi. Just a fishing village, a farming town, like most along this stretch of coast. Small houses, old houses, huddled together against the ever-present wind from the sea.

Smashed apart.

Once they passed the southern boundary of the village, the street was full of hollow, blackened skeletons of what had once been houses. Fires had started, then, after the shelling – impossible to stop in a place that had relied on wood burning for fuel. Here a wall stood, there a pillar and a few bricks, in another place a corner, completely unscathed, with half a mural on it, of an olive harvest. The cottages had been stripped, mostly, of whatever was left – Rebecca remembered the carts piled with household goods, the ash and wet wool smell of the blankets, and understood it better.

Each of these houses was once a home. A place of thought, of rest, of happiness, of work, of love.

She mustn't cry. She was here to do a job.

'This is a good spot,' Mr Baker said, very subdued. He was pale; his mouth tight as he set up his equipment.

She wandered on, up a side street, leaving him to do his work. The fires had missed a couple of houses here; she went to

116

look over a partial wall at a small kitchen, barely large enough for the table that had fallen on its side, one leg broken off, and a tall dark dresser on the wall, clearly too heavy to move.

Clambering over the wall, she went in, careful not to dislodge any of the rubble; knowing she was being foolish, but wanting to see what it was like to stand in the middle of this devastation, to try to imagine how it would have felt to have run from the shelling in the night, and then to come to this in the light of day, to come to the beloved place only to find ruin.

No. She couldn't imagine it. Couldn't really let herself imagine it, because if she did she wouldn't be able to go on.

She left that house and found another, a larger place, where great beams had come down, leaving dark caves filled with bricks and wooden shards. This place had a courtyard garden; the rosemary bushes, astonishingly, were grey–green in the morning sunlight; a blaze of chrysanthemums in one corner was shocking in its vibrancy.

Drawn to that one sign of life, she went into the courtyard. It was barely touched. Only a double shutter had fallen from the window high above across one corner. She should leave this place better than she found it. She positioned herself underneath the shutter frame, then hauled it upright and rested it against the wall.

There was a child underneath. A little girl.

Perhaps four or five years old. In an ash-covered white nightgown and scarlet wool slippers. Asleep. Even in that first moment, Rebecca knew that was a lie she was telling herself. She kneeled and touched the child's cold forehead, where a dark bruise showed; the shutter had hit her as it fell. For a moment, a vivid flash of the night before went across her mind. The noise, the fear, the shelling, perhaps a parent shouting a warning, this little one running for the safety of the courtyard and then, the next shell, the fall of the shutter . . . and in the chaos, the parents running, searching for her . . .

Her heart contracted, squeezed so tight it felt like stone, and she felt a rush of hatred for the Austrians and Germans so strong it felt like acid. To kill civilians like this. Babies. Just a baby. Killed like a rat in the dark.

The parents. They would think she had gone with the others, to the lord's fort. They would look, and not find her, and they would come back. They shouldn't find her like this, dirty and torn, her hair a mess, everything about her screaming horror and fear and a terrible death.

No. She couldn't do anything, but she could do this. She could save them from finding their daughter like this.

She touched the little cheek gently and said, 'I'll be right back.'

Mr Baker had moved his camera a little further down. He came towards her, leaving it there, when he saw her.

'Mrs Quinn? What's wrong? You're crying.'

Rebecca touched her face. Yes, she was crying. That was all right.

'Come and help me,' she said. She thought briefly. 'There was a table, up here. Set it upright.'

Without asking questions, Mr Baker followed her to the hollowed-out kitchen and together they turned the table upright and found some bricks to prop up its lost leg.

'Now what?' he asked quietly. Had she been behaving like a madwoman? He had that look, of wary expectancy in the face of unreason. Well, he would see.

She led him to the courtyard. To the child.

Like her, he dropped to his knees and touched the little face. She stood behind him, feeling strangely distant. He smoothed the little one's hair away from her face, his hand shaking.

'*Povera piccola*,' he whispered, voice choked. For a second, she imagined how Jack or her brothers would have reacted in this moment. They would have held back the tears, she thought, kept a stiff upper lip, comforted her by being stoic and manly and showing no feeling, and encouraging her to do the same, to 'buck up'. She had been taught to be contemptuous of men who showed their emotions, but in this moment, she thought, Mr Baker was right and all she had been taught was wrong. A man *should* cry at this; a small sliver of warmth slid into her as she relaxed into his tears. She wouldn't have to pretend to be strong with him.

'I want to get her cleaned up before her parents come,' she said.

He wiped his tears away with his shirt sleeve. '*Si, si*,' he said. 'I will find the well.' Gently, he lifted the girl and gave her to Rebecca; the weight brought her back to the here and now, to the needs of the moment.

She carried her carefully, so carefully, to the kitchen. The table was dirty, but Mr Baker appeared only a moment later, with the two blankets he had wrapped around his tripod, and laid them on the table like an altar cloth.

From her bag in the wagon she took her comb, and gently brushed out the girl's tangled hair until it lay like a satin cloak. Mr Baker came back with a battered bucket of water. Her handkerchief was too small for anything but the face. His was large, and white. She shooed him out of the kitchen when she realised that the girl had wet herself in her fear, in her last moment. That almost broke her, but she bit her lip and carried on, taking off the nightgown, washing her thoroughly.

This was women's business. Birthing and dying, lying in and laying out. Women had been preparing the dead for the entirety of civilisation; she was just the latest incarnation of an ancient duty. This wasn't a place for men, and Mr Baker seemed to respect that.

'Mrs Quinn! I climbed up to the floor above the courtyard. I found some clothes.'

The floor above the courtyard had been broken and dangerous; but she took the clothes from him with an approving nod, and he pressed his lips together and nodded back in acknowledgement.

He had found a dress a little too big, but that didn't matter. And socks. Little white socks. The body was stiffening. Rebecca's hat had a gold ribbon; she used it to bind up the girl's jaw. And then she wrapped the little one in the top blanket, the clean one, realising that Mr Baker had thought ahead to this moment and had wanted to shroud her cleanly. It wasn't big enough to be a winding sheet, which was good, she thought; the girl's mother would want to do that.

A small flap of blanket would cover her face. Before Rebecca folded it down, she kissed the bruised forehead and whispered, 'Eternal rest grant unto her O Lord, and let perpetual light shine upon her. May she rest in peace, Amen.'

'Amen,' Mr Baker echoed from the doorway.

She carried the little form back to the cart and Mr Baker took her while Rebecca climbed up, then handed her up. He had packed his camera and tripod in the back, wedged them without the blanket left behind in the kitchen.

He took the reins and flicked them. The donkey, patiently, turned around and walked off.

'We'll go up to Serranova, yes?' he asked. She nodded. The parents were probably up there. And if not, someone would know which family the child belonged to.

But halfway to the turn off to Serranova they caught sight of a group of people coming the other way, a family group, one woman crying into her shawl as she went. When she saw the cart, and Rebecca holding a body, she stopped dead and waited. It was the woman they had met earlier, who had said she wouldn't let her daughters go back to the village. Rebecca's heart, which had seemed to hurt as much as it could, squeezed tight in greater pain.

It was excruciating, the time between seeing them and getting close enough to stop. Mr Baker halted the cart a little way away and came around to help her down, but the woman rushed forward, and a man, shouting, 'Christina, Christina! No, *nonononono*.'

Rebecca handed the little girl down to the woman, who tenderly turned back the flap of blanket, and then sank to the ground, clutching the body, rocking back and forth. Rebecca and the other women crowded around her, crouching down, rubbing her back, the three of them united in wordless sympathy, in aching tears.

After a while, the woman looked up at her husband and spoke in an Italian so thick that Rebecca could follow only a couple of words.

'She says that the *bambina* must be buried at Serranova, not in the place where she was murdered,' Mr Baker translated.

So, they helped the woman into the wagon, and the father got up to drive while the rest of them walked behind the cart, like the mourners they were. Mr Baker walked with his eyes down on the ground, his face pale. He was a good man, not merely a man good at his job. That was a new thought for her, but this wasn't the time to consider it.

Going into the square at Serranova was like walking back in time. The stone fort rose up several storeys, connected to other buildings by flying walkways that made arches through to the garden behind. The funeral procession went through one of these, but Rebecca hesitated. She had come as far as was proper, she thought. The interment should be a family moment.

The fort looked dark and forbidding – but in the square there were many people, who came forward, exclaiming, crying, wailing. For a moment, Rebecca felt entirely foreign. The language, the gesticulation, the women's ululations, even the smell of the air, the scent of chestnuts roasting, of cold stone and wild garlic, it was all *wrong*. She longed for home. Or even just to hear English spoken.

'Mrs Quinn,' Mr Baker said behind her, in English, touching her arm. 'They want us to stay for the midday meal. To thank us.'

How could she eat? But to say no would be an insult, she was sure.

The men were bringing trestle tables out, an important-looking man directing them.

'The conte is at sea. Near Libya, they say, so his *maggiordomo* is organising everything.'

She nodded her understanding and came to sit at the table, between the major-domo and a gaunt man who introduced himself as the mayor of Strettabaia, which she realised after a moment was the name of the town that had been destroyed.

'I am a journalist,' she said in Italian. 'I will tell the world of what has been done here.'

He caught up her hand and kissed it with gratitude. What could she do? She smiled, and nodded, and withdrew her hand after a polite moment.

But she meant to keep her promise.

A Letter from Italy

Coastal towns shelled

The Austrians are continuing their campaign of terror against civilians through the bombing of coastal towns in the Adriatic.

These towns are mostly fishing villages of no strategic or military importance.

On 20 November, the village of Strettabaia, north of Brindisi, was shelled in a display of defiance against the Navy flotillas stationed there.

The town was completely destroyed (see photographs) and around a hundred men, women and children were made homeless. There was at least one casualty, Christina Trappola, aged 4, who was killed by debris when a shell hit her home.

Nina Trappola, the child's mother, has declared that she cannot return to the site of her child's death. 'Murderers, they are murderers,' she said.

Our correspondent was an eyewitness to both the shelling and the aftermath of this terrible attack.

She took the article and the photographs, barely dry, down to the British base that evening. It would go by the morning mail boat, and reach England in under a week, all things being well. It felt short – but if it were any longer, Evans would cut it back anyway. No matter how important it seemed to her, one child's death and the shelling of a small fishing village wasn't big news when thousands of men were dying on the front every day, and there were bombs falling on London itself.

Even though she had worked hard over it, she had no surety that Mr Evans would approve it as 'naval news'. It might not be enough to ensure her position as an independent journalist; and after the day's events she was determined to reveal this part of the war to those back in England and Australia – perhaps, if the articles were picked up by the American papers, to the rest of the world, too.

11

What a day. Horrible. That little girl.

He never would have believed that the stuck-up ice queen could be so human.

He snuck a look at her, still upright on the wagon seat. At Serranova she'd shown him how to free the donkey from its traces, and paid one of the kids to curry it down and water it while they had lunch. When they'd got back on the road, she'd taken the reins back as a matter of course, apparently unmoved. If he hadn't seen her tears, running ceaselessly down her face, if he hadn't seen her hands, gentle on the little body . . .

God, he was tired. Maybe it was the tears. He had cried enough for one day. *Poverina*. And he'd thought Mrs Quinn would despise him for those tears. The girls he'd gone to high school would have, the American girls. They'd made fun of the Italian sentimentality, especially that of the men. *Real* men, American men, didn't cry, didn't gesticulate, didn't shout in each other's faces.

But Mrs Quinn hadn't looked down on him when he'd begun to cry. On the way out of Brindisi it had been all right, discussing growing up in New York, making small talk as if they were at a party. But now, for the life of him he couldn't think of any topic of conversation that would be decent, after that little girl's death, so he sat in silence like a dumb ox, and she shared his silence.

When they could see Brindisi on the horizon, Mrs Quinn suddenly pulled the donkey to a halt and thrust the reins into his hands before scrambling down from the wagon. He sat, bewildered, until he realised that she was vomiting into the hedgerow.

He wrapped the reins around the brake and got down, not sure what to do. Women did vomit sometimes, he knew. Maybe she was pregnant? His cousin had thrown up every morning when she was having her baby.

That brown felt hat, which had stayed in place all day, was falling off, the hatpin landing in the grass. He picked it up and caught the hat as it fell, wishing he could do more. In the end, he rubbed her back, part of him astonished that her flesh was warm through the dark wool. She was a real person, frailer than he'd realised. Alive and alone, in a foreign land at war. Her husband shouldn't have taken off like he had. Sandro felt sorry for her for the first time.

When it seemed almost over, he left her to find some dock leaves in the hedge. Smooth and cool. She nodded her thanks when he handed them to her, and wiped her face, resolutely looking away from him.

He helped her back into the wagon with solicitude, and climbed up after her. She was pale and shivering, so he put a blanket around her, covering her head and tucking it in. He figured he could drive the donkey into Brindisi; it had been easy enough on the road to Serranova. As they set off, he searched for something to say.

'Your husband will be glad when he finds out about the baby,' was the best he could come up with.

She stared at him, astonished. 'Oh, no! I'm not, not . . . *expecting*.' She blushed as she said it, and he remembered that the American girls at his old school never talked about such things. 'I just . . . it just all caught up with me.' She glanced back, swiftly, unconsciously, remembering the little one.

'Yes,' he said gently. 'It's been a hard day.'

For a moment she was silent, her hands held hard in her lap. Then she said, 'I don't know what to call you.'

'Sorry?'

She let out a breath and slumped in her seat, half-turning to face him.

'Mr Baker. Signor Panucci. Al. Alessandro . . .'

He laughed shortly. 'Yeah, I have that trouble myself sometimes.' He thought for a moment. They were in Italy, not New York or Sydney. And they were working together. 'My family calls me Sandro. Since we're . . . colleagues, you might as well too.'

'Right,' she said. 'Sandro.' It sounded odd on her lips; she didn't have quite the right intonation. But it was okay, he thought. It was fine.

'My name is Rebecca,' she said. And that was fine too.

Halfway back to Brindisi, as they came around a curve, he saw a man slip off the roadway, down into the bushes that separated them from the sea. A ray of sunlight picked up a glint of red hair. There was only one redhead in Brindisi that he knew of – Christy Nolan, the Irish reporter.

Sandro's seat on the wagon and the height of the road gave him just enough clearance to see over the bushes as they passed the spot. On the beach, about two hundred yards away, a small skiff had pulled up, and a man was waiting by it. He looked up and came towards the road as Nolan emerged from the bushes. They met halfway, on the sand. Nolan cast a look behind him, and Sandro hunched down into his collar, trying to look like any other Italian. At least Rebecca's shining hair was covered up. They looked like a couple of peasants on their way home.

He kept a sideways eye on Nolan who, reassured that no one was watching, passed a packet to the man from the boat. Papers? Money? On impulse, Sandro fished the small camera out of his pocket and took a couple of quick shots. They might not even come out; but the setting sun was hitting the beach fully, so he might be lucky.

Rebecca was oblivious, too tired to pay attention to anything, and Sandro decided not to bother her with speculation after such a difficult day. It was probably nothing more than Nolan paying for information. But then why be so secretive? And why come on foot? It was a fair way out of town. Well, it was none of Sandro's business, but it was odd. He was only new to this journalist game, though. Perhaps this was a normal way of operating.

•

The climb to the centre of Brindisi came none too soon; the sun was sinking fast by the time they arrived back at the livery stable.

She paid. He wasn't used to that, but the truth was he hadn't been paid for the first lot of photographs yet, and she could claim this cost on her expenses. It made sense, but the stable owner flicked him a derisive look, and he knew the tale would be all over town that he was her gigolo.

He saw her back to the pensione and then went straight to his darkroom; he'd have only an hour before setting up for the evening trade at the trattoria, and Jesus, Mary and Joseph help him if he didn't make that, even if this was all Nonna's idea.

The 'darkroom' was really a big cupboard on the first floor of the trattoria. It was big enough, just, to hold his trays and his stand for printing. He'd rigged up a torch with a red rag over it for lighting.

He did the dry plates from the big camera first. A couple of good shots of the people on the road to Serranova. An excellent one of the shelled-out buildings at Strettabaia. And then, while Mrs Quinn had been preparing the little one, a quick shot, taken almost at random, of the house she'd been found in. It had come out surprisingly well, the central wall stark against the sky and a forlorn curtain draping out of a half-destroyed window. He made contact prints of them all.

Now, the small camera. Film was trickier – the timing was essential, especially in the printing process. Standing back after he'd given Rebecca the little body to hold, he'd got a terrific image of her, head bowed over the small, unmistakable shape. And when the mother had rocked the little one, he'd taken a couple – one blurry, it turned out, but the other sharp. Should he make prints? He wouldn't send these to the newspaper, but he'd felt an overwhelming need to document this . . . this *crime*. This murder.

His eyes pricked with tears again, but he blinked them back. Maybe later, once this war was won, it would be important to have evidence that civilians had been killed. Maybe they could make those Austrian *bastardi* pay for their evil.

Yes, he'd make prints, and give her a contact sheet, so she could keep a copy of the evidence. Take it to Britain or Australia afterwards. Keep it safe until it was needed.

The two shots of the Irishman on the beach were clear enough, but at that distance he could have been anyone. Sandro put them away. A waste of time to enlarge them.

Time to set up for the evening's trade. A restaurant, for God's sake! He could have stayed in the Bowery if he'd wanted to work in a little dive. At least he wasn't waiting tables; he escaped most evenings to Fabrini's shop, as he would tonight, and continued his own work while the Fabrinis were upstairs. Sometimes Natalia came down to keep him company. He hoped she didn't, tonight, though. He wasn't up to telling her about the day.

He opened the door, blinking in the light, and looked at the images in his hands. This was the real work. Important work.

Mrs Quinn – Rebecca – didn't come to dinner that night, but the next morning, after the other journalists had left, she stayed to see the images he had captured at Strettabaia.

He took the sheaf of photos out of his portfolio. He'd made enlargements of the ones he thought were best, but he handed her the contact prints, and a magnifying loupe. If she disagreed with his choice again, he would have to make copies of the ones she chose.

She nodded approvingly over the pictures on the road, and the burned-out buildings, and then stiffened. He checked. The one of her carrying the little girl. And the mother, crying. Good images, both of them.

Rebecca looked up at him with pure disgust.

'How could you? How could you *think* we would use these? Feeding off people's grief. It's – it's horrible!'

He planted his hands on the table and stared her right in the eyes.

'And after the war, when the Germans say: "Prove to us that we killed children," what then? If there's no proof, they'll get away with it!'

She flinched in surprise, but she rallied, flicking the photos with her finger.

'These aren't documentary images. They're *art*! Deliberately beautiful. Deliberately . . . heartbreaking.'

He flinched in his turn.

'So, you're criticising me for being too good?' She could go jump.

'It's manipulative!'

'It's the way I see things.'

She drew in a breath but didn't say anything, as though she couldn't marshal any further arguments against him. But her gaze was still angry.

'Look,' he said, trying to find to some common ground, where they could continue to work together, 'the camera shows the truth. I haven't made anything up. I've just showed what was there. So, it's heartbreaking? It *should* be heartbreaking. This is for posterity, not for the newspaper. We have to tell the truth to the future, or they won't know how horrible it all was.'

She bowed her head, the nape of her neck looking frail and delicate. So fair, like an angel. The anger died out of him; it had been a difficult day, that one, and they were both still recovering.

'I'm sorry,' she said, raising her head, tears a shining curve in her eyes. 'I'm glad you weren't planning on sending these to Evans.'

He nodded. What could he say? Better stick to business.

'Which ones do you want to send?' he asked.

She picked three – the three he'd have chosen – and he brought copies out of his portfolio.

'I'll send them straight off,' she said. 'And then we'll see what Mr Evans thinks of this story.'

12

His grandmother didn't bother to keep a separate kitchen upstairs; they took all their meals at the trattoria, but in the early mornings, cold as they were, Sandro would have welcomed a small, cosy room in which to make coffee, instead of this dark, chilly space. Normally he started the coffee while his grandmother went out to the market to get the freshest meat. But today was Sunday, the trattoria was closed, and the smell of coffee was already in the air. Nonna must have gone to early Mass and already come back. There was no eating or drinking from midnight before taking Holy Communion.

Nonna Rosa and Marcio Fabrini were sitting at one of the tables, cups in front of them and a plate with almond biscotti between them.

Fabrini got up as he came over. '*Va bene*, we'll talk,' he said to Nonna. 'Sandro, *arrivederci!*'

He went out with his normal swiftness of movement, but this time it felt as though he scuttled.

'What was that all about?' Sandro asked. He would have killed for a coffee, but nothing for him until after Mass. He sat down with his grandmother anyway, and looked her right in the eye.

She inspected him, up and down, lips pursed.

'Fabrini thinks maybe you will make a good son-in-law,' she announced. She sat back to watch his reaction.

'Natalia?' Startled, a little panicked, he wondered if Fabrini had been offended by the way he spoke to Natalia; if Sandro had inadvertently compromised her through their evening chats.

'The girl is nineteen,' Nonna said. 'Time she was married. Her mother is worried that she will take up with one of these sailors from Britain or Australia. Or worse, France! And Fabrini doesn't have a son to take over from him some day. You marry the girl, you stay in Brindisi, you take over the studio when he's gone.'

What the—

Marriage wasn't what he'd come here for. And staying in Brindisi hadn't been his plan.

Not at all.

He'd always intended to go back to New York. Was Natalia enough reason to stay?

She was pretty enough, but . . . His sisters' marriages had both been arranged by his parents; his father had found them nice Italian boys, boys they'd known their whole life. Papa had given them the right to say no, which many Italian fathers didn't. But Mama had pushed Papa in the right directions; both of the girls had been delighted by his choice. Perhaps Fabrini had been similarly guided by Natalia? Perhaps this wasn't quite so cold-blooded as it seemed?

'What do you think?' he asked suddenly. He might not always get on with his grandmother, but she was no fool. She pursed her lips and raised one shoulder, not committing herself.

'It depends what you want. She'd be a good wife. Not all that bright, but she'd be faithful. And those Fabrini girls are fertile. You'd get a family out of her, no doubt.' It felt as though they were discussing Natalia the way you'd discuss a brood sow, which made him uncomfortable. 'The older girls have had their dowry, so you'd get the whole lot.'

Nonna Rosa's eyes were hooded. No way of telling what she really thought. Then she sighed, and looked him in the eyes.

'It would be good to have you here,' she admitted. She paused, as if to say something else, but then she sat back and shrugged. 'Your choice.'

Not for the first time, he felt cloven into two minds. His Italian background suggested to him that this was a great opportunity. A pretty girl who, he was mostly sure, liked him a lot, a father-in-law he genuinely got on with, and the prospect of inheriting a tidy little business. Why even hesitate?

His American background urged him to hold out for love. His brother had; or at least, before he left he'd got engaged to Mariana Collacci, and that hadn't been organised by their parents, although they had certainly approved.

Rebecca Quinn's face flashed before his eyes. He felt a jolt in his stomach, but he shook his head. Even if he could find an unmarried girl as beautiful, as intelligent, as cultured as she was, she'd never look twice at a little Itie with no money.

Natalia . . . she was a nice armful, for sure. Soft, womanly, delicious. Immediately, he was ashamed of his thoughts. Was that the way to think about a good girl who might be the mother of his children? He wished his father was here so they could talk it over. Or his mother. Her gentle understanding would help a lot. And could he even think about taking a wife while

135

this war was on? What if he went off to the front lines as a war photographer? Would that be fair to Natalia?

'Let me think about it,' he said finally.

'Think long and hard. It's not a decision you can back out of later.'

True. This was the most important decision he would ever make.

•

At church, he stood with Rebecca. Today she was in her good cream silk dress, with an absurd little hat worn low on her head, hiding that lovely hair. She shone in the light from the windows.

In Italy, the United States, and Australia too he guessed, everywhere, the Mass was the same, the old Latin phrases rolling off everyone's tongue. 'Catholic', after all, meant universal.

They prayed, they kneeled, they listened to the readings and the sermon, and he could see by the flicker of Rebecca's eyes that she was understanding more and more, despite the monsignore's thick Salentino accent.

Today was a day of rest. In the week since the shelling of Strettabaia, they had sent off a story almost every day. Mostly routine dispatches about ship movements, submarine sightings, with an occasional 'shot across the bows' to spice things up.

Last night, at dinner, he had had a quiet word with Commander Warren about whether he would be allowed to go out with the ships, as Jack Quinn had been when he first arrived, but Warren had shaken his head.

'No, we had a journalist killed in the Middle East last week. The powers-that-be don't want any more civilian deaths on their hands.'

He couldn't blame them.

Natalia was there, too, standing with her mother and a young married couple with a baby. One of her sisters, maybe. The sister snuck glances at him from time to time and he tried to look oblivious.

He hoped Rebecca hadn't noticed. He wanted to look professional, not like a sideshow attraction for the locals. But of course she had noticed. When they came out into the weak sunlight, shrugging on their coats against the wind, she glanced slyly at him. 'Your in-laws-to-be checking on you?'

He smiled ruefully. She saw too much, this Australian woman.

'Or on you,' he quipped. 'You're much more interesting than I am.'

'Oh, is anything more interesting to a family than a potential son-in-law?'

There was a little edge to her voice.

'Cut it out,' he said.

'They probably know everything about you by now,' she teased him. 'Everything except why you're not already married. Or are you, back home?'

Startled, he took her arm and steadied her against slipping on the cobblestones.

'No, of course not!'

'Well, there's no "of course" about it,' she said reasonably. 'You came over to enlist. That doesn't exclude the possibility of a wife.'

'I would have told you – or Nonna would have,' he said without thinking.

'Ha! Your *nonna* doesn't give anything away.' There was a pause. He was conscious of the Fabrini family's eyes on them, and wondered if they thought he and Rebecca were having an affair. That wouldn't necessarily stop a marriage, of course. Not for a man. 'So, no marriages at all?'

He knew what was behind the question. He was twenty-seven, the same age as she was. Old even by American standards to get married, and positively ancient by Italian standards. If he didn't tell her, it would look like he had something to be ashamed of. It had taken a while for them to get past the antipathy of their first few encounters, and he didn't want her suspicious of him now; didn't want to go back to that animosity.

'I was engaged,' he said. 'Well, we were betrothed, when we were kids. It was all arranged. The wedding date was set, the invitations went out. Her name was Pascalia.'

It was much harder to tell Rebecca this story than it might be to tell it to Marcio Fabrini. More of a wound to his pride.

'She ran away with an American soldier from Poughkeepsie at the beginning of the war. She wrote to me and said she knew that America would come into the war eventually, and she couldn't bear for her guy to go into battle without . . . without ever being with her. You know. As a husband.'

'What a coward!' Rebecca said. Her jaw was clenched. 'She should have told you face to face.'

Yeah, he'd thought that.

'It was only a week before the wedding. *And* she took all her trousseau, all the stuff that she'd bought to go on our honeymoon with. I'd paid for a lot of it, too!'

It struck him as funny, finally, and he snorted. 'Terrible stuff. All peach and lace, and frankly, she'd have looked like a stuffed pig with it on. She wasn't a fat girl, but she wasn't tall. And her face . . . her face was very pink.'

Rebecca bit her lip, trying not to laugh too loudly on the Sabbath. 'You're well out of it, I suppose. And, in a way, it was brave of her, to defy her family and run away for love. Do you know what happened to her?'

A carriage was crossing the street in front of them. Sandro waited for it to move on, his thoughts now more sombre. Rebecca adjusted the little hat, still listening.

'Her man was killed in 1916, in the first wave of reinforcements in France. Just cannon fodder. She came back to New York, her family even took her back in after I said I held no grudges. But she just . . . faded away. She married again, to a little tailor from Milano, but she was never herself after that. She has a baby, though, with the tailor.'

'You're kind, not to hold a grudge.'

He shrugged. 'What can you do? I'm just glad we didn't get married before she changed her mind. But of course, it put a question in people's minds: Was I so bad that she'd rather marry an Americano? So, I didn't get too many offers, and there wasn't anyone else I wanted.'

'Is that one of the reasons you came here?'

He grinned. 'It was the reason I told my mamma. I said Nonna was going to find me a nice Italian girl to marry.'

'And she has,' Rebecca said dryly.

'*Madonna mia*, I guess she has!'

The curtain in the carriage window twitched, and he caught a glimpse of Christy Nolan as he pulled the curtain closed, as if he didn't want to be seen. The carriage moved on, followed by a couple of the mangy curs that always haunted the streets of any Italian city. Sandro and Rebecca crossed over, heading automatically for the trattoria.

Sandro grabbed one of the boys who hung around outside, Niccolo.

139

'Nicky, you see that carriage?' He pointed to where the vehicle was just disappearing, rounding the corner.

'*Si.*'

'Follow it. See where it goes. Don't let them see you. There's money in it for you.'

'Okay, Al!' Niccolo liked to be as American as he could. He raced off, his friends following him in a comet's tail.

'What was that about?' Rebecca asked.

'Christy Nolan was in the carriage. Hiding his face. I just wondered . . .'

'Oh, those journalistic instincts!' She chuckled. Then she sobered. 'Good idea. I wouldn't mind finding out where Christy goes and what he does. I never see him around the station or the Harbour Master's.'

As they walked back to her pensione, she looked thoughtful, as if she had never put that information together before, so Sandro told her about seeing Christy on the road back from Serranova.

'A fisherman? Well, he could get a fair bit of information that way, I suppose.' She frowned. 'They'd never talk to me.'

He wasn't too sure of that. He doubted any man would turn down a conversation with her. Best not to say that, maybe. Sometimes he thought she didn't know how beautiful she was, but how could that be?

•

The kids came back after lunch, to say they'd lost the carriage as it left the town, heading south. He went to the Damonicas' house and reported to Rebecca.

'South. Taranto?' Rebecca wondered. 'The rest of the fleet is there.'

140

Taranto was the main base in the southern Adriatic, so there could easily be a story Nolan was chasing there. But something felt fishy to Sandro.

'Maybe,' he said. He let it drop, but the uneasiness stayed with him. Best to keep an eye on Christy Nolan.

13

The next day, after the morning newspaper meeting (no news of Linus, still), Rebecca accompanied Nonna Rosa to the markets.

As she followed Nonna Rosa down the steps and into the first aisle of stalls, she could see the effects of the war: the market stalls were drab, the canvas faded and patched, and the goods were scant. In Brindisi, of course, the best produce went straight to the Navy bases. Then the Harbour Master's office. And only then to the populace.

Her Italian was improving. She knew the names of most of the things on offer: *cipolla* for onions, *aglio* for garlic (she was getting to quite like it now), *sedano* for celery. The autumn fruits were in: apples were *mela*, lemons *limone*, pears . . .

She held one up to Nonna Rosa, asking silently for the word. Nonna Rosa laughed.

'Pears are *pera*,' she said. 'Same letters, just moved around. It is the same in Spanish.'

Rebecca tried to buy some pears, but the stallholder, an old woman, winked at her and tucked them into her string bag.

'You're the journalist? Good for you. Women are stronger than men admit,' the old lady whispered in Italian to her. Rebecca winked back, and the old lady cackled.

The pears would be even sweeter now. She would have them for breakfast, with a couple of sweet rolls.

'She's a character, that one,' Nonna Rosa said in English, moving through the crowd. Monday was a busy market day, of course; Italians didn't do their washing on Mondays, it seemed, as most Australian women did. Rebecca wondered aloud where that custom had come from, and Nonna Rosa chuckled.

'I could guess,' she said.

Rebecca looked a query at her.

'Think about it, *signora*. On Saturday night, there is the marital bed. Sunday, the Sabbath, no one washes. So, Monday is the first day you can get the smell out of the sheets.'

Rebecca blushed. And then laughed, quietly, remembering her own Saturday nights with Jack. Catholics weren't supposed to make love on Fridays or Sundays, so Saturday night was popular. Not to mention being able to sleep in a little the next day.

'That sounds about right to me,' she said to Nonna Rosa. 'But not in Italy?'

She shrugged. 'Washing you can do later. Getting the good food at the market is more important.'

She looked sideways at Rebecca, and beckoned over one of the girls who were picking over the scant offering of parsnips lying on the greengrocer's stall.

'Natalia!' she said. 'Come and meet Signora Quinn.'

One of the girls looked up and came willingly, even eagerly. *'Nonna Rosa! Buongiorno.'* She sketched a little curtsey to Rebecca. *'Signora Quinn.'* It made Rebecca feel about fifty.

'This is Natalia Fabrini,' Nonna Rosa said in Italian. 'Alessandro works for her father, the *fotografo*.'

Rebecca smiled in recognition. '*Buongiorno, Natalia*,' she said. 'It's nice to meet you.'

'Signora . . .' She glanced behind her at her friends, who were giggling behind their hands, but listening avidly. 'Signora Quinn, is it true that Australian women can vote? Signora Affini said it was.' Signora Affini, it was clear, was the full-bodied woman behind the greengrocer's stall, who shared a smile with Nonna Rosa, one of those maddening smiles older women gave that implied they knew better than everyone else in the vicinity.

'Yes,' Rebecca said. 'It's true. I've voted in two elections.'

Natalia's eyes grew wide, and her friends slid around the stall and gathered around her.

'No! I thought it was *la beffa*.' That wasn't a term Rebecca had heard, but she could tell its meaning.

'No, not a joke. We've had the vote since 1902.'

'No need to talk about it here,' Nonna Rosa intervened, with a quick glance at the gathering crowd.

'Women shouldn't vote,' a male stallholder said firmly. 'Their brains are smaller than men's.'

'If they don't fight, they shouldn't vote,' another man said.

'My boy is fighting, and he can't vote until he's thirty!' a woman retorted.

'It's not God's will!' a woman yelled from behind them.

'*Andiamo!*' Nonna Rosa said, still smiling. 'Let's go.'

Natalia waved a hand and slipped away, and they moved through the crowd, which was now vociferously discussing the issue. Nonna Rosa laughed quietly as Signora Affini held forth on how her opinion was worth any man's.

'You're enjoying this!' Rebecca accused.

'*Si*,' she admitted, and added in English, 'it's always funny when the bigmouths bring out their stupidities.'

Not for the first time, Nonna Rosa's facility with English idiom surprised her.

'Where did you learn English?'

Nonna Rosa's shoulders rose and fell in a graceful shrug, and she answered in the same language. 'When I was a girl, I looked after a mad Englishwoman. The family paid for me to be taught, so I could speak to her.'

Her tone was so matter-of-fact that it took Rebecca a moment to fully understand her.

'A mad . . .'

'*Quanto per le patate?*' Nonna Rosa asked the next stallholder, ignoring Rebecca. She took the hint, and went on to another stall to buy some golden chrysanthemums. Jack had been untidy – his clothes, especially his ties and collars, had littered the table and dresser in their room – but since he left, it felt too tidy; bland and drab. Flowers would brighten it.

She helped Nonna Rosa carry the vegetables home, and kept silent. Questions wouldn't work with Nonna Rosa.

•

When they got back to the trattoria, Nonna Rosa made a great story out of the episode in the market, and had Rebecca and Sandro laughing with her impersonation of Signora Affini. Niccolo, the boy from the train station, was waiting for any errands to run, and tried to look as though he knew why they were laughing. Rebecca wrote up a quick story with a note for Charles Fletcher, her associate editor in Sydney: *To Fletcher, an extra for your Women's Pages*. Evans at the *News* wouldn't be interested in this story.

Brindisi, Italy: Inhabitants of this coastal town found it hard to believe our correspondent, Mrs Quinn, when she confirmed for them that Australian women had had the vote since 1902. Both men and women seemed to object to Australia's choice . . . our correspondent doubts that Italy will see women's suffrage any time soon.

'Sounds like you think Australia is perfect,' Sandro said.

'I wish it were!' she said, sobering suddenly. 'We have a lot of poverty, and slums, and crime, just like New York. Greed is the same everywhere, and the poor suffer for it. And in Australia, our Aboriginal people are treated very badly.'

He nodded. 'Like the Negroes and the Indians in the US.'

'Yes, except that Aboriginal people – even the men – can't vote. Black people can in America, can't they?'

'Well, they're *supposed* to be able to, but in practice . . .' He trailed off.

'There are problems everywhere,' she said, 'and we've had to put so many of them aside until this war is won.'

She slid her story into an envelope and addressed it to *The Sydney Morning Herald*, then gave it to Niccolo to take to Commander Warren's office.

'But this young fellow will have a better world,' Sandro said, ruffling his hair.

'We have to make sure of that,' she agreed. They nodded to each other, not quite smiling, but with a shared purpose; a shared dedication.

Niccolo grabbed the coin she gave him, and took off to the base.

While Sandro went upstairs to his darkroom, Rebecca helped Nonna Rosa unpack the goods from the market, and then began to peel onions.

Without prompting, Nonna Rosa spoke.

'My madwoman was the sister of an attaché from the English embassy. I was young. Seventeen. It was just after the war of unification ended, and it suited me to have a . . . a quiet job. Out of the way. They put her in a nice house, overlooking the sea, in a little village near Torre Dell'Orso. I looked after her.'

'And she was . . .' Rebecca ventured.

'Oh, she was mad, of that there was no doubt. She had times when she would shriek and curse and bang her head against the door. During those times all I could do was slide her food through a slit at the bottom of the door. And when it was over! Faugh! Cleaning that room was not for the faint-hearted. Other days she was fine. A little *distratto*, distracted. But sane. And clever.'

She leaned against the counter behind her, lost in memory. 'A nice woman. Young, only thirty or so. They'd had a clerk in the town teach me the basics of her language, but she taught me properly.'

'What happened to her?'

Nonna Rosa cast her a quick, shrewd glance and began to chop the onions.

'I was supposed to keep her in that one room. Always. But what kind of life is that? So I started taking her into the garden. And one day, she asked if we could go for a walk.' Again, that swift, dark glance. 'I said yes. We walked by the cliffs. She ran and threw herself off.'

The image was like a punch in the stomach. Rebecca had a swift vision of a woman – a blonde, only a few years older than herself – falling endlessly to the sea.

Nonna Rosa wasn't a fool. There was no way the young Rosa hadn't known what the woman had wanted when she asked to be taken for a walk.

'Suicide is a sin,' Rebecca ventured. Nonna Rosa's eyes snapped with the pleasure of being understood.

'Not if one is mad.'

'But when you took her for a walk, she was sane,' Rebecca said gently.

They had finished the onions. Nonna Rosa smiled at her, completely unfazed. 'The Church, she does not say, "Mad one day, sane the next." Mad is mad, and she was certainly mad. And a life in one room is no life at all.'

'But you lost your job,' Rebecca said.

Another shrug. 'By then Garibaldi had marched off to attack Austria and get Venice back. I could go back home. He had forgotten about his old enemies. I had liked the nursing, so I became a midwife.'

'You fought Garibaldi?' Like most English speakers, all Rebecca knew about Garibaldi was that he had led the armies that united Italy under the rule of Victor Emmanuel, who had been until then the King of Sardinia, in the north. She had a vague sense of Garibaldi being a national hero.

'I fought him, yes. And did other things. Carried messages, observed his armies.' A cynical smile turned up one side of her face, touched with pride. 'I caused trouble for him, the traitor.'

Despite her surprise, Rebecca smiled back. This was what a free woman looked like. Unburdened by shame or guilt because she had stood up for her beliefs, to the utmost. It reminded Rebecca of her mother, but there was a difference: her mother still cared about what other people thought of her. Nonna Rosa didn't.

'And the Englishwoman?' Rebecca asked, at last remembering how the conversation had started.

'They never found her body,' Nonna Rosa said. 'That was a shame. I would have prayed at her grave.'

Rebecca couldn't find a single word to say to that.

14

On the days no press conference was held, which was most days, Rebecca made her rounds before going to Nonna Rosa's. The Harbour Master's office, the railway station to collect her newspapers, and the post office. And then, as though drawn to the sea, she went to the high piazza before the basilica, from where she could see the whole sweep of the harbour, and note any oddities in the Navy ships coming and going.

She had followed this routine, more or less, when Jack was here. Every day, she grew more worried about him. There had been no news, not even a letter. God alone knew where he was – if he was still alive. Rebecca had to face the possibility that she might never find out what had happened to him. Missing in action, like Linus. The thought left a deep ache under her breastbone, like an internal scar.

When those thoughts started, as they did in the mornings, when she woke and faced another day of not knowing, she was glad of something to do, glad of the need to get out and about.

She enjoyed the walks, despite the steep hills and the cold. They left her rosy and warm, and brought back memories of tramping around Sydney with friends. With Jack.

Today the wind had built to a gale, and she didn't stay long at the piazza, sparing only a moment to think of the poor British crews out on patrol. She missed the Sydney sea, the sandstone cliffs, the high blue sky of winter. They had said, before she left, 'Oh, Italy's climate is just like Australia's!' But it wasn't. Maybe Tasmania. But Sydney never saw wind and sleet and storms like these.

As she headed down the main stairs, a bevy of girls came up them, smiling and pointing, saying, 'There she is!' Natalia, with three friends. They all met where a narrow street formed a landing for the stairs, and Natalia, beaming, said in Italian, 'We came to find you! Let's go to Loretta's place, that's near here!'

Intrigued and somewhat amused (had she ever been that young?), Rebecca allowed herself to be guided along the street, around a corner, down a smaller set of steps and into a terrace house.

Every so often she was still astonished at the sheer age of things in Italy, and this was one of those times. The house had walls two feet thick, and the flagstones were worn hollow in the middle from the steps of generations.

But it was brightly whitewashed and cheerful, decorated in red and white, with elaborately embroidered cushions on the wooden armchairs, and a welcome fire in the hearth. Loretta's mother, Fortunata, a neat woman with a humorous glint in her eye, greeted them, and insisted on taking Rebecca's coat and laying it in the kitchen 'to dry and warm'.

Loretta bustled after her into the kitchen, and soon the two of them came back with coffee and milk and tiny star-shaped biscuits. Rebecca felt guilty eating them; flour and sugar were so scarce now that this must be a great extravagance. But she knew better than to refuse; it would be a terrible insult.

The coffee was good – wonderful. Better even than Nonna Rosa's, though Rebecca also knew better than to say that. Even the girls followed the tradition; no talk of business or whatever had brought them out until the demands of hospitality had been met. They drank their coffee and nibbled on their biscuits while Rebecca and Fortunata talked family: their son at the front, Rebecca's brother in France, Fortunata's sister's new baby, the fact that Loretta was an only girl. Rebecca didn't mention Linus; she didn't think she could cope with their inevitable sympathy. It was a profoundly soothing conversation, nestled away in the company of women. She felt rather proud that she could join in so readily in this simple, domestic talk. Her Italian had definitely improved.

Then Fortunata sat back, almost laughing at the girls, and they sat forward. Rebecca took her last sip and coffee, and raised her eyebrows at them.

'Is it true?' Natalia burst out. 'Have you really voted?'

Ah.

'Yes. I've voted more than once. There was a federal election in Australia early in the year, and I voted in that.' She felt a little mischievous. 'There were three women standing for office, one in the Senate and two in the Lower House.'

'You voted for a *woman*?'

'I wish I could have, but they weren't standing in my state.'

The girls sat back and stared at her, as if she had two heads.

Finally Loretta said, 'But . . . but women are *allowed* to be elected?'

'Oh, yes. Since 1902. No one's managed it yet, but the time will come. Maybe some girl your age now will manage it.'

They looked at each other and burst into Italian too fast for her to follow. It showed how kind everyone had been to her, to speak slowly enough for her to understand. She watched their hand movements. It had taken her a while to realise that the Italian 'hand-waving' that British people so often made fun of was actually a subsidiary language of its own, with specific movements having specific meanings. She was only just beginning to pick out those movements from the general gesticulation.

She had no chance of following the girls' hand movements, which flashed through the air like dragonflies.

After a moment, Fortunata said, '*Signorine . . .*' in the same tone of voice with which Rebecca's headmistress had called assembly to account. 'Girls . . .'

Natalia stopped speaking first, casting an apologetic look towards Fortunata, and smiled brilliantly at Rebecca.

'So, when you voted, did your husband tell you who to vote for?'

Rebecca laughed, imagining what her reaction would have been to that.

'No, of course not! But we discussed politics, of course.'

They nodded like a row of dolls.

'So . . .' Loretta prodded her. 'You picked for yourself?'

'Voting is a privilege,' she said soberly. 'You must research each candidate and decide how much you agree with their views. Then you vote according to your conscience.'

As one, they drew in a deep breath and let it out. Their eyes shone. Maybe this next generation of Italian women would be more active than the last.

'We only got the vote because we worked for it,' she reminded them. 'The men won't just give it to you.'

'*But*,' Fortunata put in firmly, 'wait until after you are married. No man will marry an agitator.'

Each girl sighed and cast her eyes to heaven. Rebecca and Fortunata exchanged bitten-back smiles. They were so serious at this age; as they should be. It was this idealism that would transform the world.

That was all they wanted to know – perhaps it was all they could take in, in one sitting – so she got up to go, snuggling into her beautifully warmed coat, thanking Fortunata for her hospitality. Two of the girls were staying, but Natalia decided to walk back with her.

Natalia, it seemed, while no Rhodes Scholar, was interested in making her own decisions. As they walked back towards Nonna Rosa's, she blurted out, 'My father wants me to marry Sandro.'

'I know.' At Natalia's quick glance, she elaborated, 'Nonna Rosa told me.'

'Not Sandro? He doesn't talk about me?'

Cautiously, Rebecca shook her head. 'No.'

Natalia sighed. 'That's good. Maybe. I don't think I want to get married.'

'Then don't.'

'It's not that simple!'

'Sandro won't marry you if you don't want to.'

'*Si*, I know that. But if I'm going to get married, it might as well be to him. He's lovely. But . . .'

'But?'

'Once you're married, your husband tells you what to do!'

'So, don't get married. Or find a man who won't do that.' Jack never ordered her around. He was very good at persuading

154

her, though. She wondered what kind of husband Sandro would be. She suspected he could be stubborn, but probably not bossy. He seemed to cope with Nonna Rosa all right.

Natalia walked along a little further, the wind lifting the edges of her traditional cap.

'If I don't get married, who will support me?' She fretted at the edges of her shawl.

'Support yourself. Sandro won't be here forever. Your father will need an assistant, and he won't get one as long as the war is on. Learn from him. Help him. And then *you* can take over the business when he's gone, and make your own pick of husband, *if* you want one.'

From her expression, it was clear that this simple solution had never occurred to her.

'Sandro will teach you the basics, I'm sure, if you asked him.'

Natalia cast a quick, almost furtive look up from underneath her cap. 'Would *you* ask him for me?'

Rebecca laughed, her heart unaccountably light. That wasn't the look of a potential wife, but of a nervous little girl. She might be nineteen, but Natalia had seen very little of life, and had had no control over her own at all. No wonder she seemed young.

'No. But I'll be there when you ask him, if you like.'

Natalia straightened up. 'Yes! That would be wonderful. And then I will be a professional woman.'

'Exactly. Just make sure your father pays you a wage once you start helping him officially.'

'And then, if I *like* Sandro, we can still get married.'

This gave Rebecca an unpleasant little jolt. She should wish them well, but something in her doubted that Natalia was the right wife for Sandro. She was nice and attractive, but . . . on the trip to Strettabaia, it had become clear to Rebecca that Sandro lived the life of the mind, expressed through his art, his photographs. Could this child understand and share in that life?

'Do you like art?' she asked Natalia. 'Or poetry? Dante, say? Or Shakespeare?'

'I like stories better. Exciting ones, with bandits and murders.'

There were murders enough in Shakespeare, Rebecca thought, but she doubted Natalia would like the plays otherwise – except for the romance, and who could blame her for that?

It was another two blocks to Nonna Rosa's. They fell into silence, except for the calls of a street vendor selling chestnuts, and the wail of the wind at their backs.

At Nonna Rosa's, Natalia came in with Rebecca; apparently the conversation with Sandro was going to happen right away.

Sandro wasn't there.

'He's gone to the fishmonger for me,' Nonna Rosa said. 'Natalia, *buongiorno*.'

'*Buongiorno*, Nonna Rosa.'

'Have you come to help?'

There it was, the decision point. Was she here as a potential wife for Sandro?

'No, Nonna Rosa. I have to get back to the shop and help Papa. Sorry.'

Nonna Rosa gave a genteel grunt. 'Off with you, then.'

Natalia hugged Rebecca, surprising her and almost knocking off her hat.

'*Grazie, signora!*' she said, and almost sprinted out the door and down the hill.

'So,' Nonna Rosa said as Rebecca took off her coat and hat and put on an apron, 'have you talked her out of the marriage yet?'

156

Rebecca stopped to look directly at Nonna Rosa. What an odd thing to say. 'No. She'd already talked herself out of it. She doesn't want to be parcelled up like a leg of lamb and sold off.'

Laughing, Nonna Rosa slammed some pasta dough down on the counter and began to knead it. 'I don't blame her.'

'It doesn't mean she won't pick Sandro, though,' Rebecca felt obliged to say. It was impossible to tell whether Nonna Rosa was in favour of the marriage or against it.

'Doesn't mean she will.'

Nonna Rosa brought the pasta maker out and clamped it to the bench. She was proud of it; it let her make pasta much more quickly.

Rebecca came and stood in position, ready to take the long strands of fettucine as they were cranked out of the rollers and coil them into individual portions.

'She and her friends came to ask me about voting,' she said.

'Good. Time some of the women around here got stirred up. They've let the Church and their husbands tell them what to do for too long.'

'They?' she asked, teasing a little. Nonna Rosa's eyes crinkled, and her mouth tucked itself in at the corners.

'They,' she said.

Both of them were laughing when Sandro came in the door, laden with a crate of fish.

He kicked the door closed and stood there for a moment, his dark hair ruffled by the wind, his face ruddy with cold, his eyes dancing in response to their laughter, and she thought, *He is lovely. He really is.* And then, *Remember you're a married woman.*

15

The French flotilla was back in port. Of all of the sailors, the French were the most enthusiastic about having their portraits done. Sandro tried not to make the assumption that it was because they all had a girl in every port and needed photos to send to them. But he wondered.

Studio portraits weren't cheap, considering what French sailors were paid. The Australian sailors had more ready money (the Australians, he'd discovered, were the best-paid defence force in the world), but they preferred to spend theirs on wine and women and gambling. A few of them came in from time to time, but, as one of them told him, 'Most of us had ours done before we left home, mate.'

This fine autumn afternoon in Fabrini's studio, they had six *matelots* in the studio. They wanted one portrait each, and then a group shot, and then two lots of two brothers. It was taking both Sandro and Marcio Fabrini to herd them and keep them still in the right position at the right moment, and it wasn't helped by the fact that, one and all, they wanted to flirt with Natalia.

'*Ma'mzelle*,' one said. '*Trés jolie.*'

'*Bella, imbecile!*' his friend said, gazing soulfully at Natalia. '*Bella donna!*'

'Belladonna's a poison, my friend,' Sandro said in English.

'Natalia, out of here,' her father said. 'Go upstairs!' Natalia scuttled past them all, giggling, and raced up the stairs. 'That girl will be the death of me,' Marcio said *sotto voce*.

Sandro grinned and adjusted a light. The French sailors arranged themselves in a group, chins up and looking proud. Most of them had a moustache, but be damned if he was going to make those moustaches gleam. *They should keep their hands off our girls*, he thought, and then wondered when he had started thinking of Italian girls as 'ours'. Maybe he always had.

Half an hour later, the sailors left in a convivial group, heading for one of the wine bars by the docks, where no doubt they would find the kind of Italian girls who would know how to handle them. *Gather ye rosebuds while ye may, old Time is still a-flying* . . . Shakespeare knew all about that kind of girl, he figured.

It was late afternoon but not yet time for them to shut up shop. Marcio Fabrini, it seemed, didn't care.

'Come have a coffee,' he said, locking the shop door. They went upstairs, to a cosy living room-cum-kitchen with a table sitting on a red-tiled floor just near the stove. Marcio waved him to a seat at the table. It was as warm as toast and he sighed, leaning back with pleasure.

Signora Fabrini he recognised from church. She was an older version of Natalia, better padded and softer spoken.

'*Buongiorno*, come in,' she said. 'Coffee is just ready. Natalia, get the cannoli.' She smiled at Sandro. 'I'm from Sicily,' she said, which he could have told from her accent, 'and I like to make the traditional things.'

He told her he hadn't had cannoli since he'd left New York, and she beamed. It was funny, all the Italian traditions swirled in together in America, so that the Florentines liked cannoli from the pasticceria on Mulberry Street as much as the Siciliani. Like pizza. That was a Napolitano thing, but now everyone ate at Lombardi's pizza restaurant and was proud of it. This mixing up was one of the reasons the Americans thought of 'Italians' as one amorphous lot, instead of as the Italians thought of themselves: Sicilians, Apulians, Venetians, Florentines . . .

Signora Fabrini poured him an espresso, dark and redolent, and Natalia handed him a plate with a cannolo on it. He bit into the rich ricotta filling with deep pleasure.

It was maybe not a good idea to visit like this, like a suitor, but . . . well, how else was he going to make up his mind? And at the moment, his stomach thought that marrying a girl who could make cannoli like these was a wonderful idea.

Like a good girl, Natalia helped her mother around the kitchen and let the men talk. She was noticeably more subdued in her mother's presence. It was so familiar to him, this separation of the male and female realms, that he only barely noticed it. But a niggling thought kept coming back: Rebecca would sit at the table, join in the discussion. He wasn't at all sure which he preferred.

'More coffee?' Natalia asked, blushing a little.

To accept would be a declaration. One coffee, he was a friend and colleague. Two, and he was accepting more than a beverage.

'*Scusi*,' he said, getting up. 'Nonna Rosa will be waiting for me. *Grazie*, Signora Fabrini. The cannolo was delicious.'

Natalia's face was blank; had he offended her or was she relieved? He wished they could talk this out between them. He would never get involved with another girl without a proper discussion.

Marcio came down with him to let him out. Before he unlocked the door, as Sandro was putting his coat on, he said, 'You've never been married? Your father didn't arrange anything for you?'

There it was, the question he'd been expecting. He wished Marcio spoke English; it would be easier to explain in English, somehow.

'Yes, he arranged a marriage. But, er . . .' How to put it? It was a tricky subject. Maybe blunt was best. 'The girl was in love with an *Americano*. A solider. She ran away with him the week before the wedding.'

Marcio swung open the door and spat into the street. 'These girls. They are getting wilder every day. Well. Better the week before than the week after, eh?'

Sandro made himself laugh. God knew that was the truth, and he'd thought it himself more than once. 'At least they hadn't started cooking the wedding breakfast!' he said, and clapped Marcio on the shoulder. Here was a chance to slow things down. 'But you can see,' he said, 'why I'm not rushing into anything.'

Marcio grunted. 'Natalia's a good girl. She knows her duty.'

'So did Pascalia,' Sandro said gently. 'She knew her duty. She just didn't want to do it.'

He walked away on the thought and headed up to the trattoria. He wondered, not for the first time, if anyone had been brave enough to arrange his grandparents' marriage. He couldn't imagine Nonna Rosa, even at Natalia's age, accepting someone else's choice for her.

By the time he got back to the trattoria, he was feeling put upon and brash. Tying his apron on, he grinned as cheekily as he could at Nonna Rosa and asked her: 'Did your father arrange your marriage?'

'Cold feet?' she said, with a hint of a smile. 'Are they pushing you?'

'No,' he admitted. 'Just feeding me coffee and cannoli.'

'Sicilian, that Agnese Fabrini,' Nonna Rosa said with a sniff. 'But she's a good woman and a good cook.'

He'd never heard higher praise from her. He set the tables in silence, thinking. It felt to him as though he were being asked to choose between being an Italian and being an American. To live here or in New York. To make his own decisions, or to bow to the authority of *la famiglia*. Both were good systems. The American way had the get-up-and-go, the dynamism, the excitement, the sense of carving your own destiny. The Italian way had stability, warmth, continuity, tradition; and the sense of being part of something larger, something solid and real.

The American way could be lonely; the Italian, stifling.

He wondered what the Australian way was like. It was the New World too, but with such a British influence, would it also insist on tradition?

He set up and then went up to his darkroom, to develop some of the pictures he'd been taking of Brindisi, and to look over old contact prints to see if there were any worth enlarging. He found the contact sheet of the first roll of film he'd taken here – and there was Rebecca in the church.

He got out his jeweller's loupe and examined the image. Perfect. She stood in a shaft of light, her pure profile turned up, her mouth just open a little, not enough to show that she'd been crying, not enough to look odd. Her figure, so beautifully curved, was outlined by a kind of halo. Behind her, the shadows of the church and, in the depths, the shape of the chapel to the Madonna. She was like a Gibson Girl: that combination of fine lines and voluptuous body, of purity and allure. He could make money selling this print.

He was immediately revolted. Even if she gave her permission – which she wouldn't – how could he parcel her off for other men to fumble in their sweaty hands?

For a moment he just stood there, observing the rush of feeling. This wasn't good. Not good at all. She was married. That was an end to it. Married.

He put the contact sheets away and went down to the trattoria to help. Better to get his mind off – things.

The British were out on patrol, but the Australians and the Italians were all there, and so were a lot of the French. And the journalists, of course, including Mrs Quinn. When she was here, a customer, he thought of her that way. It was only when they worked together that she became Rebecca.

He longed to ask her about Australia and tradition, but of course he couldn't. He couldn't bear to wait on their table, to see the men stare at him with such condescension. He went out the back instead and chopped wood to keep the stove going, and brought a handful of lemons in from the tree in the courtyard.

As he came in, all the talk in the restaurant was about a German spy caught in France – a baron, at that! *Le Monde* had reported on it – had broken the story, in fact. Lemaitre was looking wistful, and rather envious of the reporter, a friend of his, who had written it. Mrs Quinn looked envious, too – all four of them did. They all loved getting to a juicy story first.

163

After dinner, she smiled at him as she left. Maybe it was looking at her photograph from the church, but that smile . . . *Madonna mia*, she was beautiful! Perhaps he would make an enlargement of that shot.

Commander Warren walked out with her. An interview, probably, but Sandro watched out the front window as they spoke for a few minutes, and then parted. She was safe to walk back to the pensione, but he took off his apron and went out anyway, ignoring the cold. She had already turned the corner and gone.

He went back into the trattoria soberly. He would be a fool to fall in love with a married woman – and he wasn't a fool.

•

Rebecca watched Commander Warren walk down the hill and then turned to her own homeward path, a little puzzled.

That had been a strange interlude.

She hadn't always liked Jack's friends, but she'd liked William Warren – he was a gentleman, through and through. It showed in everything he did and said. And tonight he had said, 'Are you sure Jack would want you to do this work while he's away?'

'Of course!' she'd answered. 'We work together, you know, to write our stories.'

This had been at the door of the trattoria. He'd paused a moment while he helped her into her coat, and then said, 'No, I didn't know that.'

His voice had been odd. Hesitant, as though afraid of hurting her.

'I was a journalist in Australia,' she explained. 'And we worked together here in Italy.'

'Ah.' As they walked out to stand on the narrow street, he nodded slowly. 'That explains how Jack knew so much about this place without speaking much Italian.'

'Yes. I have my contacts in the town.' During opening hours, the trattoria kept a lantern burning on a ledge outside the front door. Its light sent planes of colour over Warren's strong jawbone, but left his eyes in darkness.

'Look, Mrs Quinn, I can see that you would be an able assistant, but would Jack wish you to take the whole burden on yourself?'

'Commander, I don't understand why you're so worried. I've been a reporter for four years now.'

'So long?' His voice was surprised, no doubt about that. 'But . . .'

'But *what*?' she asked, exasperated. These men, trying to coddle her into compliance.

'Jack spoke of you as, as . . .'

'As *what*?'

'As, er . . . dependent,' he said simply.

She barely understood him. 'That can't be right.'

'Someone to be protected,' he explained.

Relief washed over her. Well, of course he would have thought that. All men thought that about their womenfolk. That didn't mean he didn't respect her work.

'Men think that about their women,' she said, smiling.

His face closed off, as though he'd said all he was going to say but could have said more if he'd chosen to. Some bee in his bonnet about women working, probably. It was disappointing, but not surprising. She'd met that reaction from so many different men.

165

They said goodnight and went their separate ways. Rebecca was aware of Sandro watching them from the window, and was obscurely comforted, and then annoyed with herself. She did *not* need a protector!

As she walked up the winding street to the pensione, she wondered how Jack had given Warren the impression she was 'dependent'. It set her teeth on edge a little. Admittedly, she had earned less than Jack, as women did, but she had always paid her own way. Or had he meant emotionally dependent? Ha! The shoe was on the other foot there. It had been Jack who had turned to her for understanding and reassurance. Of course, she missed him, but she coped. Surely she was coping?

16

It was days like today that made Rebecca long for Sydney, where even in winter the sky was a deep cobalt blue. It would be summer there, now, and her friends would be at the beach, surf-shooting, or sailing on the harbour, or gathering up a picnic after work and heading for Bondi Beach, to sit and watch that huge semi-circle of sand and sea glow in the twilight. She sat back in her armchair and looked out the window at the steel-grey sky and the slanting rain.

Siesta, even in winter, was the norm, so she had come back to her room to rest. The Italians seemed to ignore the clock, except the Angelus bell. She respected the custom, but she hadn't quite adjusted to lazing around in the middle of the day.

She considered using the time to write a story about Italian fashions – a woman journalist could always write a story about hemline lengths – which brought to mind her rant to Jack about hemlines, back in 1915.

'The world is in the middle of war, and some people are still obsessed about seeing a woman's ankles!'

He had laughed, sitting cross-legged by the fire on the Turkish rug his parents had given them. 'Calm down, sweetheart! I can think of a few times I've been obsessed with a woman's ankles,' he said. He reached out and pulled her down with him, kissing her deeply and running his hand down her leg until he cupped her ankle. 'This one, for example.'

She'd kissed him back, a little frustrated that he wouldn't take her seriously but, as always, delighted by the touch and taste of him.

'Besides,' he said, letting her pull back and settling her more comfortably in his lap, 'just think about it. For thousands of years high-status women have kept their limbs swathed. Thousands of years, back beyond recorded history. It was the one sign of civilisation you could count on. And then, suddenly, in a matter of months, the skirts went up. When the men first went away to war, the skirts were down to the top of the shoe. Now, the injured are coming home to find their wives and sisters wearing skirts only a prostitute would have been seen in when they left. It's no wonder they have trouble adjusting!'

This was what she loved about him: the quick mind, the understanding – and the knowledge that let him take a long view of history. She kissed him again, lingeringly.

'I just wish they didn't want me to write about it.'

'Yes, you're better than that.' He kissed her again, and she sank into his arms with enthusiasm, warmed by his belief.

How she wished he would come back – or at least send word of where he was, what he was doing. That he was safe.

'*Signora! Signora!*' Angela's voice cut through her memories.

'*Si, Angela, sono qui.*'

Rebecca opened the door to see Angela coming up the stairs, with letters in her hand. She looked tired, with circles under her eyes. And had she put on weight? Her dress seemed too tight and rather uncomfortable.

'Oh, Angela, there was no need to bring those up! I could have got them when I came down again.'

'But there is a letter from Australia!' Angela said. She proffered the letters with a smile. She was a nice girl, Angela. Not especially bright, but pleasant and helpful. Unlike her father.

'Thank you so much.'

Angela smiled and went away slowly. Rebecca had wondered why Angela wasn't married, whether she had a suitor. Italians never seemed to shy away from asking personal questions, but Rebecca just couldn't. She would ask Nonna Rosa.

In the meantime, excitement curled in her belly at the thought of a letter from Australia; not that she was expecting much, but anything ... it brought home to her how alone she was, when her only contact with home was letters.

One from a friend, Evelyn Northey, who was nursing in Egypt. Oh, she was glad her mother had redirected that one! Rebecca had played hockey against Evelyn when they were schoolgirls, and they had become friends when she came to Sydney to work at the Repatriation Hospital at Randwick. There were very few people she respected more than Evelyn.

She read about Evelyn's adventures with her ANZAC patients with great pleasure. Eve was always amusing. How nice it would be to work in a team, to have other women for company! The letter was over too soon.

The next was from her editor at the *Evening News*. Rebecca opened it with dread, but it was merely a short note – *Copies of Jack's stories* – attached to a number of newspaper clippings.

When journalists were 'stringing' for a newspaper, the editors often sent them their clippings for their scrapbook. It was kind of Evans to send them. She laid them out on the small table by the window, pleased to see the results of her and Jack's work. That was the problem with being a foreign correspondent – you rarely got to see your work in print. It was good to see the stories in the flesh. They had various headlines, but they all started, *From our correspondent in Italy, John Quinn.*

She had written more than half of these stories.

The editor had made a mistake. Had assumed Jack had written them, because it had been Jack who had sent those stories off, through Commander Warren's mailbag. But on her stories, she always – *always* – put her name at the bottom of the page. For the editor to believe that Jack had written those stories . . . Jack must have removed her name.

Her heart was thumping too loudly. Someone would hear it. She sat down, pressing her hand onto her chest to slow the rush; to calm down, the way Jack had always told her to. Perhaps there was another reason. Perhaps the editor just put Jack's name on the stories because they rarely, if ever, used a woman's name as a correspondent. Even Louise Mack's stories had been titled: 'Mrs Mack speaks to our correspondent', although it was obvious to anyone with a brain that the article had been written by her.

But in that case, why weren't her stories labelled: 'Mrs Quinn speaks to our correspondent'?

Because the editor didn't know she had written them. The conclusion was inescapable. No wonder he had assumed she would come home now Jack was off adventuring. No wonder he thought she would want a job on the Women's Pages. As far as he knew, she had been playing housewife while Jack did all the work.

So much for Jack's protestations of support for her career! When it came to the crunch, he had undermined her. He was just like all the others – no, *worse*, because the others didn't pretend they thought otherwise. Worse, to encourage her to be a foreign correspondent, and then to take – to *steal* – all her work so that she might as well never have written a word.

Oh, and now she knew why he had been so insistent on her coming! He had a tin ear for languages; always had had. She'd had to tutor him intensely in the Latin terms he'd needed for his law courses at uni. The only reason he'd been able to go with the smugglers was that their captain spoke rudimentary English. Knowing she already had Latin and French, knowing that she picked up vocabulary quickly, he'd brought her so she could do all the work he'd have trouble with himself. Making local contacts. Reading press releases from the Italians and French. Scanning the local papers for fresh stories.

And she had done it all, so faithfully. Like a – a *servant*.

A servant he'd got to sleep with, as well. How bloody convenient.

She was shaking with anger. She ripped the pieces of newsprint apart, tearing again and again until the stories lay in shreds around her. She cast the last scraps onto the fire and wiped her hands on her skirt as though they had been soiled.

Unforgivable. What he'd done was unforgivable.

If he'd been there . . . but he wasn't. She couldn't *do* anything. Couldn't write to Evans and declare that she had written more than half of these stories. He would never believe her – and how would it make her look, anyway? Like a fool. A trusting, stupid woman. Her own pride wouldn't let her.

She stood by the table, her fists clenched so tightly her arms ached. What good was her anger? It wouldn't change anything – at least, not until Jack came home. Slowly, it died out of her and she sat down, unutterably weary. What good was it to tear up the stories? It didn't change what he'd done.

And then she cried for the loss of him; for the loss of who she had thought he was.

All those moments of tenderness – they hadn't been lies, surely? No. He had meant that, meant the caresses and the protestations of devotion. But he hadn't meant his rhetoric about women's rights.

She had thought their marriage was one of equals; but he hadn't. He loved her as a helpmeet, not a partner in their mutual work. Not as a mind that stretched his own, but only as a body.

·

She didn't want to broadcast it, but this was something she desperately needed to talk about to someone. A woman, preferably, but definitely not Nonna Rosa. No, not her – and there was no other woman she knew well here, which was in itself sad.

There was only Sandro. Perhaps a man's opinion on this would make her feel better. Perhaps a man could explain to her that this wasn't really a sign of base betrayal.

She knew he was at the photo studio this afternoon, so she went in after the siesta, the *riposo*, and found Natalia behind the counter.

'Signora Quinn,' the girl said, smiling.

'*Buongiorno*, Natalia,' Rebecca said.

'*Vuoi vedere*, Sandro?'

'*Si.*'

But Sandro, it turned out, was in the darkroom. (Darkroom, it turned out, was *la camera oscura*, which was pleasing in a historical way.)

172

'One half-hour, *magari*, maybe?' Natalia was keenly practising her English, and Rebecca couldn't help but wonder if it was intended to impress Sandro. The girl was young, but not that young – most women her age in Brindisi were married by now. And Sandro was a good-looking man; really, quite good looking. And American. Exotic.

Thoughts of marriage reminded her of Angela Damonica.

'Angela?' Natalia said in reply to Rebecca's enquiry. '*Si*. *Poverina*. Her father is, *come si dice*, *avaro*?'

'*Avaro* . . . avaricious? Greedy?'

'*Si*, like that . . . but . . .'

'Mean? Doesn't want to give money away?'

'*Si*, *si*, mean.' Natalia beamed at her as though she had solved a particularly difficult problem. 'So, he no want to pay for cleaner, for cooking. No *dote* for Angela.'

No dowry for Angela meant no husband. Her father got to keep her services for free. *Poverina* indeed. And Angela wasn't like this charming little bundle. If Natalia had no dowry, which seemed unlikely, she could still find herself a husband. But Angela . . . with her buck teeth and her dumpiness – who would take her without a *dote*? In some ways, Italy was still in the Dark Ages.

'*Terribile*,' she said. 'Selfish.'

'Self—' Natalia stumbled over the word.

'Selfish. *Egoista*.'

'Ah, *si*. Selfish.'

They stood together, nodding at male infamy. It was nice to speak to a young woman. Even with the language difficulties, there was an unspoken accord, a way of looking at the world, that she had missed, being always with men or with Nonna Rosa, who had her own opinions.

Natalia was dressed in the local traditional way, and it suited her: the big skirts with a tight waist, the white blouse with a scarf around her shoulders tied at the breast. She wore a headscarf but had left off the cap that usually went over it: it made her look even younger. Rebecca was aware that, in Italy, she herself might be almost old enough to be the mother of a girl who could dress like this. If she had married at fifteen, as some girls did here, she could have a eleven-year-old now . . .

She wished, desperately and without any sense at all, that she had accidentally fallen pregnant in the weeks before Jack left. But that hope was gone, and just as well. Particularly now she wasn't sure of him, of their marriage, of anything. Anger bloomed again in her, and she fought back equally insistent tears. She had no one here. No one at all.

'Signora Quinn!' Sandro's voice, providentially pleased to see her. If he'd been noncommittal, she might have burst into tears on the spot.

'Signor Panucci,' she managed. The tears receded. She put on her best face, and smiled cordially at him. He smiled back, and handed a contact sheet to Natalia.

'For your father. I think we got a couple of good ones.'

'*Grazie.*' She smiled up at him, but not flirtatiously, as Rebecca had half-expected. It was the demure smile of a good Italian girl. He gave her a smile in return; it was hard to tell how much warmth was behind it.

Rebecca and Sandro went out, together, into the cold. She tucked her hands into the sleeves of her coat; Sandro had put on a pea jacket. It made him look like a sailor on leave, and there were more than a few of them around.

Their steps turned, without speaking, towards the piazza at the top of the hill. It was a habit, now, to go there whenever there was free time, to count the ships in port, to note any unusual absences.

How to begin? Professional, that was the key. Keep it professional.

'I thought I should tell you,' she began. 'My editor in England, from the *Evening News* . . .'

'Evans, right?'

'Yes. Yes. He sent me the clippings of the stories Jack had submitted since we came here.'

'That was nice of him.' Sandro's voice was tentative. It was clear he could see something was wrong. Was she so transparent?

'I understand now why he expected me to come back to England. All the stories had Jack's by-line. Even the ones I wrote.'

Sandro stopped in his tracks and looked at her. 'Sorry? You mean he never got your stories?'

She stopped too, and gazed down at her shoes. 'No. I mean that Jack submitted my stories under his name.'

'Mother of God!' She cast a quick glance at him. He was thunderstruck. A part of her clenched heart eased. She wasn't overreacting. 'What a bastard – excuse my French, Becca, but gee, that's low.'

Low. The perfect word.

'Yes. I thought so too.'

'And he didn't do any work on them?'

They began to walk again, falling into step easily.

'Oh, he proofread them, changed a comma here or there. Nothing substantial. I did the same for him.' And, she thought, he'd been good at his job. But not better than her. Perhaps that was what he couldn't admit. Perhaps he couldn't take the risk that the editor would prefer her stories.

That theory made more sense to her than the idea that Jack had deliberately set out to use and betray her. Much more sense, and it was easier to bear if it were pride, not base ambition, that had prompted him. She put the idea to Sandro.

'Yeah,' he said. 'Yeah, I can see that. He's a proud kind of guy.'

'You don't know him . . .'

'Well, I met him. Just the once. The night I arrived. I got the train from Rome through Bari, and it was pulled over to wait for a troop train going north, so I got in late, maybe eight o'clock, and Nonna put me to work straightaway. Your husband was there, on the journalists' table. I think it was the night before he took off for wherever he is.'

She remembered. She'd been cross with him, because that night he'd hinted he was onto a story, but he wouldn't tell her what it was.

Rebecca had gone home early from the trattoria, as she usually did when the men started smoking. Later Jack had come home, smelling of wine and tobacco and garlic. She hadn't denied him the solace of her body – she had never denied him, partly because of a sense of duty, but mostly because a friend of hers had lost her husband in France, and had bemoaned the fact that they had never had a chance to say 'a proper goodbye'. 'You never know,' she'd said. 'You never know when it might be the last time.' So, she'd opened her arms to him even though she was a little miffed at his secrecy.

And then, the next day, he'd rushed in during the siesta and had been gone in only a few moments.

'And you're pretty good,' Sandro continued. She had lost the train of thought. Pretty good? 'I can see how he might think you'd overshadow him.'

176

Yes. She could see that too. She'd always done better academically, for one thing. He hadn't like taking her help with his university courses, but he'd done it, just as she'd taken his advice in playing hockey for the university team. She'd guided him in his essays – sometimes she'd thought she knew more about the law than he did. Perhaps he'd just seen this situation as an extension of that. He might even have convinced himself that she would understand and approve.

It had been stupid, and cowardly, but perhaps it hadn't been intentionally cruel.

They arrived at the top of the hill and moved out onto the piazza, near the wall. The harbour below was grey and windswept, and the wind bit at her ankles. Sandro's voice cut across her thoughts.

'Probably told himself that it was more important for *him* to build up his reputation. After all, you were just going to have kids and settle down to being a housewife one day, right?'

She glared at him and he stopped, hands out as if to ward off a blow, mouth twisted in a wry smile.

'Hey, I didn't say *I* thought that! But a lot of men would tell themselves that to make it sit okay in their head.'

He was right. So often, Sandro saw the truth of things.

'So, that's why Evans has put me on probation,' she said. 'As far as he's concerned, I haven't produced anything since I arrived.'

Sandro stared out at the horizon, and then turned to her, moving closer, head bent, taking her hands. He spoke softly. 'I'm sorry, Becca. I'm really sorry.'

It was exactly the right thing to say. Uncaring who might see them, she leaned her head against the hard ridge of his shoulder, where the sleeve joined the body of the coat. Just for a moment. Just a moment to pretend she had someone to rely on. Someone who called her Becca, a name only her closest friends ever used. It brought unexpected comfort.

Behind him, a group of French sailors hooted and made encouraging hand signals to Sandro.

She pulled away, cheeks flaming. But he smiled at her, and she was reminded of their first walk up here, and how looking straight into a man's eyes had seemed oddly intimate.

'Ignore them,' he said. 'They're just boys a long way from home.'

But she was breathless; she could feel his warm breath against her cheek.

'Let's go back to Nonna Rosa's,' she said. 'I haven't done my share of chopping onions today.'

That sweet smile, the rare one, broke across his face. 'Brave woman!'

They walked back down, their steps fitting easily together.

17

After a particularly long press conference, about supply chains through Naples, Niccolo was waiting for Sandro outside the base. The boy raced over as soon as Sandro came out, running right past Rebecca, who was talking with Christy, smiling as though he'd told a joke.

She said goodbye to Christy and followed Niccolo over, still looking amused. Sandro hated to do anything that would wipe that smile off her face, but it looked like Niccolo had discovered something. Sandro had been paying him to follow Nolan; he just had a gut feeling that the guy was into something fishy.

'Signor Panucci!' Niccolo said, high voiced with excitement.

'*Si*, *Niccolo*. What do you have for me?'

'*La rossi* is meeting Leon.'

'The cafe owner?'

Rebecca had come close enough to hear, and flicked him a glance – clearly she had realised who '*La rossi*' was – the redhead.

'What's so surprising about that?' she asked.

'They are meeting in an old house up on the hill,' Niccolo said. 'Yesterday morning, before dawn. And again today.'

'Why didn't you tell me yesterday, eh?'

'I wanted to be sure.'

'Fine, fine.' He slid a coin into Niccolo's hand, and said, 'Come get me before dawn, and we will see if he goes again tomorrow, eh?'

'*Si, signore!*' Niccolo grinned widely and ran off, trailed by a couple of his buddies. Sandro knew he was a good kid, but like all kids, he thought playing at being a detective was only fun. The dark side of it hadn't hit him yet, and Sandro prayed it never did.

'Are you really suspicious of Christy?' Rebecca asked. 'Enough to have Niccolo follow him?'

'Yeah, I am. Something's not kosher.'

She walked with her head down, studying the street, and not only because her boots were slippery on the cobbles. He knew she didn't like the idea of a friend of hers being crooked.

'I'll go tomorrow morning, I'll see what he's doing, maybe take a couple of snaps.'

She seemed wistful, as if she wanted him to ask her to come along. But it was a lot easier for a man to blend in – a blonde in long skirts . . . no chance.

'I'd take you, if I thought he wouldn't spot you.'

Surprise flashed over her face, with a little pleasure. 'That's a nice thought.'

'I'll see you back at the trattoria afterwards, then.'

'No. Better not,' she said, looking up. 'Come to the Damonicas'. You don't want Christy coming in while we're talking.'

That was what he liked about her: a soft heart, but a tough mind.

The next morning was misty. As he got up in the last hour before the sky began to lighten, he could see nothing past the back wall of the courtyard, the top branches of the lemon tree losing themselves in the fog.

He placed his small camera in his pocket, then let himself quietly out the back gate and went around the front to meet Niccolo. The boy was hopping up and down, from gutter to pavement, and scurried over as soon as he saw Sandro, rubbing his gloveless hands together against the cold. Sandro's pea jacket wasn't much defence against this dampness, but at least he had pockets to ram his fists into. He gave the boy his own knitted wool gloves.

'*Grazie, signore!*' Niccolo said. He wriggled his fingers into the gloves with a look of bliss.

'*Andiamo.*'

They climbed and then went down again – they were on the landward side of the big hill that formed the centre of Brindisi. The mist was still thick, and as the sky greyed towards dawn, walking through it became like walking in a dream, where depth was an illusion and nightmares hid behind flattened houses.

He knew he would never be able to capture this illusory essence on film; there was always the gap between the human eye and the camera's. Even coloured stereoscope images couldn't give the *feel* of walking through the misty world in the early morning.

But by God it would be fun to try. To concentrate on the feeling of the image, not just on its information. After the war, maybe.

Niccolo took him to the back of the house in question, a paling fence half burned away. The old outhouse was still there, untouched, covered by a leafless wisteria vine. They moved around it, and stood between it and the side fence, hidden from anyone who wasn't especially looking. Sandro prepared his camera, and they waited.

The world was bright grey now, the sky to the east sending fingers of rose and white through the mist.

Steps. One man, walking fast and lightly. He came down the laneway and paused at the broken fence.

'Nolan?' he hissed, in an Italian accent, then made that very Italian sound of annoyance, a kind of *tcchst* Sandro had never heard from an American. As the man moved into the small yard, avoiding the fallen beams and crunching charcoal under his feet, Sandro edged along until he could get a look at him.

Yes, it was Leon.

A moment later, Nolan arrived, much more quietly, surprising both Leon and Sandro as he slipped into the yard. Sandro's heart beat faster.

'*Sterco!*' Leon said. Next to Sandro, Niccolo clapped his hands over his mouth to stop laughing at this crudity from an adult. 'Don't startle me like that!'

'Grow up,' Nolan said in English. 'What've you got?'

Leon leaned close, speaking rapidly. Christy listened. Sandro wrapped the end of his scarf around the camera, over everything but its lens; with any luck, it would deaden the sound of the shutter. He took two quick snaps, and then pulled back. The other two didn't react; the gradually growing noises of donkeys and carts and a long fog horn from the harbour had covered the sound. He edged closer to the corner of the outhouse and listened hard.

'Fessenden?' Nolan said. 'You're sure that was the word?'

'*Si.* The young radio operator, he got drunk, too drunk to do the naughty deed, hehe.' Leon laughed. 'So, the girl went through his pockets. She said there was a diagram, with the word "Fessenden" on it.'

'Good. Here.' A rustle as some money changed hands.

'This will make a good story, *signore*?'

'Oh, it'll be a nice wee story.' There was a grim amusement in Nolan's voice. A diagram from a radio operator? That sounded like classified information. Sandro had no idea who or what 'Fessenden' was, but it looked like Nolan did. And Sandro would be damned before he bought that guff about a 'nice wee story'. Combined with Nolan's furtive encounters with fishermen and secret trips out of town . . . it all added up to treason. The Austrians and Germans were paying big money for any information about Allied affairs. Espionage was everywhere, and he'd bet Nolan was on that game.

Sandro was just relieved that Leon hadn't knowingly engaged in it. He liked Leon.

They waited until both men had moved away.

'So, *signore*, was I right?' Niccolo looked at him with bright eyes, proud of himself. As he ought to be.

'Yep, buddy, you did a good job. Here.' He handed over some notes of his own. 'But – no word of this to your friends, all right? This is top secret.'

Those brown eyes grew large. 'Truly?'

'Truly. You just keep your mouth buttoned, okay?'

'Okay!' Niccolo said.

'And I wouldn't be at all surprised if you got yourself a better coat one of these days,' Sandro added. He would talk to Niccolo's mother, maybe suggest the boy should be in school. He was too bright to waste on the streets. How much could it cost to keep a kid in an Italian school? He could probably afford it.

'Come on,' he said. 'Home.'

'I don't believe it,' Rebecca said. She stood stock still in the middle of the street and gazed at Sandro in reproof and astonishment.

'Calling me a liar?'

She looked at him for a moment, and sighed. Of course he wasn't a liar. Nor was he incompetent. No one could look at that intelligent, alert face and imagine that he had misunderstood, or misinterpreted. Still, for Christy's sake, and maybe for her own, she tried.

'But we don't have any proof that it's more than . . . than aggressive journalism. Shady, yes, but—'

'Stories about radio operators spouting classified information?'

Tears were threatening; why should it matter so much to her? Except that Christy had been, she thought, her friend. Her only friend, really, of her own kind. She had unconsciously relied on his promise of support if she should need it.

She ardently wished Jack were back, despite her anger with him. This was the kind of decision that should be shared. It would have to be shared with Sandro.

'We need to report him,' Sandro said firmly.

For a moment, she quailed. Even if Christy turned out to be innocent, this would destroy not only their friendship, but his reputation. A journalist had to be trustworthy, or who would give him information? It came down, in the end, to whom she trusted more: Sandro or Christy?

She realised abruptly that she would trust Sandro with her life; with everything. Heart and mind and body. *No!* She stared at him blankly. She was married. This rush of warmth for him, it had to be reaction against Jack's deception. It *had* to be no more than that. She couldn't – *mustn't* – fall in love with another man. She felt herself begin to tremble, and took a deep breath to quell it.

'Becca?' he said. She'd been standing there silent for too long.

'Yes,' she managed to say. 'I'll send a message to Commander Warren.'

Perhaps her internal struggle showed in her voice. Sandro moved closer and touched her arm. How long it had been since anyone had touched her – Sandro on the way back from Serranova, that's when it would have been. That was the worst of loneliness; the body itself grew hungry for the simple comfort of human touch.

Of course! *That* was why she felt like this. Simple loneliness. The thought made her feel better, less guilty.

'I'm sorry, Rebecca,' Sandro said. 'I know he was a friend of yours.'

He used the past tense, as though sure that Christy was beyond the pale. He was probably right, but she couldn't relinquish friendship so easily.

'Let's see what the investigation turns up before we say "was".'

His mouth twisted awry with that element of cynicism she thought of as being *so New York*, but his voice was gentle. 'I know you like to trust people, honey, but don't get your hopes up.'

She swatted him on the arm as though he were one of her brothers, pretending that nothing in her had changed. That nothing important had happened just then, although she could still feel her heart beating fast and light, her cheeks warm with a mixture of embarrassment and dread as they moved on for their daily check of the ship positions in the harbour.

It wasn't until she was undressing that night that she realised he had called her 'honey'. But Americans did that to women, didn't they? Like a shopkeeper in Sydney calling you 'love'. It didn't mean anything.

Whatever she felt for Sandro, she had to forget it. Not only was she married, but they were working together. Professional. She had to be professional. And act like a lady.

She prayed that night to the Virgin Mother for strength and purity of spirit, but she dreamed of Sandro smiling at her as he touched her cheek. 'Honey,' he said, and kissed her.

In the morning light, she woke flushed and horrified, and wished, suddenly and completely, that Jack would walk through the door and sweep her up in his arms. That would put an end to this nonsense.

18

When Commander Warren came into the parlour at her pensione, Rebecca could see he was surprised to see Sandro there.

At least there was food to offer him. She had bought some delectable Italian biscuits; the room smelled of vanilla and chocolate. The new government was going to introduce more rigorous rationing, so best to have these now. Sugar was already vanishingly rare – she had only managed to get these by being at the door of the pasticceria before it opened and paying a surprisingly large bribe to the baker.

'Come in, Commander,' she said. The parlour was a dingy place, its walls marked by nicotine stains and redolent of pipe smoke. But it had chairs and a small table, which was all they needed.

Commander Warren took off his cap but left his coat on. She didn't blame him. It was freezing, even though she'd paid for extra wood to be laid on the fire.

'Mrs Quinn. Mr Baker. What can I do for you?'

She poured the tea she had made. 'Before we talk, have some tea and biscotti.'

He cast her an amused glance, but he dutifully sipped his tea, and then drank it with real enjoyment.

'You can't get good tea in Italy,' he said. 'That's a grand wee drop.'

Rebecca couldn't drink, or eat, or anything else until this was over. It was horrible to accuse someone who had been so nice to her. So supportive, when the rest of the men had been . . . dismissive was the nicest word she could use. She exchanged a glance with Sandro; he was diamond hard in his condemnation of Nolan, glad to have the chance to act.

She poured the commander another cup as Sandro put his photographs from outside Serranova on the table. He'd made an enlargement that showed a blurry Christy handing over a packet to the fisherman.

'We have reason to believe that Mr Nolan is . . . is collecting information that he may be supplying to the Austrians,' she said. 'We don't know for sure, but we thought it right to tell you.'

There. Done. Warren took a long breath in and leaned forward, examining the image.

'What proof do you have?'

They told him, each in their turn. Seeing Christy sneak to the first meeting. His trips to Taranto, to other places along the coast, when there was no story to be had – but from where shipping could be watched.

'It's more than can be explained by chance,' Sandro said. 'And – well, I've seen him a few times, buying drinks for sailors and pumping them for information.'

'Which is something that journalists do,' Warren observed. His face was expressionless now.

'Yes, it is,' Rebecca agreed. 'But, yesterday . . .'

She trailed off to allow Sandro to explain. He had been the eyewitness.

Sandro laid out what he had seen and heard, and showed the photographs of Leon and Nolan in the blackened yard.

Warren sat for a moment. 'You're sure the word was "Fessenden"?'

'Positive.'

Warren let his breath out slowly, as if that were very bad news.

'The censor checks every piece of mail that leaves the base,' he said, as if he were thinking aloud. 'I've had no reports of anything suspicious in his mail.'

'Of course not,' Sandro said. 'He gives it to that fisherman to be sent from Albania.'

Warren nodded. 'Yes,' he said. 'Which gives us the advantage.'

Rebecca sighed, torn between being glad they hadn't suspected an innocent man and devastated that Warren believed they were right.

'What will you do?' Sandro asked, leaning forward, his face intense.

'He'll be watched, of course. We'll follow the information. We have sympathisers in Albania. They'll find the perpetrators. We have the chance to round up a whole ring, not just Nolan.' He looked seriously at them. 'We've had warnings about sensitive information from Italy showing up in London. Which is why you must say nothing to Nolan. Continue to act as you have been. Stop following him. Don't risk alarming him in any way. When we have the ringleaders in London, then we'll take care of Mr Nolan.'

'Yes, of course,' Rebecca said numbly. How could she – they – do that? She wasn't an actress!

'I'd appreciate it if you would forget the word Fessenden.' He looked very grim. Some kind of war machine, some new technology, top secret. She had enough national pride not to consider breaking *that* story.

Warren continued, collecting the photographs. 'And this must be so far off the record that, ideally, it will never see a newspaper.'

'Oh, Commander, you can't mean that! Once they're arrested . . .'

He couldn't be serious. The newspapers were full of stories about spies. Mata Hari, that baron in France . . . And the story would blow out of the water any ideas about her not being capable of doing her job. Sandro would be sure of a staff photographer's job. Warren couldn't mean for them to just ignore it, not when every other journalist in the world was free to write about spies being caught.

'Morale is more important than selling newspapers, Mrs Quinn,' he said. 'It's a critical time. With the disaster of the Battle of Caporetto, Italy does *not* need to hear about German spies informing on their shipping. This country needs hope, not despair.' His Scottish accent was very strong, as though his feelings were getting the better of him.

Sandro broke in. 'Commander, this is an important story. Do you have the right to decide what Italians should know?'

Warren was unmoved. 'I'm sure my Italian colleagues would say the same thing.'

'But when the spies are arrested in London, that will be reported there,' she objected.

'There'll be no mention made of Italy. Britain will cope.'

'You're not being fair. I can report on this story for the British papers. We can avoid mentioning Italy, if you like, but we need to break this story, Sandro and I need to.'

He looked at her in amazement. Of course, their careers meant nothing to him.

'Don't you look at me like that,' she continued. 'This is my bread and butter, remember? I have to support myself! God knows when Jack will be back. A story like this would make sure I have a job after the war. And Sandro, as well. It would make all the difference to him.'

And show the world that women could break *real* stories. Important stories.

'After the war, you can report on it all you like.'

'Oh, get out!' she said, astonishing both of the men. 'Go on, take your bloody photographs and get out of here.'

'Mrs Quinn—'

'You're being unreasonable, and you know it. The war won't be lost because we report on yet another spy story. But now we've done your work for you, you won't let us do ours. Off you go. And be glad I don't just ignore you wholesale and publish whatever the hell I like!'

Commander Warren took his captain's cap and the photographs and stood up stiffly. 'I'm sorry you feel like that, Mrs Quinn.'

'How did you expect me to feel, Commander? How would any other journalist have reacted?'

He stood, for a moment, considering that, and unbent just a little. 'In much the same way, I'm sure. But I would not have trusted them to consider the public good – I would have slapped a D-Notice on their editors.'

A D-Notice was an advisory request not to publish something that was likely to have a negative impact on the war effort.

Although obeying a D-Notice was voluntary, Rebecca had never heard of an editor ignoring one.

He was trying to mollify her, but she wasn't mollified. Behind him, still sitting, Sandro was laughing, which made her even angrier.

'You thought I'd be easier to influence, then?'

'I thought you had better sense and a higher moral compass!'

'Because I'm a woman.'

'Because you're a *lady*.'

Oh, class. Yes, the Navy relied on class, particularly the British Navy, where Warren had trained.

'Give me a good story,' she said. 'Before Christmas. Give me a story I can *use*.'

He looked at her with resignation and a kind of disappointment, which infuriated her.

'I'll see what I can do.'

As he left, she rounded on Sandro, who was still laughing into his biscotti.

'What's so funny?'

He turned a face full of mirth and admiration to her.

'He came in here with all these expectations about you, and you stripped them off one by one. He didn't know if he was on his head or his heels! It was *splendido*!'

Her mouth twitched.

'When you said: "publish whatever the hell I like!" I thought he'd have kittens!'

The anger slid away from her as she stared into Sandro's dancing eyes.

'Because I'm a *lady*!' she reminded him, and couldn't help but laugh. '*And* not a word of thanks from him!'

He chuckled again, until he was breathless, and then he sat back in his chair.

'Let's eat every single one of these biscotti,' he said. 'We've earned them!'

19

After Mass on Sunday, Rebecca liked to stroll down to the harbour promenade, where families brought their children, even in winter, for a walk and perhaps a gelato, if the shop had any.

She was confident by now of the winding turns of the street. She and Jack had come this way a couple of times. Thinking about that, she was saddened to realise that she'd given up expecting him to turn up any day, any moment. It had been more than three weeks, now. Almost four, and no word. Soon she would give in and ask Nonna Rosa to find out what she could.

She still worried about Linus. No news, still no news. Her gut tightened at the thought, and she pushed back the need to cry. It was so easy to torment herself with wondering, with imagining . . . She couldn't do that. It wouldn't help anyone. She had to live in this moment, without Jack, without knowing about Linus. That was what war did; it made you live day to day, not knowing what might happen tomorrow.

It was a rare day of sunshine, with flitting clouds up high sending shadows skittering across the sea. Was she wrong for not missing Jack more acutely? Was it a sign she had come to care for Sandro?

That thought discomfited her deeply, which was perhaps why she didn't notice the men until they closed around her.

A dozen of them, in their Sunday suits and Homburg hats. Older men, grandfathers, with grey hair, and some youths, maybe sixteen or seventeen. All of them scowling. All of them puffing themselves up.

Terror knifed through her, sharp and instinctive. A group of men and a lone woman; the stuff of nightmares. But she was on a public street, and there were people nearby. Surely they couldn't intend her any harm? She swallowed against her fear and spoke in Italian.

'*Signori?* Can I help you?'

One man, the leader perhaps, with a ragged moustache and mean eyes, stepped forward and pushed her shoulder.

'You stop talking to our girls. You stop infecting them with your Devil's ideas.'

So, that was it. The young ones started shouting insults at her: whore, bitch, white devil, and worse, she figured, because they were words she didn't know. The man who had shouted at her in the market was behind them, egging them on.

They crowded her, and one of them put his hand on her shoulder and shook her.

She'd never thought so fast. If she pushed him off, he would grow more violent. She stared into his stupid little angry eyes and spoke. 'Let go of me.'

For a moment it hung in the balance. He still had his hand on her shoulder, and he'd raised his other hand as if to strike her. Wanting her to cower. Be damned to him.

'Take your hand off me.' She'd never heard her voice so cold. She'd never been so enraged. 'I know you. Keep your hand on me and I'll have you arrested for assault.'

He froze, clearly unsure if that were even possible.

She shrugged that shoulder, and his hand dropped. They were growing angrier, because she hadn't given them the fear they wanted. She didn't care.

'*This* is why the rest of Europe thinks Italy is a backwards country,' she said, loudly enough for people outside the group to hear. And they were there, she was sure, though she couldn't see them over the press of the men's bodies. They were all around her, she could feel and hear them behind her, but she couldn't look. She must not lose the attention of the ringleaders.

Her mother had dealt with this kind of thing so often, and Rebecca frantically tried to remember how. With humour, usually, but that was Australia, and this was Italy, and she wasn't part enough of this community to know how to make them laugh.

And then she saw the *carabiniere*, the policeman, standing at the back of the group, hands tucked into his belt, watching with appreciation. Appreciation for the men. For a second, she wished frantically that Sandro would come, would scatter them all before him. Save her, like women have always waited to be saved.

She barged through to stand before the *carabiniere*. The men, startled by her movement, let her through.

'This is how you treat women in your town?' she demanded.

'This is how we treat—' She could just imagine what he was going to say next, when a girl's voice cut through.

'Papa?'

Loretta. And two of her friends, although not Natalia.

The *carabiniere* turned to shoo her away. 'Go on, Loretta, this is none of your business.'

Uneasy at the interruption, and suddenly conscious that not all the eyes on them were male, that there were family groups from which some of the women stared condemningly at them, that children were pointing fingers, the men began to move away from each other, easing back, so that what was an incipient mob became just some men standing in a street.

Rebecca saw a bruise on Loretta's cheek. Because of talking to her, no doubt. Rebecca closed her eyes for a moment, so angry and guilty and sad that there was no room for fear.

'I'm leaving now,' she said to Loretta's father. 'It would be a very good idea for you to let me.'

He sniffed and spat right next to her foot, but as she brushed past him he didn't move.

'Stay away from our girls!' a man yelled, and the group of men, briefly in solidarity, shouted the same.

She smiled at the girls as she went past, but she didn't speak. What could she say? *Patriarchy is based on violence?* Loretta already knew that.

Walk slowly. Head high. Don't let them see you shake. Her mother had said those words to her more than once, as they walked to a demonstration for Aboriginal rights, or a protest march against the terrible divorce laws, or a court case against some woman arrested for protesting.

Don't let them see you shake, because you always *did* shake, afterwards. And cry. And stare into the mirror, asking yourself, 'Why do they hate us so?' because it had been hate in their eyes. Hate and fear.

She stared into the small mirror in her bedroom and wondered what they had seen when they looked at her. White devil, they had called her. It was only now, staring at the hair that had been only half-hidden under her hat, that she realised they had been talking about her blondeness. Alien, that's what she was.

And those girls! So brave. So full of youth and idealism. They made her feel far older than twenty-seven.

For a moment, she allowed herself to imagine going home. Back to Sydney, to her mother and father, to her aunts and uncles and cousins, to her colleagues at the *Herald*. To the warmth and comfort of her privileged life.

To Louise Mack, who would be so disappointed in her. Well, bad cess to Louise Mack, as Christy would say. Bad cess to all of them who tried to tell her what to do and who to be.

She would do what she believed right, and at this moment, that was reporting honestly and fearlessly on the Adriatic war.

But she hoped, hoped so badly, that none of those girls would suffer for standing up for her. That there would be no more bruises on Loretta's face.

20

'Osso bucco,' Nonna Rosa announced, hefting two large beef shins onto the kitchen bench. 'A good autumn dish.'

She bent down to pull out a long meat saw, grunting a little as she stood up. For a moment, bent over, she looked her age, but standing again she shed twenty years.

'Onions, celery, carrots, garlic,' she added, gesturing to Rebecca to begin chopping.

Obediently, Rebecca took the big knife and began to cut up stalks of celery, stringing them first and then slicing them into half-moons. The sharp, cleansing scent was pleasant, reminding her of summer afternoons with her father in the vegetable patch at the back of their garden. They'd had a man for the heavy work, the mowing and hoeing, but her father had done all the planting and manuring. She had loved, as a child, to go with him, big wicker basket in hand, to see what was ripe and ready for the kitchen. To eat tomatoes fresh from the vine, broad beans spilled out from warm furry pods, carrots pulled up and brushed off. And celery, snapped from the head after her father had cut it, and crunched immediately.

'So, you went to Mass this morning?' Nonna Rosa asked, sawing industriously. They spoke only in Italian now; there were words, occasionally, that Rebecca didn't understand, but for everyday purposes they were few and far between.

'No,' Rebecca said, puzzled. Why would she go to Mass on a Monday? Except maybe to pray never again to be accosted as she had been yesterday. She shivered with the memory.

The saw stopped its harsh scraping for a moment, and then started again.

'I thought maybe you would pray for your husband. It's the day of San Andrea today.' As if explaining to a child, she added, 'He is patron saint of fishermen. And your husband, he left with fishermen.'

Yes, he had left with fishermen who were also smugglers. Rebecca's stomach jolted. She dragged in a great breath of air against a tight throat; this fear for Jack came up sometimes, but she could control it.

'I doubt Saint Andrew would look after those particular fishermen.'

Nonna Rosa smiled sourly and shrugged. 'You English are strange.'

She'd given up explaining that she wasn't English. In some ways, Nonna Rosa was right; her upbringing had been as English as her parents could make it. They were part of Empire, and they never forgot it.

'Have you heard . . . anything?' It went against the grain to ask. Jack should have written to her, or sent word.

'Nothing,' Nonna Rosa said. 'But they haven't been back in port since he left.'

So, no chance for a letter to arrive. It wasn't Jack's fault, and it was silly to be disappointed that she couldn't blame him. Childish.

'You don't worry much. Of course, you don't love him,' Nonna Rosa acknowledged, as if trying to find an excuse for her.

This time the jolt went all through her, and it was anger.

'How *dare* you?' she said. She put the knife down deliberately. She should not stick it into Nonna Rosa's face, she really shouldn't. She glared instead.

'But—' Nonna Rosa said, puzzled. 'Your marriage, it was arranged, yes?'

'No,' Rebecca said. Her voice was clipped. 'I married Jack because I loved him.' A fleeting expression went over Nonna Rosa's face; was it derision? 'I *did*.'

Nonna Rosa shrugged, a full-shoulder shrug that conveyed disbelief as clearly as words.

For a moment, they worked in silence, the shriek of the saw as it got to the larger bones the only sound, while Rebecca swept the celery pieces into a bowl.

The saw stopped as Nonna Rosa cut the meat around the next piece of bone before she sawed it.

'Why would you think I didn't love him?' She felt a fool, weak, for asking, but she had to know. She *had* to know.

Nonna Rosa paused, knife in hand, and then went back to slicing through the shin meat.

'You are sleeping well without him.'

It was true. She didn't know why, but after that expedition to Strettabaia, she had begun sleeping through the night again. Perhaps it had proved to her that there were worse things than being without a husband. Now she slept all night through. And sometimes dreamed of Sandro.

Her hands were shaking and she had to stop cutting the carrots in case she cut herself. She stood for a moment, head bowed, hands still. She had never felt so lonely.

'Maybe you loved him like English people love,' Nonna Rosa said magnanimously.

Italians didn't believe you felt anything unless you screamed and shouted and wailed about it. But still . . .

'Why did you think it was an arranged marriage?'

Nonna Rosa flicked a look sideways at her, and then looked back to the counter. The first shin had been reduced to neat rounds of meat and bone, like filled-in Os. Nonna Rosa pulled the second shin towards her. Without turning to Rebecca, she said, 'He had no sweetness for you.' The word she used was *dolcezza*, which could just as easily mean tenderness, or kindness.

'*Dolcezza?*'

'He treated you like another man.'

'He treated me with respect,' Rebecca countered.

'Yes. But no sweetness. Like a man treats an arranged wife.'

She couldn't bear this kitchen, with its raw meat and garlic smell. Pulling off her apron, she reached for her bag and gloves. She'd been there for more than the allotted hour, anyway.

'I need some fresh air,' she said. 'I'll see you tonight.' At the door, she turned back, half-wanting to apologise for leaving so abruptly. Nonna Rosa was staring at her with an expression of deep pity. Rebecca flushed. How dare she. She went out the door without a word, prevented from slamming it behind her only by its weight and creakiness. Under her breastbone, a canker bud began to unfurl.

Jack loved her. The fact that this small-town provincial woman couldn't see that was no evidence at all. Anger and hurt swirled in her mind. He loved her. She knew he did, despite everything.

He would be able to explain why he had stolen her stories. He would. Surely. Because if he loved her, he wouldn't have done that. She pushed that thought away.

Nonna Rosa wasn't right. She *couldn't* be right. Despite her anger with Jack, Rebecca had never doubted that they would stay together. That was what you did, when you married – you stayed together, no matter what, and worked to build on the love you had. If Nonna Rosa was right, life with Jack wouldn't be worth living.

Halfway up the crooked road to the piazza, she realised that she hadn't once thought, *I love him.*

Was it because she was so sure of it that it didn't need to be said?

Of course she loved him, despite her doubts. She summoned her memories of him, ignoring the old man who sat selling matches on the corner and who always said rude things to her. Jack. Golden-haired, laughing, the one who entered a room and made it come alive. Jack, the sportsman, the spin bowler, his white shirt always untucking itself on his run-up so that glimpses of his bare flesh showed as he let the ball go. She remembered when that glimpse of flesh had kept her sleepless all night. But that wasn't love, was it? That was desire.

Jack the intellectual, arguing with her and his friends, including her brothers, about God and morality and the repression of women by the Church. He had been so right about the oppression of women, so eloquent on their behalf, that she had felt an uprush of hot adoration. But she had worried about him, too, about the state of his soul. He'd rejected even the broken truths of his Protestant upbringing, and his free thinking was dangerous, she felt in some dark, sacred way. But he'd been so earnest, she'd known he couldn't possibly be in any real danger of losing his soul. He was just taking another route to God, through philosophy.

Adoration, worry, desire. And then, after marriage, after the astonishments of the marriage bed, had come a great and unexpected affection. Surely it was love when every time she saw him she felt her spirits lift?

Of course it was.

Once he'd explained himself, she would feel it all again. And there would be no more dreams of Sandro.

21

Sandro still wasn't used to the late nights. His grandmother slept during the *riposo*, but he couldn't bring himself to nap like a toddler, and used the time for his own photography – taking images of Brindisi while the streets were empty. So each morning he dragged himself yawning out of bed and staggered down the back stairs to the outhouse, then inside, following the aroma of coffee to the kitchen.

Normally, no one was there – his grandmother made the coffee and set it back to keep warm, then went to the market. But this morning she was sitting at a table with one of the Italian *tenenti*, heads close together, murmuring to each other.

He hadn't realised his nonna knew any of the Italian Navy contingent so well, and as he came in, they moved apart, smoothly, as if they had rehearsed it. Perhaps this was the officer who organised her flour supplies. The *tenente* nodded to him; his grandmother tilted her head towards the coffee, which, unlike most mornings, was still perking on the stove, next to a saucepan with milk just warmed.

'I will have some too,' she said. 'And some for the *tenente*.'

Sandro poured coffee into three glasses, filled them with milk, and brought them over, along with the rolls and butter Nonna had left on the counter.

'*Grazie*,' the *tenente* said. Sandro looked inquiringly at Nonna Rosa, who shook her head very slightly as the *tenente* sat back and sipped his cafe latte. So, there was a secret. Well, if he couldn't talk about why a *tenente* in the Italian Navy was having a clandestine rendezvous with his grandmother, he could talk about something else.

'You were out on patrol yesterday, right? How'd it go? Any submarine sightings?'

The man seemed happy to break the silence. '*Si*. The *U-14*. That cunning von Trapp bastard. He was after one of the convoy ships, the *Spiritus*, but we herded him away.'

'Von Trapp? That's the captain?'

'*Si*. He's dangerous, that one. He sank three ships last month, the *Good Hope*, the *Eliston*, and the *Cape del Monte*.'

'How do we know who the captain is?'

He and Nonna Rosa exchanged a quick glance.

'They make no secret of it,' the *tenente* said.

He drained his coffee and stood up, sliding an envelope into his pocket.

At the same time, the outer door opened and Rebecca walked in. Every time he saw her he got a jolt; in between their meetings, it was hard to believe how beautiful she was. For the first moment when he saw her, he was speechless, and then the world clicked into place, and she was a colleague again.

'Signora Quinn!' he said. He got up and moved a chair out for her to sit in, and then went to get her a cafe latte – but he paid attention as the *tenente* bowed to her and smiled. She nodded back, also smiling.

'Nonna Rosa,' Rebecca said. '*Buongiorno.*' Nonna Rosa nodded and sipped delicately at her coffee.

'*Signora,*' the *tenente* said.

'*Tenente,*' Rebecca said, seemingly delighted to see him. 'Tell me, what are the plans to move the Barrage to interfere with submarines more efficiently?' Her Italian was getting better every day.

He laughed. 'Oh, signora, you know too much! Yes, we are shifting the Barrage to cover a wider passage. Your Commander Warren, he's not satisfied.' He shrugged. 'It's good. We've been suggesting it for months, but they don't have to listen to lowly lieutenants. The Australian Commander, though – no one ignores Cocky Warren!'

Rebecca laughed. '*Cocky* Warren? That's what the men call him? That's wonderful!'

Sandro couldn't help but wish she was laughing with him rather than the *tenente*. And that she wasn't even more beautiful like this, all lit up and warm.

This *tenente* was a handsome man; he would draw women's glances as he walked down the street. Sandro wondered what it was like to have the looks of a hero. And of course *he* was hardly looking his best: unshaven, in yesterday's shirt, not even a collar on yet.

He brought the coffee and another plate of rolls back to the table.

'*Arrivederci, donne, signore,*' the *tenente* said, putting on his cap in order to lift it and bow.

'*Arrivederci, tenente*,' both women replied. Rebecca sat as the door closed behind him, and Sandro put her glass of coffee in front of her.

'Thanks, Sandro,' she said. He was pleased she'd spoken in English. Sometimes it felt as though that was the only thing that connected them.

'You're welcome,' he said, and sat down too. His coffee was only half-drunk, and he was suddenly starving. The rolls were delicious. And he had something to tell Rebecca. 'They stopped the *U-14* yesterday from taking out a convoy ship, the *Spiritus*.'

'Excellent. Another story.' She smiled and drank her coffee. 'That's what I was coming to see you about. They've called a press conference for nine o'clock.'

It was past eight now; he'd slept even longer than usual. He swigged back his coffee and got up.

'I'll be right down,' he said. He rushed through his morning routine; he'd got so used to shaving in a hurry that he rarely cut himself. A new shirt, a fresh collar, clean socks; Nonna Rosa made sure his gear was well kept.

A bit of pomade in his hair and he was ready.

Rebecca and Nonna Rosa were still at the table, chatting amiably about what was in season at this time of year. Not much; they were past the autumn harvest. It looked so normal, but it wasn't. Nonna Rosa didn't sit around and drink coffee or entertain Italian *tenentes*. All this normality was a cover for something.

•

He and Rebecca walked sedately down to the harbour.

'I heard about those bullies the other day,' Sandro said. He didn't tell her how Leon's story of her being accosted by the men had filled him with murderous rage; how much he had wanted to rip into all of them. It was only not knowing the names that had kept him controlled until reason could get the better of his anger.

She shrugged. 'People don't like change, and women voting is a big change for a society. Of course there'll be resistance to the idea.'

So brave. It astonished him how someone so slight and slender could have physical courage to match her moral courage.

'If it happens again, send one of the boys running to me.'

She smiled up at him and his heart stuttered. *Dio*, he couldn't feel like this about a married woman.

'Thank you. But I don't think it will be necessary.'

The press conferences were short; she liked to be outside, ready to rush to the post office if there was important news. Some telegrams got through, but it was hard to know which ones would and which wouldn't. Worth sending them, but always necessary to write a follow-up story that went out in the naval mail. His thoughts drifted back to Nonna and the *tenente*. Was there a story there?

'Something was up this morning,' Sandro said. 'Why would that *tenente* come to have coffee with an old lady?'

'Yes,' she said, nodding. 'It was a bit odd.'

He told her about the moment of silence when he asked about Captain von Trapp, and Rebecca laughed.

'Well, perhaps your nonna is up to her old tricks!'

'What do you mean?'

'Her spying!'

'What?'

Rebecca told him what she had learned about Nonna Rosa's part in the war of unification. His nonna, a spy! A grey marketeer, he could stomach, just. But this!

'I wish *my* grandmother had been a spy,' she said regretfully. 'She was a very proper woman indeed.'

A spy. He laughed, properly. 'And you think she's still at it?'

'She seems to be very well informed, I have to say.'

Sure. She was informed, all right. And the trattoria was suspiciously well stocked with what had become luxury items during the war: the best olive oil, eggs, butter and, of course, flour. And where was she getting cinnamon and nutmeg? They were imported goods.

'Don't mention it to her,' he said. 'Let's just keep it back until we need it.'

Rebecca smiled. Oh, that smile, mischievous and clever. Her husband was a fool to ever have left her side.

'*Capisco*,' she said.

•

The press conference was unusual in that only the Italian commander, Rear Admiral Acton, was present. He repeated much of what the *tenente* had told them, but with no mention of von Trapp. When it came time for questions, Sandro asked, 'Is this the submarine that is under the command of Captain von Trapp?'

'*Tenente*, not *Capitano*,' the commander said automatically, and then looked chagrined. 'We have no comment on enemy personnel.'

Afterwards, outside, Sandro rejoined Rebecca, while Christy Nolan, Mark Coates and Ambroise Lemaitre and two Italians from Bari all tried to find out how he had known about the submarine commander.

Rebecca tapped the side of her nose and winked at them. '*Esclusivo*, gentlemen!'

They grumbled and went away to write their stories, except for Christy Nolan.

'I don't understand where you're getting your information from,' he said sternly.

'I speak better Italian than you do, Christy, my dear,' she said, and grinned at him.

'Oh, you're a terrible woman, Rebecca Quinn.'

They both chuckled. He walked away, and Rebecca immediately stopped smiling.

'I hate this,' she said to Sandro. 'I hate all this jockeying for position and trying to scoop each other. I understand why it happens, but it's so *tiring*. I enjoy going hard for a story – but this is just – I don't know the word for what it is.'

'*Maschio* is the Italian word,' Sandro said, taking her arm. 'They like it.' Together, they walked back to the Damonicas' house so she could write her story. She was paying extra so they could work together in the parlour.

'Oh, I know. Jack is the same. Loves all the competition.' A shudder went through her. 'Yuck!' she said, like a child. He couldn't help it, he laughed.

'Yes, go ahead and laugh at me.'

'I feel the same,' he said. 'What I'd rather do is work alone, instead of all this jostling.'

She looked at him thoughtfully and he tried not to stare into her eyes, gazing past her to the soft peach walls of the shops they were passing, the dark-coated women who went by, the sailors cruising along as if they owned the earth. A ship's horn sounded from the harbour, a long, lonely note.

'I suppose a war photographer *can* work alone,' she said.

'At the front, sure,' he said. 'But that's not what I meant.' He struggled for the words. 'Afterwards. After the war. I want to travel. America and the rest of the world. Travel and take photographs.'

'Oh. Yes. I can see you doing something like that. You get on with people.'

'Faint praise,' he said, unsure of her meaning.

Her grip on his arm tightened. 'No, no, I mean . . . to do that kind of work, you have to be able to, to step back and pay attention to other people. To make them feel comfortable, not to be the centre of attention. You're good at that.'

'Like a waiter,' he said bitterly.

'Oh, don't be ridiculous!' she said. 'Anyone less like a waiter I can't imagine.'

He was taken aback. Once again she had taken him and shaken him up so that he didn't know if it was tomorrow or Christmas. But on the whole it sounded like she approved of him, so he would take that and enjoy it, even if it was a perilous enjoyment.

•

In the Damonicas' parlour, they sat at the table and Rebecca crafted her story from his notes and the mimeographed paper he'd been given at the press conference. She had a folder that included all the papers given out since she and Jack had arrived, and as she went over them, she frowned.

'That makes twenty-one sightings of U-boats since we got here,' she said. 'The Austrians are being very active.'

'They have the advantage. Their submarines can evade our ships much more easily than our ships can damage their U-boats.'

'Yes. At least the tide is turning in France.'

America's entry into the war had been the deciding factor. The news of the capture of Passchendaele had just come through from the Western Front. But the outlook from Russia was not so good. The Bolshevik revolution was likely to succeed; if the Tsar was gone for good, who knew what the revolutionaries would do?

'We're going to lose the Eastern Front,' Sandro said gloomily.

'The Bolsheviks have taken over, but that doesn't mean they'll side with Germany.'

'Even if all they do is sign a cease-fire, Germany will have more troops to release for France.'

They fell silent. Since the Americans had come in to the war it had felt like only a matter of time before the Allies would win. But now, it was once more in the balance. The Italian front was wavering. Sandro itched to be there, fighting. Maybe this wasn't his home country, but it was the home of his fathers – and his mothers – back to the dawn of time.

His paper credentials hadn't come through yet; he was still riding on Rebecca's coat tails. When they did – could he just leave her and take off for the front? That would be a lousy thing to do.

Every time he heard news from the Isonzo line, he chafed with impatience. So it would be dangerous. There were worse things than dying doing what you loved. Like being stuck here, taking portraits of fresh-faced sailors to send home, with the occasional shelled village as seasoning.

The memory of that little girl they had found sobered him. The war was happening here as well as anywhere else. Maybe he was just being *maschio* himself, wanting to be where the action was.

'Sandro?'

He smiled at her automatically. 'Sorry, miles away.'

She touched his hand gently. 'The work we do here is important, too.' The featherlight touch nearly unmanned him. How did she read him so well?

'I know,' he said. 'I know.'

For a moment, they were still. Her hand on his, her scent around him, her mouth soft with understanding. And then she blushed, the flush sweeping up over her neck and face, and pulled away, pretending to study her notes, not looking at him. His heart beat so hard he could feel it shaking his whole body. This wasn't just desire.

Leaving might be the only way to get away from her before she tore his heart out entirely.

22

Some commotion on the stairs. A man's heavy tread, Angela's voice raised in – welcome? Was it—

Her bedroom door opened wide and Jack stood in the doorway.

For a moment Rebecca was frozen with astonishment. She waited for an avalanche of feeling to hit her, but it didn't come.

'Is that all the welcome I get?' he asked, grinning.

'Jack,' she said. He didn't seem real. He had a beard, and his clothes gave off a rank odour of fish and old sweat she could smell right across the room. She stood up and went to him, putting a hand out to his face to make sure he was real and this wasn't another of her dreams.

'Like it?' he said about the beard, then he pulled her into his arms and kissed her.

It felt absolutely wrong. The smell, the beard, the heavy padding of his clothes, his breath, full of garlic and spirits . . . none of it felt like her husband. But it was, no doubt about that. Something in her squirmed to get away; another part wanted to press against him and jump up and down in delight.

The two urges seemed to cancel each other out, and left her uncomfortably neutral. She let him kiss her. She held onto him. And then she remembered how angry she was with him, and pulled away.

'So you're home?' she asked. She had to say something. Anything, while she got her thoughts in order.

'Just for an hour,' he declared. As she let him go, he threw off his coat and moved immediately to their steamer trunk in the corner, where the rest of his clothes were packed. He pulled out drawers and flung their contents on the bed, sorting through until he found what he wanted. His back was to her, and for a moment all she wanted to do was kick his bottom.

'An hour? An *hour*?'

'Now, don't be like that,' he said, not turning around. He grunted with satisfaction as he found some heavy socks. 'It's a great story, and there's still so much more to come of it.' He untangled a sheaf of paper from his pocket and handed it to her, glancing up with a bright blue eye. Even with the beard, he was good looking. Reassuring. If only he would stay! If he could explain why he'd taken credit for her stories, and stayed, maybe she could go back to loving him as she had.

She put the papers down on the small table by the window, and kept watching him, searching for the man she'd fallen in love with.

'Jack,' she said. 'Look at me.'

'Hold on a minute. Ah, there they are!' He flourished a pair of long johns at her. She'd always hated them, so he'd rarely worn them since they married, but he swore they were the best in winter.

He stayed crouched down, gathering his clothes together – only the ones he wanted. The others he left strewn around.

'Jack. Why did you put your name to my stories when you sent them to Evans?'

Her voice was steady, she was pleased to note. He looked up, startled. His face shifted subtly and she realised that she'd seen that expression before. When he was at university, and hiding his journalism work from his father, his face had looked like that whenever he talked to Mr Quinn.

It was his lying face.

'I wanted to get them published,' he said. 'And you know, they're more likely to print a story from a man.'

'That's not true,' she said flatly. 'Evans only cares about the news value.'

He laughed, a shade nastily. 'Don't blind yourself to the truth. The newspaper industry is one of the tools of capitalistic patriarchy. I just did what I had to do to get the stories out there.'

Trying to blind her with politics. She stared at him. 'And all your talk about supporting my career? About women moving into journalism as professionals?'

Her breath halted; her whole body was poised, waiting. His answer was so important.

'Well, you can still do that, can't you? You *are* doing it!' He got up, moving impatiently to the door. 'I expected a better welcome than this, not to walk into an inquisition!'

'You're a liar,' she said. He stopped dead, then turned to look back at her. A flicker of alarm ran through her. He was so *big*; she had forgotten how he loomed over her, how large his hands were.

'A wife should trust her husband,' he said, trying for a light tone, but failing. There was a strange look at the back of his eyes; could he be hurt that she didn't trust him? She felt a pang of guilt, but denied it. He was the one who should be guilty.

'A husband should be trust*worthy*,' she answered.

They stared at each other for a long moment, long enough for her to hear that the bath across the corridor was filling, long enough for her to see the scars of sleeplessness and perhaps hunger in the leanness of his cheeks under the beard, the redness around his eyes – or had that been caused by too much drink?

'You promised that we would be working here together, as equals,' she said. 'Did you ever mean that?'

He relaxed, as though she'd let him off the hook. 'Of course I did! But this story – look, read it while I'm in the bath, and you'll see. It's the story of a lifetime!'

She kept looking at him, but he didn't drop his gaze. Whatever he felt, it wasn't guilt.

The bath water was turned off and a moment later Angela tapped on the door, 'Signor Jack! The bath is ready.'

'Read the story,' Jack said, and went out.

She left the clothes where he had scattered them, the drawers half pulled out, his coat puddled on the floor, and read the story.

It wasn't written, as such – it was notes only, but complete notes that would take her perhaps two hours to write up into an article.

An article about smuggling – the smuggling of food, information and, worst, arms, across the front line. Or, rather, *around* the front line, through neutral countries that were supposedly staying out of hostilities, but that allowed arms runners and black marketeers free rein through their territories – indeed, often helped with visas and passports and customs stamps.

How far had Jack travelled in the past month? By the look of his notes, across half a continent.

It was a good story. Not earth-shattering – she'd be very surprised indeed if the Allied powers didn't know about all this – but a very good news story. And, clearly, there was more to find out. Who on the Allied side was co-operating, for example.

Reluctantly, she realised that Jack did have to leave again. That if she were following this story, nothing would dissuade her from going back.

But still, an *hour*! And just because this was a good story, that didn't excuse him lying to both her and Evans. Or stealing her work. That was misrepresentation at the best, outright theft at the worst.

It took her ten minutes to read the notes, then she put them down and absentmindedly began to pick up Jack's clothes from the floor, to slide them back into drawers. By the time she realised what she was doing, the room was tidy again. Why had she done that? She should have made him do it!

He came in, clean and dressed, rubbing his wet hair with a towel. It was shaggy, as shaggy as the beard, but it suited him. She looked at him calmly, but with a deep anger still smouldering inside.

'Well?' she said. 'I've read the notes. I can see you're going back.'

'The skipper wants to catch the tide.' He checked his watch. 'I only have another twenty minutes.' He glanced suggestively at the bed and cocked an eyebrow at her. How dare he.

'Not a chance, buster. I want an explanation that I can believe about why you stole my work.'

'Oh, for God's sake, what does it matter?' he cried out in exasperation. 'We're *married*. My success is your success! You should be glad I'm making a name for myself.'

'Off *my* stories. I counted the column inches. My stories had twice the space of yours. Is that why you did it?'

His mouth was set tight, and he glanced again at the bed, as if weighing up whether he had a chance of talking her into making love. He gave a little shrug, more a settling of the shoulders, giving up that idea. 'The truth is, the world isn't ready for female war correspondents.'

'No excuses. Why lie to me? Why lie to Evans?'

'Figure it out for yourself,' he snapped. 'If you won't accept my company here, I'm going to grab something to eat.'

'Aren't you going to write your story?' She couldn't believe that he wouldn't take the chance to get it written and sent off to Britain. He hesitated, abruptly uncertain.

'Well, I thought you could . . .'

'You thought I could write it for you. And send it off under your name.'

The anger was getting closer and closer to the top. Building. She had once seen a gum tree go up in a bushfire, and she was afraid that if she let the smallest spark of anger get loose, she would go the same way, in a conflagration that lit up the sky.

Jack was suddenly serious, speaking like the man she'd known for so long. 'This is an important story, Bec. Important for the war effort. I don't have time to write it up now. I have to be on that boat in seventeen minutes. I *have* to be, or we only get half the story. I'm asking you, not as your husband but as a colleague – write that story up for me. Be my sub-editor.'

She wanted to fling the sheaf of papers back into his face, but she was a journalist first and foremost, and it was her duty, no way out of it, to write that story.

'All right,' she said. 'But the next time you get back . . .'

'We'll have to have a talk?' he asked, a glint of humour showing through, an invitation to her to smile back at him, to melt into his arms again, as she always had.

'Yes,' she said, not smiling. 'If I'm still here.'

She had never understood murderous desire before, but it was as though everything he had done since he walked in had been designed to inflame her; as though he were deliberately causing an estrangement between them. Yet she knew him well enough to know that wasn't true. He was just being what Jack had always been.

It was she who had changed; partly because she had discovered some truths about him she hadn't known, and partly because living without him, working on her own and with Sandro, had made her more independent, more likely to question. Jack had always relied on her never questioning him. It was a shame she'd only figured that out now.

He kissed her cheek and she let him, holding still.

'I'll telegraph you if I can, to let you know I'm all right.'

'I'd appreciate that,' she said.

Just outside the door, he turned back.

'If you want to go to London, or even back to Sydney, I'd understand,' he said. Clearly he thought he was being magnanimous.

'How kind of you,' she said with dreadful courtesy. 'Have a safe trip.'

She closed the door in his face.

•

Should she tell Nonna Rosa and Sandro about Jack's – well, visit was the kindest word to use. She didn't want to. Wanted to ignore it, thrust it down into the past and go on as though it had never happened. She had written up the story and handed it to the guard at the base for the outgoing mail, as usual. She hoped the censor didn't chop it to pieces. She would send another copy through the Italian mail, just in case. It was a good story, and worth reporting.

Worth Jack being away. She could admit that. She could let go of any resentment she felt about his absence, because it *was* an important story.

But her anger over him stealing her stories had grown dramatically. *Figure it out for yourself,* he had said, as though any man would have done the same. But she didn't believe that. Her father wouldn't have, nor her brothers. Nor Sandro.

Had she just experienced the end of her marriage?

Walking up the hill from the base, heading for Nonna Rosa's out of habit, she could feel nothing but a kind of blank fear. Marriages were for life. That was God's law, and she would not, could not, go against it. As long as both she and Jack lived, they were married. But relationships . . . relationships could and did end. Look at Louise Mack, who had lived apart from her husband for years before his death. She'd been shunned for it by polite society, but she'd built up her own set of friends, mostly in the women's movement. Of course, Louise had also been known to take lovers, so the comparison wasn't complete. Rebecca wouldn't do that. Couldn't. An image of Sandro sped across her mind, but she shook it away. Even if *she* could bring herself to, *he* wouldn't.

On an impulse, she veered uphill from Nonna Rosa's and went to the little church in which she'd first met Sandro.

It was quiet, as it had been then. Morning Mass well over, midday Mass an hour away. She knelt in the Madonna chapel and bowed her head on her hands, and for a long moment merely existed. Not praying, or thinking; just being.

She raised her head and looked at the Virgin Mary's face. So patient, so loving. Without trying to make a decision, she knew she had. When Jack came back she would try to resolve their differences. Try to create a happy, harmonious home. But she wouldn't have children with him. Her whole body rejected the idea. Not now. Not yet. Not until she was sure they could be settled and happy together.

Perhaps it was hypocritical of her to continue to use contraception, which was forbidden by the Church, and still cling to the Church's other teachings. But if she'd learned anything in the women's movement, it was that women's bodies were a battlefield over which men wanted control. Contraception, her mother had taught her, was a woman's right. And it wasn't forbidden in the Bible; only by the Fathers of the Church. Oh, this was a decision she'd made long ago – no need to go over it all now.

But for the first time she wondered why Jack had encouraged her to use contraception. *He* had said that it would be bad for her career to have children before she was established; which was true. Now it was clear that he didn't give a tinker's cuss about her career – so, what was his real motive? So *he'd* be free to gallivant all over the world without a care?

Highly likely. All the more reason not to have children with him, just yet.

She prayed for the ability to forgive; but anger stayed tight under her breastbone all the while, and she knew that it would be there until Jack came home and they fought it out properly.

•

Nonna Rosa's smelled good, welcoming, with coffee and red gravy the dominant scents. It was empty. Nonna Rosa was at the market, probably.

Rebecca had missed the morning newspaper meeting, but the papers had been left for her. Should she tell Sandro about Jack?

223

Sandro came in from the courtyard with an armload of wood, and smiled at her, then looked more closely. He put the wood down, and said, 'Are you all right?'

The concern in his voice unlocked the tears she hadn't been able to shed. She just stood there, tears welling up and falling. He came over and took her by the shoulders.

'What's the matter? *Cara*, what is it?'

'Jack,' she said. 'He came back and we had a fight and now he's gone again.'

She hiccupped as the tears took control. He pulled her into his shoulder and let her weep. He was in shirtsleeves, not even a waistcoat, so she was immediately conscious of the heat of his body through his shirt. Her body split in two, it seemed; one half crying inconsolably, the other aware of his heat, his strength, the smell, so different from Jack's that morning, of clean, washed male. His hands were on her back, rubbing comfort into her. He felt so *good*.

As that thought hit her, she pulled back and scrubbed at her face with both hands. She couldn't afford to let herself feel anything for any other man. Not now, when things were so precarious.

'He just lost his temper and walked out?'

'No, no,' she said, searching blindly for a handkerchief in her purse. Sandro handed her a napkin, and she took it thankfully, wiping her tears away. She could see her own handkerchief now, and she turned her back to him politely and blew her nose on it.

'He was going anyway – following the story.'

He guided her to a chair and found some coffee for her in the kitchen, then sat and listened as she described – very sparsely – what had happened.

'But you asked him about stealing your stories? About why?'

224

'He said, "Figure it out for yourself."' She paused. 'He was very annoyed with me for not trusting him.'

Sandro grunted. She realised with a shock that he was angry; blazingly angry. It set his eyes alight and tightened his mouth; he looked dangerous. It warmed her that he could feel so strongly on her behalf, but she stopped herself. She couldn't think like that. Must *not* think like that.

'What are you going to do?'

She shrugged and for a moment thought, *I'm turning into an Italian*.

'I've written his story and sent it off. It's a good story, Sandro, and one that needs to be told.' She outlined the content to him, and he nodded. 'So, I'll just keep going as normal, here,' she ended. 'After he comes back – *if* he comes back . . . or after the war . . . we'll have to regroup and try to live happily together.'

He sat back. 'Yes,' he said, quite formally. 'Yes, of course, that's what you must do.'

Their eyes met. A long quiet moment passed, and she saw in his face pain and frustration and the determination not to touch her. Tears rose in her eyes again, and she dashed them away.

'There's nothing else *to* do, is there?' she asked. The centre of her chest was hard, as though her heart had been squeezed into a solid mass. She dragged in a breath, and let it out again.

'No. Nothing else.' His expression softened. 'But if you need *anything*, ever . . .'

'Thank you. It's good to have the support of a colleague.' She used the word deliberately, to set up a barrier as much for herself as for him, but it hurt her when he flinched at it, and she rushed on to add, 'And a good friend.'

Before he could answer, the door opened on a gust of cold air and Nonna Rosa walked in, laden with string bags of onions.

Sandro jumped up to help her, and the moment, whatever it had been, was over.

•

Nonna Rosa sent Sandro to tap a barrel of wine in the cellar and fill some carafes, while she and Rebecca cut crosses in the bottoms of chestnuts and put them to soak in hot water.

A nice, clean job, which gave her a chance to collect her thoughts and pack away her disappointment and anger with Jack, and all her other unnamed feelings for Sandro. Nonna Rosa glanced at her from time to time, but said nothing.

A clatter of glass roused her as Sandro came up the stairs. He smiled at her as he passed to put the tray of carafes on the serving table. Nonna Rosa cleared her throat and spoke, for once, in English.

'So, has Sandro told you his news?'

'Nonna, there's no news—'

'Yes, there is news. Of course it is news when a young man is formally offered a bride.'

A bride. Natalia. Rebecca was surprised to feel her hands go cold. She put the chestnut she was holding into the warm water. Ripples went out from it, as though she had trembled.

Sandro cast his eyes up to heaven and tucked the tray under his arm, coming over to the counter and leaning on it.

'I haven't been "offered a bride",' he said with exasperation.

'The negotiations have begun,' Nonna Rosa pronounced.

'I am not interested in getting married at the moment,' Sandro said.

'Natalia Fabrini is a good girl. With a good *dote*. And the shop to inherit after her father has passed.'

It was impossible to tell what Nonna Rosa was thinking. She said all the things you would expect an Italian *nonna* to say, but did she mean them? Rebecca couldn't tell, but she was sure that Nonna Rosa had brought this up because of the way Sandro had smiled at her. So, who was being warned here? Sandro? Or herself?

She took a deep breath. 'Natalia is a lovely girl. You could do a lot worse.'

Nonna Rosa regarded her with dour approval. Sandro looked at her with something very like hurt in his eyes.

'A man isn't meant to be alone for his whole life,' she added. There. That should be clear enough.

'Fine.' His voice was tight. He tapped the tray against the counter, one two, and was suddenly serious. 'I'll marry when I'm good and ready, ladies. *Capisce?*'

Nonna Rosa smiled, not quite sourly.

'*Si, Don Alessandro*,' she said. '*Capisco*.'

He nodded in mock authority, and ran lightly down the cellar steps for another load. Rebecca kept cutting chestnuts.

'He's all right, that one,' Nonna Rosa said in Italian. 'Better man than his father.'

Rebecca wasn't touching that with a ten-foot pole. But she wasn't above poking Nonna Rosa with one.

'And his grandfather?'

For the first time since they'd met, Nonna Rosa laughed out loud, a joyous laugh.

'Oh, Carlo! He thought he was a man, and he was good at some things . . .' She cast a look full of insinuation at Rebecca, and Rebecca's lips twitched. 'But in other things . . .' She shrugged. 'No head for business, but he wouldn't take orders from a woman.'

That snagged on her just-buried anger with Jack. 'Some men are like that.'

'Si. He took his sons to America so he wouldn't have to take any more orders.'

Sandro's head appeared as he climbed the stairs. His face was shocked.

'Nonna? Nonno left you? I didn't know that.'

'You must have known!'

'No,' he said simply. He perched on a stool next to the counter and laid his full tray on the countertop. The wine gleamed richly red in the carafes; the sky was growing dark as clouds gathered outside, and the glass picked up the flames from the lanterns already lit on the walls.

'He was dead when you were three,' Nonna Rosa mused. 'You don't remember him?'

Sandro shook his head. 'Only photos. Of you and him, here. Of your wedding day.'

She grimaced. 'Your father, he always liked things to be happy, no fuss, no arguing. Like *his* father. I suppose he thought it was a nicer story, without your nonno leaving.'

'Why didn't you go with him?' Sandro asked. 'Why not come to America?'

There was such pain in his voice, it made Rebecca want to hug him.

Nonna Rosa snorted. 'I wasn't asked.'

She grabbed the big bowl of chestnuts and dumped them in a colander in the sink, and then spread them out on a baking tray and slid it into the oven, slamming the door closed behind it.

When she straightened up, she rolled her eyes at the two staring at her. '*Madonna mia*, such long faces! I wasn't asked because he knew I would say no. This is my home. *Fine.*'

Rebecca thought Sandro might have said something else, but the door opened and the first of the lunch customers arrived.

From now on, she wasn't welcome behind the counter. She wondered, as she took off her apron and sat down at the journalists' table, why she felt as though she were leaving something precious behind.

23

There was a telegram from her editor the next morning. He would have received her story on the shelling of Strettabaia by now.

NOT BAD STOP SOMETHING BIGGER NEXT TIME MORE SHIPS IN
IT STOP EVANS

Something bigger. She was filled with rage. The death of a little girl, the destruction of a whole village and the life of the people who lived there, that wasn't *big* enough. No doubt he would love Jack's story, with its political implications.

They would call her sentimental. All those men, all those 'objective' reporters out there, Christy included. They would say, 'Reporters can't get involved. We just report the facts.'

This was her vocation, as well as her war work. And for the sake of every girl in the world who might like to be a journalist, of every woman who wanted to stop writing about fashion and hairstyles, and engage with meatier stories, she had to succeed.

She *had* to. She was her mother's daughter in this, at least: she didn't give up. No matter what.

She needed a *big* story.

•

At Nonna Rosa's, half an hour later, she strapped on her apron and picked up the big knife, to cut up preserved peaches for the dessert. Nonna Rosa was seasoning the pasta sauce, pork and veal mince in tomato with basil and thyme.

'They call it Bolognese sauce in America, but we have been making it here for hundreds of years,' she sniffed. She moved to the big counter and started to make the pasta – a mound of flour into which she cracked an egg and began to knead.

'I need a big story, Nonna,' Rebecca said. 'And I think you can give me one.'

Nonna Rosa looked sideways at her. 'No story from me,' she said.

'No story about smuggled information?'

'*Niente*.'

'No story about keeping open an intelligence corridor to behind enemy lines?'

'How many people you want killed for your story, heh?' Nonna glared at her. Rebecca was unrepentant. She didn't owe Nonna anything. She'd more than paid for her Italian lessons by the work she'd done, and Nonna had her own reasons for everything she did. She'd done Rebecca no favours.

'So, give me something else.'

'I'll see,' Nonna Rosa said. That was all, but that was enough. They worked together in amicable silence for another fifteen minutes before Nonna rolled her dough in a damp cloth and put it near the stove to rest. 'That Marcio Fabrini, he's increased Natalia's *dote*,' she said. 'He surely wants Sandro for his son-in-law.'

'Sandro says he doesn't want to get married.'

'Hmm. Maybe. She's there with him, every afternoon. She's a pretty girl.'

'What does Natalia think about all this? Anyone asked her?'

Nonna Rosa looked thoughtful. 'I don't know.'

The last of the peaches was sliced into the baking dish, ready for the covering of oats and honey and butter. Rebecca washed the knife, dried it, and placed it on the counter before she spoke.

'Do you want him to marry her? Stay here, in Brindisi, with you?'

Nonna Rosa smiled, and her expression was unreadable.

'Do *you*?' Nonna countered.

'It's nothing to do with me.'

'No?'

'I have a husband, Nonna. What Sandro does or doesn't do isn't my concern.'

'Hmm. So, I will ask differently. Do *you* think Sandro should marry Natalia?'

Annoyed, pushed well past any decent reticence, she snapped, 'No. The girl has a mind like a day-old chick. Sandro is far too intelligent for her. The marriage would be unhappy. Is that good enough for you?'

Nonna Rosa smiled again, this time with satisfaction. '*Si*.'

•

That night, she sat at the journalists' table, but only Christy Nolan arrived. She had forced herself to put all that she knew about him to one side, and had discovered that it was almost easy

232

to treat him as a friend. After all, they hadn't delivered any solid proof to Commander Warren; they could have misinterpreted perfectly innocent journalistic activities. At least, that's what she would try to believe.

'Lemaitre and Coates are off to Rapallo, though I doubt me they'll get there in time. Still and all, they might pick up some crumbs of stories.'

'Rapallo?'

'Aye. Their editors sent them – apparently they've announced a conference of the Allied powers. You didn't get wind of it?'

God*dammit*. Her editor asks her for something 'bigger' but doesn't bother to tell her about the biggest story of the month. Her discomfort about Christy's situation disappeared, dissolved in annoyance.

'No use to me.' She brazened it out. 'I'm not allowed in press conferences, remember?'

He harumphed a little, perhaps with laughter, and looked at her with bright blue eyes. Before he could say something that would annoy her further, she jumped in. 'Why aren't you there?'

'My paper has a Roman correspondent. He was closer.'

It was odd, dining alone with a man, especially a man she couldn't trust. She'd never done so before with anyone but Jack. And Sandro, she supposed, but those had been working meals, and not in public.

Tenente Somma, the young officer who had insulted her on her first night here without Jack, was glaring from his table. She tried not to catch his eye, but every nerve on that side of her body was electric with his gaze. When he got up to come over, she pushed back a little from the table, as though she felt the need to run.

But Sandro appeared, blocking access to their table.

'No, lieutenant. Not now, not here,' he said quietly.

The whole room was looking at them. The Australians were out on patrol, and there were no British; it must be the formal mess night for them. Only Italians and Frenchmen.

'She degrades her husband!' the *tenente* hissed.

'Her husband is the one to decide that, and to upbraid her for it if he wants to,' Sandro said quietly. Good Lord! How *could* he? He sounded like the worst of men. Surely he didn't *believe* it? 'You know I'm right,' he said. The *tenente* paused, uncertain. She risked a look at his face. It was rigid with distaste.

Her heart was thumping and her cheeks were aflame. Christy just looked amused, and she wanted to hit him.

'She degrades women!' the *tenente* announced.

'Well, she's not degrading *your* women, so it's none of your business, is it?' Sandro prodded. 'Sit down and I'll bring you an aperitif.'

'That's right, lad,' Christy said in terribly accented Italian. 'Off you go and settle down. I'm a friend of her husband's, too.'

'Oh!' the *tenente* said. 'Excuse me.'

All his anger had vanished. Meekly, he went back to his seat and Sandro brought him a drink. Murderous with rage, she glared at Christy.

'Ah, don't you put a curse on me with those blue eyes!' he said. 'Begorrah, it's not my fault the young feller-me-lad thinks he's livin' in the Dark Ages.'

She closed her eyes and opened them again. 'Next time,' she said through clenched teeth, 'I'm going to tell him where he can put his ideas about women.'

Christy laughed, a great shout of laughter. 'Oh, lass, you deserve better than that spalpeen Jack Quinn!'

She thought so, too, if he'd made friends with idiots like that Italian *tenente*.

As she walked out the door on her way home, she became aware of a small huddle of men on the corner. Christy, behind her, chuckled and touched her arm to guide her to a different route.

'What's happening?' she asked, reporter's curiosity roused. There were noises: thuds, grunts, harsh whispered encouragement. The huddle of men shifted and parted, showing two men throwing punches. One was tall, effortless and tight in his moves; the other, looser and less certain.

'Oh, looks to me like Sandro's just sorting out that Tenente Somma,' Christy said.

'Because of me?' she cried. 'Oh, no, we have to stop them!'

She moved forward, but Christy pulled her back. 'He won't thank you for interfering, lass. He's been itching to lay into him all night.'

The taller man threw a one–two combination that reminded her vividly of Sandro hitting the lemon-tree branches. She had known it was him, of course; even in the shadowy street, the way he moved was unmistakable. Another punch. The other man – Somma – went down and stayed down.

His friends crowded around him. They didn't seem to be angry with Sandro – one of them slapped him on the back and another shook his hand. Men were very strange; she would never understand their enthusiasm for violence.

Sandro raised a hand to the men and came back towards Nonna Rosa's, stopping dead when he saw the two of them standing, watching.

He was bleeding from the lip, and he had a bruise mushrooming on his cheekbone. But he grinned.

'Evening,' he said. He looked at her with dark-enlarged eyes, and she moved away from Christy towards him.

'You're a fool,' she said, but her voice didn't come out hard, as she'd intended. He smiled in a way she had never seen from him, tender and satisfied all at once.

'I enjoyed that,' he said. 'Goodnight.'

'Goodnight, Sandro,' she said.

Christy walked her all the way home, and she was glad of it as she heard Somma and his friends stumble off into the dark. Even knowing what Christy was, she felt safe with him.

'There'll be talk about this,' she said at the gate. 'Scandal.'

Christy patted her shoulder. 'Don't blame the boy too much, Rebecca. He's got enough troubles with that hand of his. I'm thinking he wanted to prove he was just as capable of fighting as any of them.'

'Yes,' she said, grateful that he hadn't seen below the surface. 'I won't say anything else to him.'

'Ah, you're a grand lass,' he said, and tipped his hat to her before moving off into the night.

As she brushed her hair before bed, she thought that Jack would never have challenged Somma like that. He would have laughed it off, and expected her to do the same.

She was ashamed that she liked Sandro's way better.

24

Coates and Lemaitre were still away in Rapallo, so it was just Rebecca and Christy at the morning newspaper reading at Nonna Rosa's. She turned immediately to the casualty list, as she did every morning, but there was no mention of Linus.

This was the worst moment of the day, looking in the papers and not finding his name. A relief, but it also prolonged the torture of not knowing. Every morning she imagined him dead, or worse, still lying wounded, dying slowly in the desert heat, alone.

Her letter to her parents would still be on its long way to Australia, but she knew they would have telegraphed her if the Army had sent them any news. So they must be living in this same terrible suspense.

She clasped her hands in her lap to stop them trembling, and Sandro must have seen, because he came over and poured her a cup of coffee, which he didn't normally do.

'No news?' he asked. She shook her head and took the coffee cup.

'No news is good news,' Christy said, but she knew that wasn't true. The longer he was missing, the more likely it was that he was dead.

The door swung open as Christy was handing her the Bari paper. Four *carabinieri* at the door, Commander Warren leading them inside. Her breath caught and she looked instinctively at Sandro. His face reflected none of her ambivalence; he was alert and eager.

Had Warren brought the *carabinieri* now so she could see the effects of her actions? She wasn't sure if that was fairness or cruelty.

As Warren and the police came in, Christy jumped up from his chair and looked around – but there were two more policemen coming in from the courtyard. Rebecca sat still, so tense she almost trembled. Sandro was beside the counter; he stepped aside to let the *carabinieri* past. Nonna Rosa was behind it, watching, impassive.

Warren stood, waiting.

Christy looked at her, sitting there so unsurprised, and his mouth twisted. 'So, you turned me in, did you?'

'We intercepted the last packet you sent to Albania,' Warren said.

'Know what was in it?' Christy challenged her. Silently, she shook her head.

'Details of the next convoy to leave Taranto,' Warren said. 'Instructions on the best place to ambush those ships. Ships carrying civilians.' No mention of Fessenden, whatever or whoever that was.

Christy ignored him, looking instead at Rebecca.

'I found out about you,' he said. 'Your grandparents were Irish. How can you work with the British now, after what they

238

did at the Easter Rising?' His Irish accent was stronger than ever, but he showed no trace of shame. Of course not. In his mind, he was a patriot. And maybe he was, for Ireland. Maybe the destruction of Britain and every one of its citizens was a price he would pay, to have Ireland free.

'My brother is fighting on the Somme,' she said, standing up and facing him down. 'Another brother is in Egypt. Damn you and all your bloody plans.' She meant 'bloody' in every sense of the word.

Sandro came forward. 'You sent information so that Italian ships would be torpedoed, no? So that Italians – *Italians*, not British, would drown.' Deliberately, he spat in Christy's face. Rebecca swallowed at this show of raw enmity.

Christy swung at him, but the *carabinieri* had been closing in, and they grabbed him.

'Coward,' Sandro said. 'Hiding here while better men die.'

Rebecca felt tears rise, too hot, her throat too tight to say anything.

Christy stood still, each arm held by an officer, and wiped the spit off his cheek on his shoulder. He raised his chin defiantly.

'My cousin's boy was one of the rebels at Dublin Post Office,' he said. 'Where were your tears when he was shot like a dog? What do you think *that* felt like, eh?'

'You'll find out,' Warren said, and nodded to the *carabinieri* to lead him away. Sandro pulled his camera out and took a shot. The *carabinieri* froze, looking proud. He took another, with Christy scowling but powerless, and then Warren jerked his head to the door, and they left.

'You can't use those,' he said to Sandro. 'We're keeping this quiet.'

'I won't use them *yet*,' Sandro replied. Warren nodded, and followed the *carabinieri* to a closed carriage outside. No march down to the prison; this was secret.

Rebecca waited until the noise of the carriage wheels faded away into the general bustle of the streets, then sat down, shaking. She couldn't help but imagine: the imprisonment, the interrogation, which wouldn't be gentle, the trial . . . the end. Treason was a hanging offence. She had condemned Christy to death. He had condemned himself, she told herself, but it didn't make her feel any better.

Nonna Rosa brought over a pot of coffee and sat, an almost unheard of event.

'You did this?' she asked Rebecca.

'We did,' she answered. 'Mostly Sandro.' He sat beside her on the bench. Nonna Rosa looked at him, and nodded, then poured them coffee.

'Drink. After a while, it will be easier,' she said with the authority of experience. The older woman held her gaze, and nodded, as if confirming her thoughts. Nonna Rosa had been responsible for the death of more than one man. No matter who you were, or what you did, war dragged you down to its level.

Rebecca drank her coffee, hand still shaking. But after a while, just as Nonna Rosa had said, the trembling stopped.

25

A crash woke her. She started upright, heart racing, and waited, hearing nothing but rain on the shutters and roof. Then a voice, moaning. A shriek. Angela's voice.

Without thinking, she grabbed her dressing gown, dragging it on and tying the belt, and slid her feet into her slippers. The house was pitch black. She fumbled her way to Jack's bedside drawer for his electric torch, and now she could hear Signor Damonica's voice, shouting.

The torch gave a blessed light, lifting the sense of being in a nightmare. She opened the door carefully, and the shouting became instantly terrifying; loud and full of the potential for violence. For a moment she wanted nothing more than to shut the door behind her and pretend she had heard nothing. But Angela was still moaning. Rebecca went out onto the landing.

Shining the torch down the stairs showed a tableau out of a melodrama: Angela slumped on the floor in her nightgown, her father standing over her, hand raised, shouting what were probably obscenities in Italian.

Rebecca was frozen in fear. Did she have the right to interfere? But Angela was a grown woman, not a child to be chastised. Thinking the word 'woman' gave Rebecca courage. Women should not be beaten by men, and the only thing that would stop it, as her mother had often said, was women rising up together to stop them.

She went down the stairs, walking heavily so he would hear her coming, her heart beating so hard it shook her whole body.

He scowled up at her, saying something she was sure meant, 'Mind your own business.' She could almost feel her mind make its adjustment to Italian.

'Signor Damonica,' she said. How weak her voice sounded, how small. She breathed deeper to strengthen it. 'Leave her be.'

'She's a whore!' he shouted. 'She has brought disgrace on me! Me! I have raised her and fed her and clothed her and now she whores herself out and disgraces me.'

'Signor Damonica . . .'

He whirled on Rebecca and raised his hand as if to strike her.

'Don't you *dare*!' she hissed. She stared him down, eye to eye, anger flooding in and replacing fear completely. She shone the torch right in his eyes. 'Don't you *dare* raise your hand to me.'

He stopped, hand up, and then retreated a little and spat on the floor at her feet to show his disgust, hand lowering. She stooped to Angela, who had a great mark across one cheek, already discolouring. As she moved, the light of the torch flickered and jumped across the room, a dizzying lightning-glance of bright followed by dark.

Angela clutched her, but she wouldn't meet Rebecca's eyes. Ashamed. Rebecca was flooded with sympathy; no doubt some sailor had seduced the poor woman. Rebecca could hardly blame her. What kind of life did she have here, stuck with a father who treated her like a servant, and no hope of a properly arranged marriage, no hope of a husband and children? Well, she would have the child, at least.

'We'll find the father, Angela,' she said. 'We can make him take care of you.'

'Ha!' Signor Damonica said. 'You'll have to go to Hell to find that one.'

Oh, no. Dead. That's why they weren't married. Compassion swept through her and she gently pushed back the hair from Angela's eyes.

'Then we'll find some other way—'

'You won't be so kind to her when you find out the truth, *donna*!' he shouted, as if she were putting on airs.

'No, Papa! Don't!' Angela shrieked.

Puzzled, Rebecca paused, her hand on Angela's arm.

'Your friend the Irishman,' he said with dreadful satisfaction. 'He's the father, and now he has gone and deserted her and left her shamed before the world!'

Rebecca drew back from Angela, just half a pace, and dropped her hand. She put the light of the torch onto Angela's face. The beam of light shook as her hand trembled.

'Angela?' she said gently.

'*Si*,' Angela whispered, hanging her head, her dark hair falling to cover her face. 'Cristiano.'

Something about that 'Cristiano' rang true. It spoke of whispered conversations in the dark, or in the back courtyard. It spoke of flirting, not whoring.

Rebecca's lips were cold. Anger at Christy blossomed in her; he had seduced as well as betrayed. But he wasn't there, so she turned it on the next most appropriate target.

'This is *your* fault,' she said with deadly quiet, facing Signor Damonica. 'If you had given Angela her dowry, as you should have, instead of keeping her here to cook and clean for you, she'd be married by now, with a husband and half-a-*dozen* children.' She could hear her voice rising, but she didn't care. 'If you'd arranged a marriage for her, as a father *should*, this would never have happened!'

Astonished, he leaned back, away from her fury. 'She's a whore!'

'It's your greed and laziness that have put her in this position!' Some part of her brain was admiring her own ability to insult him in Italian. As though a switch had been thrown, and all her hesitancy in using what she knew of the language was gone. Abruptly, she knew what had to be done.

'You are going to pay her that dowry.'

'He will never do it!' Angela wailed.

'No! Pay a whore to disgrace me—'

'Shut up. You're going to pay her that dowry, and she is going to take it to Australia.'

Both Angela and he were struck dumb.

'I will give you a letter,' she continued, now looking at Angela. 'To my mother. She will find you a job where you can keep the baby with you.'

Of course she would. She'd done it a dozen times before, for girls far less innocent than Angela. It was part of her settlement work in the slums. Their home help had always been a procession of pregnant girls, or women with a child or two at foot.

Angela dropped to the floor and grabbed Rebecca's hand, kissing it, sobbing with gratitude. It filled Rebecca with a deep disgust, but she didn't move away. These people had the Latin temperament; they couldn't help themselves.

Signor Damonica pulled at his lip, and nodded. 'Maybe, maybe,' he said. 'I'll pay for her fare.'

'You'll do more than that. You'll give her whatever she would have got from you on her marriage.'

'Why should I?'

She sighed, but she knew her part. 'If you do, I will tell everyone I have organised a good job for her in Australia. No scandal. No one need know. Buy her a ring and have her pretend to be married.' She made a face. 'Mrs Nolan. A war widow.'

'You British, you are mad. All of you. She whores and you *reward* her?'

The room was growing paler, she realised. She could see his face, a little, grey in the dawning light. She shut off the torch.

'Do you really think *she* was to blame?' In her mind's eye she saw Christy, as he had been the first day she'd met him: blue eyes bright, red hair lifted by the wind, handsome in that Irish way, and full of life. It wasn't possible that poor, dumpy, plain Angela had seduced him.

'Your friend is a sinner. A fornicator.' Signor Damonica took some comfort from that, it was clear.

All she could say was, 'Apparently so,' in English. But he caught her meaning. He glared at her.

Enough of this. Rebecca pulled her hand away from Angela, and turned and went upstairs, not giving the woman another look. She had reached her limit of kindness.

Inside her room, the door locked tight, she paced, back and forth, unable to sit or lie, unable to concentrate enough even to get dressed. Poor Angela. Should she tell her the truth? Surely it was better if she and the child never knew it was the offspring of a traitor? Or would Angela prefer to know that Christy hadn't abandoned her voluntarily? Would she bring up the child with stories of its father being an Irish patriot?

It wasn't something she was calm enough to decide now. She should write that letter.

My dear Mamma,

I hope you and Dad are well. I pray every day to hear news of Linus; please telegraph me if you hear anything, anything at all.

I have a sad case here I hope you will help with, Mamma. This girl, Angela, is the daughter of my landlord, and has been seduced and abandoned by an older man, and is now expecting.

Of course, I knew you would be willing to help her, and so I send her to you. I have advised her to travel as Mrs Nolan, that being the name of the man involved – an Irish journalist here reporting for the Dublin Times. *There is more to the story, but that will have to wait until we see each other once again. I look forward to the day we can sail back to Australia across seas clear of submarines and mines. After the war . . .*

Jack is off in Albania in hot pursuit of a story, so I am keeping the flag flying here – at least I am reporting on war news, not on fashion!

Please give my love to Dad.

love,

Rebecca

Angela could explain the rest, if she could find someone to translate. Rebecca addressed the envelope in capital letters, to make it easier for Angela to read.

That task done, she realised with dismay that she had unhoused herself. She couldn't stay here without another woman in residence as a chaperone. There were rarely male guests, but she really did not want to live alone under the same roof as Signor Damonica. Even without the likelihood of gossip, her flesh cringed at the thought.

Dragging their big steamer trunk out of the corner, she packed, leaving out only what she would wear that day. She pulled out a dark brown winter walking dress, warm and subdued to suit her mood, and changed, then thrust the nightgown, dressing gown and slippers into the top drawer of the trunk, along with her hairbrush and toothbrush. After Jack had left the last time, she had buried everything belonging to him in the bottom drawer of the trunk, unable to look at anything that reminded her of him.

Except for the little icon. It was a diptych, a bit like a large square locket, cased in wood, with an image of the Madonna and Child on one side, and a small crucifix on the other. Jack had bought it for her in Rome, at a stall outside St Peter's, on their way here. She had loved it then, and loved it still, despite everything. She slipped it into her purse.

It was still early, but she couldn't bear the room any longer. Since Jack had left the last time, it had become a reproach, not a refuge, and she discovered that she was glad to have an excuse to move.

Her instinct was to slide out of her door quietly and creep down the stairs, but she didn't have anything to be ashamed of and she was damned if she was going to act as if she did. So, she walked down in her normal way, but she was grateful beyond belief that neither Angela nor her father was visible.

The rain was over, and the high cloud was beginning to clear. The air smelled of the sea, a curiously calming scent.

Early as it was, she knew Nonna Rosa would be there, preparing the slow-cooked ragu for the night's pasta. Sure enough, the door of the restaurant was ajar, and the scent of wood smoke and cooking tomatoes and garlic wafted out.

The smell of food made her feel sick, and that made her think of morning sickness, and that made her push the door open a little hard than was necessary.

Nonna Rosa looked up from behind the counter as she entered. She was cutting onions; as Rebecca approached her, their sharpness cut across the heavy smell of the garlic and seemed to clear her head.

'I need somewhere to live,' she said in Italian. 'Not a pensione. An apartment, or a small house.'

Whatever switch had been thrown in her head the night before seemed to have stuck in place. The Italian she had been so hesitant to use now rolled off her tongue.

Nonna Rosa inspected her closely, but asked no questions. 'I know somewhere. Come and help me, and then I will take you.'

She wasn't sure why Angela's plight had affected her so. Perhaps it was a reminder of how alone she herself was, in a foreign country, without her husband and family. Whatever the reason, it was a relief to pull off her gloves and hat and jacket, put on the big apron and settle into the familiar processes. She shelled beans and cubed speck, and made *cotoletta* – breaded veal – dipping the thin slices into flour, then egg and then into breadcrumbs as if she were making lamb cutlets at home.

Nonna Rosa moved the big pot of sauce off the stove and closed the flue, banking the fire. They washed their hands, took off their aprons, put on their hats and gloves and jackets.

'I know a place,' Nonna Rosa said as they went out the back way, past the privy and the garbage cans. 'Small, but clean. Dannillo Bartolacci's wife was in it, but she went home to her mother's to have the baby.'

248

Babies again. Everyone was having babies except her. So often in the past, she had yearned to be pregnant, had wished with all her heart that Jack hadn't decided against children just yet. Now she couldn't be more relieved that she wasn't than if she had never been married.

Around a corner, up a steep flight of steps. A tiny terrace house, plastered the warm cream of most houses in Brindisi. A stream of sunlight broke through the clouds to hit the front door, and she hoped it was an omen. Nonna knocked at the house next to it and spoke rapidly to the woman who answered.

'*Si, si,*' she said, disappeared for a moment, and returned with a key.

'*Grazie, signora,*' Rebecca said. The woman waved her thanks away with a toothless smile.

'Better it not be empty,' she said in Salentino so accented Rebecca could scarcely understand her.

Nonna unlocked the door and ushered her in.

Small, yes. Possibly the smallest living room she'd ever been in, but big enough for two armchairs and a tiny table.

Beyond, a passage and a stairway, and then a kitchen, longer than the living room but no wider. An open hearth, not a stove, no taps over the sink of course, free-standing cupboards, an oil lantern on the mantelpiece. There was a back door, no doubt leading to the privy and the pump.

Turn again and up the stairs. The top floor was one room containing a double bed, old, wooden, sagging, but topped with a blindingly white coverlet. Another bed, for a child, was positioned near the chimney front. No wardrobe, but there was space for her trunk, if it could be got up those winding stairs.

She sighed with satisfaction. Solitude.

'Yes,' she said. 'How much?'

It turned out to be only a little more than she was paying Signor Damonica. More than worth it.

'You pay Signora Carlona next door. Later will do. I'll send someone to get your trunk,' Nonna Rosa said, seeming to know that Rebecca didn't want to go back, and with a lack of curiosity that deserved an answer.

'Angela is leaving,' she said. 'I can't live there with just Signor Damonica.'

Nonna Rosa nodded, eyes sharp. 'Leaving?'

'She's going to Australia. I'm giving her a reference.'

A quick, unkind smile went across Nonna Rosa's face. 'Wants to get out before she starts showing, eh? Good idea.' Rebecca flinched, and Nonna shrugged. 'I was a midwife. You get to know the signs. But don't worry. There's no talk about her yet. Serve that father of hers right if there were.'

'Angela—'

'You won't find me bringing a woman down, especially not that girl. She's had enough trouble with that scum of a father.'

They went down the stairs, and the back of Nonna Rosa's head gave Rebecca the courage to say, 'Why do you hate each other so?'

At the bottom, Nonna Rosa smiled grimly. 'We were on different sides during the last war.'

That was all, but what did it mean? Surely she hadn't fought? But it was clear that was all the information Nonna Rosa was going to share.

•

Alone in the tiny place, Rebecca took off her hat and gloves, but not her jacket. The small room was freezing. So much had happened: Jack, Christy, Angela, the animosity of the men of

Brindisi, even her feelings for Sandro, and all of it wrong, all of it battering at her. It was exhausting. Again, she wondered about going home. Just giving up and living an average, ordinary life back among her family and friends. It would be so easy to give up and surrender to the tiredness that pulled her down.

She went out to the kitchen and laid the fire with newspaper, kindling and wood that had been left ready beside the fireplace. She always carried matches. That was for Jack, who was a pipe smoker and constantly mislaid his matches.

Thinking of him, wondering where he was and if he was still angry with her, the match burned her fingers and dropped into the fireplace, but the flame vanished before it hit the paper, and she had to start again.

She *would* start again, here, and build the life of a journalist working on her own. When Jack came back – well, they would deal with that when it happened. But in the meantime, she had her job and she had her own home and plenty to eat, and there were millions of women who would have given their right arm for that. And she would stay out of the Women's Pages, if she had to emulate Jack and go behind enemy lines to do it.

26

Sandro arrived with her trunk on a donkey cart and a couple of hefty cousins to help haul it up the stairs.

'Teamsters' Union, reporting for duty,' he said, teasing her.

She smiled back. 'Come right on in, gentlemen.'

They had to take the drawers out of the trunk first and open it up so it would slide up the narrow staircase. Afterwards, the cousins left with the price of a bottle or two of wine in their pockets, and Sandro sat at the table with a sigh.

Rebecca was glad to have him here, but she had nothing to offer him but black tea – she kept a caddy for her own use, unable to drink the tepid wash that Italians thought was tea. But there was a saucepan, and a pump in the shared courtyard out the back, and she had a little loaf of sugar tucked away in one of the trunk drawers. She brought it down and shaved some off while Sandro watched her quietly. So peaceful, this moment. Like a gift, or a promise that life would go on.

'So, new lodgings.' He sipped carefully from a chipped cup, and cast a glance up at her, curious.

She sat down and cradled her cup between her palms. It was the only warm part of her. Her chin trembled, and she bit her lip trying to stop it.

'Yes.'

'Is something wrong?'

Were all men like Christy? Degraded? Sandro was the only male she could imagine asking that question of; it would have made her father or brothers profoundly uncomfortable. *Now, now,* they would have said, *no need to talk like that.*

Sandro would tell her the truth. Those clear brown eyes were honest.

'Angela Damonica is pregnant with Christy's child.' Said straight out like that, it sounded even worse.

'Whoa,' he said, sitting back in his chair. And then sitting forward, touching her hand as it clenched the cup. 'That's – that's disgusting.'

Yes. Yes it was. Disgusting. It wasn't a word she would have expected from a man, but it was right.

'Yes.' She paused, then broke out with, 'We've condemned that child's father to death.'

'Oh, no,' he said, his mouth set but his eyes kind. 'Don't you think we're to blame in this. Christy Nolan has got what he deserved. And this child – it's all on him. He should have kept his pecker in his pants.'

She drank a little, embarrassed, but driven to know. She had to know. Had to ask. Because Jack had been away a long time, and she couldn't bear to think of him leaving bastards all over Europe. 'Are all men like that? You know, they say that men can't help themselves?'

'Any man who tells you that is just looking for an excuse.' It was a flat pronouncement, like a judge delivering a verdict.

He pushed back from the table and stood up, but there was nowhere to move in the tiny kitchen: a pace forward, one back.

'What a bastard!' he muttered. He looked down at her, and grimaced. 'Sin is sin, no matter who commits it.'

'There's an odd kind of equality,' she said, her mouth twisting awry.

'The only *real* equality,' Sandro said. There was an undertone in his voice, a kind of suppressed meaning she didn't understand.

'Sandro?'

'No real man needs to seduce a girl. I never have.' He said it shortly and to the side, but he meant it. She got up and stood before him, trying to look into his eyes. He turned his head back and met her gaze as his meaning sank in slowly.

'Never?' she whispered.

He shook his head. 'I wanted – I wanted to come to my wedding night and offer my bride the same thing she was offering me. I guess equality *is* what I wanted. To be able to say: I've been as constant as you. It's hard – of course it's hard. But any man who says he can't do it is lying to himself.'

Tears came to her eyes and she took his face between her hands, holding him fiercely.

'You're a good man, Sandro Baker,' she said. For a moment they were suspended, his skin against her palms the only point of contact. He smelled of lemons and shaving soap. A flush rose in his cheeks.

The troubled day had driven all physical awareness out of her, but her palms were warm and she felt, for that moment, alive and emotional and ready to keep on living.

His breath against her wrist was even warmer. She knew she had to put her hands down, but he was looking at her with something in his eyes. Gratitude? As though she had given him something, but she didn't know what.

He took a breath in and released it, and on the exhale they both moved back, just a little, and Rebecca dropped her hands.

'Thank you,' she said. Nodding, he went to the door. It was still so early, the street was quiet when he opened it.

'The fleet will be coming soon,' he said.

Back to normal. Right.

'I'll meet you down there.'

And he was gone. She stood watching the door, bereft. Facing the truth. She had been pretending she didn't care, that her feelings were a reaction to her anger at Jack, to her loneliness with him gone, but of course that wasn't true. She raised her hand to her face: the trace of lemon was still there, bringing back the way her pulse had jumped at the touch of his breath on her wrist; his warmth, his strength, his *maleness*. Love was supposed to feel like this. Like all of you reached out to all of him. This wasn't how she'd felt about Jack. No. She knew now that that had been desire and liking mixed up with social expectations.

Marriage was more than social expectations. It was a solemn, holy vow, for life. She made herself drop her hand and sit down at the table.

Astonishingly, the tea in her cup was still warm, although it felt like an hour since she had stood up to face him.

No matter how she felt, he was not for her. He would have some young, pure, untouched girl, who could offer him the same gift he gave her. Someone like Natalia. At the image of the two of them, pure and in love, as she and Jack had once thought themselves, she lay her head on her arms and began to cry.

27

Sandro Baker.

You're a good man, Sandro Baker.

She had named him, and as she had, all his doubts about his identity had fallen away. That name was the right name. It was as though, for the first time in his life, someone had truly seen him.

As he walked down to the harbour to get an espresso from Leon's cafe, he thought about Pascalia, the girl who had jilted him to run away with an American doughboy. She was the only girl he had ever kissed. Of course she was – they had been betrothed almost since the cradle. They had gone to school dances together, had walked down to their First Communion together, had made each other Valentine's cards. He had thought he had known her well.

But she had never looked at him like Rebecca Quinn had looked at him. She had never *seen* him; just Al, the boy she was being forced to marry.

Maybe no one had ever seen Sandro Baker before.

He was different, he knew, to when he had left home. His Italian side was stronger, but so was the American. Living here had clarified for him why he loved America. What he liked about Italy was the ability to *feel* everything as strongly as he wanted to. Except fear, of course. Italian men didn't admit to fear.

His hat almost lifted off his head with the wind, and he became aware that the weather was worsening, the winter sky presaging another storm, probably complete with sleet and hail. His pea jacket was thick, but he had left his umbrella at home. He hoped Rebecca would check the sky before she came out.

Poor Becca. That husband of hers was a real bastard, leaving her to cope with everything alone. He hadn't even joined up, although he could have. Sandro wondered if he'd boxed. As the middleweight champion for his school team, Sandro reckoned he could have taken Jack, even with the other man's advantage in height and reach. He itched to try, but he had no right. No right at all.

He turned in to the cafe and raised a hand to a table of crew from the *Regina Elena*, the Italian battleship. The cafe owner had his order ready by the time he crossed to the counter.

'*Ciao, Alessandro!*'

'*Ciao, Leon. Come va?*'

'*Sto bene, grazie.*' The everyday greeting and response was soothing, reminding him that the world went on as it always had, no matter how much his skin felt raw from touching her, no matter how much he burned inside.

The cafe was crowded, but he found a small table by the street window and sat, nursing his coffee, his rucksack with its precious camera safely between his feet. Rebecca. He was a fool to even think her name. The urge to kiss her had been so strong. Who was he kidding? Even if she had been single, he was a poor dago guy from New York. Yeah, he was trying to make it as a photographer, but anyone could see she was from money. Her clothes, her attitude, even the way she walked showed she had class.

He wouldn't have had a hope even if she had been available. From now on he must treat her like a colleague, and nothing else. It would have been easier if she wasn't so beautiful.

Someone tapped on the window, giving him a start. Rebecca. She smiled at him, although her eyes were red and her cheeks pale, and despite his resolution he smiled back, heartfelt. That beauty of hers ran more than skin deep.

He left the cafe with a light step. She was out of his reach, but he could spend time with her and learn from her and make himself a better man, and have no expectations at all.

So, he would probably get his heart broken. There were worse things.

The ships on patrol normally got back to the harbour mid-morning, and as usual they walked down to the best vantage point, Le Sciabiche promenade east of the fort. There was always a crowd of boys waiting for the ships, and a few others – sweethearts and prostitutes and, for the Italian ships, families waving tea towels.

Today it was the Australians coming back. They sailed in looking much the worse for wear, ice on their rigging, rime crusting every exposed surface, so that it almost looked like the ships had been sprinkled with sugar. The crew were in their Lammy suits, cold wet-weather gear that bulked them out like a child's toy and made them seem rather like Humpty Dumpty with a sou'-wester on.

'They look tired to death,' Rebecca said, making notes.

'The weather warning was for a gale out east last night,' Sandro said.

'Yes, I saw. The poor things.' They both checked the Harbour Master's weather noticeboard every day. It was part of the pattern of their lives, like seeing the patrols come in, and helping Nonna Rosa.

Sandro had set up his camera on one of the stone bollards; he'd found it a perfect steady surface to work from. Two shots were all he had time for, but he was ready. He got a good one of the *Parramatta* as she sailed past, the icicles on her shrouds showing up beautifully in the morning sunlight. And then, one of the crew on the *Warrego*, waving for the camera, dolled up in their Lammy suits, beards iced up. Commander Warren had agreed that his sailors could grow beards against the fierce cold, although he kept himself clean shaven – that was the way to earn men's loyalty; give them what they needed but keep yourself to a higher standard.

The ships tied up to the trot line, manoeuvring to be bow out, ready for any emergency call.

Gangplanks came down from their sterns, and crew began to file off. The sweethearts went around to the main gate, to wait for them – although it would be a long wait, because Warren insisted on the vessels being shipshape and Bristol fashion before anyone was granted leave. The ones disembarking would be walking wounded heading for the first aid station.

They walked around to the gate with the others, meeting Mark Coates and Ambroise Lemaitre on the way.

'Press conference in fifteen minutes,' Coates said.

'It can't be anything from this patrol,' Rebecca answered. 'There hasn't been time.'

Lemaitre shrugged. Sandro didn't like the way he looked at Rebecca. Assessing, like a director auditioning chorus girls. He had no idea what she thought of Lemaitre, but he hoped it wasn't good. Just because he knew *he* couldn't woo her didn't mean he wanted a slimy Frog like Lemaitre doing so. And then he laughed at himself, because Lemaitre probably thought of him as a dago.

'Have you seen Nolan recently?' Coates asked.

Rebecca bit her lip.

'Gone back to Ireland,' Sandro said, jumping in. She smiled at him.

'He didn't say anything about leaving,' Coates observed; suspicious, always suspicious, that one.

Rebecca had herself well in hand, though. 'His mother,' she said. 'Some kind of family emergency. Commander Warren let him go on the mail boat. The message came while you two were in Rapallo.'

Coates looked dissatisfied, but the gates opened for the press conference and he and Lemaitre went in.

'It's too cold to wait out here,' Sandro said to Rebecca. 'Go home and I'll find you there.'

She shook her head. Usually so neat, this morning some strands of her hair had come loose and fell around her face. He resisted the urge to stroke them back.

'I'll go to Nonna Rosa's,' she said. 'I need to work. To keep my mind off . . . things.'

'*Certo*,' he said. 'I'll meet you there.'

•

It was the British commander Commodore Kelly today. With Admiral Acton. They looked pleased with themselves all round.

'The British flotilla will be setting up a hospital here on the British base,' Kelly said. 'Fully equipped. And we will, where necessary, offer our facilities to our Italian colleagues.'

The Italian commander said, 'This generous decision by our British colleagues will relieve the pressure on our own hospital and allow collaboration on health matters for the good of all.'

They must be pleased to have something nice to announce. Well overdue, though, Sandro thought. Those poor Johnnies who had come off the ships this morning, probably with frostbite on hands and noses, would have welcomed a proper hospital.

Sandro asked for a photo and they gladly agreed, standing proudly in their dress uniforms, for once united, with none of the sniping or suspicion often seen between the navies.

Camaraderie, that was what was best about men in war. It dragged up the old disappointment in him; being rejected from the services had been hard, and it didn't get any easier, not when he was surrounded by men in uniform. There were days, when he was walking down the street, the only young man not in uniform, when the unfairness of it grabbed him by throat. Then the desire to go to the front, to share in the danger and the work that had to be done, became almost overwhelming.

'Smile!' he said, and clicked.

28

Rebecca did her rounds on her way back to Nonna Rosa's. She started at the Harbour Master's, to check the weather and the news, then moved on to the train station, where she paid her informant the few coins he expected and learned that no one exciting had arrived today on the morning train from Bari. She would go to the post office and then back to Nonna Rosa's to check the newspapers for any mention of Linus.

Just before she had come here, she had heard from her Red Cross chum Barbara that the Red Cross was spending some time and energy in trying to find soldiers who were missing in action in France; but when she went to her editor with the idea for the story, he had shaken his head. 'People have enough to bear at the moment,' he said. 'Let's not make them weep until they have to.' Now she wished she had at least researched the story, so she would know what was being done on Linus's behalf.

She was almost sure he was dead. Almost all the missing *were* dead – particularly near Beersheba, where a white-skinned man stood out. They would have heard by now if he'd been found. It was different in Europe, where an injured man who had lost his uniform jacket could be almost anyone, and be gathered up by the medics from the other side. There were so few missing men in the Sinai who turned up either injured or safe. But she couldn't let herself cry until they knew for sure; instead, she carried this knot of grief in her at all times, ready to be let loose at any news.

People have enough to bear, she thought. Let's give them some good news. Let's give them a story. But what story?

When she got to the post office, the clerk waved a telegram flimsy at her. 'Just in, signora.'

Poor Mario, no tip for him today.

She took it lightheartedly, expecting a compliment from Evans on her last story, an account of a tense submarine hunt by the *Warrego*. It was too soon for him to have got Jack's story.

DAILY HERALD BROKE IRISH SPY STORY BRINDISI STOP WHY
HAVENT I GOT IT STOP TRIAL OVER COME BACK WOMENS
PAGES WAITING STOP WAR NOT WOMENS WORK STOP EVANS

The *Daily Herald* was Mark Coates's paper.
God*dammit*.
She hurried off a reply:

WARREN PUT D NOTICE ON STOP WE UNCOVERED NOLAN STOP
STORY TO FOLLOW WITH PHOTOS OF ARREST STOP AM NOT
COMING HOME STOP QUINN

Warren couldn't prevent her publishing now.

263

She went home and wrote the story, trembling with anger and dismay. Yesterday's news. And by the time it got to Evans, last week's news. Not good enough.

She went to Nonna Rosa's, the story in an envelope.

'Is Sandro here?'

'No. He has gone somewhere.'

'I need some of his photos for a story. Where is his portfolio?'

Nonna Rosa looked at her, assessing. 'In his room.'

Defying convention, Rebecca marched up the stairs and into Sandro's room, following the scent of his shaving soap.

Neat. An unobtrusive organisation. His portfolio was on the desk. Despite her defiance, it did feel odd to be in his room. Seeing his slippers, tucked under the bed, felt very intimate.

She opened the portfolio, looking for the enlargements of the *carabinieri* taking Christy away. Part of her still found Christy's betrayal hard to believe. He had been so *nice*.

Sorting through the images took longer than she had expected. Sandro had taken more than she had known. Images of Brindisi, surprisingly beautiful. Images of townspeople. Old, wrinkled faces with gap-toothed smiles. Mothers with babies. Natalia, in the Fabrini studio, looking shy. Nonna Rosa, one hand up, turning away, but the line of her jaw and the straight line of her arm eloquent of her personality.

With each image she more fully appreciated that he was an artist. Every photograph was imbued with some element of him; compassion, maybe, for his subjects. The truth of each person shone from their eyes.

In a paper bag underneath the others, were two pictures of her.

One was when she had held the small body of the girl from Strettabaia. She couldn't look at that one. The other, she had almost forgotten he'd taken. It was in the church, the day they'd met. When she'd prayed, not knowing he was there.

Madonna mia. Her legs were shaky and she put one hand out to steady herself against the desk. This photograph was of an angel.

She didn't know how to react to it. She *wasn't* that beautiful. Pretty, yes, but not this ethereal loveliness. Was this how Sandro saw her? Or was it just a momentary trick of the light, which he had captured like the professional he was? She had been so angry that day; but who could be angry, looking at this? She had been the professional teaching the new recruit when Sandro started working with her, but looking at this – at all his photographs – she was achingly aware that he went far beyond her own capabilities in this. For the first time, her admiration for him was unrelated to his kindness, his looks, his maleness, his strength. She admired him now as she would admire any great artist; humbly and with a kind of deep yearning.

She could have looked at his work all day, but this wasn't what she had come here for.

Underneath those images were the photos of Christy being arrested. She grabbed them and pushed them into the envelope, checking to see that Sandro had written his name and the date on the back, as usual. Yes.

She went down the stairs and out quickly, raising a hand to Nonna Rosa as she went past.

'I'll be back later,' she said.

•

At the base, Commander Warren was grim-faced when he came out to the gate to see her.

265

'Don't blame me,' she said at once. 'Coates got wind of it somehow. *Your* security's to blame, not me.'

'I see.' He rubbed his eyes as if it had been a long night. 'And now?'

'And now my editor's fired me for not having the story.'

He winced.

'I told you my career was on the line, but you didn't care. Or you didn't believe me.'

'I really didn't think . . .' He looked genuinely sorry for her, but not in the least regretful.

She thrust the envelope at him. 'Here. That's *my* version. You can check it if you want, but the story's out already, so you might as well let it go.'

He took the envelope. 'I'm sorry. I'm not sure what we'll be able to release.'

'Sandro's photos?'

'Yes, probably they will be all right.'

She breathed in and let it out. 'Well, then. Go back to your ship, Commander Warren, and next time let me do my job.'

He shook his head firmly. 'No, Mrs Quinn. No. Not if it interferes with the security of my men. Nothing is more important than that.'

She had to admit that was admirable. But not to him.

Sandro, when she saw him that evening and told him the news, was appropriately annoyed that they'd been scooped. Coates smirked at them all and it gave her a good deal of satisfaction to tell him they had photographs of the arrest.

'Old news,' he said, but he looked perturbed.

He was right. Old news. They had better find some scoops of their own.

She counted the days until Jack's story reached Evans. Sure enough, nine days after she had sent it off, a telegram arrived, addressed to Jack.

GOOD STORY STOP MORE LIKE THAT STOP BIG ANNOUNCEMENT
COMING FROM NAVY IN VENICE HAVE ARRANGED TRAVEL
PASS STOP GET THERE BY 9TH INST STOP GLAD YOURE BACK
STOP EVANS

She wasn't even angry. But she wasn't going to let herself be sidelined, and discounted, and overlooked. She was damned if that big announcement would go unreported just because Jack was away. It was *imperative* that she present Evans with this story.

Today was the fifth. She had to get travel passes, which normally took at least a week, if one could get them at all. Perhaps she could use Jack's? But when she walked up to the train station, the Station Master confirmed that the travel pass he had arranged would be in Jack's name, and only Jack's. He was *desolato* that he couldn't help the signora . . . It didn't really change things; they needed two passes anyway. Sandro would want to go with her, she was sure.

She had to go elsewhere for the passes.

Nonna Rosa was stringing some peculiar-looking rhubarb. It was very thin and desiccated.

'I dried it out in summer,' Nonna said. 'It holds its flavour that way.'

She had apples in a saucepan already, cut up, with a little brown sugar. Rebecca's mouth watered. She hadn't had anything to eat that morning. Had she? No. Only some tea, before the telegram came. No wonder she was lightheaded.

'You're too pale. Eat something,' Nonna Rosa said.

Rebecca helped herself to some bread and sat at the nearest table. Bread and oil and salt; that was the stuff of life. She began to feel better. Stronger. She got up and made herself a pot of tea, then sat again.

'Rosa,' she said, and the woman looked up sharply at the change of name. Rebecca met her gaze calmly. 'You owe me. You were the one who put Jack in touch with the smugglers, weren't you?'

For a moment, Rosa just looked at her, and then she nodded.

'So, you owe me for all the weeks I haven't had a husband. Now's the time to pay back. You have to get me to Venice.'

Rosa took in a large breath and let it out through her nose. She put the knife down, wiped her hands on her apron and came around the counter to sit opposite Rebecca.

'That's a fool's errand.'

'There's a big story happening in Venice, and my editor wanted to send Jack. The travel permit is in Jack's name, and they won't let me travel on it. My editor will fire me if I don't get a good story. I need to prove that women can do this job as well as the men.'

'Faugh! I don't understand you, always trying to impress men! Just live your life, do what you want. Ignore them.'

'This *is* what I want! To be a war correspondent!'

'A man's obsession, not a woman's.'

'Like intelligence gathering?'

They locked eyes. Rosa's lips gradually curled up at the corners. She spread her hands, hunched her shoulders and wilted into an old lady, harmless and ordinary except for the spark of mischief in her eyes.

'Who, me?'

Rebecca couldn't help it: she laughed.

'Yes, you. You get correspondence from all over the Adriatic. I've seen you. You're getting information to the Italian Navy. You're getting the names of the submarine commanders and God knows what else out of Trieste and Grado.'

Rosa shrugged.

'So,' Rebecca said. 'You can get us to Venice.'

Rebecca never had been able to read Nonna Rosa's expression, and today was no different. Sitting close together at the table didn't help at all. She poured tea for both of them.

'We need travel permits,' she insisted.

Nonna Rosa took a sip of tea and made a small grimace. Rebecca pushed the pot of honey over to her and Rosa put a teaspoonful into her cup and stirred, slowly.

'What makes you think I can get them?

'Am I a fool?' Rebecca asked. 'If you wanted to, you could get them.'

Nonna Rosa sat back in her seat and looked her over carefully.

'You are not trying to prove how brave you are?'

She would need to be brave to go to Venice – the Austrians were only a few miles away from it, and the front got closer every day. After a disastrous battle at Caporetto, the Italian army had fallen back to just the other side of the Venetian lagoon.

'No,' she said.

'Because my grandson will go with you, and I want him safely back.'

Restless, Rebecca got up and walked to the window. It was raining; sleeting. The benches outside had a fine film of ice on them; it must be terrible out at sea. And up north, in Venice. The snow would lie heavy on the ground up there; it would be hard going, and dangerous. If Venice fell, Italy might fall.

Why *was* she going? Just to prove to herself, to her editor – to Jack – that she was a true reporter, not just the wife of one? And because the war here was out on the waves, where she couldn't go. But she *could* go to Venice.

'I just want the story,' she said, turning back to Rosa. Then, hesitantly, she added, 'He won't stay, you know. After the war. He'll go off again.'

'I know. Like his grandfather. Always wanting to see foreigners doing foreign things.'

Rebecca laughed. She herself had wanted to see foreigners doing foreign things on her trip here, via Aden and Cairo and Rome. Oh, yes, she liked seeing foreigners doing foreign things.

Rosa sniffed, but she wasn't really annoyed.

'So,' Rebecca said.

'You must go by train to Venice,' Rosa instructed. 'You can leave in two days. I will give you instructions. An emergency contact.' She glanced sharply up at Rebecca. 'Can you manage a code?'

'I don't know! I've never tried.' Codes. Good Lord, what had she got herself in for?

'Sandro can do it. We will see. You will not read the instructions until you are in Venice.'

Rebecca sat down and took Nonna Rosa's hands in her own. 'You've already planned this. You've already set it up.'

'Am *I* a fool? I've heard the news from the north. I knew Sandro would want to go. Maybe if he goes with you, he won't get himself killed.' Rosa leaned back and regarded Rebecca with a cynical gaze. Her tone was scornful, but the old hands in Rebecca's returned her clasp.

'Men are fools,' she said. 'If I get you the permits, you must stop him doing stupid things.'

How was she supposed to stop a grown man doing whatever he wanted? She hadn't been able to stop her own husband. She let go of Rosa's hands and gripped her own in her lap to stop them trembling.

'Tell me how, and I will.'

Nanna Rosa looked over her shoulder at the window. Her eyes became unfocused, as if the falling rain were taking her mind somewhere else.

'Women don't want a man they can control, but they want their man to *be* controlled,' she said. She sighed, pushing her cup away from her. 'I didn't want to control my husband, but he wanted to control me. So, he went to America, because I am not for controlling. And Sandro has been brought up in the same way of thinking. Be careful. He is romantic, like all the Panucci men.'

'Oh, for Heaven's sake! I'm not *eloping* with him!'

Smiling wryly, Nonna Rosa raised her eyebrows. 'Travel brings people together. Enjoy him, I say, but don't expect him to accept you the way you are.'

Enjoy him? *Enjoy him?* Oh, that was just disgusting. She wanted to lash out at a world that had that idea in it.

'Don't judge others by your mistakes,' Rebecca said sharply. 'I'd love to hear Sandro's grandfather's side of that story.'

Nonna Rosa actually flinched. Then smiled just a little, that smile with the corners tucked back in, which could mean satisfaction or anger.

'So would I,' she said. 'But he's dead. My mad Englishwoman had a saying. She said it just before she threw herself over the cliff. "Gather ye rosebuds while ye may." It's good advice. Come tomorrow for the permits.'

Rebecca went to the kitchen and washed up the teacups, shaking with something very like rage. Gather ye rosebuds!

No. She would *not*. She would *not* think of Sandro as some wartime interlude, some exotic affair.

'He'd be wasted on Natalia,' Nonna Rosa said, and got up, returning to the kitchen to finish her rhubarb.

'What can I do?' Rebecca asked. But this time she meant the food.

'Get some chestnuts ready.'

They worked in amity until Sandro came in, flushed with cold.

'The British are setting up a hospital.' He grinned and waved an envelope. 'And my accreditation's come through from the *Evening News*!'

'That's wonderful!' Rebecca beamed at him. No matter what happened now, Sandro was established in his career.

'*Bene*,' Nonna Rosa said. 'Go call the boy next door to chop the firewood. Then come back and set the tables.'

He grinned at Rebecca and obeyed, going out to the back courtyard.

For a moment, it was so normal, so natural, so family like . . .

But after the war, the three of them would part company, and never see each other again.

29

'You're going away? With that woman?' Fabrini asked.

'Just for a few days, to Venice. Following a story her editor wants.' Sandro finished washing out the developing tray and stacked it to dry. Fabrini leaned against the counter, trying to peer into his face.

'What's in Venice?'

Sandro turned to face him, shrugging. 'Some announcement the newspapers want covered.'

'You can't travel with that woman without people talking.'

'I know. But it's my job. That's why I thought it was best that Natalia and I . . . well, best if she's not caught up in this.'

It was a good excuse. It was a *great* excuse. He didn't want to insult the girl, and it would be an insult, to simply say, *No, thanks*.

Fabrini sniffed and pushed off the counter, heading for the stairs.

'Natalia!' he shouted. He turned back to Sandro and regarded him with an ironic eye. 'You can tell her yourself,' he said. He went up the stairs without another word, but the set of his shoulders showed his disapproval.

Darn it, he hadn't wanted to hurt Fabrini's pride, either.

Natalia came down slowly, her traditional skirts brushing against the stairwell walls. She had picked up on her father's mood, that was clear in her questioning eyes and solemn face.

He couldn't talk about this here; every word they said would float up the stairs, and he'd bet his right hand the parents would be sitting there, listening.

'Come into the studio,' he said.

Natalia preceded him, while he tried to talk himself out of this. *Marry Natalia*, his mother's voice in his head said. *Settle down*, said his father. *Give us grandchildren*, they both said.

Natalia sat in the big armchair, trying to look grown up, and looking instead like the girl she was. She gazed at him, searching his face.

'Alessandro?' she asked. Her voice was so young. He really hated to hurt her. Best not to pussyfoot around it.

'I'm going away on a story with Signora Quinn,' he said. 'There will be talk.'

A smile broke across her face. 'Oh, I don't mind about th—'

He cut her off, as gently as he could. 'We can't get married, Natalia. It wouldn't be fair to you.'

She raised her chin, defiant. 'I'm the only one to make that decision. Besides, I haven't made up my mind.' She was putting on a brave front, but there were tears in her eyes. She was afraid the gossip was true. He half-wished it was, and that made him feel worse.

There was no way to get out of this without hurting her, at least in her pride.

'You're in love with her,' she accused him.

'She's a married woman – and a *virtuous* woman.'

Nodding, she smiled bitterly. 'But that doesn't answer me,' she said. 'Don't be a fool, Sandro.'

Natalia deserved a whole heart. 'Do you want to marry a man who loves someone else?'

Abruptly, she looked older, more like her mother. The lines between her mouth and nose deepened with a kind of disgust.

'No,' she said. 'No.'

He couldn't meet her eyes.

The moment was broken by footsteps on the stairs, and the Fabrinis came into the studio. Signora Fabrini clearly hadn't liked the idea of Natalia being left alone with him.

'Natalia and I have decided . . .' What was it they said in those old novels? 'We've decided we do not suit.' He hesitated, carefully not looking at the girl. 'It would be better if people believed that Natalia refused me.'

'*Si*,' Signora Fabrini said, pinching her husband on the arm. '*Si*, we will tell people she did not want to go to America with you after the war.'

'Thank you.'

He bowed over Natalia's hand, nodded to her parents, and walked out.

So, that was it. No Natalia. No happy Italian family gathered about the big table upstairs. No nice secure job in the studio, no inheritance. No children. He was a fool who was in love with a married woman. He would probably die alone and unloved, still a virgin.

He felt perfectly poised between a dark, deep horror at what his life might hold, and an uplifting, flying relief.

Both true. Both true.

30

The train huffed steam at them and smoke filled the platform, making Rebecca cough. They had only taken tickets as far as Bari, the first stage on their journey, to throw anyone off their scent. Rebecca had paid extra to Mario, her source at the railway station, for him *not* to tell any of the other journalists that they had left.

'If they find out, signora, I will tell them that you have left with your lover for a—'

'No! Say nothing.' Mario looked disappointed, and she hedged. 'You have to protect my reputation.'

He put a hand on his heart. 'With my life, signora!'

She had no confidence in his ability to carry through with that, but she let him kiss her hand. At least he didn't know exactly where she was going.

Niccolo ran onto the platform and thrust a telegram at her. She opened it swiftly, hoping against hope that it wasn't a message from Evans cancelling the trip.

ARRIVED IN PARIS STOP WONDERFUL STORY STOP WILL TAKE
PERSONALLY TO EVANS STOP MEET ME IN LONDON STOP JACK

Paris! What was he doing in Paris? No doubt she would find
out in the pages of the *Evening News*. Meet him in London!
As if she could just leave her work here. As if it had no value.

Her anger was mixed with a kind of despair. It was hard
to believe that her marriage could ever recover from this long
absence – but wasn't that what every wife had to fear in this
war? What every woman around her could do, she could do.
They would work it out, once there was peace.

Sandro had stowed his camera in a compartment and came
to get her. She showed him the message, and he went very still.

'Will you go?'

She sniffed in disdain. 'After the war, then I'll go. When
my work here is over.'

He frowned, looking at the flimsy yellow paper. 'Your
husband might not approve.'

'He gave up the right to approve when he left me to go
gallivanting over Europe!'

Her words were more forceful than her thoughts. Sandro
glanced sideways at her a couple of times, but he said nothing.

This, the only train to Bari that day, was already an hour
late. As everywhere, troop trains and hospital trains had priority,
and the usually chaotic Italian train system was barely coping.

The train had only two carriages, and they were full, having
come up from Maglie and Lecce. But they had paid extra for
one of the forward compartments, which at least had bench seats
and luggage racks. It was only supposed to hold six, of course,
but they squeezed in and the family already there rearranged
themselves so Rebecca and Sandro could sit side by side, facing

backwards. She was grateful that her gloves were tight enough to show her wedding ring, because it was the first thing the matriarch of the clan had checked for.

The last time she had been on a train, she and Jack had journeyed from Rome to Brindisi. It had been so much fun, watching the Italian landscape unfurl out the window, exclaiming at medieval villages, both of them drinking in the sheer age of the place. Pain twisted through her at the memory. It didn't seem fair that she should have both kinds of pain – the pain of missing him, and the pain of being angry with him. Surely one should cancel out the other.

There was the whistle, the guard's call, and that first lurch that, no matter her destination, always filled her with excitement. This time, though, the excitement was close to panic. What on Earth had possessed her to commit to this insanity? Was she only here because she wanted Jack to admire her professionalism, to admit that she was as good a journalist as he was?

She turned to Sandro, wanting to tell him they should get off at Bari and come straight back home. But he smiled at her with such genuine delight that she couldn't do it to him.

'We're off!' he said.

•

They made it into Bari as the sun was setting, to find that the Venice train, which had been due to leave two hours before, wasn't expected to go before midnight.

They found a trattoria run by one of Nonna Rosa's friends, and ate. The first time, really, they had sat alone in a restaurant, lit by candlelight. She was aware of the glances her blonde hair was getting, and suddenly saw them as others must: Sandro so handsome, herself exotic, eating together like a married couple.

'Why photography?' she asked him, desperate to fill a sudden portentous silence.

His hand went automatically to his jacket pocket, where he always kept his small camera.

'I used to go to the art galleries in New York on the weekends,' he said, surprising her. 'The paintings were beautiful, but they were . . . separate from my life. People with money painted them, most of them – or at least, people with the kind of education no one I knew was ever going to have. But photography . . . anyone can buy a Box Brownie and take shots.' His eyes were alight; she had never seen him so passionate. 'Photography is the art of the people. Painting is all fancy and flowers, but photography's *real*. And available to anyone. The first democratic art form since they drew on the walls of caves.'

She had never been more conscious of her privilege. She had had that education he spoke of so wistfully. Her parents had commissioned paintings – one of her brothers and her, when they were children, and a portrait of the two of them on their silver wedding anniversary. When she had gone to the art gallery in her childhood and youth, it had given her a comfortable feeling of being somewhere familiar and intimate. Some of the artists on those walls had come to her mother's soirées, and it had been pleasant to recognise their names, and be glad for them that the gallery had bought their work.

The first democratic art form.

With anyone else, she would have challenged, said, *Are you sure it's an art form?* But she had seen those images of his, and they were Art.

Photography was just one thing that was changing everyday life. She was aware of standing on a precipice of time.

'This century is going to be like nothing that has happened before,' she said, and Sandro nodded solemnly.

'Who knows what will happen after the war? We may see the greatest civilisations that have ever existed,' he agreed.

'Thriving in peace.'

Together, they contemplated it. This was the war to end all wars. No one would ever be stupid enough to begin such a conflagration again. German militarism would be curbed; demolished. And peace would reign. What wonders could man be capable of once the threat of war was taken away?

'That's why war photography is important,' Sandro added. 'So we don't forget the horrors.'

After the meal, the owner, an old man called Nunzio, let them use his flat upstairs to wash up. Her thoughts were running around like scared rabbits. She realised how tired she was. This was the third night since she had left the Damonicas' pensione, and she had slept badly in the new bed, and from anxiety about this trip. She caught her reflection in the mirror over the wash basin. She looked like a hag. But what did that matter? She was a married woman, and shouldn't be worried about how she looked to other men.

•

The train to Venice was cold, despite gas heaters, but they had forward-facing seats this time, and huddled together, coat collars turned up.

From time to time, the train just stopped and waited. Usually, after a half an hour or so, another train would pass – filled with troops, or freight or, once, completely empty – and then they would jerk into movement again. At one of these stops, Rebecca rested her head on the high seat back and closed her eyes. She was aware of Sandro's warmth seeping through that old pea jacket of his; his leg pressed against hers as the carriage filled up and she thought, *That's comforting*. She was almost asleep when the train began to move again, far more smoothly than the Bari train, picking up speed quickly. She slitted her eyes to peer out the window – the landscape was rushing by. Good. It was a long, long trip to Bologna, where they must next change trains.

Her head dropped onto Sandro's shoulder and she slept, lulled by the rhythm of the train wheels and the simple security of being in a rushing room where she had to do nothing at all but sit and wait.

31

Sandro carefully took the folded paper out of his pocket, trying not to disturb Rebecca. Having her sleep on his shoulder stirred up too many emotions and desires – time to distract himself with the coded message.

It wasn't that complicated, and it took about twenty minutes to decipher. Nonna Rosa had given him the key – the first letters of the words of a lullaby his father used to sing to him. It made him smile to think of his nonna singing it to his father. Despite her hard surface, underneath – no, it would be nice to think she was sweet and soft underneath, but she wasn't. She was as tough as old oak all the way through.

Unlike Rebecca, who had her sweet side, all right.

She had told him the plan as they walked to her home after dinner two nights ago. It was longer than her walk to the Damonicas' had been, and he persuaded himself she needed his protection.

'So, will you come?' she had asked him.

'Try and keep me away!' She'd punched his arm in response as if he were her brother, and he swallowed the bitterness of that and tried to be glad of it, for her sake.

The little house was very cold, so he'd started the fire while she sat in a chair at the kitchen table. She looked very tired, but there was a light of purpose about her, and he was secretly thrilled to share in her adventure.

'Goodnight,' he'd said, wishing he could kiss her. She had turned her head and given him a gentle smile.

'Goodnight, Sandro. Thank you.'

For the rest of the night he had felt stronger, more stable and, yes, manly, even while he was helping Nonna Rosa do the dishes.

On the other hand . . . Venice! It was crazy, heading straight for a city only miles from a wavering front line. The newspapers reported everyone was running *away* from Venice. He'd been raring to get to the front since he left New York, despite knowing that it wouldn't be pleasant once he got there. Venice was better than nothing – better than Brindisi – and anything could happen. He might get a chance to fight after all. He'd become aware that he was smiling in anticipation of the danger, and laughed at himself. Maybe his nonna was right, and men were all fools, including him.

But he knew he would go, all the same. He'd thought to himself that he would need to take a lot of film, in case they got the chance to go to the front . . .

'Alessandro!' Nonna Rosa had said.

'Sorry, sorry, just thinking.'

'It's dangerous up there. Your father would tell you not to go.'

She wasn't saying no. She looked at him solemnly, but without any judgement.

'I can't let her go alone,' he'd said. But that wasn't the only reason. He had come to Italy to join the Army, to risk his life, not to sit comfortably in a town while other men did the real work. Maybe he couldn't fight, but he could still contribute. For a moment, he'd faced the thought of his own death. He was a young man still, and death had always seemed far off, an academic certainty without any weight to it. Heading north brought the idea closer. But if he gave in to fear of death, he would be less. Not just less of a man, but less of a human being.

'Death will find me alive,' he said. It was an old Italian saying. It meant that it was best to live as fully as one could, every moment.

His nonna smiled a secret smile, as if he had passed a test.

'*Sì*. So, make sure you have warm clothes. It's cold up north.' Everything was clean and back in its place, ready for the next day. She passed him to go up the stairs to bed and paused behind him, her hand on his shoulder. 'I knew you took after me,' she said.

Apparently, all he needed to do to earn his nonna's approval was risk his life on a whim.

Sandro had stood in the kitchen and laughed.

•

The coded message Nonna had given him was a simple address. *Calla Lunge San Barnaba.* And a clue: *The sign of the bull.* A shop sign? An inn? They would have to go there to find out. It was an emergency contact, Nonna had said. Hopefully, they wouldn't have an emergency. With luck.

He tucked the original and the decoded messages away carefully and let his head fall back and slide until his cheek rested against Becca's hair. He prayed, as he slipped into sleep, that he wouldn't disappoint her on this expedition. That he would be the newsman she thought he was.

32

Venice!

That was a name to conjure by. The queen of cities, the jewel of the Adriatic. *Serenissima*. Romantic, beautiful, mysterious.

Unbelievably cold and damp, and smelling of ash and bad fish. The sunlight showed up alarming cracks in the railway station walls.

The station was crowded, beyond capacity: soldiers everywhere, old men in suits, entire families waiting to board the train, pushing past them as Rebecca and Sandro got out of the compartment, desperate to get away. Children wailed, porters shouted, a goat in a crate bleated with annoyance.

Beneath the racket, in the distance, Rebecca heard a dull boom; it was only when Sandro said, 'Those are close,' that she realised it was artillery fire. The booming of cannons.

The front line was nearer than they had known.

'Let's go,' Sandro said, and took her bag. He pushed through the crowd in front of her, making a path she could follow. She grabbed one of the straps of his rucksack, frightened of losing him in the crush of people that surged around them. There were so many people, all focused on the train in which they had arrived. The smell of fear was everywhere; terrified eyes, faces that flinched with every distant thud of cannon fire.

With a final push, they made it to the wall, and Sandro reached out to pull her to him, an arm around her waist. She clung to him unashamedly, deeply unsettled by the fervour of the mob.

They wormed and shoved their way through to the entrance. Near it was a *tabaccaio* booth, with an old man behind the counter, a gold tooth glinting. His stock was almost gone, but he also sold maps. They found the address of the small hotel Nonna Rosa had recommended. This wasn't her 'emergency' contact, merely a friend who kept a place to stay.

They would have to take a gondola – if they could find one.

The canal was chock full of private boats, some apparently abandoned by their owners, who were inside the station, trying to escape the pounding of the guns. The noise was incredible; not just the guns, but the shouts and cries and sobs of the crowd.

They found a gondola, piloted by a man with one eye. When they told him the address, he simply grunted, so they got in and sat together in the stern.

Sandro was huddled down in his coat, collar up around his ears. They shivered together as the gondola traversed a wide curve. Ahead was a bank of fog, threading through the palazzos on the side of the canal, and hanging low over the water.

As they went into it, around them the world disappeared slowly, until they were breathing water, it seemed, and droplets weighed down each of her eyelashes. The gondolier began to call out regularly, in a surprising, clear voice, warning that they were there. Other gondoliers called back.

The clammy chill was settling into her bones and her thin leather gloves were doing nothing to help. Her wedding ring was so cold she was afraid she might get frostbite. She had to find some gloves lined with lambskin. And maybe a Lammy suit.

The calls across the water came from all directions – they were out in the middle of the canal now. There was no way to judge how fast they were going, or how much distance they had covered.

She tucked her hand into Sandro's arm and he pressed it against his side, smiling at her. Her eyes were level with his ear, which lay flat to his head, its warm olive skin blued with cold. To be in Venice . . . she had planned to come here with Jack; to have a romantic interlude sometime or other. A few golden days they could look back on and sigh over. She hadn't imagined coming in winter, and with another man.

But still . . . Venice! Of all the European cities, this was the one with the most allure. Deep down, she was thrilled to be in a gondola on the Grand Canal. Not that deep down, in fact. Happiness bubbled up inside her and she wondered how long it had been since she'd felt this way.

With one last call, the gondolier brought the craft closer to the right side of the canal, until they could just make out the boarded-up windows and sandbagged churches they were passing.

'Up there.' The gondolier pointed with his chin towards a street that led into what looked like a picture of a medieval town.

She paid the man and Sandro hoisted their bags.

They found the pensione, which was double the size of the Damonicas'. Even so, there was no room to spare, but the woman, Nonna Rosa's friend, told them that her friend Vanni had a small hotel just down the street.

'They're all gone, they've shut the big hotels, you know,' she said. 'Cowards.' She took a step forward and spat into a smaller canal that ran alongside the pensione. 'Still, good for business!'

Vanni assured them he had a room, 'Only one, so you're lucky!'

He had assumed they were husband and wife. Rebecca wasn't sure what to do. Of course, if they weren't husband and wife, no one would rent them any kind of room, except in the sort of low slum she wouldn't want to stay in. No decent hotel would rent a room to a woman, unless she were travelling with her husband or father or brother. Restaurants were the same; the good ones refused to serve a woman on her own. All single women were assumed to be prostitutes unless proven otherwise.

'*Grazie*,' Sandro said, and carried their bags up to the room. Fortunately, it was a large one, with a double bed and a single.

She still wasn't sure where to look when Sandro put her bag on the double and dropped his own backpack on the single.

Two chairs and a small table sat near the window. She took off her coat and lowered herself into one gratefully, pulling off her gloves even though it was still chilly in the room.

A moment later, Vanni came in to light a fire in the closed stove.

'Soon have you warm!' he said. 'Just close the flue when you go out.' He spoke good English – Venice was a beloved travel spot for the English, and the Venetian hoteliers had adapted.

There was a washstand that held both a ewer of water and a billycan – though they wouldn't call them billycans here, Rebecca thought. She wanted warm water to wash in more than she wanted to sit down, so she struggled up and filled the billy, putting it on top of the stove to heat.

She stood for a moment in front of the fire, not thinking about anything, her hands out to the heat, vaguely aware of Sandro behind her, changing his socks.

The room seemed smaller now it was filled with the sound of his breath, the faint rustle of his clothes as he put his shoes back on. She could imagine every movement, but she kept facing the fire, not wanting to watch him – it was too intimate, too domestic.

They were still for a few minutes, warming up, and then Sandro's stomach gurgled loudly. Rebecca turned to him and laughed, covering her face with her hand. Face red, Sandro threw up his hands.

'I admit it, I'm starving!'

'I'll just wash, and then we can find somewhere. Vanni will know.'

It was amazing how much better she felt with clean hands and face and warm toes.

Vanni directed them down a couple of narrow alleys, and they found a cafe miraculously open, serving soup and brown bread; and if the soup was thin and the bread chalky, at least the cafe was warm.

'The announcement is tomorrow, according to Evans. We'd better check with Naval Command and present our credentials.'

'Not that it will help *me*,' Rebecca said. 'No press conferences. Just as well you're here.'

They smiled at each other; the smile was a little warm for colleagues, and she flushed and looked away.

'We need to go to the naval headquarters,' Sandro told the cafe owner.

'You want the Arsenale,' he said. 'You'll get lost. Better take a gondola.'

Their gondola was smaller than the one they had taken from the station, so they sat close together, and she was vividly aware of the long line of his thigh against hers the whole way. It wasn't far, but through several turns and double backs. They probably *would* have got lost, especially since the fog was still hanging in corners.

The gondola pulled in to a small landing stage at a piazza, just before one of the little stone bridges that joined all the islets of Venice together. The piazza looked as though it should be thronging with people, but there was no one coming down the street that led into it, and the canal was empty except for their gondolier, who was slowly moving away, counting their fare.

The guards on the gate merely pointed to a notice on the board outside that stated: *L'ammiraglio Thaon di Revel darà un annuncio pubblico domani alle ore 10 in Piazza San Marco.*

'Public announcement ten o'clock tomorrow in St Mark's Square,' Sandro said. 'What do we do now?'

'Find where they've taken the wounded, and try to get a story,' Rebecca said. Why not? It had worked before for them, and it was clear no one from the Arsenale was going to give them an interview. At least – at last! – she could be at the announcement tomorrow. It must be important, if they were using the Square, making it public. A thread of excitement crept through her. What if she were actually there for one of the turning points of the war?

They went into a nearby tabac and asked directions to the hospital where the wounded were cared for.

'You want Giovanni e Paolo,' the woman behind the counter said. 'You'll get lost.'

'I know,' Sandro said, 'we'd better take a gondola!'

The woman barked a short laugh out, and shook her finger at him playfully. 'It's true, it's true!' she cried.

Sandro winked at her, and she made flapping motions with her hands, delightedly pushing them out. She'd hardly looked at Rebecca. That easy charm of Sandro's was something she rarely saw. He was scrupulous in treating her altogether differently; as a colleague and, lately, as a friend. Those few moments when they had looked at each other with something other than friendship in their eyes ... they shouldn't have happened. Colleagues, that was what they had to be. Which was right and proper, if not satisfying.

'Oh, let's get out of here!' she said, and strode to the dock where some gondolas were waiting.

The gondola took them through small canals to the hospital, at another small piazza near another bridge. But here, before them, at right angles in the square, was a tall dark basilica and another building that looked much like a church, of paler stone than the cathedral. They went through its huge double-arched rococo entrance.

Inside, people rushed past in every direction. Doctors, orderlies, nurses. There didn't seem to be any reception desk, and no one to ask, so as an orderly pushing an empty bed on wheels came past them at a leisurely pace, Sandro intercepted him.

'We're looking for the soldiers' wards,' he said.

'Si,' the orderly said. He looked them up and down, assessing their travel-worn appearance against the quality of their clothes. Clearly Sandro's pea coat didn't impress him, but the cut of Rebecca's clothes did. 'You'd better follow me,' he said. 'You'll get lost otherwise.'

Getting lost seemed to be a perennial threat in Venice. She could understand why; even though Sydney wasn't laid out on a grid like some modern cities, it was a hundred times easier to navigate, by land or by sea. There was something about the high Venetian houses on either side of the narrow canals that made her lose her sense of direction, and on days like this, when the sun hid behind clouds and mist, she had no way of orienting herself.

This hospital, she suspected, had been a monastery – probably attached to the basilica. It was laid out in the classic monastic square, so they had to walk around two-and-a-half sides before they got to the right ward. The area in the middle was given over to a kitchen garden, with big red Entry Forbidden signs at every door that led out to it.

Above them, high vaulted ceilings echoed their steps; there was an air of past magnificence, both sad and uplifting. Melancholy. And everywhere, there were signs of making do. Equipment wired together. Wheels off trolleys, the legs held up by bricks or books. Damp patches on some outside walls, and low lighting, every second lamp turned down.

The wards they passed were mixed: a maternity ward, the thin cries of hungry newborns coming through the open door; an old people's ward full of coughs and wheezes; and then a surgical ward, with thin children in casts and a young woman in a sling, staring out the door and smiling at everyone who passed.

Finally, they came to another door, not marked, and the orderly jerked his head towards it and stood waiting. Rebecca tipped him; too generously, by his pleased reaction, but he had saved them time.

This door was shut, and so heavy that they didn't hear any sound until they opened it.

The moans were so loud that Rebecca instinctively turned to make sure the door shut, so as not to disturb the rest of the hospital.

Here were soldiers. Blood-soaked bandages, men missing a leg, or an arm, a young boy tossing in fever, the smell of decay fighting that of disinfectant. At first glimpse, it was the most horrible thing she'd ever seen, far worse than the ward of *Orione* passengers at Brindisi. Like one of the Circles of Hell, chaotic and impossible to grasp. At second, it resolved itself from chaos to order, of a sort. The beds were ranged along the walls, facing each other, and medical staff worked among them. But the pain was still there, and the misery, and the despair.

A nurse looked up from sponging down the feverish boy.

'Yes?' she said, sharp and unwelcoming.

'May we speak to the sister in charge?' Sandro asked.

'Pina!' the nurse shouted, and went back to her boy, speaking steadily and quietly to him as she sponged, until he calmed and lay still.

From the far end of the ward, a young woman approached them, dressed in the uniform and apron of a nurse, but without a cap on her head. Her skirts were shorter than they wore in the south, more like the length Rebecca had worn before coming to Italy, swinging at mid-calf. And underneath, Rebecca was delighted to see, were sturdy drill trousers in dark blue, tucked into equally serviceable flat boots.

Now, that was dressing to suit your circumstances! Her mother would have approved.

The nurse stood poised on the balls of her feet, eyes bright, as though ready for anything. She was fairer than most of the

Italian women Rebecca had met, with the reddish-brown hair that northern Italy sometimes produced.

'*Si?*'

'We're journalists,' Rebecca said in Italian. 'We'd like to interview your patients; to allow them to tell their stories. It will be published in British and Australian papers.'

A sly smile came onto the woman's face. 'We've had a directive not to speak to the Italian or British newspapers,' she said, 'from the admiral himself. But he didn't say anything about the Australian ones! Can you tell me truly that you will send your stories only to Australia?'

Rebecca exchanged glances with Sandro, and shrugged. The *Herald* would share their story with Evans at the *News,* probably, but they could certainly *send* their stories only to the *Herald*.

'*Certamente,*' she said.

The woman grinned; she seemed to take a positive relish in bending the rules, and Rebecca and Sandro had to smile back.

'I'm Seppina Rizzo,' she said, and went to a man – a doctor? – who was lancing some kind of infection on the leg of an older man. She spoke to him quietly. Rebecca looked away. She admired those who could nurse the sick, but she just couldn't do that job. It made her ashamed. If Linus was lying somewhere, injured, she would want some woman to take care of him . . . but she knew that it would kill her to work in this environment, day in and day out.

'Let's go,' Seppina said. 'I'm due a break.' She led them through two passageways to a smaller room that held a small stove with a kettle and a coffeepot.

'This is the room for the staff,' Seppina explained as she made tea. 'My husband Luigi laughs at me. He says a real

Italian should drink coffee, but my mother always drank tea, and I like it.'

'So do I,' Rebecca said.

'I never had it before I came to Italy, but it's okay,' Sandro added. 'Coffee's the American drink.'

They sat at an old, scarred pine table and cradled their cups. 'I have no food to offer you, I'm sorry,' Seppina said.

'We've just eaten, thank you.'

Seppina gave them the information they needed on the men and where they had been wounded. 'Better to get this from me; you must not tire them with questions.'

Sandro nodded and sipped his tea cautiously while Rebecca wrote down the details of a battle by the Piave River.

'So, you are an Australian journalist?' Seppina asked. 'Are you here to get the big story tomorrow?'

Rebecca and Sandro exchanged a quick glance.

'You know what it is?' Sandro said.

She sat back a little, as if unsure what she should say.

'My editor told us to come to Venice by the ninth, and we would get a good story,' Rebecca added quickly.

Laughing, Seppina shook her head. '*Che scherzo!*' she said. 'So, that is true. By tomorrow, there will be a good story.' She dimpled. 'A very good story, about my husband.'

That was all she would say, except that the story would come from naval headquarters, from Admiral Thaon di Revel, who had been a witness at her wedding, only six weeks ago. And that her husband's name was Luigi. Tenente Luigi Rizzo.

'A very good story,' Sandro mused as they walked back to the ward.

'No use guessing. We'll just have to wait until tomorrow, like everyone else.'

It irked her, to have come so far and still have to wait.

They spent the next hour interviewing soldiers, getting first-hand accounts of the battle of the Piave: the Italians on one bank, the Austrians on the other, and the rest of the Allied forces far behind because they didn't believe the Italians could hold their line. But hold it they had, despite desertions from their own ranks, despite too many deaths. The stories brought tears to Rebecca's eyes, and to Sandro's too, she noticed.

She would write the stories, but she was pretty sure that the parts about deserters and Allied forces hanging back would be edited out. She felt the way Sandro had about the bombing of Strettabaia – that these men and their truths should be commemorated. It reinforced her belief that what she was doing – both this kind of interview, and the work she did in Brindisi – *was* worthwhile. She was a witness to the war, and that was important.

Sandro set up and took a photograph of the whole ward, the doctor, who turned out to be Seppina's father, and his three daughters, the only nurses working here.

'This is just the overflow from the field hospitals,' Seppina's sister Maria said. 'Just the ones they couldn't take or who wouldn't last the journey by road.'

The doctor allowed them some time, but not too much, with each patient who could talk. 'It helps them, to describe what has happened to them,' he said.

The doctor excused himself, answering a call from the other end of the ward, as they arrived at a bed where the young man looked very bad, although he had no obvious wound.

Seppina came over to them. 'Leave him. He hasn't long,' she whispered. 'Internal bleeding from the gut; he got infected, and there's nothing we can do.'

The boy gestured weakly to Sandro. 'Take a photo of me,' he said. 'My mamma, she wanted one, but I was too keen to join up. Take one for her, and send it to her.'

'Sure,' Sandro said. He positioned the camera carefully, to get the best light, to make the boy look as good as possible. Seppina propped him up on his pillows, combed his hair, and pinched his cheeks to bring them some colour.

The click of the camera was very loud.

Sandro took the boy's address and promised faithfully to send the photograph – a good-size one – to the mamma. When the boy tried to pay him, he waved it off, in tears.

'No, no, I am in *your* debt,' Sandro said.

Walking beside her on the way out, Sandro was lost in a brown study.

'A penny for your thoughts,' she said.

'Those boys' stories, they ought to be told.'

'They will be.'

'But how many more are there at the front, whose stories will never be heard?'

As they came out into the square, he looked north, towards the sounds of the guns, and she knew he was thinking of going to the front. The idea clenched at her heart. *Not yet*, she thought. *Not yet.*

•

As they made their way down the street, in search of somewhere she could sit and write her story, they passed a menswear shop, its lights blazing out into the murky afternoon.

'Right,' she said. 'Come in here.'

She dragged Sandro in and presented him to the owner, who was both surprised and delighted to have customers.

'My husband needs a warm coat,' she said. 'Something serviceable.'

It was odd, speaking of Sandro as her husband. Oddly believable. Sandro cast her a quick look, his face unreadable. Had she offended him? But he smiled a little wryly and allowed her to keep going.

The manager was enthusiastic. Yes, yes, he had just the thing. Half an hour, and several arguments later, they had decided on a knee-length greatcoat in dark brown – 'So he won't get mistaken for a soldier' – which looked wonderful against his olive skin. If he had to go to the front, at least he would be warm.

'And gloves,' Rebecca added. 'For both of us.'

She paid. 'A birthday present,' she insisted, and the manager indulged her.

'You can't buy me things,' Sandro said softly, so the manager wouldn't hear. 'I'll pay you back.'

'You can buy me a birthday present, in April,' she said.

She fell silent as they went out arm in arm, wondering where they would be in April. Perhaps he was wondering the same thing, because they walked quietly, through little streets, over small bridges and alongside canals, until they came to a row of shops with both a cafe and a photographer's. She went to the cafe to write her story; Sandro to the photographer's to have his film developed. He took a few shots of her at the cafe table to finish off the roll, and she smiled for him.

She was so thankful that he had come with her. Prepared to relish every moment of his company. Which she was enjoying too much. Far too much.

33

The late afternoon light, combined with the lamps in the cafe, had given Rebecca's hair a halo of light. And when she smiled at him . . . He was coming to learn her smiles. The polite, the annoyed, the wondering, the kind – but this was a different one. Affectionate, he thought; and sometimes, remembering how she had pushed and prodded him – physically! – into this brown coat, the finest he'd ever worn, sometimes he was afraid that she thought of him as a brother.

Not that he expected anything; no. But he'd at least like to be a temptation.

The photographer was delighted to have an American colleague to chat with as he developed the images. Business had been pretty good – although over the past few weeks, even business from the sailors and the soldiers had dropped off. Still, if the Austrians took over, as they had threatened to do, he would still be in business. There was nothing victorious soldiers wanted so much as photographs – he would go out in the street and get them to pose in St Mark's Square. They'd had the gall to drop pamphlets to say that they would be attending Mass in San Marco's next Sunday. Ha! They'd better hurry up, that's all he could say.

Sandro let him ramble on, watching as the images came up through the developer. He'd chosen four: the one of the dying boy (a blow-up that the mother could put on her mantelpiece and adorn with black ribbon); and one of the ward, showing the boy in his bed; one of Seppina he had taken surreptitiously, in profile, which he thought her father might like; and one of Becca, smiling at him as though he were the centre of her world.

A trick of the light.

He waited until they had dried, and then bought as much film as the photographer would part with. He tucked the photo of Rebecca into his wallet, put the others in a couple of envelopes, and went back to the cafe, where Rebecca was waiting. They went to the post office, she with her very long telegram to the *Evening News*, and he with his photographs.

The post office clerk at the telegraph counter looked at her sheaf of forms, onto which she had transcribed her story, with dismay.

'Is this a newspaper story?' he asked suspiciously. 'All newspaper stories to be approved by Admiral Thaon di Revel's office.'

'Do I look like a newspaper reporter?' Rebecca said, smiling.

The clerk scowled at her, but then the inner Lothario that lived in every Italian man's breast broke through, and he smiled. 'You look like an angel!' he said, and charged her an incredible number of lire to send the telegram.

Sandro sent both photographs, of the ward and the boy, to the boy's mother, with a note Rebecca helped him compose. He was better with images than with language.

When I saw him, he was thinking only of you and his loved ones, she had him write. *He was brave and strong and had made his confession.*

'Should you say that? Did he?'

'Yes. Maria told me while you were taking the shot. This morning, the priest came. His mother will want to know. Put: *He wasn't in any pain.*'

'But he will be.'

'Yes, but put it anyway. They'll give him morphine when the pain gets bad.' He thought of the groans of some of the wounded men, but he wrote it. The memory of the ward, full of pain and courage, made him angry. They'd been so *young*. The best of their generation, cut down like wheat at harvest time.

Becca had tears in her eyes. She shouldn't be here – not because she was a woman, but because none of them should be here. None of them. They should be home with their families.

But without the war, he would never have met her.

34

The bathroom of the hotel, which was on the first floor, was beautifully warm, because it was directly behind the main chimney from the kitchen. Rebecca had an actual deep bath, better than any she'd had since leaving Sydney, and dressed in her thick flannel nightdress in some relief at being clean again. With clean teeth! No one could like the texture of tooth powder, but the results were wonderful. She put her overcoat on to go to the room, and hesitated.

Sleeping in the same room as Sandro. An unexpected intimacy. She felt a blush rise in her cheeks at the thought, remembering his lean strength as he helped her from the gondola, and the way his boxing outfit had clung to his legs. At least the cold meant they had to cover up completely.

She went back to the room with her overcoat buttoned firmly around her, her nightgown covering her underneath it to her toes. She tapped at the door, in case he was changing.

'Come in.'

Opening the door felt far more important than it actually was. Sandro looked up as she came in and smiled. She wondered what he saw when he looked at her: she knew her cheeks were flushed. Pray God he assumed it was from the bath.

'Off to the bathroom with you,' she said lightly. 'The hot water is fine!'

He passed her on his way and although he didn't brush against her, her skin was as alive as if he had.

The fire had been stoked up, but it was only small and did little to take the chill off the air. She threw her overcoat on top of the covers for extra warmth, and sat cross-legged under the blankets, getting some snarls out of her hair. She would brush it until it crackled, and then plait it for the night, as she always did. Normality. Routine. That would calm her down.

Sandro came back unexpectedly soon, with a knock at the door before he came in. She flung the brush onto the night table and slid under the covers, heart racing. She pulled her hair in after her. It would get all snarled up again if she didn't plait it, but sitting up in her nightgown while Sandro was watching . . . she just couldn't do it.

Sandro pulled his boots off and placed them outside the door for the boot boy to collect. He did the same for hers. It was an ordinary, domestic action, and emphasised the peculiar intimacy of their situation. Strange that respectability was forcing a kind of dissolution on them.

Spending the night in the same hotel room as Sandro would give Jack cause to divorce her. Adultery by the wife was about the only cause for divorce that the courts would accept. Adultery by the husband . . . they didn't take that seriously. But even if he divorced her, it wouldn't change anything. Marriage was more than a legal contract; it was sacred. She would be cast out of the Church if she remarried – out of every church, not just the Catholic one. But even that wasn't the point. The point was that she had given her solemn, sacred vow, and she would hold to it. No man but Jack, until death parted them. No matter how her heart ached and her skin flushed when she looked at Sandro. No matter how much more she felt for him now than she had when they'd started this journey.

After closing the door, he stood at the window for a moment, looking out as if mesmerised by the movement of the rain, his brown coat over winter pyjamas, his dark hair having lost all its pomade, and curling wildly. His shoulders were tense, hunched forward as though he were worried, or angry.

She couldn't see his eyes. He turned to look at her, and then he took in an audible breath, and moved to his bed, and everything was back to normal, except that she was breathing too hard.

Thank God the bedclothes covered her so completely. In summer, it would have been much more embarrassing.

'May I turn down the lamp?' Sandro asked, so politely.

'Yes, of course,' she answered. She wanted to sit up and brush her hair again, but she couldn't do that while he was awake, especially as the closed stove sent flickers out of the edges of its door.

A brief orange glow highlighted Sandro's cheekbones, the gleam of his eye.

Her breath caught sharply and she was uncomfortable with how physically aware she was of him. And why? Sandro wasn't even . . . well, he wasn't the type of man she had ever admired. Perhaps she was just rebounding from disappointment in Jack. Sandro was everything Jack wasn't: quiet, steady, reliable as bedrock; and dark, muscular, instead of Jack's long rangy blondness. Perhaps she was attracted to him, in a way, to spite Jack.

But that's not what it felt like. Being with Sandro felt like coming into a peaceful harbour. He required nothing of her but that she be herself. Jack – and, she had to admit, her brothers were the same – needed women's admiration, women's praise. Her praise. Sandro didn't have an inflated opinion of himself.

At one time, she had thought that Jack's opinion of himself had been deserved, but now she knew differently. He hadn't been a – a *gentleman*. Staring into the darkness, she faced it, made herself admit it. She had married – loved! – a self-glorifying liar. Was that too harsh a judgement? If only he'd taken her seriously, if only he'd *explained* why he'd stolen her stories. What was she to make of *Figure it out for yourself*? Only that he was contemptuous of her.

The long weeks without him had lent her a clarity of vision. In that clear sight, Jack was a clever, ambitious, unscrupulous man. Attractive, oh yes! But only on the outside. She remembered, suddenly, that when she had asked him why he hadn't enlisted, he had said, 'Newsmen do an important job in any war. Besides, can you imagine me stuck in a foxhole? I'd go mad!' He had laughed as he said it, but looking back, she thought it might have been the most honest thing he had ever said to her. He was devoted to his craft, but he would much rather risk his life chasing a story than in defence of his country. Thinking of Linus, of Charles, she was angry with him in an entirely new way.

Sandro stirred and turned over and she froze, her whole body becoming aware of his, of his every movement and breath. He settled with a long sigh, and she relaxed.

In the darkness, she stared at the flickering reflection of flames on the ceiling, and admitted the truth. She'd been a fool to marry Jack. She let the admission sink into her, and began to wonder why. She was no fool. Her work had showed her that. So, how had Jack cozened her so easily? She edged up in bed, keeping the covers high, and began to brush her hair.

She had assumed that someone – say it, someone of their class and race – wouldn't lie, or steal. She'd been brought up to blithely believe that a tall, breezy bronzed Aussie *had* to be honourable. Or a redheaded Irishman, for that matter.

Even Jack's ongoing lie to his father about becoming a solicitor hadn't alerted her to the truth. Jack had made it seem funny; and she had let herself be persuaded by his laughter into thinking it not so bad. But it had been bad. Jack had taken his father's money without any intention of going into the family firm. That was a kind of theft; similar in its familial nature to his theft of her stories.

It should have warned her. But she had fallen for an ideal of Empire, not a living, breathing, fallible human being.

The only excuse she had was youth – she'd been eighteen when she'd first met him.

As she braided her long plait and settled down to sleep, she wondered what their marriage would be like now she had seen the real Jack. Could she find the compassion to help him find his own way back to a steadier course? To a more manly, upright way of behaving? Until she knew that, until she knew herself and him better, she could not decide what the future might hold for them.

The fire died down during the night, and the gentle flickers gave way to a small, steady glow. At odd moments, when the wind outside howled, or a shutter banged somewhere nearby, she would rouse, and hear Sandro's reassuring breathing, and sink back down into sleep.

In the morning, she sat half up in bed, covers high, and shook her head hard to wake up, her plait flying from side to side. Sandro laughed. She scrunched up her nose at him.

'Good morning,' he said, still sleepy. He looked particularly good in the morning, tousled head and warmed lips, his skin picking up the light filtered through the shutters, warm as honey, those capable hands relaxed on the blankets. Oh, she had to stop looking at him like that!

As she replaited her hair while Sandro visited the WC, she admitted to herself that she had been mightily tempted to crawl into his bed last night.

Would anyone believe she hadn't? Would Jack believe it? Perhaps that would be the test for them, when they met again. How much could they trust one another?

She wondered where he was, and how much danger he was in. Travelling now, even between Paris and London, was dangerous; the German planes targeted train lines and main roads. Thinking of Linus always made her stomach clench tightly with worry, and thinking of Charles only slightly less so; but wondering about Jack in danger had little effect – was it that he wasn't a soldier? Or that she couldn't really imagine him in a situation he couldn't talk his way out of?

Or was it simply that she had ceased to care?

•

After breakfast, having asked the way to St Mark's Square, and being told they would get lost, they took a gondola there, to where Admiral Thaon di Revel, Seppina had said, would give them news.

In the square she and Sandro had cafe lattes and watched the people go by – just as she had imagined she would do with Jack. The fact that St Mark's four great horses had been taken to Rome for safekeeping, and that the basilica was boarded up and sandbagged, only put a small dent in her satisfaction.

She had virtually smuggled a solid war story out of Italy to England, she was set to get another good story today, and the morning sunshine was warm enough that she could take her gloves off to eat the flaky pastry without fearing her fingers would turn blue. And Sandro was here.

It was a little frightening, the extent to which she had come to rely on him. She must learn to stand on her own two feet. After the war (soon, please God), she would go to England and convince Evans or some other editor that she could be trusted to cover bigger stories than hemline lengths. Would Jack be with her?

'Are you all right?' Sandro asked. He didn't talk much, but he always said the right thing.

'Just thinking about after the war.'

He grimaced, which she hadn't expected, and she laughed.

'I know,' he said. 'We're all supposed to want the end of it. I do. But . . .'

'But what then?'

'Yeah.'

They sat for a moment, sipping their coffee. 'I thought Jack and I would go to England together,' she said. 'But who knows what he'll want?'

'I thought I'd be a hero,' Sandro said dryly. 'We live and learn.'

'We learn too much, sometimes.'

His smile died and he took her hand.

She would be calm and collected and professional. The best possible defence. The best possible disguise. She was a fool. A fool who fell in love too easily.

She withdrew her hand and refused to meet his eyes.

'They're setting up,' she said, pointing to where some sailors were erecting a small stage. 'Best get our places.'

Sandro paid and they went to stand right in front of the stage, side by side but not touching, as the crowd gathered. Sandro took out his large camera and extended its focusing slide, ready.

Admiral Paolo Thaon di Revel was an upright man in his late fifties, with a truly impressive moustache that spread out from his face like wings. He wore an old-fashioned high collar under his uniform jacket, and his face fell naturally into stern lines.

He bounced a little on the tips of his toes, clearly impatient to make his announcement. Around them, journalists and citizens gathered; the reporters only known by their notebooks and cameras. Rebecca and Sandro duly took out their tools of trade, and Sandro took a shot of the admiral, who was flanked by several aides, all wearing suppressed smiles. Whatever this was, it wasn't bad news.

To one side, Seppina Rizzo waited behind the stage, with her father and sisters. She saw them and wiggled her fingers at them, smiling broadly.

The admiral cleared his throat, and the murmurings in the crowd died away.

In that moment of silence, Rebecca felt oddly disconnected from everything. Here she was, in St Mark's Square, in Venice, a journalist, under a cloudless pale blue sky. The buildings around her were those she had dreamed of seeing her whole life. But it all felt so distant; unreal, like a theatre backdrop.

She blinked rapidly, as if that would clear her thoughts as well as her eyes. Sandro leaned towards her and whispered, 'Are you all right?' and she thought *Why does he keep asking me that*? But then she caught his eye and suddenly everything was back as it was supposed to be: the flagstones firm under her feet, the wind real on her cheeks, St Mark's itself a towering, solid edifice instead of a flimsy backdrop.

The admiral spoke: 'I am delighted to announce a stunning victory for the *Marina Militare*. Last night, the ninth of December 1917, two Italian torpedo boats left Venice, towing *MAS 9* and *MAS 13*, under the command of Tenente Luigi Rizzo and Chief Quartermaster Ferrarini.

'At 22.45, *MAS 9* and *13* were detached from their tow ten miles from Trieste harbour.'

At the mention of Trieste, the Austrians' big base only ninety miles from Venice, the crowd stirred, and Rebecca felt the excitement start to build. The admiral smiled, and nodded, as if to encourage it.

'Tenente Rizzo led a team into Trieste harbour itself, and sank the Austrian battleship, the SMS *Wien*, and brought his entire crew home unharmed!'

Cheers broke out in the crowd. People were hugging each other, jumping up and down, waving small Italian flags.

As the news spread through the piazza more people came running, shouting to their neighbours. Someone started a chant of '*Italia! Italia!*' and half the crowd joined in.

The admiral stayed still, basking in the news; finally, *good* news to share with the people of Venice. And what news! My God! Trieste harbour was closely guarded, one of the most important Austrian ports in the Adriatic. And the MAS boats were tiny! What a story. No wonder Seppina was smiling proudly.

The journalist in Rebecca came to the fore, and she pressed closer to the stage.

'Admiral!' she shouted. 'Where is Tenente Rizzo now?'

'At Grado, celebrating his victory, signora!'

The admiral waved to the crowd, and headed off. The Italian journalists rushed away to the post office or to the nearest telephone, to try to get the story into the evening edition, but Rebecca had more time. A telegram couldn't possibly get to England early enough for that. She followed the admiral towards the edge of the piazza, where an official navy launch was waiting for him. He was shaking hands with Seppina Rizzo and her father. Her sisters stood nearby, as proud as punch.

'Admiral!' she called. '*Ammiraglio!*'

He turned and smiled benignly on her. 'Signora?'

'Rebecca Quinn, with the British *Evening News*,' she said in Italian. He blinked, and frowned, casting a glance at Sandro that darkened when he saw the camera. He had a reputation for disliking the press.

'When can we interview Tenente Rizzo?'

'No women on base,' he said. 'We're bringing Signor Percy Gibbon down from the front line to Grado tomorrow. Signor Gibbon is a trusted correspondent and will be given the *only* foreign interview. *Signor* Gibbon,' he added, 'is from *The Times*.'

In other words, he's quality and you are trash, she thought. *He's a man and you should be at home having babies.*

'That's hardly fair to the large part of the British public who don't read *The Times*. The *Evening News* has a larger circulation.'

He smiled with a patronising air. 'My dear, even if you represented Reuters, the answer would be the same. No women are allowed on any base, or into any press conference. Now, if

311

you could get yourself to Grado and persuade Tenente Rizzo to leave the base to give some unknown *lady* an interview . . .' He shrugged, half-laughing.

'So, I have your permission?' she asked, anger building.

'*Si, si*, you have my permission.' He waved her away, heading off to the launch. 'Go home and tend your house, woman.'

Sandro sniffed in disgust, and Rebecca shared a glance with him, full of anger and resolve.

Seppina was gazing after the admiral with narrowed eyes. 'He is a good friend to Luigi,' she said, 'but he is very old-fashioned.'

Everything from the past few months – every frustration, every snide comment from Coates, every dismissal by Evans, and yes, every word of hers that Jack had stolen, built up behind Rebecca's eyes. This was *the* story. The one that could establish both her and Sandro. She *would not* let it go.

'You know what we're going to do, right?' she said to him.

'Sure,' he said, hefting his camera and smiling. 'We're going to Grado, and we're going to scoop everyone else. You've got permission.'

Jack would have said, *I'm going to Grado*. But not Sandro. Even though she had once thought of him as the typical disapproving male, he had changed – or now she was seeing him better. At every step he supported her – no, it was better than that. At every step they moved together, as equals. She couldn't think about that now, or she would cry, the emotion swelling in her heart and making her eyes hot with tears. She swallowed, and got herself back under control.

Seppina regarded them with approval. 'If you can get to Grado, Luigi will come out of the base to you. He will come because I will give you a letter for him, and because you will tell him you are my friends. You can use our house,' she added, and gave them a key and the address.

Grado was on the coast between Venice and Trieste – hours away by boat, and even further by road, because it was on the tip of a long peninsula. It was the last Italian port before enemy territory, and the waters were heavily patrolled by U-boats.

'If you ask for an official permit to take a boat there . . .' she added doubtfully.

'The admiral will cancel any permission he's given me,' Rebecca said. 'We have to get there by less official means.'

'Smugglers,' Sandro said. 'Black marketeers.' They looked at each other, sharing a smile.

'Time for Nonna Rosa's contact,' Sandro said. 'I have an address. I decoded it on the train.' He explained to Seppina, 'My grandmother is connected.'

'Ah, so you have a way? Good!' Seppina said.

The two women stood there, smiling at him, and the way they stood, their confidence, the intelligence in their gaze, the laughter in their eyes . . . they were the picture of the New Woman. The twentieth-century woman. And he was an American, a twentieth-century man.

He grinned back at the both of them.

'*Ecco!*' Seppina said. 'Go to the address and see if they can help you. But wait . . .'

She ran back to her father, borrowed his notebook and scribbled a note, folding it in three.

'Here.' She gave it to Rebecca. 'Give this to Luigi with my love and tell him I'll see him tomorrow.'

•

Rebecca was possessed by a lightheartedness she would never have expected. Death was possible, likely even, if they went on. She was surrounded by desperation. But this story was so important. If ever there was a time in this war when the Allies needed good news, it was now. And this story had everything the Allies valued: independence, courage, teamwork, and a kind of self-reliance that, for her, was the very heart of a democracy. This story ought to be in *every* paper, not just in *The Times*. She was damned if she was going to let the admiral deny it to the rest of the newspaper world.

A gondola was pulling in a little way up the street, and Sandro jerked his head towards it and started to plough through the crowd coming for noon Mass at the Basilica. She followed, close behind.

This gondola was rowed by a woman in her thirties, with a small rugged-up child at her feet. Husband at the front, probably, and she was keeping the family business literally afloat.

'Signora,' Sandro said, 'we need to go to the Calla Lunga San Barnaba.'

'*Si*,' she said. Her face was mostly covered by a scarf worn over a shawl, and as Rebecca stepped gingerly onto the deck and sat on a narrow bench, she saw that the woman was wearing trousers under her skirt, like Seppina. Good for her. It was so cold that Rebecca wished she had a pair of her own. The wind whistled off the water, sharp and mean, and up her dress. Wool stockings weren't much barrier to it.

The little bundle of child at her feet stared at Rebecca with wide brown eyes. Rebecca smiled at it. Impossible to tell if it was a boy or a girl. Now, somewhere she had a bun left over from breakfast . . . she found it in her purse, unwrapped it from the waxed paper, and held it out to the child.

Without a pause, the child snatched it, pulled down the scarf that was wrapped around its mouth and nose, and tore into it. Poor thing; hungry as well as cold. The gondolier looked down at her expressionlessly, but then nodded. Rebecca nodded back. Once again she was struck by the solidarity between women who had only just met. An unspoken understanding.

They travelled through a network of small canals, taking turn after turn, and then, they were out, onto the Grand Canal. They began to make a slow, winding way through boats and gondolas going in the other direction. The streets became emptier as they went, and the boats fewer. When they had first arrived, it had been so foggy that she had seen very little, and now she looked around eagerly. The canal was wider than she had expected, more like a huge river, choppy and challenging for the gondolier. Even the word was exotic, bringing back snatches of Gilbert and Sullivan songs, memories of the Turners in the National Gallery of British Art, of countless stories.

She hadn't known how shabby some of the palazzos would be, or expected to see the results of bombing. But why should Venice, the *Serenissima*, be different from other cities in this war? That was romantic thinking. She was near the front line, and there *was* danger here.

The boat followed the curve in the canal around to the right, deftly avoiding short piers and other boats tied up, and drew in to a large wharf. The gondolier named her price, and Sandro paid her; but Rebecca found a five lire note in her purse, and pressed it into her hand. 'For the little one,' she said. The woman nodded her thanks, swallowing tightly, clearly unable to speak.

They clambered out and stood on the wharf while she drew away up the canal.

'You're sure about this?' Sandro asked her.

She thought of Jack, haring off with smugglers halfway across Europe. She had been angry, but right at this moment she understood perfectly. When the story was good, when it dangled in front of you like a shiny Fabergé egg, you had to chase it, no matter what the danger. In retrospect, she forgave him for leaving her alone in Brindisi. If their positions had been reversed, she would have gone on that smugglers' boat too.

'I'm sure,' she said.

There was a signpost on the street nearby: Calla Lunga San Barnaba.

A long name for a tiny alley. Rebecca doubted three people could have walked abreast in it. Ancient houses and shops, most with their windows boarded, alternated with tiny terrace houses whose front doors opened straight onto the street. Brick and plaster, iron bars on some windows, and a few shop signs, hanging out over the alley just above head height.

They went down, fog swirling around their feet, checking the signs, getting colder and colder.

'The sign of the bull,' Sandro said in frustration. 'She couldn't give us a street number?'

'I don't see any here,' Rebecca said. They walked together, each checking their side of the street. Suddenly, the alleyway opened up into a piazza, with a church, San Barnaba, presumably, but then kept going on the other side. Rebecca sighed. Even with Sandro insisting on carrying her bag, she was exhausted. Her feet hurt, her hands were icy, and the exhilaration she had felt at the press conference had been washed away by the cold.

They went on.

On the other side, there were more signs, mostly shops that were closed, even boarded up. A few were open: a tobacconist, a cobbler, a bar. Then, on a corner, was a cafe, and the delicious scent of coffee and bread. Over its door was a strange outline drawing. It *could* have been a bull. She didn't care if it wasn't – there was coffee. Nothing short of an Austrian battalion could have kept her out of that shop.

Without even looking at each other, they turned in and sat at the table closest to a small fire. There were only a few other customers; the place looked bare.

The owner came over, an old man, towel over his shoulder, beaming at them, speaking in a fast, colloquial Italian. She was rather pleased with herself that she could understand him.

'Signore, signora. What can I get for you?'

'Whatever you've got,' Sandro said. 'We're hungry and we need coffee quickly!'

The man laughed, showing he still had two teeth. '*Si, subito!*' He mock saluted and left.

'Sandro,' Rebecca said. 'Look.'

On the wall was a mural of a bull. Not one of those fiery Spanish bulls, but a pretend bull, a construct of papier mache, sitting upright like a man, with its front legs stuck out straight. Around it were small human figures apparently about to light it on fire. The painting seemed very old. There was no perspective, no naturalism.

'Aha!' the owner said, returning with a pot of coffee and two cups. 'You like our bull, yes? In the old days, they used to kill an actual bull, and later they made the pretend one and set it on fire on the last day of Carnevale, like it shows in the picture. But now, no more. Carnevale still happens, but it's a poor thing to what it used to be.'

'I think my grandmother would like that bull,' Sandro said cautiously. 'Rosa Panucci?'

The man stopped, mid-gesture, and brought his hands slowly back to his body, tucking his thumbs over his waistband and rocking on his heels.

'Rosa? She is a lovely woman.'

'Ha!' Sandro said. 'Is that a test? Anyone who ever met her would pass it!'

The man grinned. 'You're the grandson, no? She told me about you.' He bowed in a most courtly fashion. 'And this is your young lady? I am Marcello.'

Better to let him think so. 'A pleasure to meet you,' she said.

He bent over and whispered to them. 'We will talk. But first, food!'

'And coffee!' Sandro said with feeling, pouring a cup for her.

'And coffee!' she echoed.

Before they could take their first sip, the Angelus bells began to ring, waking the city and drowning out the cannon fire. Together, the three of them made the sign of the cross.

'*Angelus Domini nuntiavit Mariae*,' Marcello said.

'*Et concepit de Spiritu Sancto*,' Rebecca and Sandro replied. '*Ave Maria, gratias plena . . .*'

They went through the whole prayer; Rebecca's responses were automatic, from long practice. Every day of her school life, every day since she'd come here and had heard the Angelus bells ring out. The words flowed through her, calming and uplifting. Everyone in the cafe was doing the same. She saw their lips move as they muttered the words. It gave her a sense of belonging she would never feel in Australia, which was so heavily Protestant, where Catholics, although a quarter of the population, were considered somehow inferior, strange and suspicious, under the sway of the Scarlet Whore of Rome.

'Amen,' said Marcello.

'Amen,' they answered, and then it was over and everyone went about their business as though it had never happened.

'So, what can I do for you?' Marcello asked.

'We need to go to Grado,' Sandro said. 'Tonight.'

'Pwha!' Marcello pushed all the air out of his lungs in an expression of astonishment. 'You know the Austrian U-boats are on the hunt all up and down this coast? You could be blown out of the water!'

Rebecca looked at Sandro, troubled. Did she have the right to drag him into danger? But he was smiling at the cafe owner.

'A man has to die some day,' he said.

'You're Rosa's grandson, all right. I won't ask why you want to go.'

He tapped his teeth with his waiter's pencil, thinking. 'Okay. I think we can do it. Let me make some calls.' He disappeared into the back room.

'A telephone?' Rebecca said, surprised.

'I guess, if you're a smuggler, a telephone is handy . . .'

After the meal, the cafe emptied out and Marcello came to usher them into the back.

After the simplicity of the Brindisan furnishings, the room's opulence caught her by surprise. The furniture was ornately carved, and the walls were painted, not whitewashed, in a deep red. On the floor, a Turkish carpet, old but still vivid. Heavy silk curtains over the one window. There were even some small figurines that were clearly Chinese in origin, next to a very modern telephone. The room was a reminder of Venice's long maritime past, its dominance in world trade for centuries.

The sense of age swept over her, filling her with awe as it had in the church when she had first met Sandro. This room had been occupied for longer than Australia had been settled.

The walls had seen generations come and go, and each generation had brought a new treasure to add to the total. Perhaps only one treasure every fifty years; but after so many generations the room was luxurious, astonishing.

She sat down on a horsehair sofa with armrests carved into lion's heads.

'It's nice, yes?' Marcello said, looking around with pride. 'No one looks for spoils in this little alley, eh? So we survive.'

In that remark, Rebecca saw war after war, invasion after invasion. France, Austria, France, Austria, and finally Sardinia in the form of Garibaldi.

'You're survivors in Venice, for sure,' Sandro said, sitting opposite her in a deep red armchair.

'Yes! And we will survive this,' he answered, cocking his head to listen to the sound of the distant guns. 'Rest, now, and I'll come and get you after dark.'

Even with the early winter sunset, that gave them a few hours.

'Lie down,' Sandro urged. 'No one will mind.' But she couldn't put her feet on this sofa. She took off her hat and arranged herself so that she could rest her head back against the antimacassar, and closed her eyes, comforted by the knowledge that he was there with her.

35

He let himself look at her for a while before he rested his eyes.

Knowing they might die in this exploit made every feeling sharper.

The two sides of her fascinated him. He had seen both, in their first two meetings. In the church. And outside the base, where she had harangued him about women and the war, her passion harnessed into a cause. He had interpreted it as coldness, arrogance, an unpleasant personality, but he'd been wrong.

She had so many flaws, and so many good points. Her naiveté about people balanced by shrewdness. Her temper matched by her compassion. Her pigheadedness undercut by her rationality.

He was a lost cause.

•

Marcello shook Sandro's shoulder and whispered, '*Andiamo!*'

He jolted awake and sprang out of his chair to help a sleepy Rebecca stand up.

As she came fully awake, her smile seemed to say, *What an adventure we're having!* He smiled back. It *was* an adventure.

They visited the outhouse before they left, then grabbed a quick meal, standing up in the kitchen at the back. Eating standing up in a kitchen – it was so unusual for Italians that it gave the whole night an air of urgency.

Marcello parcelled up some bread and hard cheese for them, and they went out through a side door that gave onto an even narrower alley. The city was eerily quiet, the only noise the guns to the north and the constant lap of the water in the canals.

How many people had left? From the scenes at the train station this morning, there were still a lot trying to get out.

Then the bells started. He had heard them, on and off, waking him from his doze, but they had been muffled. Out here, the sharp tintinnabulation was a shock to the system, bouncing from the walls and the water and fading away only gradually. When it ended, it took him a few moments to make sure his ears weren't still echoing with the noise.

It was first-rate cover for their movements, and the moon was in its last quarter, so the shadows were deep. They went by mean alleys and by canals so narrow that they could jump across them. Marcello knew his city, and he was making sure they weren't followed. Several times he pulled them into some dark niche while he waited to hear footsteps, or maybe oars.

The caution was necessary because all trips outside the Venice lagoon were supposed to be approved by the Arsenale. Marcello could be arrested for helping them, and they would probably be kicked out of Italy. Was it worth the risk? Sure. He wanted to be a war photographer, so why should he bellyache about a little danger? Besides, he couldn't do much for Becca but he could do this: support her in her valiant effort to make it to the top of her profession, where she deserved to be.

Marcello eventually stopped in front of a pair of red wooden doors, big enough to let in a cart, or a car. The building was the last in the alley, which ended in a blank wall just beyond the doors. He knocked softly. The left door opened a crack, and then wider. A woman, standing behind it, beckoned them and they slid in.

She was young, with a sharp nose and a wide, smiling mouth. 'Tio Marcello,' she said, kissing him on the cheek. 'Come.'

It was a warehouse of some kind. The girl had a lantern, which sent shadows advancing and retreating across a row of over-sized gondolas up on wooden cradles, their curving sterns carved and gilded in astonishing ways.

He and Rebecca stared at the boats; they were glorious, and amazing, and unnerving. One day he would come back here with studio lights and a camera, and take some shots which would stun New York.

'For the Regata Storica,' the girl said, gesturing to them as they went through the large, unearthly shapes to a set of double doors, open to the water beyond. A boatshed – no, a *loading* bay.

At the small dock they came to a motorboat not much bigger than the gondolas they had just passed. A new ally was waiting – a young man. He jumped in and gestured to them to follow.

Sandro steadied Rebecca as she stepped down and wondered, not for the first time, how women got anything done in long skirts. He climbed in after her and the two sat on either side, on benches that ran the length of the boat. There was a small cabin, and the man stood in it at the wheel.

Speaking low, he said, 'I'm Abelardo.'

'Sandro.'

'Rebecca.'

He smiled, and even in the starlight his teeth flashed white.

'We're going quietly,' he said, his voice a murmur only just above the waves. 'We go north.'

That was all. He flipped a switch on the dashboard and motioned to Sandro to cast off. Sandro grabbed the mooring line and flipped it off a low bollard, and they nosed out to open water in silence. This was an electric boat, and the noise of the engine was more than covered by the sound of the waves and the rising wind.

On this side of the island, there were no lights. He tried to remember the shape of the Venice Lagoon. There was the big island of Venetia itself, near the mainland, then a few small islands and then a gap before the long, thin arm of the Lido stretched out to protect the huge lagoon, which was more like an enormous lake.

The Lido, famed pleasure ground of Venice, where surf bathing and promenading and fine dining were the order of the day. Now, according to the Italian newspapers, the bathing huts were boarded up and the beach was barricaded with barbed wire. He couldn't help but imagine Coney Island like that, and shivered.

There was a passage through to the open sea on either side of the Lido island, and they were heavily guarded. Surely they weren't expected to run under those guns? Thinking the word, he became again aware of the far pounding of the Austrian cannon. His confidence faltered. Why had he encouraged Becca to come? It was too dangerous.

He looked across at her. She had her face turned into the wind, and she was smiling.

Smiling.

Madonna mia, she was wonderful. He was seething with something too big to push down. A blazing admiration, a tender yearning, a deep desire. The longing was so strong that he couldn't breathe. *This is the beginning*, he thought. *This is the start of my heart being broken, or of . . . something too great to even name.*

Rebecca turned and smiled again at him, inviting him to join her enjoyment. He smiled back, unable to even imagine his previous fear.

His disobedient heart was filled with exhilaration.

36

The wind was strong, and even here in the lagoon the waves were high. Abelardo handled the little boat confidently, though, seemingly unworried.

There was nothing Rebecca could do to influence the outcome of the next few hours. And she was at sea again! Jack had introduced her to sailing, back in their university days. His father had a 33-foot sloop, and they had sailed on Sydney Harbour, setting off from a mooring just down from the Quinns' Rose Bay house. Jack and his father Valentine and his brother Ted, his brother's girl Mavis, and Rebecca. To sail on Sydney Harbour on a summer's evening, to goose-wing back from the Heads down to the Quay, spinnaker stretched in the gentle breeze . . . her love for Jack had been bound up in times like those, in sailing on the harbour and rowing on the river, in shooting the surf at Bondi Beach, in lazy picnics in Centennial Park. Perhaps she had fallen in love with Sydney rather than with Jack . . .

They went north, towards the sound of the guns. From the Lido, getting closer, great searchlights cut across the water in long sweeps. There were other lights pointing out to sea; Rebecca could see them shining out from wooden towers. And the shoreline, lit by the reflections from the lights, was a jumble of barbed-wire coils, jagged and evil looking. No soldiers on this side, but there would be in those towers.

After Caporetto, Italian soldiers would be on the alert and likely to overreact. Best never to be seen. The searchlights swept past them, and then one circled back to pin them with light.

A sudden staccato noise. The water before them sputtered with shots. Holy Mother! That was machine-gun fire. A warning from the lookouts on the Lido.

Her heart jumped and cold sweat broke out on her brow. Would they be shot out of hand?

Abelardo thrust down on the throttle and pulled an Italian flag from under the cockpit. He waved it with his whole arm, back and forth. They stayed still, in silence, knowing nothing but the glaring light in their eyes. She wished desperately that she could hear past the wind in her ears; her heart was jumping, hard and fast.

Then the light moved on.

Sandro was holding her hand. He had moved, without her realising, to put his body between hers and the guns, pulling her down to make a smaller target. Shaking, she squeezed his hand, and he touched her cheek, softly, with gloved fingers. Even so, his touch brought the blood rushing to her face.

'Okay, *cara*?' he asked.

'Yes.' As she said it aloud, it became true. 'Yes, I'm fine. Are you?'

'Sure.' But his voice wavered a little. 'If they'd shot you . . .'

327

Abelardo, with one last wave of the flag, set the boat in motion again, making way against the growing waves.

He turned his head to grin at them. 'I come this way every night. I live on Sant'Erasmo.'

'You might have warned us!' Sandro said.

Abelardo shrugged and spread his hands. 'Sometimes it happens, sometimes it doesn't.'

She had been ready for submarines on the Adriatic, but not being shot at by Italians. Now it was over, though, all she could feel was the warm place on her cheek where Sandro had touched her. They sat back up and he let go of her hand, leaving it feeling colder than before.

They were past the last bit of Venice proper and heading towards a channel between the peninsula opposite the Lido and another island. Further north, and the wind dropped a little now that they were between two stretches of land, but the current was stronger. They were running with the incoming tide; she could feel the strength of it on the stern, pushing them forward, with the wind against their bow, pushing them back.

The tide won, of course; nothing could resist it. The boat ran, fast and silent, past houses and piers on the banks of Sant'Erasmo, and fields and farmhouses on the eastern bank. There were few lights; this close to the front, people were taking no chances.

God help them all. This expedition of Rizzo's was important not only strategically, but also in terms of morale. If a little Italian motorboat could sink the Austrians' biggest warship . . .

What a story it was!

•

Half an hour later, they were past San'Erasmo, and in the salt marshes. No enemy could come through here; only a local could

328

know the twists and turns, the passages that would take the boat and those that would leave them stranded.

'We go slow to wait for the tide,' Abelardo explained. 'Then we take a back way, through to the Fiume Sile, and to the sea.'

'In this boat?' she asked, disbelieving.

'Just to the ship,' he assured her. 'You will get wet, maybe, but you will be safe. Trust me.' He slapped hand on his chest, full of bravado.

'Of course,' Sandro said drily, but in fact Rebecca did trust him. He knew his job.

With wavelets slapping hard, they were in a world of sound and movement, through channels so narrow the seagrass scraped against the hull, past silent fishermen's huts, the sky grey above them, the wind always complaining. Finally, they were moving between the banks of a small river, lined with bushes and trees. The wind was calmer here, and the smell of the sea lessened.

A bridge formed an arch of darker shadow above them. Abelardo put the engine into slow reverse, so that they hovered underneath the bridge. Was there a man on it? It was so hard to see, the shadows and darkness bleeding into one another.

'*Ho!*' a quiet voice came.

'*Come stai?*' Abelardo said. From above, a line snaked down, some kind of bag on the end. Abelardo grabbed it and took something out; bottles chinked, then the rope was hauled up. And on they went.

'Do we find out what that was all about?' Sandro asked him.

'Not from me,' Abelardo said with unimpaired cheerfulness.

Another bridge, a larger one, with a sentry hut, its small light shining brightly. What would happen if they were caught? Arrested as spies? With her blonde hair, she could be taken for Austrian, or German . . . Spies were shot.

Abelardo crouched down as they approached the bridge, motioning them to do the same. A smaller target, but the light wooden hull would be no protection.

As they approached, they heard guards talking in the hut. She held her breath as slowly they crept past. Sandro crouched next to her, and held her hand firmly. He was so dependable. Solid and real and human, always calm. She could rely on him. But she mustn't.

Then they were past. She squeezed his hand and let go. Haltingly, because they were stiff with sitting still, they edged back onto their seats.

After that came smaller passageways, with Abelardo cutting the motor down to its minimum so as not to foul the propeller. Ahead of them, growing brighter as they moved on, a lighthouse split the night with a series of flashes sent out to sea, and the noise of waves on a beach grew louder. A lighthouse meant a perilous passage. How safe were they really, in this little boat?

The waves grew larger. A low white beach on the left, and a wall on the right. The waves were running fast up the river, and the boat lifted and thwacked down again over and over. Abelardo turned to the left and ran the boat up on the beach, leaping to the stern to pull the propeller up before it scraped on the sand. Sandro hauled it up with him.

'I thought we were going out to sea,' she said.

'I am brave, *signora*, but I am not a fool. The sea runs too high for this boat. They will send a *canotto* to the beach for you.'

'They can come up in this?' Sandro asked.

'Not *up*,' Abelardo said, as if that was too much to expect. The wind whipped his words away, and again she had a feeling of being in something surreal, unbelievable. What was a girl from Sydney doing standing on a barbed-wired beach in Italy in the darkness of night with a Venetian smuggler and a photographer from New York?

He led them further up the beach. In some places, the wire had been put as far down as the high-water mark; with the tide coming, they had to manoeuvre around these carefully, and her skirt ripped on one, sending a draught of cold air right up her thigh.

A half a mile or so up the beach, as far as she could measure it, Abelardo stopped and took a torch out of his jacket pocket, pointing it out to sea, and waving backwards and forwards three times, just as he had signalled with the flag.

Was he a patriot, she wondered, or just an opportunist? Because an opportunist might think that handing them over to the Austrians could be good insurance against possible invasion.

An answering light came, and soon enough a splash in the dark announced another electric motorboat, a bigger boat, thank the Lord, which nosed in, riding the waves, until it beached just up from them.

She kissed Abelardo's cheek, and pressed some notes into his hand.

'*Grazie, bella signora!*' he said, and winked at her, just as the lighthouse flashed, so that he was suddenly bright, his teeth and eyes gleaming, like a film hero. Sandro shook his hand.

They would have to walk through the waves to get to the boat. Either they trusted Abelardo or they didn't – they had cast that die a long time back.

She kirtled her skirts up high, but Sandro picked her up against her protests and carried her out to the skiff. A couple of slight figures turned out to be young men, fishermen in their teens, who were astonished when they saw her.

'*Una donna!*' one exclaimed.

Abelardo shone his torch onto the side of the boat, the beam pointing down. 'Hurry up, you fool! The guards at the lighthouse are due to make their rounds in five minutes!'

Chastised, the boys dragged her on board, and then Sandro behind her, complete with backpack, and one jumped out to help Abelardo push the boat out until it could make way. The boy clambered back on board just in time to see Rebecca lower her skirts. His eyes almost fell out, and she tried not to laugh.

But the cold wasn't funny. Now her feet were thoroughly wet, and the chill crept up her legs to ice her body. This boat had a small half-cabin, and the young crew herded her and Sandro into it, away from the wind. It was a relief, but there was nowhere to sit; only just enough room for the two of them to stand. Without thinking, she put her hand on Sandro's cold cheek.

'You're freezing!'

Startled by the touch, their bodies close together, his face revealed desire. Rebecca stood still, not breathing. Her own body leaped to answer the need she saw in his eyes. Ridiculous. She was a respectable woman, a *married* woman. She shouldn't be *able* to feel like this. It was the tension of the night bringing this out in her.

But she knew she was lying to herself.

'I'm okay,' he said softly, putting his hand up to cover hers. 'Thank you for asking.' Such polite words. Such a different meaning.

She lowered her hand slowly, and his came with it, gripping hers. The mists of their breaths mingled; in the small cabin light she could see his pulse beating fast in his throat. The boat went up over a wave and came down hard, and they grabbed one another for balance. Sandro leaned back against the cabin side, and pulled her to lean against him. She nestled her face into his shoulder, allowing the weight of her head to rest against him. It was a magnificent relief. His arms came around her. *Just this one moment*, she thought. *Out in the darkness, where it doesn't count. Just a moment to remember*. They stood, feet braced against the climb and descent of the boat, against the waves and the wind, his mouth against her hair, her hand over his heart.

•

It took hours for them to get to Grado. Along the way their hosts offered them hot coffee in a thermos, and they ate dried fruit and nuts with relish, sitting on a bench just outside the cabin, oilskins buttoned up tight. The small respite they had had in the cabin had rejuvenated them both. Rebecca wasn't sure if it had been the rest or the . . . the connection they had formed.

'We're not far now,' the oldest of the boys said, with an accent she couldn't place.

'For you,' the other said, 'one hundred lire.'

It was a huge sum of money, but they were risking their lives. Before she could get it out of her purse, Sandro said, 'Fifty,' and they were off, haggling in the way she had never quite got used to.

The boy at the stern had throttled back, watching the bargaining with amusement. From seawards, without warning, a deep bubble and hiss came, like a warning from a sea monster. The sound slid under her nerves and brought up the deepest kind of fear, the kind only felt in the dark. She trembled and clutched the side. What *was* it?

Twenty yards away from the boat, the monster emerged, moving up, the water streaming off its smooth grey side.

'U-boat!' a boy yelled.

Rebecca was frozen in place. She had no idea what to do, except look for Sandro, to make sure he was all right.

A bright light cut across them. The sharp sound of machine-gun fire. Bullets spattered in the water ahead of the boat.

'Down!' Sandro yelled, lunging at her and pulling her to the deck and covering her body with his own.

Peeping over the edge, Rebecca saw the long, low shape of a submarine, a bright yellow searchlight on its stern pinning them in place. Another light swept back and forth; as it moved briefly across the hull, she saw *U-14*. Von Trapp's boat. A voice came, in German, demanding they identify themselves.

'We are Serbian!' the oldest boy cried. 'Out of Trieste! The fishing boat *Vesna*.'

'Show yourselves. All of you.'

The boy gestured frantically to them to stand up. Slowly, Sandro raised himself and put a hand down to her. Her heart was skipping and pattering with fear; her breath caught short at the thought of bullets tearing through him, of the torpedo breaking apart this flimsy old boat, and abandoning him to the killing cold of the sea. The air was suddenly sharp in her lungs, and her knees were shaky as she stood up, outlined in the glare of the light. Chatter broke out on the sub.

'*Gott im Himmel! Ein Madchen!*' A girl. For some reason that astonished tone, the dismissive word, took away her fear.

'*Nein!*' she shouted. '*Eine frau!*'

There was some laughter, and a deeper voice – von Trapp's? – said, '*Geh in freidan, Frau.*'

Go in peace.

'*Abschied, mein Herr.*' Farewell. Goodbye. Yes, go, go on, leave. Her heart was speeding up again and she could feel her hands shake. She clasped them together.

Sandro stared with hatred at the submarine. Hatred and frustration, as though he would have liked to have had a machine gun of his own to use.

The lights clicked off, and the dark sparkled against her eyes. Sandro's hand came up and he swept her into his arms, holding her tightly. His other hand found her face and then he kissed her, hard and strong, and God help her, she kissed him back; relief and desire mixed up so that she couldn't pull them apart.

Then he tore his lips from hers and buried his face in her hair. She clutched his shoulders and hid her own face against his sleeve, her face flaming with shame; with need.

The boys muttered to each other in Serbian.

'One hundred lire,' the oldest said firmly.

'*Si*,' Sandro said. 'One hundred.' He roused, letting her go. 'When we get there.'

•

For the rest of the trip they sat apart, no matter how cold it got. She couldn't even look at him. She had behaved like a slut. And he . . . no, she couldn't blame him. Not when she'd responded so ardently. What must he think of her!

At Grado, they tied up at a wharf near the naval base, a large snow-covered building whose wire fence was patrolled by guards. This time, the sight of the guards reassured her. They had safely arrived – even if they were arrested for being here, no one would shoot them on sight on dry land.

Sandro paid the money from his own pocket. She didn't object. They were in this together.

'Okay?' he said to her, looking at her but not meeting her eyes.

'Yes,' she said.

He nodded almost brusquely, as though those shared moments hadn't happened.

He didn't offer to swing her up onto the dock, so she scrambled out as best she could, and he followed, still not looking at her.

The boys stowed their gear and headed up a path that had been shovelled out towards a building from which lights shone. The sound of voices and the chink of glasses came softly down to where she and Sandro stood on the dock. Her legs were unsteady, now she was back on solid ground.

'Food?' Sandro suggested, his voice a little more relaxed. 'A hot drink?'

They walked up the path, which was covered by a light dusting of snow. Their feet made no noise, as though they glided along.

The lighted building was a taverna; although almost midnight, it was half-full of off-duty sailors, drinking steadily and making free with a number of women who were clearly professionals.

Sandro established her in a corner table and went to the bar to get drinks and some food. He came back in a lightened mood.

'Come on, drink up. It's mulled wine,' he said. 'And some Montasio.'

Montasio was a pale cheese, much softer than the bread, which suffered from the problem experienced by everyone in Italy – with the exception of Nonna Rosa, apparently – of not having enough white flour.

As they raised their glasses, their gazes caught and held. Sandro swallowed a good gulp and put the glass back on the table with a little more force than necessary.

'Back to reality,' he said.

She closed her eyes against the resolute stoicism in his eyes, but that was being cowardly. Opening them, she nodded to him, and spoke as gently as she knew how.

'Yes.'

His mouth turned awry, but he said nothing, and they ate in silence.

After the meal, they went out into the cold reluctantly, but if they were to get that interview in time, she had to see Tenente Rizzo now. All they had to do was persuade the man on the gate.

As they approached the guards, the two men snapped to attention and then lowered their rifles, complete with bayonets, towards them.

'*Fermati lì!*' one said.

'*Buonasera, signori,*' she said, comfortable in Italian now. 'I have a letter for Tenente Rizzo from his wife.'

They looked at each other. The lights were pointed down on the guardhouse, so they couldn't be seen clearly from a plane, but she could see that they were unsure of what to do.

'Signora Rizzo gave it to me today, and asked me especially to get it to her husband tonight.'

They looked at each other again, and one of them shrugged, but they said nothing and made no move.

Sandro stepped in. 'I think Tenente Rizzo would probably like to have this letter immediately. Don't you?' There was a faint warning in his voice.

'She is not Italian,' the older of the two said, pointing at Rebecca.

'I'm Australian.'

They gaped at her, unable to imagine what an Australian woman was doing in Grado. She had to admit, it was unlikely.

'I'm a friend of Tenente Rizzo's wife.'

Again, they looked at each other.

Sandro took a photograph out of his backpack and showed it to them. Rebecca hadn't seen it before – it was Seppina, in the hospital. The guards both nodded and smiled.

'*Va bene*,' the older one said, taking it from him. 'I'll get him. You, stay here.'

The younger man brought a stool out of the guardhouse and set it for Rebecca. 'Here, signora. Seat yourself.'

'*Grazie*, signore.'

She felt ridiculous, sitting out in the street on a stool in the snow while Sandro and the guard stood nearby, but she couldn't refuse the kindness in the gesture. Grado was younger than Venice – at least, near the harbour, it looked as though some upgrades had been carried out in the past few years. The roads weren't cobblestones or flagstones, for a start, but asphalt. It gave her a vague sense of coming back into reality, as though her time in Italy had been in another century. The sound of guns and shells in the distance was another reminder.

The older guard arrived back in a rush.

'*Si*, signora, signore, Tenente Rizzo is coming!' He caught his breath, and smiled at them now he was assured of their bona fides. 'The captain is a great man,' he said. 'A true hero!'

'Yes,' Sandro said, and Rebecca echoed him. Yes, he was, and she itched to find out exactly how *much* of a hero he'd been.

A man appeared, tall and good looking, moving with the smoothness of an athlete. Next to him, the guards looked slovenly and unfit. He looked, in fact, like a hero. He had not been asleep, she thought, but his collar was open and his hair was mussed. He stood in the gateway and stared at them with hilarity in his gaze, as though they had performed a magic trick.

'A beautiful photograph of my Seppina?' he asked. 'And a letter brought by a friend? But, signora, I do not know you.'

'We are new friends,' Sandro said. 'But I assure you, Tenente, we come from your wife.'

'I do have a letter for you,' Rebecca said, conscious of the guards. She proffered the note from Seppina, which he read, and then smiled and tucked it away in his breast pocket. 'And I'd like to interview you.'

'Alas, signora, I cannot give any interviews without Admiral Thaon di Revel's permission.'

Sandro grinned. 'I am here to tell you that the admiral told Rebecca: *If you could get yourself to Grado and persuade Tenente Rizzo to leave the base to give some unknown lady an interview, you have my permission.*'

'After that, he told me to go home and tend my house,' Rebecca added. 'So, the question is, Tenente Rizzo, are you really a brave man or not?'

Rizzo laughed, and patted his pocket. 'My Seppina would be cross if I did not help so valiant a lady!'

He came with them, back to the taverna, and they sat in a corner, drinking mulled wine while Rebecca interviewed him. She had prepared the questions in her head long since, and Rizzo spoke easily and openly about the extraordinary operation. What a story this was. Two small motorboats, sixteen crew members, cutting down the great steel net which protected the harbour of Trieste, invading the Austrians' prized base, destroying one of their greatest ships – and then escaping with all hands! Incredible. She wouldn't have believed it in a novel, but this was real.

She was in the presence of someone who made history, and it gave an odd sharpness to every sense. It was like meeting Nelson, or Wellington. What a wonderful job this was!

Sandro persuaded the tavern owner to bring over every lantern in the place and, after Rizzo had combed his hair and fixed his collar, took a photograph.

'Since you had the admiral's permission,' Rizzo said, 'I will give you a lift back to Venice in the morning.'

But before that, she had to write her story, and send it.

'Is there a post office? A telegraph?'

'Signora, the Austrians have cut the lines. Listen.' He jerked his head to the west, where the sounds of cannon fire came intermittently. Could it be closer than before? 'We have advised the residents to evacuate. You will have to wait until Venice to send your story.'

She sighed and rested her head back on the wall behind her, tired to the bone and disappointed. She'd have a start on the *Times* reporter, but only by a few hours. Still, any advantage was good – and at the very least the *News* wouldn't be scooped. If she had waited like a good girl in Venice, Admiral Thaon di Revel would have made sure she never got anywhere near Tenente Rizzo.

She sat up straight. If she wrote it now, she could send it off as soon as they got to Venice, before Mr Percy Gibbons from *The Times* could take out his notebook. But there was one final question she had to ask.

'Weren't you afraid?'

'I would have been holding onto my rosary, or at least a rabbit's foot!' Sandro laughed, and Rizzo laughed with him.

'I only believe in these mascots,' he said, pointing at his head, wrist pulse and heart. 'Brain, nerves and courage. These are the right mascots.'

It was the perfect quote to end the story on.

By then, they were calling each other Luigi, Rebecca and Sandro. Luigi walked them to Seppina's family home and came in to show them the bedrooms and light a fire in the kitchen for them.

After he left, kissing Rebecca's hand and slapping Sandro's shoulder, they sat at the kitchen table with glasses of water. Rebecca took off her shoes and stretched her toes to the fire as she wrote the first draft of her story. She finished, yawning, and passed it over to Sandro, but he didn't read it. He was looking into the flames; they painted his face with slabs of orange and gold, and left his eyes shadowed.

'I wish I'd met you before—' She stopped. She couldn't finish that sentence. Her throat ached too much.

'If you'd met me *before*,' he said, not pretending to misunderstand her, 'you wouldn't have looked twice at me. You couldn't take me home to your parents. What would they say to a penniless dago American? They'd have had conniptions.'

Yes, they would. Her entire social circle would have been appalled, and completely flummoxed. She could just hear them. *My dear, what* were *you thinking?* And that patronising, sideways smile. Oh, yes. They would have had conniptions.

'I wouldn't have introduced you as a penniless dago American,' she said, chin out. 'I would have said, "This is Sandro Baker, a modern artist. His medium is photography."'

For a moment, they both contemplated that scene; and almost at the same instant, they let it slide away, sighing.

'I'll take the chair down here,' Sandro said quietly.

She nodded. What was there to say?

Upstairs, in what was surely the daughters' room, she lay on the top of the bed and pulled a spare quilt over her. Every part of her wanted to go downstairs, to walk into Sandro's arms, to kiss him, to lie with him.

Not quite every part.

There was still a faint sliver of honour, somewhere, that told her it would be wrong. Not only a sin for herself, but a worse sin in seducing Sandro. He had struggled so long to stay free of taint; and she knew that one touch from her would shred his good intentions. She knew he would not, could not, say no to her. And that was the most important reason she would stay in this bed until morning, even though her thoughts were downstairs, near the heat of the fire.

37

Luigi came to collect them, bouncing into the house just after dawn, full of vigour and energy. *'Andiamo!'* he called.

Rebecca changed her blouse and underwear quickly and straightened the bed. She came downstairs to find Sandro coming in from the privy, with no collar on and his hair tousled every which way. He looked . . . wonderful.

She greeted Luigi, who smiled benignly on them, and went out to the privy herself. And then they were gone, locking the door and heading down to the harbour. Sandro was very cheery this morning; and if it seemed a little false to her, it was clear that Luigi Rizzo didn't notice.

Luigi had brought the *MAS-9* around to the public wharf so they could board, and his crew were waiting – seven men, lounging around, eating cheese and sopressa rolls. Rebecca could smell the salami, and it made her mouth water.

'We can eat on the boat,' Luigi said. 'And we will be in Venice by lunchtime.'

'What about your interview with Percy Gibbons?' Rebecca asked.

'Oh, I think I will be so very happy to see my new wife again that I will not have time for Signor Gibbons until tomorrow!'

Laughing, they boarded, and then Sandro stood straight and bowed, very formally, to the crew and Luigi. 'On behalf of our fellow countrymen, I thank you for your great victory,' he said.

They nodded, smiling, and the first officer came over to kiss Sandro on both cheeks, hands on each other's shoulder. Sandro had never seemed so Italian – or so handsome. She wondered if he might even come to grow a moustache, in time.

Casting off, they made their way out of the harbour, paralleled by the other MAS that had taken part in the Trieste exploit, captained by Chief Quartermaster Ferrarini. The MAS were smallish boats – no larger than the fishing boat Rebecca and Sandro had been in the night before. The big difference was the two torpedoes, which were held up by braces, one on either side, pointing, oddly, backwards. They were rigged with gear so they could be lowered in the water.

'They point to the stern,' Rebecca said to Luigi.

'Si. It's annoying, getting into position to fire, but the advantage is you can run away faster!'

The whole crew laughed uproariously. They were buoyed by success, and so they should be. She would have loved to interview them, but Thaon di Revel had only given her 'permission' to interview their captain, and she didn't want to get them into trouble.

•

After a quick breakfast, Sandro took advantage of the great opportunity, and shot two rolls of film of the crew and Luigi in various poses, including having them simulate battle positions. They were in high spirits and the conditions were great, with thin clouds scattering the light so that he didn't have to worry about shadows on their faces. *Excellente*.

The work stopped him thinking about Rebecca.

After last night, the submarine, the noise of the guns getting closer and closer – he had to go to the front. But leave her . . . he wasn't sure he should do that. He wasn't sure he *could*.

The thought of leaving her was an ache, low down, as he imagined an ulcer would feel. Something eating away at him. She sat on the side of the boat, a perfect lady in any circumstances, equal to anything. He burned for her to come with him, but he couldn't ask that of her, not without endangering her marriage, her reputation – not to mention her life.

The trip to Venice was faster than the night before, especially since they could enter the lagoon openly, through the passage at the end of the Lido. As they came in, a cannon fired in salute from the guard post, and cheers accompanied them as they started across the lagoon, which soon filled with smaller craft holding women and children and old people, all waving Italian flags, and shouting, *Rizzo! Rizzo!*

It would have turned the head of a less honest man. Luigi was blazingly happy, yes, but he took it all in stride, and there was not a puff of pride to be seen.

'Now, that's a real hero,' Sandro murmured in Rebecca's ear, and she nodded. It was good to know that there *were* heroes out there. That courage and humility could go together. 'It must be very hard for him to be separated from Seppina,' he added. His voice was laden with sadness, and she looked at him with curiosity.

They pulled into the Arsenale dock, and there waiting was Seppina and her family, and the admiral, and a crowd of dignitaries.

Sandro knew it was petty of him to enjoy the thunderstruck look on the admiral's face as he saw Rebecca and him on board. They hung back as Luigi and the crew disembarked to deafening applause. When an Italian crowd let go, it was something to remember.

He and Rebecca edged off the boat, making themselves an inconspicuous as possible – not to hide, but to keep the focus of the celebration on Luigi and Ferrarini and their men. The admiral never lost sight of them, though, glaring the whole while.

'Rizzo, explain yourself!' he said. Luigi wasn't listening; he was kissing Seppina thoroughly, to the approval of the crowd.

'You gave me permission, Admiral,' Rebecca cut in.

'I heard you,' Sandro said. 'You said, if she could get to Grado and persuade Tenente Rizzo to give her an interview, she could do it. So, she did.'

The admiral was speechless. But Seppina broke away from Luigi, gleaming with happiness and pride, and slid an arm through his.

'Isn't she wonderful, Admiral?'

Paolo Thaon di Revel might be proof against the worst that the enemy could throw at him, but he was no match for Seppina.

'I'm a man of my word,' he grunted. 'I did – I *suppose* – give you permission.'

The celebrations swept him and the Rizzos away to the church, where no doubt there would be a Mass of Thanksgiving. Sandro wished they could join in, but it was more important to get Rebecca's story out, and his photographs developed.

Sandro seemed to see the day in a series of images, as though his brain was taking snapshots to remember later. Rebecca smiling at the post office clerk as she handed over her story. Rebecca at lunch, dipping her bread in oil. Rebecca thanking Vanni at the pensione, the older man grinning at her like a fool. Rebecca in a gondola, framed by the Grand Canal as they went to the station. There, he came back to himself, jolted by the contrast with his expectations. Nowhere, it seemed, had the news of Luigi's victory made such an impact. There were still crowds leaving, yes, but not the panicked hordes they had seen only two days ago.

Sandro went to the ticket office, and then they made their way to the cafe tucked in a corner of the concourse, and sat and drank their coffee in silence.

•

The train took forever to come, and it seemed to Rebecca just as long for the passengers to disembark and the cleaners to go through it. It was getting dark outside, so that the white clouds of steam that puffed from the side vents of the engine were dazzlingly pale.

The air smelled of coal, and steam, and brick dust.

Finally the announcement was made: the Bologna train was ready to board.

Sandro picked up her case and carried it to the train, but he handed it to a porter to take on board. She closed her eyes for a moment to gather her strength, and then turned to him.

'I won't be coming back to Brindisi with you,' he said. His face was set, but his eyes were burning.

She had known. The expression on his face when he'd pulled her away from the machine-gun fire on the boat, the way he had looked as the submarine moved away . . . he had come to Italy to fight, after all. And if he couldn't fight with a gun, he would fight with a camera.

'You're going to the front.'

He moved to face her. The low lamps along the platform cast light up on his face, showing the cheekbones under the clear skin, highlighting the angles and bones. She saw the man he would grow into in twenty, thirty years. The man he *might* grow into, if he wasn't killed in action.

'I—'

He smiled gently and put a finger on her lips, and she wondered how she had ever thought him young and simple to understand.

'Listen,' he said. He raised his head and she turned to face the north, as he did, standing before him so that his warmth was at her back. The guns pounded and they could hear the shriek of shells. Explosions. The night was falling, and the sounds were startlingly clear. She almost expected to hear the screams of the wounded. Shivering, she turned to him and put her hands on his chest.

'It's true I might die tomorrow,' he said. 'But every man out there could die tomorrow. Every single one. Why should I think I'm more important than any of them? You were the one who reminded me of that. Every one of them is a hero, you said.'

'I take it back,' she said, her voice shaking. 'You're more important.'

'I can't stay with you,' he whispered. She knew he was right. It was so dangerous for them to be together. But—

Her chin was trembling. She could feel it, but she couldn't stop it. All this time, all this long journey, and she hadn't let the tears fall. Until now. Sandro made a soft noise in his throat, a *t'ch* sound that made her hiccup with laughter. He wiped her tears away gently.

She couldn't ask him not to go. She couldn't. Didn't have the right, didn't have any arguments that would mean anything, because he was right.

'I can do my job best at the front,' he said. Yes. He could. Recording the truth. Making a record of what really happened, one that governments and army HQs and staff officers couldn't explain away, couldn't brush off, the way they could mere written reports.

No war was pretty; but a war with photographers watching was a war with the world watching. It might bring peace closer, even just a little.

But how could she let him go? Tears rose again and she turned away from him. Jack's absence was nothing to this. Nonna Rosa was right; her missing him had been short-lived, superficial. But she was married, and it was no business of hers whether Sandro went to the front or not.

'God bless you and keep you,' she managed to say.

He handed her the envelope containing his photographs, and she tucked it into her purse, then stood before him, wordless.

The guard blew his whistle. Reluctantly, she climbed onto the steps. There was a pain in her chest, sharp and constant.

'Promise me you'll let me know what happens to you,' she said. 'After the war. Come to London before you go back to New York. Let me see that you're all right before you go home.'

'I will.' The tone of his voice made it a solemn vow.

The train began to move. She thought he might walk with it as it picked up speed, but he stayed still, kneading his hat between his hands. She couldn't bear to leave him

349

without – without something more. Words couldn't break marriage vows, could they?

'*Ti amo!*' she called as the train pulled away from him.

'*Ti amo*, Rebecca.' He raised a hand to her. His eyes were bright; she couldn't tell if it was love or tears. '*Ti amo, carissima.*' A shot of steam obscured him and she held her breath until she could see his face again.

She hung in the doorway until they were so far out of the station she couldn't even make out a tiny speck that was him. Then she went slowly in and found a seat, and held her bag with his photographs on her lap, and prepared herself to go on with the rest of her life.

She would buy herself some trousers to wear under her skirt, she thought, and live out the rest of the winter in comfort. She would work in her little house, and write her stories, and entrench herself as a foreign correspondent, so there would be no chance that she would ever be sent back to writing about hemlines.

She could only plan for so long. For the rest of the trip she prayed, as the train sped through the falling night and the sound of guns grew softer behind them, that the war would be over soon, and he would come safely home.

EPILOGUE

Rebecca slapped her copy down onto Evans' desk.

'Another Bolshevik arrested,' she said. 'They found bomb-making materials in his bedsit.'

Evans, who had turned out to be a compact dark-haired man with silver at his temples and pale blue eyes, grunted, then nodded to the doorway.

'Got a visitor,' he said.

She turned, expecting some suffragette matron come to complain about how her last article wasn't forceful enough. But it was a man, tall and elegant, standing in the newsroom doorway. Dark-haired, clean-shaven. Hat in hand, kneading it in exactly the same way he had on that station in Venice.

Her heart gave one great thump and seemed to stop.

He came forward, hesitantly. He was in a new suit, charcoal grey; very suitable for a newsman. He looked – older. Of course he was; a year at the front would age anyone. And how many months after that, as Europe sorted itself out? She had seen his images of the Paris Peace Conference.

She had checked on every photograph that arrived on Evans' desk, and she knew Sandro had grown in his art as well as in his technical competence as a journalist.

He looked – extraordinary. The emotion welled up and tears fell onto her cheeks. She hastily wiped them off before anyone could see.

'Becca!' he said, and started towards her then stopped a few feet off, his face wearing a worried frown.

They were watching, all the newsroom staff. She had passed her probation on general news, but she was still the centre of gossip in the office. She didn't care. She didn't have anything to be ashamed of.

'Sandro,' she said. He blinked and put his chin up, hiding whatever he was feeling. She saw his gaze sharpen on her black dress and mourning armband, and his face softened into sympathy.

'Oh, I'm sorry,' he said. 'They found your brother? They found Linus?'

'No,' she said baldly. 'Not Linus. I'm in mourning for Jack. He's been dead almost a year now.'

What could she say? How could she describe the shock, the confusion, the complicated grief of that news? Or how often, since then, she had begun a letter to Sandro, only to decide time and again to wait until she was out of mourning. Until she could come to him with both a free heart and no risk of ruining his career through a scandal. If he still wanted her. Did he?

His eyes were unreadable as the news sank in, but his hands clenched and his throat worked. Before she could take a step towards him, Evans came up beside her, still in his shirtsleeves, with those characteristic elastic armbands he wore to keep his sleeves free of printer's ink.

'Don't talk to me about Jack Quinn,' he said with feeling. 'I'm still sorting out that problem with the Serbian diplomatic corps.'

'Mr Evans!' Sandro said, outraged.

'I speak as I find,' Evans said. 'You two did good work in Italy together. I've a mind to pair you up again here. Any objections?'

Sandro took her hand and bent over it in a formal bow. She quivered as she felt his lips brush her fingers.

'No objection on my part, sir,' he said. 'What about you, Mrs Quinn? Any objection to being one of a pair?'

She smiled, and said in Italian, 'What if I had? What would you do?'

'Kiss you until you changed your mind.' His dark eyes were warm with desire and relieved delight, and she knew hers were the same.

'*Ti amo*,' Sandro said.

'None of that foreign gabble in my newsroom,' Evans said. 'Off you go, the both of you. There must be a story out there you should be covering.'

'Yes,' Rebecca said, tucking her arm into Sandro's. 'I'm sure there is.'

They walked out together, but as soon as they got around a corner and were out of sight, he stopped her and cupped her face in his hands.

'Marry me, *carissima*,' he demanded. 'As soon as your mourning is over.'

Against all odds, here they were. Both alive, both free.

'*Si*,' she said. '*Certamente. Assolutamente.*'

Their mouths met and clung.

This was real, not one of her dreams. The smell of floor polish and Jeyes disinfectant, of printer's ink, the linoleum floor beneath her feet – everything was real, and so was he. His heart under her hands pounded as it had that night on the boat to Grado, and she was alive again, burningly alive, as she hadn't been since she last saw him.

She felt such gratitude that they had done the right thing in Venice. They could come to this marriage with clean hearts and no regrets, and no illusions either. A marriage of true equals.

'I love you,' she said in English. 'Kiss me again.'

ACKNOWLEDGEMENTS

My first thanks go to Rebecca Saunders, my publisher at Hachette Australia, for prompting me to find World War I stories further afield than Sydney. Her influence on this book has been profound.

Secondly, thanks to Vicki Northey, who told me about the Otranto Barrage and its strategic importance in the war. Who knew that the Royal Australian Navy had been in Italy in World War I? I certainly didn't, but what a story it was!

From the RAN I received nothing but encouragement and support, first from Commander Peter Cole of the Garden Island Museum in Sydney, and then especially from the RAN's Senior Naval Historical Officer, Duncan (John) Perryman. I owe John many thanks for help with my research. I should also note my debt to Dr David Stevens for his book *In All Respects Ready – Australia's Navy in World War One*. The wonderful story of the *Orione* comes from there. Any errors in this text are purely mine.

As always, thanks go to my beta readers, Bernadette Foley, Melissa Sargent and (of course) my husband Stephen, and to my always supportive editor, Karen Ward.

A short note: there is no village of Strettabaia north of Brindisi. I made the name up – but Italian coastal villages were shelled by Austrian ships throughout this period of the war, so I hope you will forgive me for using a fictional example to tell my tale. Serra Nova, however, is real, as was Conte Dentice di Frasso, who was an admiral in the Italian Navy in World War I.

All other naval events actually happened – including Luigi Rizzo's extraordinary attack on Trieste Harbour. Rizzo went on to even greater heroisms later in the war and in World War II. Unfortunately, I didn't have space to tell Seppina's story in this book, but it is every bit as heroic as her husband's. You can read more about them both on my website: www.pamela-hart.com

Louise Mack, an Australian, was the initial inspiration for this story. She was the first woman war correspondent in active service – she reported from behind enemy lines as Germany invaded Belgium, and later wrote a book about it, *A Woman's Experiences in the Great War*, which is available for free download from Project Gutenberg and is well worth reading. Mack returned to Australia a celebrity and became the editor of the Women's Pages of *The Sydney Morning Herald*.

Nonna Rosa, alas, is completely fictional!